PRUE PHILLIPSON was born in Newcastle in 1928 and studied English at London University. During her working life she has been a teacher, freelance journalist and supervisor for offenders on community service.

Prue has lived for the last forty-six years in Hexham, Northumberland. Her husband, Alan, has been her mainstay in all her writing years. She has five children, twelve grandchildren and four great-grandchildren.

She has written fiction for many years, winning prizes for short stories and even having one read on the BBC. Prue spent fourteen years caring for her elderly in-laws and finally her mother. She wrote *Lesson of Love* drawing on her experience of her mother's dementia in the light of her Christian faith. Since then, Prue has had seven novels and a short story collection published on line by E-bshop and historical novels in hard and paperback published by Quaester 2000 and Knox Robinson publishing. These last two have ceased trading but information about all her books can be obtained from her website Prue Phillipson Books and orders placed via her email address: pru.phillipson@btopenworld.com

Her latest novel *The Unloved Child* is published by SilverWood Books, with a sequel, *The Unloved Wife*, to follow.

PRUE PHILLIPSON

The Unloved Child

SilverWood

Published in 2020 by SilverWood Books

SilverWood Books Ltd
14 Small Street, Bristol, BS1 1DE, United Kingdom
www.silverwoodbooks.co.uk

Copyright © Prue Phillipson 2020

The right of Prue Phillipson to be identified as the author of this work has been asserted in
accordance with the Copyright, Designs and Patents Act 1988 Sections 77 and 78.

All rights reserved. No part of this publication may be reproduced,
stored in a retrieval system, or transmitted in any form or by any means,
electronic, mechanical, photocopying, recording or otherwise,
without prior permission of the copyright holder.

This is a work of fiction. Names, characters, places and incidents either
are products of the author's imagination or are used fictitiously. Any
resemblance to actual events or locales or persons,
living or dead, is entirely coincidental.

ISBN 978-1-80042-062-5 (paperback)

British Library Cataloguing in Publication Data
A CIP catalogue record for this book is available from the British Library

Page design and typesetting by SilverWood Books

Part One

Sowing the Wind

July 1802–June 1813

Chapter 1

July 1802 Ovingham on Tyne

Jack

Jack Heron was destined to be late for his brother's wedding. There was no church in Wylam, only miners' houses and several pits forming the colliery, so the whole party had set off to walk to Ovingham when Joseph noticed Jack was wearing his work boots.

"Are you trying to make me a laughing stock, our Jack?"

From that moment he knew it was going to be one of his days of shame.

"Catch us up," their father shouted.

Hot-faced, he ran back to the cottage. Where had he put the boots he had polished last night within an inch of their lives?

He hunted about, flapping his arms in despair. At last, there were the boots peeping out from under the box-bed in the shadowed corner. He sat on the bed to unlace his work boots and pull on the others, lent by Joe and too loose for him. To be sure they stayed on, he yanked too hard on the lace and it broke. Joe must have known it was worn but Jack blamed no one but himself. It was always he who failed.

The lace was too withered to knot and hold. Was there another boot lace in their one room? The cottage had three other rooms but they belonged to different families and his mother always said, "Don't borrow from them if you can help it." He grabbed her wooden box of odds and ends from the mantelshelf and emptied it on the floor. All he found that might serve him was a piece of string. His fingers fumbled to thread it through. He had to lick the end to make a point. Would anyone notice? Of course they would. Joe would, and Joe's sharp-eyed bride, Sarah, of whom Jack was already in awe.

Ready at last, he crossed to the door and nearly tripped on the upturned box. He must put everything back and restore it to its place. His mother always said, "With three grown men cluttering up the room, *I* have to be tidy."

It flitted through Jack's head that Joe wouldn't be sleeping here after today. It would never happen to him. No girl wanted him and the ones he had small yearnings for he would never dare to approach.

He shut the door and set off at a run in the overlarge boots. As far as the pithead, a mere half mile, he ran beside the waggonway that took the coals down to the staithes at Lemington, his daily job, all the way on the bank of the Tyne. Now he must head on upstream; strange and worrying because he was late and would be in trouble with his brother and all the family.

Once he'd skirted the mine buildings and was making for Ovingham he could follow the riverside path. He looked at the dry, baked ground beneath his feet and there was not a mark from family footsteps, nor could he see anyone ahead. A fluttering of fear happened in the pit of his stomach. He was used to leading a horse, not walking alone.

A heron flapped up from an exposed sandbank. The Tyne was at its lowest. He waved to the heron with some relief, as to a relation of his, but his heart beat uncomfortably. He couldn't see the tower of Ovingham Church yet. Should he not have reached it by now? He came this way most Sundays but always between his father and mother. He liked to have one on either side of him. When he was small they held his hands and gave him a swing every twenty paces. That's how he had learnt to count. His brother Joe was older and could read and write too.

Joe was going to be angry.

Relief! There was the tower of the church among its trees. Turning from the river and up into Ovingham village, panting, he kept his eyes from knots of people greeting him with, "Hey, if you're here for the wedding, ye're late, man." There was no sign of anyone when he neared the church. The service had begun. How could he lift the great latch and have faces staring round at him?

He paused just inside the gate to listen for the singing of a hymn. Instead he heard another sound, a wrenching, choking, heartbreaking sound. Behind the wall someone was sobbing.

He slipped back out and walked round the corner of the wall. A young woman was crouched against it, her arms locked behind her head as she rocked, with her face almost touching the soft fronds of grass that sprouted at the base of the stones. Her fingers were buried in a chaos of dark curls escaping from their ribbons but he took in nothing. Her misery was all. The heaving of her body spoke of a wretchedness that engulfed Jack's whole being. Nothing in his twenty-one years of life had ever moved him with such pity. At that moment there *was* nothing else in his world but this girl and her sorrow.

"Nay, nay," he murmured. "Nay, don't cry so."

Swallowed up in her grief, she didn't hear him. He touched her shoulder. She shuddered, spun round and gazed up at him, mouth agape.

Her eyes locked on to his with absolute wonder. She sat up, her back against the wall, still gazing. He couldn't find words. He could only give her his sweetest smile, thankful that her sobs had subsided, though her bosom still rose and fell with gasping breaths. He kept his eyes from that, riveting them on hers; so intense, dark and yearning was her look.

At last she said, "God sent you?"

It was half a statement, half a question. He could think of no answer so he held out his hands and lifted her up. She was no higher than his shoulder. Supporting her, he was made aware that she was light in weight but well curved above her neat waist and that she wore a dress of silk with a lace collar and cuffs, all rumpled and grubby. Still her eyes, a dark glowing brown, never left his. She could be pretty if her face were not tear-stained and smudged with dirt. She wore no hat or cloak. Where had she come from?

"What is your trouble?" he asked. "I never heard crying like that. Can I help?"

"I am all alone." Still it was his face she studied with a kind of awe.

"Nay, I am here with you."

"I have no one at all now."

"You have me. What can I do?"

She suddenly gestured wildly with her arms, tossing back her head and looking all around. "In my world there is no one left. Everyone, everything has gone. No one is left to love me, to save me. There is only a great hole and darkness."

For a sickening moment he thought she must be an elfin creature from another world. Maybe he conveyed the thought in his eyes. Maybe there was the slightest withdrawing motion of his body.

She grabbed his hands. "Don't leave me. Oh, please, don't leave me alone. I can't go back. There is nothing there. Nothing."

She was no wraith. She was human. Her touch had no sinister power.

Jack Heron had never in his life heard any human soul express a need of him. 'Don't leave me.' He wouldn't. No one to love her? *He* could love her. He had stopped her crying. She was looking up into his face again. She was pleading for his protection. Whoever had cast her out, whoever had taken away all she had, be damned to him! He – Jack Heron – was the one she clung to now.

He put his arms round her and held her close.

At once there was a change. Her head tilted back and the awe in her eyes changed to curiosity with a hint of fear.

"Who *are* you?"

"Jack. Jack Heron. Look, don't be frightened. You want someone to love you, someone to protect you. You're all alone with no one, nothing in the world?"

She nodded. "No one, nothing."

"Well you've got me now. Jack Heron. *I'll* never leave you."

She wriggled free of his arms and for the first time began to study him, from the crown of his head to his boots. He felt his cheeks flame up. His boots. His overlarge boots with the string in one of them. Joe's wedding. He was too late now and this was more important. This would change his life. Joe didn't matter. Joe could manage his own life with no trouble. He always had.

"Jack Heron." She was savouring his name on her lips. They were pretty lips, small with the upper lip well curved and the lower slightly full. She laid her hand on the cloth of his Sunday best coat. "Where do you come from, Jack Heron?"

"Wylam. I work on the waggonway." He supposed that was still true, though the world had changed around him.

"How old are you?"

"Twenty-one."

"Are you married?"

"Nay."

"You have the kindest face on earth. I thought you were from heaven. Maybe you are. Maybe God *did* send you." She listened. "I hear a hymn. You *are* from heaven."

He beamed, though in ordinary life it was no laughing matter. "It's my brother's wedding." The church must still be on the other side of this wall. He tried saying it aloud. "The church is right here."

"I didn't know," she said. "I was wandering blindly. Why are you not inside?"

"I heard you crying. I couldn't bear that anyone should be so wretched."

"And you don't even know who I am."

"Well, no." He didn't know whether he wanted to fasten her to a name or a place. She was just someone who needed him.

She was looking at him with a twisted sort of smile. "My name's Dione. The rest doesn't really matter. I have no one at all. You are the kindest person I have ever met. You breathe love. Did you mean it when you said you wouldn't leave me? I need you so much. You are missing your brother's wedding for me. He will be angry. Your family, your parents, they will all be angry."

"But *they* don't need me. They have each other. May I put my arms round you again? That was good."

"You'll stop at that? I loved it, but you'll stop at that?"

"Ay. I know what 'tis to *want* a woman but none ever wanted *me* before. I know it's right to be betrothed first, so my mother says."

"If you are never going to leave me we'd have to be married, wouldn't we?"

"Why ay, we would that." He could feel a great smile spreading across his face. This was how he could protect her. He, useless clumsy Jack, who would never make anything of his life, who could never get a bright lass as Joseph had! Here was this girl, loving him, wanting him, praising him as heaven-sent – beautiful, too, for now a smile like paradise was lighting her whole face. He hadn't got hold of her strange name properly but that didn't matter.

"Will you have me for a husband?" he said. "I know the right words. It's love and cherish till death do us part."

"I will, Jack. Oh, how I need loving and cherishing." Her eyes welled with tears but she hid them by laying her head on his chest as he folded her in his arms. The happiest man in the whole world, he told himself.

They heard the creaking of the church door and people's voices.

She pulled away from him. "They will be angry. I must disappear."

He gasped. "No! How will I find you? You have nowhere to go."

"*I'll* find *you*."

He reached out to grab her, and catching one boot with the other he toppled over onto the ground. When he scrambled back up she had vanished. There were clumps of bushes, garden walls, but no one could disappear so quickly.

He heard his mother's voice.

"Well, I do worry for him, Joe, whatever you say."

His father said, "Nay, he goes about in a dream. He'll have forgotten where he was heading."

Joe said, "If he fell in the river today he could paddle out. He'll be at home, drying off. Let's go."

The sharp voice of Joe's new bride, Sarah, came to Jack's ears as he still stood, dazed, one hand on the wall. "It's a slight to you, Joe, missing your wedding. I'm not sure I shall forgive him."

Now Jack moved. He came round to the gate as they reached it, a small crowd of villagers clustering after them. Shouts of "Here he is" and laughter.

"Did you get lost?"

"He looks mighty lost now."

He found words at last. "I meant no slight, Joe. I had to help someone."

Joe was looking at his feet. "Ye've put string in your boot. Ashamed to come into the church, that's what it was."

But his mother – in a rare show of affection – had her arms round him. That was comforting – to know she'd been anxious.

"Who did you help, Jack? Was it a dog drowning?" He'd once forgotten to go to work when he'd seen a neighbour's old cur struggling in the river.

He shook his head. They were all starting to walk on now and he settled between his father and mother because he must tell them the world had changed.

Joe and Sarah hurried ahead, hand in hand, no longer interested in him.

He answered his mother. "Nay, it was a girl. Heartbroken, she was." He kept turning his eyes to seek her. "She has no one nor nothing in the world so I asked her to marry me."

His mother's head jerked up as a bark of a laugh shot out of her. "Eh, Jack? Ye've sat on the bank to rest and had fantasies again."

"I have not. She was back there behind the wall weeping. I had to stop."

"So where *is* this girl?" His father, who rarely spoke, grinned at him and looked across the river and up into the sky. "Is that her sitting on yon cloud?"

Jack looked but no one was sitting on the cloud. She might indeed have been caught up there, so quickly had she disappeared, but the cloud was just a fluffy whiteness drifting across the summer sky.

"She consented too," he said, nodding his head as he thought of it. "She needs me that badly. It was you all coming out of the church that frightened her away."

"Ay, that's the way o' fairies," his mother said. "They'll show to a man on his own but a crowd scares them off."

He looked at her square, solid face, unsmiling, and felt her seriousness.

"It wasn't a fairy. Fairies don't sob their hearts out. She'll come back. I know she will." But misgivings were beginning to grip him. "Do fairies have names? She told me her name."

"And?" Now his mother was grinning again. Oh, she could be a great tease, his mother.

"I had never heard such a name," he admitted. "It sounded like Deony."

"Ay, well, you fell asleep and had a dream." She looked round. "Bet Simpson" – she was addressing Sarah's mother close behind them – "You mustn't think our Jack is weak in the head. He has a good job on the waggonway."

Everyone was laughing. Jack closed in on himself, head down, shuffling the big boots along the sandy path. The summer's day was dark around him. He had been needed. He had been going to marry a young woman with a face like paradise at the thought of his protective arms. And now it had all stopped and they were walking just as planned to some sort of wedding feast spread out on the grass by their cottage. Yesterday he was excited, looking forward to that, but it had gone wrong with the boots and the string and he hadn't been at his brother's wedding.

He had been a fool again.

And yet it felt in no way like a dream…

Chapter 2

Dione

In a patch of woodland on her father's estate was a small gamekeeper's cottage and it was to this that Dione Sheradon ran when she parted from Jack Heron. She had run from it that morning as a hateful place and her parents – broken creatures – might still be there, but it was at least a roof for the night where she could clean herself up, change her clothes and present herself at the home of the Herons of Wylam next day.

Not sure how far she had wandered in her state of distress, she struggled to find her way back, all the time her mind hovering between excitement, wonder and doubt.

Had it been an angel who lifted her up? Angels could take any form they chose. She had been screaming to God that she was in the pit of despair and could sink no lower. But He wasn't listening and her sobs were wrenching her in two when the touch on her shoulder had happened.

Jack Heron. Would an angel take such a name? She went over what he had done and every word he had spoken. An angel was outside time. This was a sweet, simple young man of twenty-one. She was eighteen and all too worldly-wise now. It didn't matter if he *was* a little simple. He was kind. And no angel would have thought of having one boot tied with string. Jack Heron was real and maybe that was how God had answered her prayer. His kindness, his respecting her when his arms were about her, that was enough. He would do. Of course, she was afraid of his family but she would go to meet them next day and play a part that would make them accept her.

She ran on. There were paths at the edges of fields, baked hard, one much like another, but she headed west and when she could see the pithead buildings of Mickley Bank Colliery across the river, dark structures glimpsed through the trees from her bedroom window, she knew she was not far from the eastern gate in the stone wall surrounding Sheradon Grange.

She was too far down the hill but if she followed the wall she would come to the gate and the gamekeeper's cottage was only fifty yards into the wood from there.

What could she tell her parents? Nothing or everything? She was in sight of the cottage before she had planned anything at all. Her mother's face was at the window, distorted with surprise and anger. She appeared at the front door as Dione approached it.

"Why are *you* here? Do you think we want your shame here? You said you would never stop for one minute in this place again. Did you see your father?"

Dione stood quite still in front of the dishevelled, raging figure that had once been her mother, the lady of the manor whose philosophy of life was contained in a book of social etiquette.

Dione answered her jumble of questions. "I am here for the bundle I managed to spirit away. I have found a way of overcoming my shame and will stay here no longer than I have to. No, I have not seen my father."

Her mother stood aside so she could go in and muttered her reply without expression as she passed. "He's likely done away with himself then."

Dione went into the small front parlour, paying little attention to those words. The disaster had turned her mother's head, she was sure. At least her anger seemed to have vanished as she followed Dione in and sank onto the settle against the wall.

She said, "Where is the point in living now? You did well to run away. I thought you were going to throw yourself in the Tyne. Why didn't you?"

Dione was looking at the few bundles that had been brought from the Grange. She had tied hers up in a sheet from her old bed. She must have taken it upstairs last night but none of them had gone to bed here.

A figure darkened the window, the front door was thrust open and her father burst into the room. He flung something down on the rug in the centre of the room. There was an explosion of noise and something flashed by Dione's feet, just missing the leg of the settle where her mother sat and embedding itself in the wall behind. Her mother shrieked, tucked up her legs in a convulsive movement and fell into hysteria.

Dione, quivering, looked at the pistol on the rug. It had jumped when the spark and explosion happened but now lay like a dead thing. She didn't dare pick it up. Her father was staring at it, shaking his head. He put his hand to his temple.

"That's where the bullet was to go, but I'm a coward, Dione. I couldn't do it."

He seemed to have accepted her presence. Perhaps he'd forgotten that she had run away three hours before, in grief and anger at their hopelessness. He peered at her mother, rocking and crying out, and seemed to decide it was not worth addressing her, so he looked back at Dione. Then he stepped close and drew her out through the door to the back room, its small window dimmed by the crowding trees behind the cottage. He closed the door on her mother's rasping screams.

For a moment he stood there, a shrunken version of her confident, ebullient father. Then he flopped down on one of the kitchen chairs and began to speak as if she had just asked him why he had failed to kill himself.

"You see, Dione, my father was waiting for me on the other side of death. I couldn't cross that gulf and see the reproach in his eyes."

She gritted her teeth. It was anger she felt, not pity; anger at the shock he had just given her, but even more at his pleading for words of comfort. How dare he, when he had recklessly thrown away his father's life's work? She remembered her grandfather before his death, wizened from hard work and long hours, but contented because he had built Sheradon Grange and seen a pretty little granddaughter running about its spacious rooms.

"Do you suppose you would go to the same place as Grandfather?" she shouted at the drooping figure on the chair. "Taking your life is a sin. *That* would have been cowardly. But you are a coward anyway. You will not face what you have done to others. You think of no one but yourself. What about her in there? What about me? We had no hand in this disaster."

All he did was stare at the floor and mumble, "It was her extravagance. The dressmaker's, the milliner's, the jeweller's bills all came in together."

"Of course. As soon as they heard Sheradon's was doomed. And who doomed it? You, only you." She pulled up a stool and made him look at her. She was now bursting with words that had to be said to give her a measure of relief. "I had five years with Grandfather but they were a glimpse into a different life from the one you and Mother showed me. You gave me nothing but luxury and complacency. What has that prepared me for? And you wanted to marry me to a man who could write 'sir' before his name so you could feel grand among the 'best people', so you said. What judgment had I? He was handsome and persuasive and pretended to love me so much that I yielded to him with the wedding only two weeks away. But *he* knew what was coming to Sheradon's even if *you* ignored the warnings. So he thought he'd enjoy me and then vanish to his regiment before the storm broke over your head, and over mine and over hers." She pointed to the parlour door.

Her father did now focus his eyes on her, but it was her waistline he was looking at.

She laughed. "Father, you're a fool. It was only three weeks ago but I am as certain as I can be that he has left me with child."

He shook his head. "You cannot blame me for that, girl, even if it's true."

She stood up and turned her back on him. "I can't talk to you. I'm going upstairs. I won't be here tomorrow. I can do nothing about *her*. The two of you will have to find your own way of living." She darted a poisoned glance at him. "At least you still have your *life*. You nearly killed yourself and you could easily have killed Mother or me just now and then they would have hanged you."

She opened the other door that led to the narrow stair. At that moment she couldn't bear to go back to her mother, who was still uttering rasping cries, nor could she think what might happen with the pistol still lying on the floor. If he killed her mother and then himself she would be free of them and surely Jack Heron would love her still more for being an orphan.

But when she had clattered upstairs and shut herself in the smaller of the two attics which she had never wanted to see again, she went to the window and looked into the wood and wondered if Jack Heron had ever existed except in a fevered dream.

This has driven us all mad, she told herself. Was I so intent on finding a way out of my own trouble that I conjured him up? Could anyone like him exist?

Her bundle, saved from the creditors' men, was on the bed, where she had lain with Sir Ralph Barnet. She had viewed the experience as a sweet initiation but it was swiftly soured the day his lawyer's letter came to her father at Sheradon Grange.

Dear Sir,

I am advised that you are no longer in a position to honour the marriage settlement which you agreed with my client, Sir Ralph Barnet

Love, if it had ever been love, was engulfed in bitter fury. Why had she never guessed he was marrying her for Sheradon wealth? His 'passion' had made a fool of her.

Now, here in this room, his bodily presence came back to her. They had been walking in the woods when they came upon the cottage. She told him the place was uninhabited and he took that as an invitation. All too easily he broke down her objections. She had believed in his love and oh how she had wanted to be truly loved!

Now she clenched her fists and beat them on the windowsill as she would like to have smashed his smiling, panting mouth. She must crush his image and replace it with Jack Heron's. That tender boy had had her in his arms and gently released her.

She turned away from the window and picked up her bundle. If only she could have avoided coming up here! Why had she not fastened her bundle to a stick and carried it over her shoulder like a wayfarer when she had left that morning? She had planned nothing.

The three of them had passed the night in the small parlour. Back in the Grange men were carrying away their treasured furniture. That was why her mother had leapt up, crying, "I cannot bear this. We will go to that empty cottage. Bring our bags." There were no servants left to hear but some woman, brought to sweep up the cleared house, took pity on them and went ahead to lay a fire in the hearth and put some eatables in the larder.

Her father had slipped a flask into the pocket of his greatcoat and hastened after her mother, so Dione had been obliged to follow. She had tried that night to worm some sense from them over what was to happen next, but her father had rapidly drunk himself into a grinning lethargy. She took the chance to confide in her mother that she feared she was pregnant, hoping for some compassion, some maternal care, but all she got was a scream to her father that "The girl has shamed us too. First *you* ruin me and now *she* has shamed me for ever." So she had run from the house in the morning without a thought for how she would live.

Now she flung herself on the bed and her mind was back at the wall again with her wild prayer for help that had conjured up Jack Heron.

She blotted out the tall naked form of Ralph and struggled to trace Jack Heron, from his curly fair hair and round cherub face, past his broad chest and the straining buttons of his best coat down to the overlarge shiny boots with the string in one. He had to be real.

"Oh, I could love him for his gentleness and sweetness." She spoke out loud. "I *will* love him."

She imagined life as Jack Heron's wife in a charming cottage with a garden of roses. Her grandfather had told her how he and her grandmother had started their married life in such a place and never been happier. He often said, "God chose to bless us with wealth in our later years but that is only good if one can do good with it." He was one of a group of Quaker families who made money from hard work and wise investment. He had set up Sheradon's Bank to help his tenants with their savings and lend money to his suppliers. Dione didn't care about any of it until she discovered how her father had put the bank's money into a canal scheme that failed. He had boasted that he would make more money than his father because he didn't waste hours sitting in meetings where nothing was said, listening to a God who didn't understand the commerce of the new century.

Now, in 1802, Sheradon's Bank was bankrupt and Dione Sheradon must start a new life as Mistress Jack Heron. As she repeated this to herself over and over again, her night of sleeplessness took its toll on her young body and she drifted into a dream in which the cottage was there before her but locked up, and she was waiting for Jack to appear with the key. All sorts of people who seemed to be his family were laughing at her for standing outside. They showed her an open back door and she went in, but the rooms turned into a meandering tunnel which closed in on her with black walls running with slime and she shrieked for "Grandfather!"

She woke to find the long summer evening fading. Where was she? There was no sound. She was desperately hungry.

Looking at the small dirty window and the trees beyond, she remembered everything, including the dream. "Grandfather is dead but I am alive and I will not fall into madness like those two down there." She peeped out onto the tiny landing and saw that the door to the larger room up here was shut. She opened it a crack. Her father and mother were sprawled across the bed – asleep or dead? There was no blood and when she listened she could hear their breathing.

She ran down to the kitchen and saw the remains of a meal on two wooden trenchers. There was the heel of a loaf of coarse bread, a crock of butter and scraps of cheese. In the larder was a bowl of eggs, a bunch of watercress and a jug of buttermilk. They had been too lazy or helpless to make a fire to boil the eggs and they had not cared to call her to share their supper, such as it was.

Dione had seen fires laid because she had loved to spend time in the kitchen of Sheradon Grange with Bessie, who had been her nursemaid when she was small. Bessie was Grandfather's appointment and her mother discarded her to the kitchen as soon as he died: "You must have someone superior, my child, as befits our status."

"Bessie can read and write," Dione had protested. "Grandfather taught her. She borrowed the book of Greek and Roman tales and read it to me. *You* must have read it to find my name there."

"Oh, I glanced through it for an unusual name but *she* should not have taken it from our library or read it to you. You're far too young for heathen tales of gods and goddesses."

Unknown to her mother, Bessie continued Dione's practical education. She not only showed her how to lay a fire but how to make a stew, bake pastry and hem sheets. She also saved Grandfather's old books that were thrown out because they shamed the volumes her mother chose to display. Dione was soon reading them for herself to supplement the stilted lessons from her new governess, Mademoiselle Verrau.

As she laid a fire in the hearth, Dione thought of all the people suddenly thrown out into the world with the collapse of Sheradon's and the dismantling of the Grange. Mademoiselle, with her French nose in the air, had returned to France, saying she felt safe to do so since the signing of the Treaty of Amiens. Fortunately Bessie had long since been in her grave and the gamekeeper who had lived in this cottage had received a better wage on an estate in the Borders. But the cook, the butler, the ladies' maid, chambermaid, kitchen maid and all the outside men had suddenly found there was no money to pay them any more. How that would have grieved her grandfather!

The fire was hot enough, so Dione put a knob of butter in a pan and broke in two of the eggs. Who would buy the Grange to help clear her father's debts? That was a matter for the creditors' lawyers to arrange. This cottage was part of the estate and Dione doubted that her parents would be allowed to remain. "But I will be gone at first light," she said softly, bringing the eggs to the table and cutting herself a hunk of bread. She shook the crumbs of cheese over her supper and ate every scrap.

Before the last of the daylight faded, she fetched her bundle from upstairs, spread out the sheet and chose her plainest dress and petticoat and laid them out ready. Then she went out and filled a bucket at the pump and extracted a piece of the best soap only her mother ever used from one of the bags in the front parlour. She discarded her torn, grubby dress and petticoat and washed herself as best she could. When she was clean and dressed she lit a candle from the remains of the fire and crept up to her room with all that she wanted wrapped up again in her bundle.

There were snores coming from her parents' room. They had not slept for days. She was sure she could sleep again too, through the short hours of darkness, now that she was ready for her new life, but when she lay down carefully on a clean shawl she had spread out, and arranged her dress so she would not crumple it, she found herself wide awake and wracked by questions.

Is there a Jack Heron in Wylam? Can I find him? Will he be pleased to see me? Will he regret what he said? It will be a new day and his family will be there! Whatever will they say? Shall I admit I am a Sheradon? Will not everyone in the Tyne Valley loathe the name or laugh at our downfall? She found herself grinding her teeth. I must have him. And my true name must go in the Parish record to be lawful. I am going to marry Jack Heron. This is my new life. I *will* make it happen. He is all sweetness.

She dozed at last, then woke to shouted arguments from the next room. Faint moonlight showed her own door opening a crack. Her father's voice hissed, "Let her sleep, woman!" and it was closed again.

There was more talk and crying but she buried her head in the pillow and wrapped her shawl over her ears. Somehow she slept until a sunbeam lit the tops of the trees outside and she was instantly up. Two minutes later she was creeping downstairs. They were not about. She wouldn't look in their room. She would go.

A summer's day flooded through the wood. Wylam lay to the east. She pulled down the brim of her straw hat to shield her eyes but the brightness was good. It heralded the opening of her new life. She stepped outside and walked towards the sunlight.

Chapter 3

Jack

Jack ate his porridge on the window seat as usual, except that Joe's bulk was not beside him. His father ate his on his stool at the corner of the table. His mother had eaten hers and was stirring the fire to heat water for the washing. But nothing was as usual because of their disbelief. There was no girl for him. All night on the bed under the eaves, where he should have enjoyed the extra space, their teasing seeped into him, filling him with nagging doubts.

His mother lifted her eyes to look at him. He pouted at her and she shrugged her shoulders.

"Not a word, William," she said to his father. "Not a word has our Jack spoken this day."

His father, who rarely spoke in a morning anyway, gave only a grunt in reply.

"I tell you, William, he wants us to believe he's copying Joseph and getting wed."

Another grunt from his father.

Jack scraped the last spoonful out of his bowl and leant forward to place it on the table. As he did so his mother's gaze shifted from him to something outside the window behind his back. She straightened up, staring.

"Botheration! It's one of them gypsy girls. She's coming to Slaters' door."

Jack swung round. A young woman with a bundle on a stick was out there setting down her bundle and lifting her hand to knock. She wasn't grubby and torn and weeping but he knew her.

He drew a long gasping breath. "Oh no, Mother! It's her. She's come. It's my own girl. She's here!" He knelt on the window seat and pressed his head to the glass, his whole body alive with joy. As he waved and banged on the window she turned her head and smiled, that smile of paradise he had seen in those wakeful hours. He leapt past the table, shoving aside his father who had half risen, and pulled open the outer door at the back of the room. He ran round the house. She was still there, no fantasy, looking a little surprised to see that the door in front of her remained shut.

He took her in his arms. "You came, you found me."

Her face was all excited and laughing. "I asked the teacher at the school gate and he said to follow the waggonway from the mine and it would be the first cottage along. He said he taught your brother, Joseph. That would be the one was married yesterday? Do you not use your front door, Jack Heron?"

"Nay, that goes up to Charltons and Slaters."

She looked puzzled, but followed him when he said, "Come, meet my father and mother. They never believed me but I still hoped. All night I hoped." He was gripping her hand, pulling her round to their door. "And you've come." The door was open as he'd left it and his father and mother were looking out.

He couldn't stop a grin of triumph splitting his face. "See. See. She's here. My wife-to-be. Did I not tell you? Is she not lovely, Mother?"

For a moment his parents were speechless. Oh, it was good to see their faces! Then his father looked at his mother for her response, but Jack saw she was looking at him and shaking her head because he had amazed her for once in his life. Finally she looked at his girl, her eyes taking her all in, the straw bonnet, pushed back by his embrace, the fine bosom in its tight bodice, the neat waist, the plain cotton skirt with sensible shoes peeping out.

"Well!" She stepped aside. "You'd better come in, lass." She motioned her to sit in the rocking chair.

There was an odd silence. His girl was looking up at his mother. He clutched himself in disbelief that she was here in their home. Would she vanish? But she had sat where directed, her hands clasped in front of her, her feet primly together, a real being. And she belonged solely to him.

Then they all heard the clang of a bell from the colliery.

His father gave a great sigh of relief. "Work don't stop. Haway, lad."

Jack didn't know whether to go or stay. There was no disobeying the bell. Yet how could he leave his girl when he had scarcely had two words with her?

"Go to work, Jack," she said, smiling up at him. "Your mother and I will get to know each other. Will I see you come by on the waggonway?"

"Ay, you will that." How clever she was! She had remembered that he worked there. The two worlds were coming together.

"When we're wed you'll be going to work, just like this."

He clapped his hands. "Ay, we're to be wed, just like Joseph was wed yesterday. I'm going to be a husband, Ma, just like Joseph."

"Haway, lad," his father said again. "No more of that. Joe and Sarah we knew all about." He turned to the door, just checking himself beside the rocking chair. "The missus'll ha' words wi' ye, whoever you are." He spoke to the back of the chair, Jack noticed, and went red in the face as he hurried out.

"My bundle, Jack," the girl said. "It's still on the front doorstep." He ran round and fetched it and set it by the chair. Then he bent and kissed her. She was so calm it was hard to believe she was the same girl, but she was. He himself had transformed that weeping wretch by the church wall into this bright, smiling maiden who had come to marry him. He went out, head high, a new powerful figure, ready for a day's work.

Dione

"Well," said the short, sturdy woman standing before Dione, "this is an odd state of affairs and no mistake. What's your name to start with?"

It was happening. She was here with her heart thumping. If she moved the rocking chair rocked. She had to get out of it and look at the room and make it all real.

She tried to keep gazing at the woman.

"Dione."

"Ay, he said summat like that yesterday but it's not anything I ever heard of."

"My mother found it in a book. Dione was a goddess." Why tell her that?

"Ay, it has a heathen sound to it. What about your mother then? Where is she? Who are your people? You didn't just drop out of the sky."

Dione got to her feet. "Dear Mistress Heron, pray sit yourself here and I'll pull up that stool and explain everything."

"I have the copper boiling on the fire for the washing."

"I will help you with that. You must put me to work, but first I'll tell you everything." She drew the stool opposite the chair and sat down on it. Jack's mother pulled the steaming copper to the side of the fire and sat down.

"Ay, well, there's a mighty lot I need to know, seemingly."

Dione began to take in her face. This was to be her mother-in-law. Tough as a nut she looked, the features small and crumpled in a rough square, but there were humour lines at the corners of the eyes.

Dione knew how she must begin. "The first thing is that your son Jack is the kindest person I have ever met."

Mistress Heron sat up straight and her little eyes opened wide. "Ay, well, you're not telling me anything I don't know there. Let's have you and your family first. You don't talk like the folks round here."

"I'm a Sheradon." She looked to see if the name produced a reaction.

"Sheradon? Sheradon? Isn't there a big new house called Sheradon Grange up beyond Ovingham? You'll not be from there, I reckon?"

"But I am. And it's not so new. My grandfather built it before I was born and I am eighteen years old."

"Eighteen? You've hardly begun to live, girl. But what's the likes of you doing with my boy, Jack, and dressing up like a gypsy girl, selling trinkets and stuff, door to door?" She was looking at Dione's bundle.

"In there is everything I have in the world. The Sheradons are ruined."

Before Mistress Heron could exclaim, Dione launched into the sad tale of her father's rash speculation and losses and the desperate state of mind of both him and her mother now. She said nothing of Sir Ralph Barnet.

She saw she was being listened to but without much understanding.

"Nay, I know nowt of these goings on," Mistress Heron broke in when she paused for breath. "I only see common folks losing work when the gentry chooses to cast 'em off. Are you saying you want to wed my son Jack because you're poor yourself all of a sudden and have nowhere to go, and he's been daft enough to want you?"

"No, indeed I am not. I saw that he was – as I said just now – the kindest man on earth and when he asked me to marry him I said yes. I knew, above all things, that I wanted to be his wife."

"So how long do you reckon you've known him, Missy Sheradon?"

"My name is Dione. I want to forget the Sheradons. We met yesterday."

"Ay, well, I'm glad you're honest. And you think that's long enough for a courtship, do you? Did you go home and tell your father and mother you'd met a man you wanted to marry – a coal miner's son?"

"As I explained, I have no home. The hovel we stayed in briefly is not ours and my parents must leave and find work or starve. My father was cruel. When he was rich he tried to marry me to a titled man I did not love." Dione guessed Mistress Heron might hear that from local gossip. And, she thought, she likes my honesty. But the woman was laughing and shaking her head. She got to her feet and pulled the copper pan back over the fire.

"It's just as I said. You found yourself with nothing in the world and the first man you met what said a kind word you thought you could trap him into wedding you. You'd best get yourself off and look for work at one of the coal owners' mansions. I'm wasting half the morning listening to your nonsense."

Dione had risen too and moved the stool to its place by the table. "So let me make up for it by helping you. Will you show me the rest of the house and give me any task you need doing?"

Mistress Heron turned and faced her. "This *is* our house." She flung out her arms to encompass the room. "I don't think the Charltons and Slaters upstairs or Jenny Coxon that way" – she pointed to the wall –"would want a stranger peering through *their* rooms." She snatched a coil of rope off a peg by the mantelpiece. "If you want to help me, girl, take that out and string it between them two posts you'll see." She pulled a basket of soiled clothes towards her.

Dione took the rope and opened the back door, which she now realised was the only outer door, and went out into the sunshine. Her throat was dry. She found herself swallowing as if she couldn't take in what she had heard. Four families lived in this house. Jack and his parents ate and slept and did all their living in one room.

She had thought, when she came along in a tremulous state of excitement, that the stone house, standing four-square facing the waggonway and the river, looked solid and comforting. The brothers she supposed would have one of the two upstairs bedrooms but as Joseph had gone that could be Jack's and hers. Yes, I can live here, she had told herself, till Jack and I can find our own place. Will they let me have a sofa in their sitting-room till we are wed, I wonder? I am certain they will not turn me out for I will be so meek and helpful.

Well, she thought now, as she fastened the rope to a hook in one post and carried it over to the other, Mistress Heron has made her first big mistake if she wants me to go. She has given me a task. If I can make myself indispensable she will let me stay. She has no daughter it seems. But I can't possibly live in one room with them. She mentioned a Jenny Coxon as if she lived alone. Maybe she will give me a bed.

Looking around outside she saw a vegetable plot with leeks, onions, cabbages and potatoes. It was divided from the next plot by a few sticks and further on was an enclosure with chickens pecking about. A hedgerow bordered the plots and beyond that was a field with horses and ponies grazing and further on rising ground with clumps of woodland. If she looked west past the gable of the house she could see pitheads and mine buildings on both sides of the river, but there was country that way too. "I could bear this place," she murmured aloud. "I'll have to."

She heard the rattle of a wagon on wooden rails and darted back through the house to kneel on the window seat and wave to Jack. He was plodding along the track leading a great carthorse and his head was turned expectantly to the window. He waved back, delighted.

She thought, He's a good, solid figure of a man. His face is alive with joy and love and he's mine.

His mother looked up from pounding the clothes in the tub. "Ay, you'll hear that sound often enough. Sometimes they make three trips a day."

"Where does the coal go?" She had seen the laden wagon.

"Five miles to Lemington Staithes on the river. They cannot bring boats this far west. 'Tis too shallow. Is the clothesline up?"

"Yes."

Mistress Heron straightened her back with a grunt. "I'm thinking you'd best be off to find your father and mother."

"I'd rather stay and help you."

"Ay, but that's where your duty lies. I'm nothing to you."

"My mother-in-law, I hope."

"Nay, I cannot see that ever happening. A Sheradon indeed!"

Dione took hold of her hands, wet and red as they were. "You wouldn't break your dear boy's heart. You saw him just now. You saw his look."

Mistress Heron pulled her hands away and resumed her pounding with the poss-stick. She said without looking up, "He'd forget you after a while."

Dione heard doubt in her voice so she pressed on. "You saw him when we parted yesterday. What did he tell you?"

"Oh, that he'd met a girl he would marry. We laughed. He's given to dreams and fantasies." Again she checked her pounding and stood straight, looking Dione in the eye as if a thought had just struck her. "This time it was different though. He went silent, sulking I'd have called it, which he never does. You bewitched him. That's what it was." She waved the poss-stick before Dione's face. "I don't know you. You *could* be a witch. I'm feared now. You'd best get out o' this house." She pointed the stick at the door, her hand trembling so much the end of the stick sprayed hot water.

Dione stepped out of its reach and put her hands together in prayer.

"Dear Mistress Heron, I swear before God, I am no witch. Think how your boy was when I arrived. Did he not shed that unhappy silence you describe?"

"Ay, but you have him in your thrall. Black magic – to lure him into danger."

"I don't want to lure him anywhere. I'd like to help you all I can and be a good daughter to you. I know you have your other son's wife…" She paused for a reaction, having seen no sign today of such a person.

Mistress Heron was still appraising her with the poss-stick raised like a weapon, but at that she snorted. "Sarah! She'll never be a daughter to me, wants to get Joe away from the pit and off to Newcastle if she can."

Dione dared to take a step towards her, her hands upturned, her eyes beaming love. "So let me be your daughter, please." She looked down at the wet washing. "Tell me where to get water for the rinsing and I'll fetch it."

"Oh, ay, well – the stream comes down at the corner of the field yonder. The land there is all part o' the pit farm." Mistress Heron motioned her towards the open door and pointed with the poss-stick. "Jack built up a nice little waterfall and made a pool for filling the buckets. There's still a full one on the floor of the larder but there's two empties outside you could fill if you've a mind to."

Dione smiled and went out and picked up the buckets. She's mine, she told herself. She lives only through her daily work. I can manage her.

She followed the well-beaten path that had been pointed out, skirting the vegetable plot, and saw a woman's figure filling a bucket at the stream.

As she drew near she saw she was young with coarse yellow hair and a red blotchy complexion. She was staring at Dione, oblivious of the water overflowing her bucket.

"Good morning to you," Dione said. "I'm fetching water for Mistress Heron. I'm Jack's betrothed."

"What! It's true then. Eh, I half-died laughing at him."

The girl set her bucket down on the path, slopping water on her bare feet, and looked Dione up and down as if she were a weird phenomenon.

"I'm Dione." She held out her hand. "What's your name?"

The girl grinned and wiped her hand on her petticoat before taking hers gingerly. "Jenny Coxon."

"Ah, you live in the other downstairs room. Do you live alone?"

She pushed out her lips and narrowed her eyes. "Ay, since me man died."

"Oh, I'm so sorry. When was that?"

"Three weeks gone. Fall of rock. They're letting me stay here rent free for a wee while but no compensation. They'd like to blame him. I ask you, does anyone *try* to get crushed? And he's left me a bairn on the way too."

Dione felt instantly at one with this girl. Her face was blotchy with weeping.

"Oh, let us be friends."

"I don't know. I'd have gone for Jack Heron now me Sam's dead. Jack's never had a woman. I could bring him on, but you say he's yours."

Dione hardly knew how to answer this except with an emphatic nod and a move to the stream to fill the buckets.

"Ay, well," Jenny said, "if that's the way of it. But I cannot think how he came onto you so quick when he was the bashfullest man you ever saw."

She was turning away with her buckets when Dione called out, "Would you let me have a bed till Jack and I are wed? I could pay you something."

Jenny turned her head and her eyes gleamed bright. "I reckon I'd rather have a *man* in me bed but you might stop me crying all night. What did you say your name was?"

"Dione."

"Funny sort of name. Can I call you Dee?"

"Certainly."

She grinned again and walked off with her buckets.

Dione wondered what she had done but it was too late now. She stood looking at the little waterfall bubbling over a cleft boulder that had been placed in the stream, and the pool surrounded with flat rocks so one could stand comfortably to draw water.

"My man did this. It's good," she said aloud. "I love him."

She picked up the full buckets and followed Jenny back to the house.

"You've met Jenny, have you?" Mistress Heron was standing in her doorway.

"She has kindly offered to let me sleep there so I can help you every day."

"She has, has she? Well, we'll get the washing rinsed and hung out. The sun's on the clothesline now. I reckon you can do that, but can you cook and lay a fire?"

"I was shown how by my nursemaid who was put down to kitchen maid when my Grandfather Sheradon died. I told you my parents were cruel. They made me have a horrid French governess instead of dear Bessie."

Mistress Heron pursed up her lips and said, "My, my! French governess, eh?" But Dione saw that the laughter lines at the corners of her eyes were creasing. "We'll try you out with the fire in the morn, I'm thinking. That's if you're really stopping and won't vanish into thin air like the way you dropped into our lives, Milady Sheradon."

"Jenny's going to call me Dee."

"Oh ay, well that's easier than what you said you was called."

Dione exulted. She was a new person, Dee. Soon she would be Dee Heron and this was Dee Heron's new life, fetching water from a clear bubbling stream, hanging clothes to blow in God's good air. She had made this happen. It was a life of purpose. It was a great adventure.

Chapter 4

Jack

Jack Heron, his heart like a pumpkin in his chest, thrust open the house door and darted his eyes round the room. He turned desperately on his mother.

"You *did* throw her out. I feared that all day after she didn't wave on the second run. How could you do that? She's my betrothed."

He felt a huge sob rising and then saw that her eyes were laughing at him.

"Nay, you daft booby. She's next door with Jenny. She's going to stop there till you're wed – if it's to come to that. But she'll have to get her father's consent. I'm not having anyone descending on us and reckoning we kidnapped her."

She had to stop speaking as his wild embrace nearly choked her. But he released her at once and was out of the door and darting to Jenny's door which he opened without knocking.

He checked when he saw the two girls sitting close together on Jenny's bed and examining a piece of lace that spilled across their cupped hands.

They looked up, startled, but his own girl's face shone with delight. She dropped the lace back into her bundle which was between them on the floor and jumped up with outstretched arms. His own were round her in a moment.

"My precious, my lovely." His hands felt her firm slender waist and longed to reach higher but he was shyly aware of Jenny grinning at him from the bed.

She stood up. "I'll hide in my larder if you want to get down to business."

He stepped back, his face burning.

"Why not? You say you're betrothed. You cannot suppose I made my Sam wait for *our* wedding. Oh, he was a wonder was Sam." And she burst into tears.

"Nay, don't do that," he pleaded.

She shook her head, trying to laugh them away. He could see that his Dione was distressed for her and he wanted to know whether she had taken in what Jenny had said before the tears came. She wasn't blushing.

Jenny pulled up her apron and wiped her eyes. "Don't mind me. It was seeing you two and thinking of the good times you're going to have together – I mean it. I'll go in the larder. The shelves want scrubbing."

He stood, hands by his sides, stupidly. "I – Ma will have our meal ready."

"Come back later then. Dee and I are eating together tonight. She brought some leeks from your ma's vegetable plot and I got eggs today for minding the Slaters' twins."

"Dee?" he repeated, feeling foolish again.

"That's what I'm called now," Dione said with her angel smile. "I like it. And I was weeding the vegetables when you came back on the wagon. I ran round the house to wave but I was too late. Of course you can come back later. I'm not to go into your place." She cast her eyes down and now she did blush. "Your mother said your father has to be washed down by the fire when he comes in from the pit."

Is that why she's blushing? he thought. Aloud, he said, "Ay, he does that. I'm not black wi' *my* job. Can I come back then, just to say goodnight, like?"

Jenny held her sides, laughing. "Eh, my word, what a pair of innocents you are! Your brother Joe told me you were too shy even to look under a girl's skirt and I'll wager Dee's never been allowed to be a naughty girl in her whole life. I can see you'll both need Jenny Coxon's help. So go on with you, Jack Heron."

Jack was so hot and flustered now that he got himself out of the door so quickly that he never even glanced at his own girl's face. He felt powerfully that it was all wrong. His Dione and Jenny should inhabit two different worlds and yet she was here in his own world now, among his own people, and she was to be his. She loved him. That was the miracle.

He opened his own door and there was his mother washing his father's back in the tub, the narrow shoulders coming up white, the still-grey knees hunched up in front of him.

He looked round. "Seen your girl then, Jack? Ma thinks she might even do for you. Cut above us o'course, but seems to be set on having you. I can't think why."

"She's a worker," was his mother's verdict. "Leastways, she's worked today, and she took kindly to us calling her Dee. But I cannot let another day pass without meeting her family, whatever they're like. She's no but a wee lassie when all's said and done."

When his father was dressed he and Jack carried the tub of black water out and emptied it at the corner of the field. Jack set it down and faced his father. "How is Ma to find her family? My girl said she has no one in the world."

"Ay, well, she's told Ma she's a Sheradon from that big house beyond Ovingham."

"What?" Jack shook his head. A name and a real place snatched away all the mystery that had floated about Dione.

His father stooped to grasp one of the handles of the tub. He didn't seem inclined to say more but when Jack still stood unmoving he added, "Ay, but it seems her father threw away his wealth somehow and the place will have to be sold. The girl has naught but the clothes she's wearing and whatever's in that bundle. Your mother looked in it and said there's some good linen on top of a few bits and pieces."

And pretty lace, Jack thought. For our wedding? Of course his girl was from gentry. That was how she spoke so well. But he wanted her to have dropped from heaven. Slowly he stooped and took the other handle of the tub. He was remembering that she had asked if God had sent him. It was all a puzzle. Dione Sheradon – a great lady. His mind couldn't compass the idea.

"Haway." His father tugged at the tub. "I'm wanting my dinner."

Jack set his feet in motion. Perhaps it would all come right when she was Dee Heron.

After they had eaten he went outside and, not letting himself think what he was going to do, he took the eight paces to Jenny's door and knocked.

"Oh, come in, Jack," came Jenny's voice. "She's all ready for you."

He pushed open the door and stepped in and closed it behind him. He stood there with his back to it and looked at his girl standing in the centre of the room with one hand outstretched to him.

"Come and sit with me. We've scarce spoken two words since I came this morning." She was indicating the window seat.

"Oh ay." He moved with alacrity. "Talk."

Jenny laughed. She had sat herself in the cane-seated chair by the hearth and taken up some knitting. "Talk first and then I'll go in the larder and scrub the shelves."

Dione ignored this but sat close to him and spoke softly. He felt his thigh touching hers through her cotton skirt. He could scarcely take in her words.

"I'll tell you about my childhood and my dear grandfather and Bessie, my nursemaid. My husband should know these things."

He wasn't sure that he wanted to know anything but he loved to hear that word, 'husband'. That was what he was going to be as soon as it could be arranged. He, Jack Heron, was to have a wife, just like his brother Joe had a wife, but Dione – Dee he must call her – Dee Heron – was so much lovelier than Sarah, so sweet, so soft-voiced. Sarah was shrill and could be sharp of tongue. He looked at Dee's profile as her lips moved. His girl, his betrothed. She had a trick of pushing out her lower lip when she paused for a word. It was full and rosy and there was a dimple in her cheek when she turned to smile at him. He nodded and smiled back. He had kissed her on those lips already. That was magical. But there would have to be real action. He knew what it was, but how would it be? Jenny's coarse talk must be far away from the moment when he knew his girl and made one with her.

"So you see, Jack" – now he had to listen – "I'll go with your mother to Sheradon Grange in the morning and see if I can find out where my parents are or what has happened to them. She is most insistent on meeting them but I dread her knowing them. She may not want me then. She may try to stop us marrying. My family are not fit to meet yours. You come from kind, honest people. If only my grandfather were alive still!"

He thought hard for a moment. "It's no matter for families. Just you and me. Jack and Dee Heron. That's all."

Jenny got up and put her knitting down on the chair. "It's larder time. Them shelves want a good clean. There's the bed. Call me if you need help." She shut the door on herself, chuckling.

His face was burning. He could feel it and put his hands up to cover his cheeks. Dee was staring down at the worn rush-mat.

He touched her hands, which were clasped tightly in her lap.

"Could we?" The words squeezed out of him.

She didn't move but murmured so low he could hardly hear, "We're not wed yet."

"But betrothed. I love you. Should we not know each other better?"

"I've told you all there is to know."

But he hadn't heard it. He wanted only herself, no past, no people. Nothing must stand between them. What had struck him just now was her saying that his mother might not want her if she met her parents. That meeting was to happen tomorrow. So she must be his tonight. The belonging together had to happen. Oh yes, his body was telling him that, as it never had before in the presence of a girl. There had been dreams of course, but *she* had proved no dream. When he had been scorned for imagining her, she had come to find him. She was here, close to him. Her need of him was so desperate. Her arms had been open to him from the first moment. That was the greatest wonder. So now? It must be right that nothing should separate them.

He couldn't speak. There were no words in his head to express his certainty that this was the moment. He dare not put it off. Jenny was totally forgotten. He slid his arms round her and stood her on her feet. He didn't know how it was to happen but he began to propel her across the room to the bed in the corner. Like his parents' it was a box you slid into with cupboards above. He mustn't bang her head. He must be very careful.

She was pulling back.

"Oh Jack, we can't, we shouldn't."

He could only nod his head, then lay his cheek against hers and gradually roll his lips round to seek her mouth. She let him kiss her, then gripped him and kissed him with passion.

"I do love you, Jack."

She was yielding. She had kicked off her shoes. They were moving as one towards the bed. Awkwardly they fell into it. He knew he had to pull his boots off and sat up quickly to do it, and then his breeches. He had no idea how to approach her lovely body. His parents always had the curtain drawn. He slid next to her, his hands touching the curve of her breast.

"Oh Jack," she murmured, "I've never had anyone love me as you do. Your love is the most beautiful thing. It can't be wrong to be one with you, can it? We will be wed as soon as we can. No one can stop us."

She was untying the laces of her bodice. She wore no corset, just a shift which she drew up so that he could see one of her full round breasts.

He kissed it. Was that how you started? He didn't know but it was very lovely.

She stroked his head and the back of his neck. "I was set against it, sweet Jack, but Jenny told me what happens, what I must do. We haven't long. When we are in our own home together it will be wonderful." She was easing up her skirt. He could see her pale legs, without stockings or garters. She was touching him, drawing close.

Somehow, he hardly knew how, he was inside her, with a wonderful rush of passion, gasping, clutching her, falling away from her, panting, his head back and her eyes beaming love and with that smile of paradise that he had conjured from her tears an age ago. If this was married love he would have more and more of it.

"Get dressed, Jack," she said. "You lovely man. Your mother will wonder why you have been so long." But she herself didn't move, though her hands pushed her skirt down and fastened her bodice as she lay flat. "This is our secret, Jack, at least till we're safely married. Jenny will not betray us."

He fumbled into his breeches and boots. "I thought once we were betrothed it was…? God won't be angry, will He?"

"Nay," she said, picking up his manner of speech. "*He* will not. Does not the Bible tell us Jesus is all love? But my mother would, and my father, although he is a bad man, would think it his duty to protect his daughter's honour."

Jack felt his face crumple with dismay. "Have I dishonoured you?"

"Nay," she said again, her eyes bright with laughter. "You are to be my husband and it is you who will defend my honour for the rest of our lives. I am yours, Jack, for ever. And quite soon we will declare it in church before the minister and all your family and friends, just as Joseph did yesterday."

Yesterday! The word echoed in Jack's head. How could it have been only yesterday?

There was a tap from the larder and Jenny put her head round.

"Me shelves are clean. But do not you fret, the day will come when you'll spend much longer at it. When my Sam was not doon the pit it was all we wanted to do. I'd have had you, Jack Heron, if Dee hadn't come along, but it'll be hard to find a man when the bairn comes. No man wants to bring up another man's child."

Jack couldn't think of a reply to that. He was painfully embarrassed that Jenny should know what had been going on. Dee had now slid herself off the bed and looked as red-faced as he felt. He must take himself off, but she was truly his now and he knew when he was back in his own bed he would sleep with utter contentment. He had achieved what he had long believed would never be his – a woman who wanted him and loved him for himself.

"Goodnight, my own," he said. "Will I see you in the morning before I go to work?"

"Yes," Dee said, with a half-smile. "I have to prove to your mother that I can lay a fire."

Jenny laughed and opened the outer door for Jack. The summer night was dimming and they must all be in their beds soon to save candles.

"Do *I* not get a word of thanks, Jack Heron?" she said.

"Oh ay, I thank you, Jenny," he mumbled.

She reached up and kissed his cheek. "Go on with you."

Dione

Dione watched the door close. "Do you not bolt it, Jenny?"

"If you like." Jenny shot the bolt across. "Are you feared he'll come back for more?"

"No. I dread my parents finding me."

"But you are to seek them tomorrow, you said."

"I trust I'll find no one but their lawyer at the house."

Jenny shrugged her shoulders. Evidently it was not a subject that interested her greatly. She sidled up to Dione. "Well, did the innocent wee lad manage anything?"

Dione assumed a look of bewilderment. "I suppose so. It wasn't very pleasant. Not like you said you had with Sam. It was all over so quick."

Jenny laughed. "He'll learn to hold back. First time for you both. I should have warned you not to expect too much. Eh! I don't know how I'm to live without it. There's lads would come in to me if I asked them but I've got you now so they'll not come."

"But could you do it when you're expecting a baby? Is it safe?"

"Why, ay. You can't be caught out when you're with child already."

"I meant is it safe for you and the baby?"

"Ay, though there's women will make it an excuse for their man to leave them alone. Maybe when I get big some men won't fancy me. Maybe I won't fancy it meself then." She gave a great yawn, showing Dione some of her blackened teeth. "Let's turn in. I'm hoping I'll sleep better feeling a body next to me."

Dione had had plenty of time to see all there was in Jenny's one room, which was a mirror image of the Heron's apart from their extra bed up a short ladder which Jack and Joseph had used. The last time she had shared a bed was as a little girl when she would ask Bessie to come in with her if she was frightened by an owl hooting outside the Grange windows. But now she was suddenly so tired she longed only to be lying down.

"Sam was always on the outside," Jenny said when they were both ready. "Will you mind that?"

"Not at all."

"He never waked if I climbed over him for the chamber pot."

"It's all right. I'm sure I'll sleep deeply. I was up early after a dreadful night."

Dione could hardly wait for Jenny to slide in and curl up next to the wall. She followed her and fitted her body to hers in the cramped space.

Jenny chuckled a little. "It's a mighty odd business, you coming like this." She mumbled a few more words and then she was asleep.

Now Dione, her body quite still, found her mind buzzing with amazement at what she had achieved in this one extraordinary day. Her strongest emotion was relief. She had a father for the baby she was sure was within her. There need be no trouble over the time the child was born. If they couldn't be married for a few more weeks Jack would confess to his mother what had passed today. She felt a small stab of conscience when she recalled Jenny's remark that a man wouldn't want to bring up another man's child. But this baby would be Jack's. He was far too sweetly simple ever to think otherwise.

And I have won over his mother, she congratulated herself. She is a plain simple soul who sees no further than her daily chores. Her husband? After a day down the pit he only needs to eat and sleep. They will make no trouble over the wedding. What I do fear is that we may see Father and Mother and find that they have recovered something of their old selves. If they have, Mother will be horrified to hear I intend to marry into a miner's family. Oh, dear God, they must not meet Jack's mother and tell her I am with child. So much has unfolded so easily since I wept and prayed in the churchyard yesterday. Does it mean God truly had compassion on me or is He waiting to hurl some fearful thunderbolt at me in the morning? No, He could not be so cruel. They will be gone away.

Her mouth felt dry. She longed suddenly for the iced water a footman would bring on hot days from the ice house to the wrought-iron table on the terrace at Sheradon Grange when her mother was entertaining friends. She mustn't think of such things. They were shallow tedious days when no one truly loved her. Now she had her man who adored her and the child they would treasure together.

I can sleep, she thought, because I know I can love this man. And I *must* sleep for I have to be up to make a fire next door. Grandfather, you would be proud of me. You told me once that the overcoming of hardship makes the soul stronger and you feared you were leaving my father too soft a life, and me too. Well, this will not be soft, dear Grandfather. Whatever comes, I will remember all you taught me. I'm glad I told Jack about you today.

And on that memory Dione finally slept.

Chapter 5

Dione

Dione and Jack's mother never reached Sheradon Grange the next day. They had briskly walked the three miles to Ovingham but there they found a crowd in the village, babbling with excitement.

"What's to do here then?" Jane Heron remarked.

Dione had heard William, Jack's father, name his wife that morning in a rare moment of speech. "Why Jane," he'd said, "the lass has set that fire mighty well." And then he had gone to work with a nod to her that suggested to Dione that *he* would not object to her becoming part of the family. But, she thought, his wife, Jane – I may not call her that yet – seems wary of me today. She said little as we walked along the river path. Is she nervous of meeting my parents? Not as anxious as I. I pray to God they are nowhere about now.

An old woman at a cottage door heard Jane Heron's question and peered in their direction.

"Eh, is that Jane Heron from Wylam? Me eyes is bad. It's not Sunday, is it?"

"Nay, it's not Sunday, but it's me, Elsie. What's the commotion about?" She added aside to Dione, "She knows us from the church, Dee, but she'll have the tale wrong, I wager."

"They brought two bodies down from the Dene," croaked the old lady. "Dead as doornails they were. They wheeled them by on a cart, covered up, like."

"How could they get dead up there?" Jane asked. "There's not the water in the Whittle Burn to drown a rat after this dry weather."

"Nay, but I heard someone say there was a pistol shot. I daresn't walk out in the street when there's a crowd. If I get pushed around I fall over. Me eyes is bad."

"Ay, you stay where you are, Elsie. We'll hear soon enough. Maybe it was poachers about." She turned to Dione. "We'd best get on, though. Your place is a mile or two further, ain't it? What's up, lass?"

Dione realised her sudden sick apprehension must be showing on her face. Her mother had once told her that the day she and her father met there had been an elegant picnic in the grounds of Sheradon Grange and to draw her from the company he had enticed her on a walk to Whittle Mill, where he had been bold enough to kiss her. "As it happened," she had commented to Dione, "your father was perfectly eligible and *your* suitor, Sir Ralph, is too, but always observe the proprieties until you're safely married." Now it hit her like a blow to the stomach that her father might have chosen that place to end their lives. Horror and a fearful hope fought within her.

"Oh, nothing, nothing," she told Jane Heron. "Just the thought of dead bodies carried by here."

"If you'd seen 'em crushed from pit accidents as I have you'd not be troubled." She began to push through the chattering crowd.

A man said loudly, "Ay, they're questioning Mary at the inn. It was she that shouted 'Murderer' and then he shot himself. She's mighty upset about it."

"But did she *see* him push the woman?" another voice asked.

"Nay, you'll have to ask Mary when they've finished with her."

Dione's knees trembled under her. She caught hold of Jane Heron's arm. "Please, I'd like to stop at the inn and inquire."

"Ay, ye're curious now, are ye? Well, it'll be a tale to tell in Wylam, I suppose."

There was such a crowd in the inn doorway that Dione despaired of learning anything, but then a constable appeared from inside and began pushing them all out.

"Have you folks nothing better to do than stand gawping? There'll have to be a coroner's inquest and you'll hear no more till then."

"Do you no ken who they are yet?" a man shouted.

"We have a good idea but *you* won't be told."

"Looked like gentry by their dress," a woman said.

They began to drift away as the constable shooed with his arms as if they were a herd of bullocks. He was about to go in and shut the inn door when Dione thrust herself forward.

"Please, I have to know. I fear – they could be my parents. Oh, please!"

He reached out an arm and pulled her inside and tried to close the door but Jane Heron forced her way in too. "Nay, I'm with the young lady, Constable Martin."

Dione would rather have been alone with him. She was either about to look very foolish or receive a fearful shock.

She peered up into the constable's face. He had a great bulbous nose but his popping eyes either side of it were looking at her kindly.

"What made you ask that? Why do you suppose you know the sad couple?"

"Where are they? Are they here?" She shivered but her hands were sweating. She looked about her. There was no one in this, the main room of the inn, though mugs were scattered on the tables and some on the benches as if the drinkers had been summarily removed. She sniffed an unpleasant smell and realised it came from an old mongrel dog sprawled in front of the fire. It opened one eye to look at her, but finding her of no interest closed it again. A man's muted voice came through the half-open door to a little parlour beyond and then a shrill woman's voice pleading, "I've told you all I can. I was not near enough to be sure." That must be the Mary they were questioning.

The constable stepped over and closed the door.

Dione said as he came back, "You said you had a good idea who they are."

"There were letters in the gentleman's pocket. But, young lady, first you must tell me who *you* are."

She swallowed. She would have to say it, the name she longed to be rid of.

"Dione Sheradon."

"Ah!" His eyes popped more than ever. He indicated the bench behind her. "Sit ye down. The name *was* Sheradon."

Dione sank onto it and leant against the table for support. *Did I not pray God just now that my parents would not be anywhere about? Is He heeding all my prayers so precisely? Is this what I was truly hoping for? Is this relief?*

Her throat was as dry as the sandy path they had walked on. She moistened her lips with her tongue.

Jane Heron was at her side, babbling, "Now Dee, it may not be your father and mother. Why would you think such a thing?"

Dione turned her head and met her eyes, which were peering anxiously. This is the only woman friend I have in the world, she thought, and I scarcely know her.

"My father threatened to kill himself." She kept her voice steady. "Nothing either of them have done will surprise me now."

The constable stepped to the other door and reopened it. "Will you come here, sir? I've found a young lady reckons she's a daughter to the parties concerned."

A daughter to two corpses, you mean, Dione said to herself. What have they done with them, I wonder? I will have to look upon them or I will never be able to close the curtain on my young life.

A grey-haired gentleman stood before her and solemnly eyed her up and down. She began to get up but he gestured for her to remain seated and perched himself opposite her on a stool brought forward from the inglenook fireplace. She saw him crinkle his nose and look down at the dog with some distaste.

"I saw you in happier times, Miss Sheridan," the gentleman began, "at a party at your home. I believe it was to celebrate your sixteenth birthday and entry into society. Your father had invested well up to that point but was considering the speculation which seems to have caused his downfall. He was not pleased that I advised him against it. I understand you have been told that sadly he and your mother have met with a fatal accident."

Dione noticed his way of talking while clasping his chin and pushing up his cheeks. She remembered him speaking to her father and afterwards she had learnt that he was a Justice of the Peace, but she couldn't recall his name. Her father and mother had been at the pinnacle of their social life on that occasion. All they could speak of was their triumph in assembling so many notables to the Grange, including Sir Ralph Barnet. "You may encourage that young man, but very discreetly," her mother had told her. New curtains had been purchased for the drawing room which was lit by three chandeliers. "No one hereabouts has *three*," she remembered her mother saying.

Jane Heron was addressing the magistrate with surprising boldness. "She's not been told a thing with any plainness, Your Honour. If 'tis Mary, the miller's wife, you have in there and she saw what happened, why don't you bring her in here and let her tell the tale?"

He glowered at her over his cupped hand. "I presume you are Miss Sheradon's maidservant."

Dione shook her head vigorously. "Mistress Heron is to be my mother-in-law."

He sat bolt upright at that, dropping his hands and looking from one to the other.

"And she is right that I know nothing yet. I beg you to take me to see my poor parents and let me know how they died."

"*See* them!" He got up and walked about the room. "No, no, mighty upsetting. No, no." He turned to Constable Martin who had taken up a position with his back to the outside door. "Fetch Mary Robson in and my clerk to make notes."

The woman who was ushered in was younger and tougher-looking than Dione expected. She was bare-headed, wearing her apron, just as she must have been when she was brought from the mill.

"I've work to get back to," she began truculently.

The magistrate indicated Dione. "This young lady is daughter to the couple whose deaths you witnessed. You will oblige me by repeating to her what you saw."

Her manner changed at once. She dropped a curtsey to Dione and her face crumpled. "Oh my, I'm that sorry."

"Pray, tell me what happened." Dione looked up at the magistrate. "Could we not be alone?"

"I fear not. An inquest must be held and all relevant matter submitted in writing."

"Very well." Dione saw that the clerk, a hollow-cheeked youth, had settled with his writing materials on a stool at the end of the table where some light came through the smudged window. She looked at the young woman who had been directed to the stool the justice had vacated. She perched on it and clasped her hands tightly over a fold of her apron and turned her eyes on the somnolent dog near her feet, avoiding Dione's gaze. The justice remained standing with an elbow on the mantelshelf, watching her closely.

"Well, Mary?" he said.

Not lifting her head, she began to speak as if to the dog, repeating what she must already have said many times. "It were not long after dawn when

I went out to feed the chickens and saw a gentleman and a lady standing on the high plank bridge what crosses the Dene 'bout fifty yards above the mill. They was shouting at each other but I couldn't make out words. Then he pulled her to him and it seemed like he tried to kiss her but she wasn't having it, leastways that's how it looked. So he grabbed her hand and gave a sort of shout and pulled her off or maybe she jumped with him. I couldn't tell." She glanced quickly up at Dione. "I screamed and began running towards them along the path – to help if I could – but she'd fallen face down right in the middle of the stream on the stones and gravel. The water's only a trickle but I didn't try to climb down to her. I was feared for I saw the gentleman was still alive. He'd landed part-way down the bank and was caught astride an alder branch and was staring full at me. I suppose he heard me scream and I could see his mouth open in surprise. I wasn't certain whether he could move so I was minded to run for my husband but—"

She broke off and began to whimper with a pleading look at Dione, whose eyes were riveted on her. "As I turned to run, I yelled at him, 'Murderer!' I don't know why, my lady, but I could see the poor woman not moving and the water bubbling over her turning red, and I was so shocked. I thought he'd meant to save *himself* and the word just came out. I'd never seen such a thing happen before."

Dione reached a hand towards her. "Pray don't fret about that. Just say what happened next."

She spoke in a rush of words. "There was a bang and I looked back and he was slumped across the branch and his head – the blood…" She lifted her apron over her head and sobbed into it. "So it's my fault he's dead, isn't it?"

Dione, in tears too, jumped up and raised her to her feet and put her arms round her. "It's not, it's not, it's not."

The tale rang only too true. Oh, Father, you sorry fool, she cried in her mind as she clasped the girl to her. You couldn't kill yourself in cold blood alone in the wood so you had to decide to die with Mother – where you first kissed her. What drama, what sentiment! But of course you bungled it, saw you had been observed and now feared you would be arrested and hung – so at last you must have used the pistol. Oh Father! And oh wretched Mother! Did you agree to die with him but couldn't forgive him at the end for bringing you to this?

She became aware of the magistrate gently but firmly trying to part them.

"It is enough. We will let Mary return to the mill. Constable Martin, pray accompany her there lest she be pestered by the crowd."

Dione released her, saying, "My father was *not* a deliberate murderer. He intended to kill himself and my mother together but he made a poor fist of it and I blame you not one wit for what you shouted at him."

Mary, still rubbing her eyes, muttered, "Thank you, my lady," and followed the constable out.

"But from you, Miss Sheradon," the justice went on, "I would wish to learn more of the events of the last few days, but not of course till you have had time to recover from this terrible news. You understand that all this happened some hours ago. It was the miller who fetched Constable Martin and a messenger was of course sent to me. Mary will need to make her affidavit when an inquest can be convened and I fear we may need your presence at that too, Miss Sheradon, to shed light on your parents' state of mind." He cupped his chin with his hand, pursing his lips together. "It *might* be avoided if you are able to tell me all that is necessary." He looked over at Jane Heron, sitting very still on the bench against the wall, and lowered his voice. "Did I hear you refer to *her* as your *mother-in-law*?"

Dione forced herself to speak with great composure. Her mind was already working on how quickly she could become disengaged from her old life. She said loudly and clearly, "I am betrothed to Mistress Heron's son and eager to begin my life with my new family. As you will know, I have nothing to bring to them but my youth and health. Nevertheless they have kindly welcomed me into their home."

His eyebrows, grey and bristly, shot up. "And where is this home, may I ask?"

Jane Heron spoke out. "T'other side o' Wylam by the waggonway. 'Tis called Burn Cottage. And we'd best be getting back there."

"No, please," Dione said. "Let me tell this gentleman all I can now and then I can be done with the past." On an impulse she got up and grasped Jane Heron's hands. "*You* are my mother now and I thank you for being my strength and stay during this fearful shock, but go back now to your duties and I will follow presently."

"Nay, I'll not leave you at a time like this." She looked up at the magistrate. "If she and my Jack are to be wed, we're all the family she's got now. Is that not so, sir?"

He pursed his lips. "Permit me a few words with you alone, Miss

Sheradon." And he took Dione's arm and led her into the small parlour.

Jane Heron was left standing, none too pleased, Dione saw, looking back.

He shut the door and motioned Dione to a shabby sofa. There was no fire in here for the day was warm but there was only a tiny window and she felt closed in. He stood with his back to the empty fireplace and began, "I am truly grieved for you but feel I must advise you as an old friend. You cannot ally yourself with people so far below your station in life. You will only make yourself miserable. There must be relatives of your family, however distant, who will offer you a home when they know of this tragedy. I know not how you came to be acquainted with that woman out there but her ways, her speech, her limited horizons are far from yours."

Dione held up her hand. "Pray, go no further, sir. I have chosen my path. The only relative I loved was my grandfather and he died when I was still young. I have met a fine man who loves me and all I desire is to be with him. I beg you to ask me anything you wish to know and let me go."

"And as his wife you will never again move among educated people."

His words flowed over her. She only wanted to slam the shutters on Dione Sheradon and be Dee Heron.

He became impatient at last and his manner changed from avuncular to professional. "Now pray, Miss Sheradon, could you relate to me what happened to your parents from the moment when they witnessed the seizure of their goods to this very morning of despair when they contrived their own deaths?"

She told him what had passed in the gamekeeper's cottage but when he learnt that she had left them and knew nothing of their last two days he looked troubled.

"But you can confirm that taking his own life was certainly in your father's mind and that your mother appeared completely deranged?"

"Yes indeed, sir, and you may think me callous but to them I was only one more burden. There was guilt in my father's heart and I reminded him of it. I met Jack Heron and he loved me. That is my whole story and I will now return to his mother." She got up and then repeated her former question. "Where *are* my parents' bodies?"

"In the cellar below here. It is cold there but they will be reverently removed under cover of dark and the inquest convened as quickly as possible so they can be buried. You do not – I hope – still wish to view them?"

Dione shook her head. "From what Mary has described I cannot bear to think how they will look. I will remember them as they were on that sixteenth birthday you reminded me of. They were so fine in new clothes and with high colour in their cheeks." And how I hated them, she added to herself. They are gone and no one now knows my secret. I am free. How they died is horrible but that I will commit to God's judgment. "May I leave you now, sir?" She moved to open the door to the other room.

He stepped before her. "Well, Miss Sheradon, you know your own mind. I know where to find you and if you need my help or advice, pray ask for it."

"I have forgotten your name, sir, I'm afraid."

"Godfrey Hammond, Justice of the Peace."

She gave a little curtsey and passed quickly through to Jane Heron.

"Will Jack still want me after this horror?" she murmured to her.

Jane tucked her arm through hers. "Haway home, lass. I can answer for Jack."

When Jack came home from work and Dee told him her parents were dead she sensed at once that he wanted no distractions from their wedding day. He held her in his arms, and when she said, "Ah, but I have you, Jack. You are all I need," his face lit up and he held her closer. She added, "And you won't be ashamed of me when this story is in the newspapers?"

"Nay, never! I don't read 'em. Ashamed – of you! Shame was always *my* trouble but since my Dee needs me I shan't ever have days of shame, not one."

Jane told her none of them could read but Joe. It was a shock but she hid it well. "I'll teach you, Jack, so you can sign your name at our wedding."

He jumped with glee. "I won't read the papers though, when the story's out. We want to forget all that. Just look forward to the wedding."

Of course the story shot through the valley like a plague but the result of the inquest was not printed till their banns had been called twice in Ovingham Church.

Dee hadn't expected to meet Jack's brother and his wife till the wedding day. He was Overman at Hedley Colliery which was where they had removed to after their wedding, but one evening they walked in with a newssheet and Joe, heavy-jowled and swarthy, read the report of the inquest out loud. Sarah, sharp and gawky, gave Dee pointed glances at the verdict of suicide, but Jack, who had tried to cover his ears, sat up, all agog when it concluded, *'We understand that the only daughter of the unhappy couple is shortly to be married to Jack Heron, the son of a miner from Wylam. We wish the young couple well and trust that after a life of wealth and privilege Dione Sheradon can find happiness in a humble cottage.'*

"Humble cottage, eh!" muttered their father, but Jack was madly excited and wanted his name pointed out in the printed writing.

"Ay, there it is. That's the J and the H. Dee's been showing me how to write my name so I can sign it in the church book."

Sarah said, "Are ye not feared Dee will despair of you in a while for you never learnt at school?"

Dee was alarmed at this but Jack said stoutly, "You don't understand. I'm Dee's protector. She sobbed in my arms when she told me her parents were dead. Then she said, 'But you are all I need, Jack.' Didn't she say that, Ma?"

"Ay, she did," Jane said, "and I can tell you, Sarah, things are shouted at her in the village and when I tell Jack who it was he goes to their door and threatens them."

Jack broke in, "Yes, I say, 'If you speak about my lovely bride you'll have me to answer to' and I look big and glare at them and then they don't do it no more."

Joe laughed but Dee squeezed his hand. This frank talk in her presence was uncomfortable but in a strange way liberating.

Sarah poked her thin nose at Jane. "What do they shout? I'm curious."

His mother shrugged. "Things like 'Hoy, Sheradon girl! That's brought you off your high horse.' But I don't see she was ever on one. You was never happy with your parents, were you, Dee? Didn't like grand parties and all that. You been happier working wi' me than in your whole life since your grandfather died." She looked hard at Sarah and added, "She's got no notions of pulling Jack from his good steady job."

Sarah turned abruptly to Dee. "Who'll give you away now, Dee?"

"I've had to ask Mr Hammond, the magistrate. He said if I needed help—"

"Ooh, that'll get the tongues wagging. I'm looking forward to this wedding – though you missed ours, Jack." She wagged her finger at him. "Are you planning a banquet, Ma, since she's a Sheradon?"

"Nay, it's to be very quiet," Jane said. "Isn't it, William?"

But he was asleep.

Sarah giggled. "Oh well, we'll likely be the only witnesses."

"I've asked Jenny next door to be my attendant," Dee said, aware that Joe was growing red-faced at his wife's talk.

He got up now. "We must be off. It's a fair walk after the river ferry and mostly uphill. Nay, we'll not stop for supper, Ma. Haway, Sarah."

Jack opened the door before Sarah could object. He and Dee escorted them round the corner of the house and waved as they joined the track, Joe with a heavy plodding gait and Sarah moving jerkily to keep up with him.

Jack put his arm round Dee's waist. "Joe only chose her because she's clever. They're not the wedded couple you and I will be." The look he gave her was yearning. "Dee, do you think Jenny might scrub her larder shelves tonight?"

She shook her head. "I told her I'm holding back to make our wedding night special and she says we can have her bed then. Nan Slater will let her snuggle in with her twins."

After that, in one room with his parents, she supposed they would have to wait till the old ones fell asleep. Such a life was unimaginable but he nodded happily and repeated, "Ay, wedding night special. All that other business is past now, ain't it, Dee? All's clear till our wedding." And he held and kissed her before they went back inside.

Chapter 6

Jack

Jack was so buoyed up he was walking on tiptoe as they reached the church. He was to be wed, he, Jack Heron, and to the loveliest girl in the world. Out of all the world she had chosen to love him. He was part of a miracle.

"Bless my soul," his mother cried, "the church is full."

"Ay, Jane Heron," came old Elsie's voice among the people still pushing in, "we all want to see the great lady your Jack's to wed. Not that I'll see much, me eyes is that bad. Is there a back pew where I can have a bit o' daylight when she walks in?"

Jack saw Dee step up to the old lady and put a hand under her elbow. "I am here, Jack's bride. We just walked along together for a quiet wedding. There, you're welcome to look at me, but I'm no more important than Jack or his parents or his brother and sister-in-law, or Jenny here, who have all kindly come to support us."

Jenny giggled. "They ain't here to see me, that's for sure."

Old Elsie fingered Dee's dress. "Eh, that's a fine silk. I was a dressmaker for the gentlefolk once." She peered up at her face. "I think you're a bonny lass."

Jack burst out, "She's the most beautiful girl in the world and she loves me."

Some of the young men going in laughed and clapped him on the back.

Joe, his head held rigid by his starched collar, said, "We mustn't get caught up in this crush. Come, Sarah, we will have places reserved at the front. Jack, elbow your way ahead. You must stand by me, you know."

There was a sudden buzz at the arrival of a carriage. Jack turned round. The magistrate had come to give Dee away. He descended, stiff-backed, frowning at the noise. The people hung back. Jack saw him make his way to Dee's side.

"Miss Sheradon, I sent my clerk to fetch you so you could arrive *with* me."

Jack exulted in Dee's prim curtsey to him and her clear answer.

"I know, sir, and I thank you, but our family party had already set off and I told your messenger that I wished us to come together. The last thing I desired was to arrive in a carriage."

Jack thought the magistrate looked peeved but he took Dee's arm and motioned the rest of the family inside.

"Pray, take your places." He waved a hand at the crowd still outside. "And you people, if you are ready to behave reverently in God's house, go inside."

The vicar had now managed to make his way to the church porch. "Ah, Mr Hammond, sir. I never expected this. There are people from all down the valley, even as far as Newcastle. It was the newssheets that did it."

"Well, let us proceed, Reverend Birkett. The sooner they can all be dispersed the better."

The vicar returned to the chancel and Jack scurried after his brother, his heart swelling as the people pointed at him.

"There's the groom!"

Dee had made him a somebody when he had been a nobody.

In the front pew Jack could see only the dark chancel behind the vicar in his vestments. Then the magistrate's heavy step rang on the stones and he had to look round. Dee was on his arm, her eyes radiant, a picture in pale blue silk with the piece of lace he had glimpsed before pinned in her hair. She was to be his, all of her.

His joy was almost too great. When it came to the vows he repeated them in a loud voice, looking into her glowing brown eyes which showed him how desperately she loved him. It was unbelievable that this was happening to him. His legs trembled when they went into the vestry to sign the book. His big fingers refused to pick up the quill pen and Dee placed it between them herself, giving him her paradise smile.

"You remember how it starts. J." He made a stroke with the pen. "It curls to the *left*, my sweet husband."

That's what he was, her husband. She was his *wife*! But the order and shape of the letters had gone from his mind. Joe took out his pocket book and wrote it for him to copy while the Reverend Birkett was assuring him that it was quite in order for him to make his mark. It was done, however, a little rough and uneven, but there it was, Jack Heron, and Dee was still smiling and saying it was beautiful writing.

Joe and the magistrate signed as witnesses and they processed back out of the church with the crowds laughing and cheering.

Jack could hear his mother, arm in arm with his father, saying behind them, "I never could have dreamt our Jack would be wed scarce a month after our Joe."

His father actually broke into speech. "Ay, I've not rightly took it all in yet."

Dee pressed Jack's arm and laughter broke over her face, showing her dimples. "I've hardly took it in either, Jack, but I've never been happier in my life than I am this minute."

He swallowed tears, too exultant to speak.

Dee

Dee repeated her words to herself as they walked back to Wylam, refusing Godfrey Hammond's invitation to "A little light refreshment for the bridal pair at my house?" If he wasn't inviting the family and Jenny they were not going.

Am I happy? she asked herself. What have I done? But what else *could* I have done? There was no other road to take and Jack loves me. I need to be loved. This is my new life as Dee Heron. This solid man beside me is mine for life. I know all there is to know of him now but he doesn't know me yet and I doubt if he ever will. Nor will his father or mother or Joe or Sarah, though I am a little afraid of Sarah. Those green eyes of hers are probing, catlike, everywhere.

Most of Wylam Village was walking back with them. Will I ever again have any seclusion? she wondered. I used to have my own bedroom and all the gardens of Sheradon Grange to wander in and find solitude.

As they passed the rows of colliery houses and the pit itself the company dispersed, all but the families that lived in their own cottage. The feet tramped by the waggonway and Dee watched her own feet in her one pair of elegant shoes peeping from beneath her one silk dress. Beside them, in shiny borrowed boots with two new laces, Jack's feet bounced with the springy walk he had displayed from the moment of hearing the words 'man and wife'.

"You are walking on air, Jack."

"I am that. I cannot believe this day has come. A lovely girl loving me. Me! Jack Heron."

He was looking into her face as he said it and his foot caught in a tree root sprawling across the path. He tumbled forward, taking her with him since their arms were linked together. They landed in a heap on the sandy path.

The family and Jenny scrambled to help but they were up and Dee was laughing even as the Slaters and Emmy Charlton following behind hurried forward in alarm.

"Ee, that's bad luck," said Emmy Charlton, a matron in her sixties known as a clever midwife, with a husband coughing his life away.

"Don't talk so daft, Emmy," Jane Heron snapped. "There's not a scratch on either of them. A brush down to get the sand off and they'll be as good as new. If there's a pin on the floor our Jack will fall over it. Dee will just have to get used to it."

Dee saw Jack was red-faced with distress. She squeezed his arm. "It's nothing. I won't be wearing this dress again anyway."

He put the hand she had linked with his to his lips. "Your knuckle's bleeding. I'm ashamed. Nothing was to go wrong this day."

His father said, "Haway, I'm wanting a mug o' ale."

Dee, still holding her smiles for everyone, and linking confidently again with Jack, stepped out at once, but she was shaken up. The pit of her stomach was telling her it could be an omen. Was her baby unharmed? She was sure there was a baby for she had felt sick that very morning and laughed it off to Jenny as nervous excitement. Would she be punished now and lose it, the very reason why she found herself here now, in this group of alien beings? She had slammed the door on Godfrey Hammond, the one link with her old life. Farewell, Dione Sheradon, she said to herself now. For better or worse, I am Dee Heron and the child within me – if Jack's tumble spares it – is his own. He will be a loving father.

She looked up at him with her most radiant smile. "Dear Jack, nothing has gone wrong. We are man and wife."

"Ay, man and wife." His cherubic face relaxed.

How easy, she thought, it will be to keep him happy.

It was not so easy for herself, as she soon found in the early days of their marriage. Several times she was on the verge of screaming hysteria in the cramped living space, but she remembered how her mother had looked when she had lost all reason. She must uphold Jack's vision of her and his mother's too. When people from the village called on any excuse to see a Sheradon at work in a miner's cottage, Jane met them with, "Get ye away home. I cannot wish for a better daughter than Jack's Dee."

It felt like balancing on a pinnacle but she was valued as she had never been in her parents' eyes. In Jack's eyes she could do no wrong at all. If her stotty cakes were burnt on the griddle it was the fault of the fire for being too hot.

"You're perfect too," she whispered to him one night when they had climbed into their bed, "for I never hear a grumble out of your mouth."

"How could I grumble when I have everything a man could desire?"

Will his aspirations always be so few? she wondered. And as he fell instantly asleep after their swift love-making she tortured herself with listing her own aspirations, limiting them to what might someday be attainable by Dee Heron.

A place of their own with more than one room. A water pump in the house. A shelf with some books. Time and privacy to enjoy slow love-making. But here she found herself remembering Sir Ralph Barnet who, aware that she was a virgin, had caressed her body so cunningly that she was thoroughly aroused. How I hate him, she reminded herself. If I had him in my arms now I would tear his handsome face to shreds. And she stroked Jack's round cheeks, inches from hers, and wondered if he would ever learn more than loving her, eating, sleeping and leading a horse on the waggonway. In reading and writing, using a tray filled with sand for practice, he was making little progress. His love though was strong and unwavering.

With a stab of fear she cried in her heart, I must never ever forfeit that for what would be left? We will have the child, she thought. We will have *our* child. Soon I will tell him he is to be a father.

It was three weeks since the wedding and the dry summer of 1802 dragged on till there was only a puddle in Jack's pool. No waterfall bubbled over the groove in his rock. Now Dee crossed the waggonway every morning and scrambled down a well-worn route to fill two buckets from the river. Dione Sheradon had woken to a maid bringing in a jug of warm water to pour into the china bowl on her washstand, but that was another life.

Nausea and hard breasts increased Dee's discomfort but she was desperate not to seem pregnant too soon. An old spade with half a handle was kept stuck in the bank so that the drawers of water could dig a hole since the river itself was so shallow. In the village there was a pump but she preferred to come down here opposite their cottage where only the Charltons, Slaters and Jenny would come.

Here by the river, if she picked her time carefully, she could be alone and it was possible to be sick and no one would know. She could bury the mess with a shovelful of sand. Then she would straighten up and take several long breaths.

Jane Heron found out first. "Dee," she said one morning in late September when heavy rain overnight had at last broken the dry spell, "will you see what's making that stink in the larder? There's summat on the floor at the back. I cannot fetch it out."

Dee got down on her knees and reached her hand under the bottom shelf and felt around. Her fingers encountered something soft and spongy. Her gorge rising, she drew it out and found the decomposing body of a rat.

Her shriek was stifled by the vomit that rose up in her throat and she just had time to turn her head and expel it into a half empty bucket beside her.

Jane Heron picked the thing up by its tail and tossed it into the fire. "Must have been old or hurt by a cat maybe. So what's up with you, Dee? Did you not have rats at the Grange?"

Dee could still smell the stink on her hand. She retched again.

"Well that's water we'll have to throw out. You'd best chuck it away and get fresh. The stream should be flowing again today. That's a blessing."

Dee stood up and reluctantly clasped the bucket handle.

Her mother-in-law was staring at her face. "By, you're a mighty odd colour. Hey, lass, you didn't have your monthly, did you?" Nothing was private here. Dee knew she had in fact missed two. "Is that the first time you've had sickness in a morning?"

Dee shook her head.

"Why, bless my soul!" She prodded Dee's apron. "Ye've a bairn in there. By, I'm right pleased. Did you not guess?"

Dee managed a crooked smile. "I wanted to be the first to tell Jack – when I was sure." She moved towards the door, itching to be out and dipping her hands under the running water.

Jane flopped down in the rocking chair. "I hope it's a girl for I lost three myself. Eh, William'll be right pleased to see a wee bairn toddling about the place."

Dee left her chuckling, hugging herself, and escaped into the chill air, washed clean by the night's rain. The field path was black mud as she slipped and slithered her way to the pool where she was thankful to sink her hands into the water flowing down Jack's rock. She flung the contents of the bucket into a bed of nettles and washed it and her face and hands again before filling it up. She stood up, breathing deeply, and felt restored.

Walking back in her squelching boots, however, she was struck by Jane's glee.

"I won't let her and William take over our baby," she said between clenched teeth. "How can we get out from under their feet before it's born?"

A familiar rumbling broke into her thoughts. This time the sound was higher pitched and more of a rattle. The wagon was coming back empty. For a moment, Jack, leading the horse, was hidden behind the cottage but then he emerged heading for the mine. She set down the bucket and plunged off the path into the long wet grass, cutting across to the track, waving her arms.

Jack reined in the horse, his mouth open in alarm.

"Oh Dee, what's happened?"

She laughed. She would get her word in before his mother. "Nothing. Nay, something wonderful. Oh Jack, you're going to be a father."

There was no holding Jack after that. He told everyone at the mine. He told everyone in the village and everyone at Ovingham Church. He told the tinker who came with ribbons and knick-knacks to sell.

One late September evening he surpassed himself with his loquacity.

Jenny had asked Dee to come and sit with her.

"I've been told to expect a man from the mine owners. I need you here if there's papers to sign or owt like that."

The man came, a gruff elderly clerk with a letter which Dee read aloud to Jenny. It said that no blame for her husband's death was attributable to the management but it had been decided to offer a sum of ten shillings to the widow to help her removal now that the period of free rent had expired.

Jenny made her mark that she'd received it and the man slouched out without a word. Dee was then surprised to hear Jack waylaying the clerk before he could get away. His voice came to them warm with excitement.

"Good evening to you, sir. We too are expecting a child, just like Jenny there. I am to be a father, come April next year we reckon. Is that not cause for rejoicing?"

Dee exchanged laughing glances with Jenny.

The clerk snorted. "Rejoice if you want to but don't forget it's another mouth to feed. And if you're looking for a higher wage I can tell you there's none to be had unless war breaks out again and the demand for coal goes up."

They heard his footsteps stumping away on the gravel path.

Jack put his head round Jenny's door, his mouth pursed in a rueful pout. "I wasn't asking for higher wages. I just wanted to tell him the good news."

Jenny said, "My good news is I can get myself to North Shields now. I'll join me ma and da afore the bairn comes. If you can afford the two shilling rent, Jack, you and Dee could have this place."

Dee gasped as if she had been offered a palace. "Oh Jack, can we have it?"

His forehead puckered with thought. "Nay, I know not. I tips my wages up to Ma and we all live well enough out o' mine and Father's."

Dee had never had to manage money but since her marriage she had been prodded by rebellious thoughts that *she* should be in charge, not her in-laws.

"What is your wage, Jack?" she asked now.

"Five shillings."

She swallowed. Three to spend on everything else. "I should find work."

"Nay," Jack cried as she knew he would, "you've our baby to carry."

Jenny said, "Slaters'll give you eggs if you mind the twins for a few hours."

"And we'd have your vegetable patch. Oh, Jack, we must try." She looked round the room and pictured it with flock wallpaper and a matching bedspread. Then it hit her like a fall of rock in the pit. There would never be spare money. But to have their own space? "We must do it, Jack," she said again.

When it was put to his parents Jane stared reproachfully at Dee. "You said you wouldn't take him away from me."

"Next door!"

"Nay, but families lives *together*."

William, who had been scratching his sparse head of hair, said slowly, "Joseph's wage has gone. This would be two wages less."

Dee prevailed. She had brought writing and sewing materials in her bundle and that very night she wrote out notices that she would do repairs and fine work on ladies' and children's garments, free, but would accept payment in food, candles or bobbins of thread to be agreed beforehand.

The next morning she walked to Wylam and on to Ovingham, posting the notices on the gates of the more genteel houses and telling everyone she met what she was planning to do.

"Ay, 'tis a come-down to earn your bread," some of the miner's wives shouted at her. "Your wee one'll not be heir to a fortune."

When she got back she told Jane what she planned. "I'll still come in and help you, Mother Jane." This was what she called her mother-in-law. The term 'Mother' by itself sickened her but with Jane tagged on, there was a familiarity mixed with deference which seemed to please them both.

"Nay, wi' only William I can manage fine, but I hope you'll still give me your company and let me mind the bairn when it's here."

"'Course I will." She gave the stocky little woman a hug. Oh, she would be able to breathe now!

The day of Jenny's departure came swiftly. Dee was surprised to see the tough girl's eyes moisten.

"Eh, Dee, having you here stopped me tears flowing for Sam. I know I'll weep when I see me ma, and again when the baby's born wi' no father to bring him up. I hope you and Jack have a fine healthy child."

"I'll write and tell you."

"Ay, do that. Me da has a pie shop and I'll be helping there so I may even learn letters and numbers myself. I've picked up some of it seeing you writing in your sand tray for Jack."

The cart taking her and her few possessions came up and she clambered in and rattled away on the road to Newcastle and then on to North Shields.

Dee yearned with every bone in her body to be travelling too. Anywhere. She hadn't been outside the few miles between Wylam and Ovingham since disaster had overtaken her family. But she was mistress in her own place at last. She waved till Jenny was out of sight and then scampered inside.

Chapter 7

Winter 1802–Spring 1803

Dee

That winter as she grew bulky and the baby leapt inside her, Dee concentrated only on the task under her hand, striving for perfection. If her mind teetered towards the future she drew it sharply back. She took her sewing in to Jane and sat on her window seat for the light, waving to Jack when he went by on the waggonway, and listening to Jane's chatter. She was fighting off the questions battering her brain. How can our child be educated and grow to maturity here? We live from hand to mouth as Jane and William do but they expect nothing else. Will I become like them? How will Jack be as a father? He is so excited, laying his hand on my belly and feeling the child move. Will he chastise an unruly boy or petulant girl? Harsh words don't cross his lips unless someone pokes fun at me. Then he looks big and says, "Stop that talk. I have the best wife in the world." *He* is my child, so what will the child be?

She tried to think no further than the next meal. She made up warm dresses for the Slater twins from an old cloak and was given a sheep's head for the broth pan. She sewed lace on Mrs Hammond's pillow cases and was sent a chicken for Sunday which she shared with William and Jane because she had taken Jack's wage from them.

The days shortened and cold gripped her when she went for water and found icicles hanging from Jack's rock. She tried to keep her mind as numb as her fingers.

On Sundays they went to Ovingham Church and, until winter closed in, they sat with Joe and Sarah, who sang the hymns in a fluty piercing voice. Dee wasn't sorry when Joe came alone saying Sarah wouldn't cross the ford with the Tyne in spate.

Dee, curious about him, watched his face. He had a look of Jack but his jaw was heavier, his hair darker and his eyes only animated when he spoke of a subject close to his heart, like the running of the mine where he worked.

One Sunday in January, Dee, standing beside him in their pew, felt him exude a nervous restlessness throughout the service, which Jack, the other side of her, never noticed. As they walked out Joe bent and whispered to her, "Dee, we're away to Newcastle in the morn. Will you help me tell Ma?"

Dee didn't think he'd ever addressed her directly about anything. She looked up into his face which was puckered with anxiety.

"You're going to work for Sarah's father?"

"Ay, well, *with* him. His chest's bad this cold weather."

"Will you be coming back then?"

He shook his head, gloom apparent in every feature.

Jane, who had stopped to speak to Elsie, stepped alongside him. "So what's up, our Joe, that you're shouldering the world's burdens today?"

His eyes met Dee's with a pleading look.

"Sarah's father's not well so they'll be going to Newcastle tomorrow." She said it as if it were the most casual thing.

Jane was not deceived. She's sharper than I realised, Dee thought, and sharper than Jack and William by a country mile. Jack and his father were strolling ahead, indifferent to the drama. Jane stood still in her stolid, hands-on-the-hips pose.

"So that'll be the last we see of you, our Joe. I knew she'd get the better of you at last."

His eyes blazed. He's angry, Dee thought, and he'll say something he'll regret.

"*My* decision, Mother. I'm sick o' the pit. I know how I'd manage things if I had the chance but I never will. This way *I'll* be in charge. You've never liked Sarah but I picked her because she's cleverer than the whole pack of you and between us we'll make our fortune, which is more than you ever will. Or Jack, I'm afraid, Dee."

His father and Jack, having reached the cold air outside and found them not following, came back into the porch.

"What's to do?" William said.

Jane set herself in motion again. "We're to say goodbye to our Joe. That's all."

Joe frowned at her but was willing to walk a little way back to Wylam with them while his father took in what was to happen.

Jack kept saying, "You'll come back, Joe, won't you? You're to be godfather to our bairn."

It flashed into Dee's mind that if Joe and Sarah failed to have a family of their own that could be a blessing.

"I'd be happy to do that." Joe clapped Jack on the shoulder, shook his father's hand, gave his mother a brief peck on the forehead, a nod and smile to Dee, turned on his heel and headed purposefully back.

Dee looked after him for a moment as the others walked on, gabbling about it.

If I'd married *him*, she let herself speculate, I might have had *prospects*, but he's too calculating and at the same time too unsure of himself. His character is complex and inconsistent. My Jack is strong in his simplicity, and I love him.

She caught up to the others.

William was shaking his head. "You mean he'll not go down the pit ever again? How will he do? Ah well, we've still got Jack and Dee and there's a bairn coming." By the time they were home he had reached his customary equilibrium.

It was the last day of March with a sheen of ice on the ground when Dee went into labour. Emmy Charlton said when she examined her, "Ay, 'twill be here soon. You're lucky to have me so close. I'd not have gone out for anyone else today. I was clinging to the house wall just creeping round from our door."

Dee was too engrossed to thank her. The spasms astonished her with their force, but when Emmy said, "You weren't expecting it till April, were you? Mind, I thought you looked ready a week back," Dee knew she must answer.

"I think I brought it on lifting buckets. Jack kept telling me to leave them for him but when I needed water I couldn't wait."

"Ay, well, spare the talking, you'll want your strength for this one. He's big even if he *is* early."

"Is it a boy then?"

"I'd wager a fortune it is if I had one. Now there, push him out, girl."

It was two more hours before that could be done. Jack came home from work and walked up and down the room sobbing and wringing his hands till his mother sent him next door to vent his pain on his father.

"Eh, 'tis a tough one, my grandchild," she said to Emmy Charlton, whose face was shining with sweat.

Dee had abandoned all her planned efforts to be brave, yelling and shouting at them to let her die.

At last with a convulsive heave the head was expelled and the body slithered out swiftly after. Dee shook and trembled with the sudden emptiness but she heard Jane clapping her hands. "William will be that pleased!"

"Sit ye up," Emmy said, "and we'll ha' the afterbirth and ye can hold the clever lad for he must ha' brains in a head that big."

Into Dee's hands was thrust a smeary, bright red creature with a fuzz of black hair and a wide mouth uttering penetrating cries. Horror seized her. She wanted to thrust it away but Jane was coaxing it onto her breast.

"No, no, take it away. I can't."

Jane said, "Nay, let him suck, it'll quiet him and bring the afterbirth. You'll feel the better for it."

The thing squirmed in her arms, limbs thrusting at its bloodstained wrappings. She felt nausea as its hard gums latched onto her nipple. She squealed.

Jane was supporting the little body as her own arms recoiled from holding it. Its head was drawing back and still emitting cries.

"Ay, there'll be nowt there yet," Jane said, "but keep trying. I wonder why Jack's not appeared. He must have heard the babe's racket."

He came in as she spoke, took two strides to the bed and broke down in tears.

His mother laughed. "Don't be daft, lad. Ye've a fine son."

"I see," he gasped, "but Dee, will she live? She's suffered so."

Dee struggled to smile at him. It was perfect that his first thought was for her. "I'll live, Jack." She daren't say look at your baby, but he did then. To her the puckered red face was hideous but he put a tentative hand to one cheek and stroked it.

"Eh, he's a lusty one." He straightened his back and lifted his eyes to the ceiling. "I thank the good Lord for my son and for saving my angel wife."

Jane, still with a hand cradling the squawking head, looked up at him with a quizzical grin. "I've never heard our Jack pray aloud the way he has this night."

Emmy Charlton shooed him out while she brought the afterbirth.

Dee was intensely relieved then when she took the baby "To clean him up proper and swaddle him." Jane brought her a mug of tea which she gulped thankfully.

"Oh, Dee pet!" Jane sat down on the edge of the bed. "You've done us proud with a fine strong boy. It 'ud please me man no end if you called him William."

"Oh, by all means." Dee only wanted Jack to come in again and be alone with her, comforting her.

But now Emmy Charlton came over to the bed with a white bundle in her arms. "Here he is now, all spic and span and ready for his ma."

They were speaking of him as a human being, a person in his own right, who would make demands on her for ever. He was still squawking, eyes shut and mouth open. Emmy helped her undo her nightgown again and give him the breast.

Dee swallowed and made herself look at him as he sucked powerfully. Briefly his eyes opened and met her gaze. They were a dark blue and behind them she was shocked to see a little being with a soul looking out at her. Ralph's eyes. Ralph's soul.

The eyes closed again and soon his lips relaxed and his head felt heavy in the crook of her arm. Emmy laid him in the wooden rocking cradle that Joe and Jack had slept in and Jane tucked the shawl she had knitted for him round him.

"Ay, he'll sleep a while now for it's been hard work for him too."

Dee sat up straight, fastening herself up. "I want Jack."

For a few weeks Dee gritted her teeth and, under tuition from Jane and Emmy, taught herself to manage what she saw as a fierce little monster. As the wiry body developed he was all thrashing arms and legs when she tried to bath him in the tin tub on the table. Often she was glad to wait till Jack was home from work. He would put his great hands round the squirming shape and talk to him while he washed him.

Dee was thankful to be relieved of the task but his tenderness and joy in 'our fine boy' was agony to her soul.

One day his mother came in while he was bathing him. Dee saw in her face horror followed by amazement and then laughter.

"Eh, our Jack! I'd bring your father in to see this but *he's* in the tub an' all." Then she turned to Dee. "You're not to let wee Billy stop you putting Jack's meal on the table. Babies are to be in bed afore the man o' the house comes in."

"He took so long feeding and I am *sore*." Dee hated to offer excuses; she disliked a rare rebuke from her mother-in-law even more.

The baptism was fixed for a Sunday in April and a few days before, when a sudden shower had sent Dee scurrying to bring in the washing, Jack came home with a letter addressed to them both that had been left at the pit. Dee flung down the clothes on their bed and sat at the table, agog with excitement. Something from the world outside! Jack looked over her shoulder.

The directions were written in a clear masculine hand. Was it Joe's? Would he make Billy his heir? She broke the seal carefully and opened it up. Inside was a short letter in childlike writing.

Thomson's Pie Shop, North Shields.
April 1803

Dear Jack and Dee,

What's your news? Is your baby born yet? I have a pretty baby girl born in January. She is called Alice after my ma so we call her Ally. I cried when I saw her for she has Sam's eyes and turned-up nose. I work in the shop and we are doing well. This has taken me a half hour with my uncle's help. Can you read it, Jack? Let me know if you have your baby.

From your friend,
Jenny Coxon

"It's from Jenny." Dee read it aloud with a confusion of emotions. There was disappointment that it was not something to disrupt the dour pattern of her life; there was guilt that she had almost forgotten Jenny's existence and dismay that Jenny had learnt to write when Jack hadn't. There was envy, too, that Jenny was prospering and would certainly be managing her 'pretty baby girl' in her own happy-go-lucky way.

She beamed at Jack. "I am glad for her. I'll write after Billy's baptism."

"Will you tell her you had to read hers to me?" he asked.

She shook her head.

"I'll wager I can read her next one."

He still thinks he's improving, she marvelled.

"And we have a grand boy to tell her about. Now his eyes have turned brown he has your colouring, not mine, so he will grow up handsome."

Ralph was handsome and somewhere in the world, she supposed, he still existed. What if he came back and found her? She felt quite giddy and grasped the edge of the table but Jack was looking into the cradle and was unaware.

He gazed silently at Billy before lifting his eyes to hers and launching into the longest speech he had ever made to her. "My lovely, I am happy every day, coming home to you and Billy. I've been a new man – as you know right well – from the day I met you and you needed me. Even when I fell down on our wedding day you made the shame of it go away. And now I am a father and Joe is not! Ma says Billy reminds her of Joe with his dark hair and he's so quick to notice things. It made me think that, if we have another child, we must see that we love him as much as Billy and praise him all we can, for he is not to have days of shame like I did."

Tears came into her eyes. She had never supposed Jack could have such thoughts in his head, linking the past and the future, but, God forbid, she prayed that he should never learn Billy was not his son or his brain compass for a moment the truth that she could not love this baby. And to talk of another child! I am afraid of this one. When he is feeding, his dark eyes probe mine till I look away. I cannot bear his crying so I pick him up – but not to cuddle him. How can I write to Jenny with any honesty?

In the end it was not difficult to describe, selectively, the day of the baptism.

Joe is godfather and Sarah came too, proud of their arrival by the Newcastle–Carlisle stage. Joe called Billy a fine boy, though I think him no beauty myself. Sarah remarked, "He's a big baby considering he was a few weeks early by your reckoning." She noticed Jack blushing.

Jenny would smile at that.

Billy – as we call him to avoid confusion, like you with Ally – fought his baptism with vigour and old Elsie – remember her? – said it was good to get the devil out of him.

Back at home over a dinner of boiled mutton and kale and onions (from your patch, which is doing well) Sarah told us her father has bought the house next door to his and she and Joe are getting rooms ready for letting. They will have a parlour, a dining-room, a bedroom and a kitchen where Sarah will cook and send meals up to the tenants. She reckons they will pay handsomely for that on top of their rent.

Jenny will know I'm jealous, she told herself, for Jack has no wish for change. Puzzled, he had asked Joe, "What sort of work do you do every day then, Joe?"

Joe's heavy brow had contracted. He blustered out, "It's been carpentry, plastering, lime washing and painting, long hours to make the place really fine."

"So what'll you do now it's finished?" his mother had asked.

Sarah rushed in. "There'll be plenty to keep us busy looking after the tenants for we've six rooms and an attic to let. You should come and see it sometime."

And that was where it was left when they had to depart in time for the coach.

Jane had said when they'd gone, "Ay, it'll be, 'Joe, take up the coals for Number Three. Joe, Number Four wants a tray of supper and them stairs want sweeping down.' Ay, he's at her beck and call now."

Jane, Dee wrote, *started in service as a girl and knows the daily life Joe can expect now, but Jack and his father can't imagine him without a man's job and a wage coming in. I am glad for you that you are happy in your parents' shop.*

As she wrote she wondered if Jenny could ever have become an intimate friend if she had stayed close by. I couldn't have told her my secret, she thought. She would have laughed at the barb of guilt that stabs me every time Jack voices his pride in fatherhood. Jenny would say, "Go on with you, Dee, he *is* Billy's father in every sense that matters." And she would be right too. I must cling to that but tell no one. Maybe one day I will even believe it.

She finished her letter with news of the Slaters' twins and how Emmy's husband struggled on with his cough, and Emmy had declared after Billy's delivery that she was too old for such work now.

Jack watched in awe as she folded and sealed the letter with a scrap of wax and wrote the direction.

Billy grew. Dee was soon feeding him pap and was thankful to wean him altogether before winter set in again. Just as his first smile had been for Jack, it was to Jack that he held out his arms during his first step when the winter snows had melted and Jack held his hand and let him toddle round the house and on the gravel path. Dee could see that Jack's joy in Billy was building his own confidence higher and higher despite their hand-to-mouth living which didn't worry him at all.

Dee was getting more sewing work but Billy liked to wrench it from her hands to demand her attention. After fearing that Jane would take over their child, she was thankful to push him next door or let the Slaters' twin girls play games with him as often as they were willing. Whenever she had a moment to herself her needle was busy and she could think of the pigs' trotters or the lamb shanks she was earning.

After his second birthday Billy's tantrums became ferocious. Jane told Jack in front of her, "Dee cannot manage him. She's had no experience of babies. She cannot hang washing out or weed the patch as he's away off down to the river. You'll have to be firm and give him a good smacking when she tells you he's been naughty."

Dee saw Jack's dismay. Billy was his small playfellow who chuckled and held out his arms to be thrown up and caught or whirled about till they were both dizzy. But Dee listened to all this in despair. She had missed her monthly and was certain there was to be another child. Looking back to her first day at Burn Cottage, she could scarcely credit her confidence that she could manage her life and the people about her in this place. She had found a father for her child but never doubted her own readiness for motherhood herself. She knew what triumphant joy she would see in Jack's eyes when she told him she was with child again so day to day she put off telling him.

On an early May morning with a foretaste of high summer she was hanging up the unending washing and relishing the hot sun on her back. Billy was yanking out the row of sticks that divided their vegetable patch from William's and Jane's. She could put them back later. As long as he was occupied she was thankful.

She had pegged the last of his pinafores on the line when he lifted his head and cried, "Da-Da! Horse! Horse!"

She listened and now she heard it, an unmistakable clip-clop sound on the dirt path. It was not the measured thump of the wagon horse's hooves but a trotting rhythm and now the rider came into view from the direction of Wylam.

It was rare for a horseman to pass this way. Locals walked everywhere. She watched him approach as Billy threw down his sticks, disappointed that it was not Jack. The rider raised his hat and she saw it was Godfrey Hammond. He dismounted at the stone steps set at the corner of the house with a tethering post beside it. Dee had never seen it used.

"Good morning, Mistress Heron." Why was he here? Her mind was leaping at possible reasons while he took the few paces towards her. Had the slow-moving processes of the law found there was money to come to her after all?

Billy crept behind her skirts at the stranger's approach, a rare act of shyness.

"Good morning, Mr Hammond. My mother-in-law is not at home I'm afraid." She was visiting Elsie who had taken to her bed with a fever.

"It is you I have come to see."

"Then pray, come in."

With Billy clinging to her skirt she ushered him into their home.

He looked at the dwindling fire in the hearth. She was letting it die to save fuel now the washing was done. He looked at their bed, rumpled from Billy rolling about. He looked at Billy's ragged straw mattress in the corner, at the unwashed porridge bowls on the table and the shelves high up cluttered with Dee's sewing.

Pretending all this was invisible, she drew out a kitchen chair for him.

"Can I offer you some refreshment, sir, after your ride?" She was imitating her mother's social manner though she was sure there was nothing in the larder that he would want to drink.

He shook his head. "No, I thank you. The fine morning tempted me out for a ride before my day's work and I chose to come this way. The truth is, it has been on my mind for many months that I should pay you a visit. I imagined, wrongly perhaps from the day of your wedding, that I was not welcome in your new life—"

"Oh, Mr Hammond—"

"No, pray, let me finish. I understand your position. To avoid cruel gossip you wisely conform to your new surroundings. I trust you are happy in them, especially now you have a fine son."

Dee had sat down too and Billy still clung warily to her skirt, watching this strange new presence in their room. She murmured that they were very happy.

"I think, however," he resumed, "that a well-educated lady like yourself may feel sometimes a little out of touch with the world outside. You know, I presume, that hostilities have again broken out between England and France?"

Wherever is this leading? she wondered. She replied a little sharply, "Indeed, sir. We may not see newspapers but newssheets are posted at the colliery gates. I read them if I pass that way and I hear miners who can read talking of what is happening."

"I am pleased to hear it, but I took the liberty of bringing you the latest copy of the *Newcastle Courant*." He put his hand under his riding coat and drew out a folded newspaper. "One item caught my eye and I thought you might be interested in it, whatever your feelings about the person it concerns."

He laid the paper on the table and the headline leapt out at her – 'Captain Sir Ralph Barnet killed in a duel'. She snatched it up and her eyes began to devour the small print.

Her reading was interrupted by a crack on the side of her head. Billy had grabbed Godfrey Hammond's riding crop from the table, by the leather strap that was dangling within his reach, and had brandished it.

"No, no, my boy." Godfrey Hammond seized it back and Billy flew into one of his rages.

It was a fortunate distraction for Dee, whose inclination had been to leap up in delight at what she had read.

"Naughty Billy," she cried, trying to grab his arms as he smacked his hands on Godfrey Hammond's knees.

The magistrate demonstrated his judicial wisdom by pulling out his watch chain and dangling it before Billy's eyes. The tantrum stopped as Billy reached for the chain. Hammond popped it behind his back and produced it in his other hand. Billy was soon chuckling and Dee looked back at the paper and read to the end.

I am free, she exulted. No one else knows of my sin.

She looked up at Godfrey Hammond. "Thank you for amusing Billy and thank you for showing me this."

He inclined his head. "I had no wish to cause you pain but when I saw the name I recalled that there was an engagement between you, which he broke off at your father's unfortunate bankruptcy. I had the impression from your speedy attachment to Jack Heron that your disappointment was not too great. I trust that was the case."

As he spoke he was still tantalising Billy with the antics of the watch chain and Dee was astonished at his versatility.

"Oh yes, sir. It was an arranged betrothal against my will." That was a lie. She had been consumed with passion on first sight of his handsome looks and alluring smile. "But what a foolish man to engage in a duel! Such things are frowned upon, I believe, in the army."

He smiled. "It is indeed a waste of a life. If he had been killed in battle he would have had honour, dying for his country."

And that would *not* have been a waste, I suppose, she commented silently, but that is a woman's view, for I see no sense in us fighting France again. For what?

Her moment of cynicism was brief, drowned by the inward laughter that kept bubbling up from her huge sense of relief and her amusement at Godfrey Hammond playing with a young child.

She jumped up now and removed Billy, who was beginning to be fractious at not being able to grab the watch chain.

"You have been so kind to play with him, sir, and to bring me this news which as you rightly guess does not afford me great sorrow. Sir Ralph was a shallow, dishonest character who has met a foolish end."

Godfrey Hammond rose too. "Then I will be on my way, Mistress Heron, comforted in my mind that I have seen you in your surroundings and with a fine boy."

She gave him a little curtsey.

"Pray tell your wife I am most grateful for the work she sends me."

He bowed, patted Billy on the head and took his leave.

Dee led Billy to the corner of the house to watch him mount his horse and ride away. Then she took the boy into her arms and looked into his dark, questioning eyes. She felt a great yearning for a sudden transformation. Surely she could love him now that his father was dead and her secret buried with him? She held him close, smiling at him, but there was no response in his eyes. He squirmed and wriggled to be set down. She put him on the ground and he ran back to his pile of sticks and began throwing them in the air and scattering them.

"No, Billy," she shouted.

He looked up with a defiant grin and jumped on the kale and onions to trample them. She smacked his legs, carried him inside and, shutting the door, set her back against it. He flung himself on the floor, yelling with rage. No one would hear. Nan Slater had taken her girls for their daily walk by the river, Emmy Charlton was growing deaf and so was her failing husband and Jane would not be home for a while from her visit to Elsie. She was alone with Billy.

Was it too late to love him? His father was dead but the hatred she still felt for him for crushing her young love was as rampant as before. Ralph Barnet had known she was passionate for him and he had spurned her love without a thought. Just now it struck her that Billy had repelled her embrace with the same disdain.

She looked at him beating his heels on the floor and dreaded the daily life she must continue to endure with him. He seemed fond of his da but Jack was bewildered by his tantrums and Billy was already aware of that. His gamma's no meant no and his gampa's quiet presence seemed to be respected. But how, she asked herself, will Jack and I cope with this horrible presence in our life of love for each other? And another child? The thought of the immediate future suddenly overwhelmed her. She put her hands over her ears to stifle Billy's yells and her body shook with choking sobs.

Chapter 8

June–December 1805

Jack

Jack Heron's happiest moment of his working day was his 'click click' to Sandy the Horse at the start of the first 'run' to Lemington Staithes. The air was fresh and the piled coal in the wagon had all the shine of a new day. There was the constant flowing of the river to his right in one of its varying guises, full and strong or idly chattering. If the tide was high he smelt the sea, though his father always laughed at this. "Why, lad, we're at the tide limit here. The sea's twenty miles away."

There was joy too in the sandy track stretching ahead, for after the first bend in the river he would see Burn Cottage and Dee and two-year-old Billy waving from the window. It was one thing they did together in harmony and it made him very happy.

Jack lived most of life in the present moment and a morning in early June had everything he could enjoy at the beginning of a day: sunbeams dancing on wet grass, the river all of a sparkle, a fresh wind at his back and Sandy stepping out bravely as if the trundling weight of the coal wagon was nothing. But fighting against all this happiness was the news Dee had just told him, that she was with child again.

She had said it with smiles, all bright and cheerful, so he had been happy too, but as he walked to work with his father terror had struck him.

She had all that pain to endure again and this time she might not come through it.

"I never think o' the consequences," he said as they trudged along to the mine. "I take my pleasure but 'tis she has to face the pain."

His father grinned up at him "Nay, it's just nature. If a bairn is to come it comes. Maybe ye'll get a wee lassie this time. Jane would like that. She had two stillborn and one the fever took."

Jack had heard of his lost sisters before but the pain and grief of it had never come home to him till now. The shimmering morning became totally overcast.

All the way down to Lemington thoughts tumbled in his head, pushing out the habitual pleasure of sensation alone. Dee had trouble with Billy. Soon there would be two. A child was not the pure joy and pride it had seemed at first. Billy was a tough, rough little person. His grandfather said he would make a fine hewer one day, and he could be down the pit earning his pennies as a trapper boy in four years' time. But how, Jack wondered, would such a fierce wee character take to a brother or sister?

He thought of Joe and himself as boys. Joe was eager to be down the pit like his mates, or so he had boasted, and Jack had expected to feel the same after his sixth birthday. But when they began to lower him into the darkness and the sides closed in he found himself screaming and couldn't stop. No one could stand the noise so he was taken up again into God's good air and open spaces. It was his worst day of shame. Even now, striding along the towpath with his lungs expanding to the frisky breeze, he could feel that black panic again and broke into a sweat of terror. And that brought him back to the terror he had set out with – the memory of Dee's screams when Billy was born. If Dee were to die in childbirth there would be no point in living.

At Lemington Staithes, he yearned to recapture his daily delight at the sight of the waggonway running to the end of the staithes built out into the river, and watching the coal Sandy had hauled for five miles tip into the keel boat. They were a rough lot, the keelmen, and Jack always marvelled at the cascade of swear words that flowed from their mouths. Today they should be happy. The tide was on the ebb and with the west wind behind them they would be able to hoist sail as soon as they were loaded and be spared the labour of rowing the heavy shallow-bottomed keel boat downriver to the waiting collier. He always waved to them with his most beaming smile before hitching Sandy up again to the empty wagon and starting on his return journey.

Today he was too oppressed with his worries to smile or enjoy the wide river with its endless bustle of traffic, the raucous shouts and the slapping of the water on the mud banks. Like a child cheated of a treat, he found tears pricking his eyes as he headed westward. Must be the wind, he told himself, but he knew it was not the wind. Life had become complicated. The freedom his new-found confidence had given him was mangled with fears. He was seeing life without Dee. He would have to bring up Billy and the other child if it lived. A sense of his uselessness fell about him like a suffocating blanket. Dee was already showing Billy letters written in the sand tray. Only that morning he had heard Billy shout, "G for Gamma and Gampa!" And then he had picked up the tray and emptied the sand onto the floor.

Jack had heard the pit bell and had had to leave Dee to deal with him. But if she wasn't there? He would be despised by a clever child, two children perhaps. Was it not a miracle that Dee still loved him? She had been engaged to this gentleman who had died. She said she was glad, that he was a deceiver and she hated him, but no doubt he had been able to read books and discuss the world's affairs.

There was a niggle of worry in his mind that she hadn't told him of Godfrey Hammond's visit. It was Billy who had said, "Man on horse" and pointed to the mounting block and then Dee had explained, but casually as if it were nothing at all, when in fact the visit of a gentleman was an extraordinary event.

Jack shook his head to get rid of the thoughts. Dee came from another world. She had come into this life of his, where from boyhood he had taken coals to Lemington, at first with a driver and then alone when they thought him ready. If she were to go out of his life as suddenly, leaving him with fatherhood, how would it be? He had prayed the awful night of her labour and God had spared her, but would He spare her again?

It was a long day before he could go home and the dark premonitions didn't leave him till he opened the house door and saw her sitting on a stool by Billy's bed, reading him a story. She looked up, smiling, and Billy jumped down and ran to him in his little nightgown and clasped his legs. On the trivet over the fire he could see and smell a pan of rabbit stew. Thoughts flew away. He was hungry and life was good.

Dee

Dee was happy that she had found one thing she could do with Billy that kept him quiet. She had no children's books but she still had writing materials. She made a little book of folded pages and stitched the back. On it she wrote a story about Sandy the Horse and Billy lay quiet, listening. She couldn't say, looking at his impassive face, whether she could now begin to love him, but she was thankful for the peace.

For the rest of the time life with Billy was a battle. Even William and Jane found him difficult and when he had hit the Slater twins in one of their games Nan Slater forbad them from playing with him any more.

Dee tried to wear him out with walks into the village or along the towpath, pointing out and naming flowers and trees. He appeared to rebuff her efforts at the time but days later he would pluck a flower and shout at her 'Daisy!' or 'Dandelion!' as if scorning her ignorance.

One late October day he was excited by flags hung in the windows of houses and people laughing and cheering. Dee wished he was older to understand when she said, "Our country has won a great sea battle at a place called Trafalgar." This meant nothing to him and made him cross, and even more so when a man with a long face came up and posted a paper on the pit gates with a black edge and everyone ran to look, exchanging groans and headshakes, some of the women lamenting loudly.

"Admiral Nelson has died of wounds," she told Elsie at her house door. The old woman threw back her head and uttered a wild wail.

Billy stepped up and slapped at her skirt, shouting, "Stop that."

Elsie was contrite. "I've frightened the wee bairn."

Dee had to hurry him home, protesting.

When winter came on and her advancing pregnancy slowed her down she longed to flop in their basket chair, patting the small being moving inside her. She found herself yearning to have this baby in her arms, caressing it. She was now sure she would love him or her for being Jack's child and not being Billy.

She was pondering this one cold morning when Billy, who had been coughing in the night, had crawled back into his bed and fallen asleep. How blissful, the silence! She sat herself down with a shawl round her shoulders and a rug on her knees. The daytime sounds of coals settling in the fire and the occasional clucking of the Slaters' hens in their run soothed her and she was soon asleep too.

It was an hour later that she woke, startled to find she had been asleep at all and even more alarmed when she looked at the clock on the mantelshelf and saw the time. Fancy Billy sleeping so long!

She heaved herself up and went over to his corner. The crumpled blanket was empty. Her eyes darted over the whole room. He was mischievously hiding, but where? He was not squeezed under the larder shelf. He couldn't possibly have lifted the lid of the chest but she looked inside. Then she heard a creaking sound and felt a cold blast of air. The outer door had stirred open. It was not properly latched and the rising wind had caught it. Billy had gone!

She pulled her shawl over her head and looked up and down outside. William and Jane's door was firmly shut. She banged on it but there was no answer. Jane had spoken yesterday of taking some of her stotty cakes to Elsie. Dee tried the door and it opened on an empty room. All the same, she went in and searched every corner.

She had to face it. Billy was out there somewhere, in only his nightgown, with a bad cough on a bitter November morning. She was too ashamed to rouse the Slaters or Emmy to help her look for him. No one must ever know she had let him escape.

She ran round the house looking in all directions but he was not in sight. She was marvelling that he was now tall enough and strong enough to lift the heavy door latch. She must shoot the bolt across in the future to keep him in. If he had a future…

How long had he been out? She could find him dead from cold. She crossed the towpath and the waggonway calling his name. It was the river she feared most. In summer he could splash in little pools among the pebbles and grassy islands and she could sit on the bank and watch him, but today the river was a strong pulling body of water halfway up the bank. He could easily miss his footing on the frosty grass and be gone in a moment. She clambered back to the house, gasping with frantic sobs, and panted along to the stream where they drew water. She ran by the wall of the field where the mine horses grazed, looking for loose stones where he might have climbed up. He was a desperate climber within the house, pulling stools to the shelves to reach forbidden things. His determination not to be thwarted was frightening.

She ran back and looked both ways along the towpath. If he was not being swept away by the river, which direction could he have taken? But he could also be hiding nearby. If he had heard her calling he was quite capable of creeping under a bush and staying still.

She heard voices and footsteps and shouted "Billy!" but round the house from their front door came Emmy Charlton and the Slaters.

"We saw you wondering about. What's up?"

"Billy got out." They had taken time to get all wrapped up, Dee noticed, and realised she was shaking with cold in spite of the shawl.

"Where would he go?" Nan Slater asked her girls.

"To seek his da," they said in unison.

"The pit! Why did I not think of that?" Dee tried to sound hopeful as they all set off together, alight with the novelty of a hunt. Her disgrace would be known all over the village now but there was no help for it.

"I didn't believe he could lift the latch," she kept saying.

Emmy Charlton asked the question she feared. "How long has he been gone?"

She shook her head. "He was asleep and I fell asleep too. I was so tired. We all had a bad night."

"Ay," Nan Slater said. "We heard him coughing." Nan Slater always let her know when she'd heard him shouting too, but she didn't moan as much about Matt Charlton's coughing in the next room to her.

Her girls made a great noise calling "Billee! Billee!" darting from side to side of the track. They soon covered the half mile to the pit head but Dee had no hope that he would be here. His body was floating downriver to the sea.

She had never gone in past the main gates and the jumble of low wooden buildings dwarfed by the tower with its winding gear bewildered her. She stepped across the end of the waggonway and called in a croaking voice, "Is there anyone about?"

A man emerged at once from a doorway with the sign 'Mine Office'.

"Is it the wee lad you're after? Come away in. Nay, just the mother," he said as they all surged forward in an excited bunch.

Dee, not believing her eyes, looked into the room and there he was, huddled in a grubby hearth rug by the fire, scowling round at her.

"Want Da-Da."

"Didn't we say he'd come to the mine?" crowed the Slater twins behind her.

"Ay, well, ye're all right now, Dee. We'll away off home," said Emmy Charlton. "It's too cold for my old bones to be out."

"Will you manage to get him back?" Nan Slater said. "He's heavy for you to carry in your condition."

"I'll manage," Dee said. "Thank you all for your help."

She walked over to Billy, fighting tears of relief, but there was dismay too at his defiant little presence, very much alive and careless of the fright he had given her.

"He was so cold," the man said, "he collapsed in the doorway. When he'd had a mug of hot tea he could tell me his name was Billy and he wanted his da-da. I reckon you're Jack Heron's wife."

She nodded.

"Jack's not back yet from the first wagon run and his Grandfather William is at the coal face. So off you go with your ma, Billy, and don't come wandering again."

"Thank you for your care of him," she said, and repeated, "I didn't believe he could lift the latch."

"Keep him wrapped in the rug. Jack can bring it back in the morning."

She reached out a hand for Billy but he drew back. "Want Da-Da." But then he was seized with a fit of coughing ending with a loud gasp as he struggled for breath.

"That's croup he's got," the man said. "He needs to be in his bed."

Dee tried to pick him up but he fought her, crying, "Da-Da."

The man grimaced. "I'm the banksman. I can't leave the mine or I'd take him for you. You'll be near your time, eh?"

She felt her cheeks burn. "A few weeks," she murmured.

Then Billy shrieked out "Da-Da," scrambled off the chair, and evading them both, shed the hearth rug and ran to the door.

"By, he's got good hearing. He's right. It's the wagon. He mustn't run onto the tracks."

They were both out in a moment and the man grabbed Billy, who was jumping up and down looking along the rails for the first sign of the horse.

Dee was astonished at the speed with which men appeared from other buildings and she heard the harsh grating sound of a load of coal being hauled up the shaft. She was glimpsing Jack's world.

He appeared in the distance.

"Da-Da with Sandy!" Billy yelled, and was again engulfed in coughing.

Jack was obviously dumbfounded to be greeted by his wife and son.

The banksman told him he must take them both home at once and be back as quick as possible for his next run. "And keep the boy wrapped up but bring me hearth rug back w' ye."

Billy was happy to be lifted onto his da-da's shoulders and Dee couldn't wait to get away from the clanging sounds and shouting men.

"But what happened?" Jack asked as they scurried away. "Is Billy ill?"

Dee had to confess her carelessness and of course Jack said, "Eh my lovely, you shouldn't be left alone with him in your state. Of course you were tired. We'll have to manage better than this." But she noticed he didn't scold Billy for running off.

Billy *was* ill, very ill. The mine doctor came to look at him when he was hot as a furnace and rolling in his bed coughing and gasping.

"I'm pleased to see there's to be another one soon," he said to Dee, "for I fear you're going to lose this one."

Jack was frantic but helpless, unable to stop Dee 'wearing herself out' as he moaned to his mother. Jane wanted to take her turns with the nursing but Dee only asked her to make the poultices the doctor ordered and cook Jack's evening meal.

One evening when Jane had come in with two bowls of mutton stew on a tray, she told Jack, "Your Dee's been sat by him all day, cooling his head, keeping the poultice on him for he will cast it off. If anyone can bring him through this she will."

Any other time Dee would have been thankful for such praise from her mother-in-law but this brought new stabbings of guilt. In the dark hours when Billy coughed and she rose to replenish the fire and lifted him to help him breathe, she would be weeping and muttering desperate prayers for him, because she knew there was an evil thought lurking in her mind that she would be glad to be rid of him.

William came in one evening and shook his head over Billy.

"He'll knock himself to bits with that coughing. You have to face it, Dee. He'll not come through this."

But Dee fought to keep him alive and Billy fought too.

A day came when the doctor looked in and saw him lying utterly limp and pale. He felt his head and listened to his breathing.

"Well, God be praised, Mistress Heron. The fever's left him. Thanks to your nursing and his fighting spirit. All he needs now is feeding up."

Dee was astonished at the speed of his recovery which was greatly helped by the little offerings that kept arriving from people in the village she scarcely knew. Godfrey Hammond's wife came in person with a basket which contained two books as well as foodstuffs. Tall and elegant, she looked round their one room and took in the crowded shelves with the only book visible being a worn old Bible.

"My dear girl," she said, "I can't think why I never thought how you must long to read. I picked two at random from our library, Milton's *Paradise Lost* and this *Life of Sir Francis Drake* by a cousin of mine who is a vice-admiral." She laughed lightly. "Drake is a hero of his, second only to Lord Nelson, of course."

Dee took them gratefully but she was thinking, Not picked at random at all. *Paradise Lost* is what she believes has happened to me and the other is just to boast that she has a relation of high rank who can also write a book.

Fortunately, Billy was next door with his Grandmother Jane at the time, so Dee invited Mistress Hammond to sit down but she declined. Her groom was turning the carriage in the lane and she wouldn't keep him waiting in the cold.

She said, as she pulled on her gloves, "Well, you are truly part of the community now and I trust all goes well with your imminent lying-in."

"I thank you, but I know not that I am accepted here yet."

"My dear, your character is known. As far as Ovingham mothers speak of how you fought for your boy's life when there seemed no hope for him. And taking on work for offerings of food or sewing materials has impressed men too. I heard a young man say 'I'd take a wife tomorrow if I could find one like Dee Heron.'"

This was amazing to Dee. She escorted Mistress Hammond round the house to her carriage and then stood watching it drive away, wondering if she could do so now without a twinge of jealousy.

As she walked back Jane emerged with Billy. "We made some stotty cakes together and I give him one but he wants the lot. You'd better have him back now."

Dee's delight melted away. She looked at her son and saw how his wasted limbs had filled out, his dark hair had grown profusely about his stolid face and his eyes were alight again with the old belligerence. His presence was back in her life with a vengeance.

"Want more stotty cakes," he declared.

He was now so active and eating so well that he slept long hours every night. As Jack was coming in early during the dark days of winter, Billy was content to go to bed after a brief romp with him. Dee then had the pleasure of reading by precious candlelight while Jack dozed by the fire after his days of fresh cold air. She set aside Milton after reading of the forbidden fruit. Billy was the embodiment of *her* sin and all too strong evidence himself of original sin. She picked up the other book and was soon absorbed in the life of Drake, marvelling that he dared to risk ocean storms in so frail a vessel as the *Golden Hind*. She was utterly taken out of herself till the candle burnt too low and they had to go to bed.

Chapter 9

Winter–Spring 1806

Dee

It was an oddly balmy day in January when Dee felt the first labour pains. She was reading the newssheet account of Nelson's funeral with Drake in her mind. My life, she thought, is as far removed from London today as it is from the Elizabethans. We win battles at sea and it matters to me not one jot. Today I will give birth. I am excited, not fearful. I want to love this son or daughter. And how will *he* take to it?

He was playing quietly for once. Jack had told the schoolmaster that Billy could say his letters when Dee wrote them in the sand tray so the schoolmaster had given him a set of wooden letters, worn and chipped but usable. "If he's so clever," he said, "bring him to school when he's three." Dee thought it must be a joke but what bliss it would be to have quiet days alone with a new baby, Jack's child!

Billy's play came to an end when he said "E – Egg" and it was an F. Dee glanced up and corrected him. He shouted, "Egg," and swept all the letters onto the floor and began hitting her bulge. She stood up and backed away to the outer door. Feeling behind her, she pushed back the bolt and lifted the latch.

"You go to Grandmother Jane."

He dropped his hands and jumped up and down. "Make stotty cakes."

"If you're a good boy."

She led him in and Jane looked up from tending the fire.

"Ay, is it the baby coming?"

Dee nodded.

"Emmy has said she'll come down for you but would you rather I fetched the doctor? Billy and I can run to the village."

"Make stotty cakes," said Billy.

"I'll do well with Emmy. This one's coming quick."

"Happen it'll be a lassie then." Jane took the pole she used as a clothes prop from the corner and banged three times on the ceiling. "That's the signal Emmy asked for. She'll be down directly."

Billy stamped his foot three times. "Make stotty cakes."

Jane cried, "What? Giving your orders, eh?" But she was laughing.

Dee retreated thankfully next door.

"Well," Emmy said, only an hour later, "I can see a fair head. Another push should do it. Eh, it's a canny wee one this and no trouble at all."

Dee was in control of herself this time and knew the moment had come. She exerted all her power and expelled the slippery shape with a great shout of triumph.

Leaning back, she waited for Emmy to say, "Ay, 'tis a wee girl like I thought."

But Emmy was carrying something over to the table and slapping it and dunking it in the tin bath.

"Emmy!" she screeched.

There was a sickening five seconds' wait and then a tiny cry. Emmy rubbed the back, tipping it head down, and small gurgling sounds followed. She wiped the face and enveloped the little form in a warm towel and brought it to Dee.

"He'll do very well now," she said.

Dee swallowed. "He?"

"Ay, he's Jack over again. I didn't say before but the birth went just the same. For all he's a big man now, Jack was no but a shrimp newborn."

Then Dee studied what she had taken into her arms. The little round face topped with a smudge of fair hair was serene, the skin soft, the blue eyes open and a little surprised, the way Jack sometimes looked.

"Oh," she said, tears welling up, "he's beautiful." She held him close and kissed the velvety cheek.

Emmy stood before her, hands clasped. "Eh, that's what I like to see. Have you and Jack got a name for him?"

"I was thinking of Elizabeth after great Queen Bess but now—"

"You ain't disappointed I hope."

"No, never. He's here. He's his own little self. I won't have Horatio, not with Heron. He shall be Francis after Sir Francis Drake."

Jack

Jack came home with his father and, as often happened, his mother looked out to greet him. Behind her came Billy, shouting, "Da-Da."

"Ay, he's been asking for you," she said, "as soon as it began to grow dark. I wouldn't let him in to bother Dee. She has his wee brother to see to now."

"What? What? The baby's here? And Dee? She lives!" Relief was like a great burst of sunlight.

"Ay, Emmy said she dropped him easy as a lamb. Nay, stop a moment." Jack was leaping towards their door. "What do you think she wants to name him? Francis!"

His father repeated, "Francis! There's no miners' sons called Francis!"

Jack was hopping with impatience. "If Dee wants Francis that's what he is. Now will you let me go in and see them, Mother?" Billy had already seized his hand. He looked down at him. "You've not met your little brother yet? Haway in then. Heaven be praised they're both well."

"I'll not come in till I'm cleaned up," his father said, "but I'm right glad for you, though Jane here fancied a wee girl, didn't you?"

"Ay, well, you take what the good Lord sends," she said. "There'll be time enough for daughters."

Jack opened the door to see Dee in the basket chair with one foot rocking the cradle. She greeted him with her paradise smile.

"Oh Dee, you look wonderful!" He knelt down beside her and tears flowed. "I was so afraid after last time." He looked in the cradle. "Why, he's a beauty!"

Billy stepped up to the cradle and jumped on the rocker.

"No!" cried Jack. "Poor baby." The little head bounced on the pillow.

Billy peered into the cradle. "What's that?"

"Your little brother," Dee said, "and you are to be very good with him."

Billy promptly stamped on the rocker again and a tiny wail came from the baby. Jack swivelled round on his knees and caught Billy with a slap on the head.

"No! Bad!"

Billy's outraged face shocked him.

"Eh, Dee, I shouldn't have done that."

"Of course you should. He's got to learn right from wrong."

Billy hurled himself into the far corner of the room and howled.

Dee said, touching the baby's cheek, "This one will do great things. I want him to be Francis after the Admiral Francis Drake and he could have Godfrey if we dare ask Mr Hammond to be godfather. That might help him on in life."

Jack, still torn by Billy's howling, said, "Whatever you want, angel."

Then his mother walked in with the stew-pot and set it on the table.

"What's this noise, Billy? Fetch the bowls or you don't get any dinner."

"I smacked him, Ma," Jack whispered, "for bouncing his wee brother."

"About time too," she said and bustled out again.

Billy, hiccupping, brought the bowls and looked at Jack with reproachful eyes. Jack was sorry but couldn't stop joy bubbling up as Dee rose and came to the table with baby Francis.

"Oh good," he cried. "One happy family. Us and our boys."

A great sob of thankfulness broke out of him. Billy stared at him and didn't look at the baby.

Jack was glad then that the weather had turned cold and the country was plunged in snow. He kept Billy busy, helping to clear the waggonway, though the snow beat them at last and coal piled up at the pithead. They made snowmen by the track and little caves in the piled up drifts. Joe and Sarah couldn't come for the baptism, but Godfrey Hammond and his wife had the pavement cleared the short distance from their house to Ovingham Church and Jack knocked together a rough sledge on which he pulled Dee and the baby from Burn Cottage, with Billy riding on his shoulders.

It was not till Billy's third birthday in March that Joe and Sarah paid a visit. Jack was gleeful because Joe was still not a father and *he* was a father twice over. His only worry was Billy's behaviour but Dee had a plan.

"I've made him two new books and told him if he is very quiet over dinner with Grandpa and Grandma he will have a special birthday present afterwards."

Jack was delighted at the thought of more stories. He almost knew the Sandy one by heart, so he welcomed Joe and Sarah without a qualm of anxiety.

Sarah peered into the cradle. "This one *is* like his father," she said with one of her sharp looks at Dee. Jack found Sarah odd so he thought nothing more of that.

Billy remained unnaturally still and silent and Joe said, "He's shy," when there was no response to his genial greeting of "My, you're getting to be a big boy."

Jack saw his father and mother exchanging bemused looks and was excited because he knew what the surprise was to be.

As soon as they were finished eating, Dee slipped next door with a special glance at Billy who sat up all agog.

She came in with her hands behind her back and everyone's eyes followed her movements as she held out the books, one in each hand, across the table to Billy.

Billy stared.

Jack cried, "Look, Billy, your clever Ma has made you some more stories."

Billy grabbed at them and turned the pages. He frowned. "Where Sandy?"

Dee pointed to the pictures she had painted. "Here's Susie the Sparrow who lives in the hedge and this one is about Freddy the fish down in the river."

Billy's face puckered up but he didn't cry. Instead he let one book fall and ripped the front page off the other, shouting, "Want more Sandy stories."

Joe didn't hesitate. He slapped Billy's hand and rescued the book. "Pick up the other."

Billy did, but tore at it too before handing it over.

Joe slapped him again. Billy glared at the heads shaken sadly over him and stamped to the window seat where he buried his face against the threadbare cushion.

Grandmother Jane said, "Oh Billy!" and then, "I'm afraid he's often naughty."

Grandfather William nodded. "Ay, I doubt he'll not be proper tamed till he gets down the pit. Hard work will soon mend him."

Jack's eyes welled with tears. He saw Dee's lips trembling at her wasted labour and the old shame came back that his brother and Sarah had witnessed this.

But Joe sat down on a stool by the table and was studying both the little books. He looked up. "Would you mind if I took these away with me, Dee?"

She tried to smile at him. "Why, Joe, you can't mend them."

"No, but the stories can still be read and the pictures are not much damaged."

Sarah was laughing. "You want to read them at bedtime!"

He frowned her down and turned to Dee again. "One of our lodgers works for a printer in Newcastle. He could show them to his master. No one is printing anything as charming as these for little children. They would sell. You will be asked for more."

Jack clasped his hands in amazement. Only he, Jack Heron, had a wife who could earn money by writing and drawing.

Dee herself was wide-eyed but she said, "I have little paper left and I know not where I could buy more if I could afford it."

"The printer will send you paper if he wants your work," Joe said. "These are dainty watercolours. He has a man can trace them and make woodcuts so they can be printed. You brought pencils and paints and brushes from your home?"

"Yes, I bundled some into my needlework bag at the last minute."

"You poor dear," Sarah said. "Your father had no head for business of course. But now that evil Buonaparte can't bring his army over and invade us everything will look up and Joe will make your fortune for you, you'll see."

"No I won't," he said, "but these might bring you a small income."

"Which would be most welcome," Dee said. "I thank you heartily, Joe."

Jack threw out his arms to embrace them all. "Did I not always say I have the loveliest and cleverest wife in all the world?"

Dee lowered her head down, blushing, and Jack guessed Joe might not care for that, but Francis woke up then, reminding them all of his existence. Dee clasped him to her full bosom, murmuring, "So soft, warm and wet" with the utmost tenderness. "If you will all excuse me," she said, "I'll take him next door to feed him."

Jack knew she hated to have Billy near at those times. He would try to pull Francis from her breast, shouting, "Stop doing that!" If he, Jack, picked up the baby to dandle him Billy would pummel his legs with his fists and cry, "Put him down."

It was like trying to protect a lamb from a prowling wolf. His father would shake his head. "Ay, they'll be fighting when little'un is big enough."

His mother said, "Francis'll not stand up to Billy. He'll be too feared o' him."

"Nay, Billy will be all right when he's had a taste o' the pit." His father repeated this prophecy now and Jack shivered at his own memory. Would Billy scream as he had done?

Joe was now saying they must leave for the Newcastle stage and Sarah slipped out to the netty. While she was gone Joe admonished Billy. "I am your godfather and I want to hear you are a good boy. That was very bad, spoiling your lovely books."

Jack hoped Billy would be sorry but he only grumbled, "Want Sandy story."

Sarah came back then, complaining, "You want to get that door fixed. One of the Slater girls tried to come in."

Jack was relieved when they had gone for he felt shame piling on his head. Joe could bring his wife by the stagecoach and live in a tall house with an inside closet and many rooms while his own angel had to earn money because his wage was so small with two boys to bring up – and all in one room! Even worse, Joe had had to scold Billy when their plan to keep him quiet had failed.

He looked sorrowfully at Dee. Her eyes were bright.

"Oh Jack, I might be a published author one day and if Mr Hurst is really willing to take Billy for lessons, I could do more books and we could afford the school penny. Oh Jack, things are looking up."

She gave him a hug and life was instantly good again.

Dee

Two weeks later, when Dee had taken Billy to the school 'to see how he does' as Mr Hurst put it, she was handed a package that had just come by the mail coach from Newcastle. She tucked it into the folds of the shawl which held Francis on her hip and hurried home. She laid him in his cradle and he looked up at her, apparently amused by her excitement. Fumbling with agitated fingers she extracted a letter, a pack of fine paper and a replica of a book cover.

Moral Tales
The Story of Susie the Sparrow
By Dione Sharon

Dione Sharon! What was this? She opened up Joseph's letter.

My dear sister-in-law,

Pray do not be offended by the decisions I have had to make on your behalf. Mr Septimus Brandling of Brandling Printers was so eager to have your stories that he was not prepared to wait while I communicated with you. He was also reluctant to use your real name, requiring as he phrased it, "Something more refined and elegant for the upper-class market." I recalled your classical name of which he heartily approved and I was murmuring "Sheradon" to him, being in some doubt of your feelings on that subject, when he exclaimed, "Ah, Sharon! Dione Sharon," emphasising the second syllable, "that has a beautiful flow to it."

In only a few days he had set up his press for the cover of what he says will be the first of many books from your pen under his imprint of Moral Tales. This he says will entice the Sunday School market.

I am an innocent in the printing business but initially he will undertake the costs of publication and distribution and offer you twenty-five per cent on each book sold. I accepted this as quite generous so that he could go ahead at once.

I beg your forgiveness if I have acted over hastily and trust I may remain your affectionate brother-in-law,

Joseph Heron

Dee's first impulse was to whirl round the room clutching the letter. Her second was to study the wording again and marvel at the scholarly letter by a former miner, and finally to wonder what twenty-five per cent would actually mean.

Before she did anything else she wrote a swift, informal reply, her gratitude exploding on the page and endorsing every decision Joe had made. When she had sealed it she wanted to run back into the village at once but it would not go before the noon mail coach when it would also be time to collect Billy from the school.

Francis announced feeding time so she put him to the breast with her eyes on the cover of her first book, recalling the old art master who had taught her for a year and whom she had secretly giggled at for his wisps of grey hair and paint-stained smocks. Her mother had said, "We really can't have him about the place any longer. If he doesn't care to wear a neat wig he could at least look clean." So she had told him, "My daughter shows talent and I believe we can dispense with your services now."

"Ah," he had protested, "it is because she has talent that I can teach her so much more." But her father dismissed him as a needless expense.

Dee knew now that he had been a blessing. His great theme was 'life'. "Put life into your drawings. Dog, bird, fish, are all alive. A flower has life and a tree."

When she had begun drawing Sandy she had remembered this and watched his movements, straining at the wagon or frisking in the field. She was pleased when Jane peered at her work and said, "Ee, William, that horse fairly leaps off the page." But that anyone in the wide world might want to see her work had never entered her mind.

She cooed to Francis, "Your ma is an artist and a writer. We're not going to be frightened of Billy any more, are we?" And when it was time to go she tucked him on her hip, took her letter and marched out like a soldier to battle.

Mr Hurst, young and abrupt in manner and wearing his own flowing locks, brought Billy to the school gate. He had offered to have him for a trial morning and his opening words were, "Well, Mistress Heron, you have a crocodile here."

"What's a crocodile?" demanded Billy.

Mr Hurst bent down and gnashed his teeth at him. "A creature who bites."

He straightened up and said to Dee out of the corner of his mouth, "A clever crocodile, but I must keep him away from the others till he's learnt to behave himself."

Dee nodded sadly.

He added, "He likes a task but is soon impatient. The rest are older and bigger which makes him more aggressive. Maybe he's gentle with wee Francis?"

Dee shook her head. "I don't know how to deal with him." Her confidence had ebbed away. Billy was tugging at the shawl as if he wanted to dislodge Francis.

Mr Hurst turned on his heel. "I must return to the others. Bring Billy back at four o'clock when school closes. I'll give him an hour then."

"Oh, thank you sir. And the cost?"

He waved his hand and went inside.

So began a daily pattern when Dee could write without interruption as long as she had Jack's dinner simmering on the fire. Mr Hurst kept Billy mentally active for his full hour, varying the tasks and cunningly turning them into games.

Billy showed Jack and his grandparents what he was learning but when Dee fetched him she always had Francis with her and Billy's resentment of the baby was palpable. When Francis began to crawl and pull himself up by the furniture, Billy would push him roughly down. Jack didn't hit him again and was at a loss as to how to punish him. What Billy loved best was to be outside, running, climbing and throwing pebbles into the river, but to shut him indoors was a worse trial for Dee. William and Jane gave swift slaps but he only pouted and seemed to forget quickly. They rarely witnessed his worst behaviour to his brother since Dee kept Francis to herself.

Joe's letters reporting the progress of her stories were a small comfort in the daily trial of life with Billy. She tried to interest him in the first printed copy of *Susie the Sparrow* but he slapped it away with, "Don't like Susie Sparrow." Perversely she wouldn't show him her drawings for a new story of Sandy the Horse.

It was late summer when she received a letter from Joe saying that he had found a messenger to bring her the first payment she was owed by the printer. He added, *We are very busy with the renovations to a property we have acquired next to my in-laws otherwise Sarah and I would have been delighted to come ourselves.*

Dee wondered when this messenger would come and more importantly how much he would bring. She hardly liked to leave the house, but one soft September day when the Tyne was drifting lazily to the sea she dared to bring her boys to the riverbank to see if they could play among the pools and grassy islands without mishap.

She set Francis down on a sandy patch where he could crawl about and Billy hunted for flat stones to skim. He had seen Jack skim them and though he hadn't mastered the action of flicking his wrist he kept trying.

When he grew cross with repeated failure, Dee said, "The river's too low. There are no stretches of flat water today."

He stopped and looked at her and for once he seemed pleased at what she had said. He nodded. "I do it when there's more water."

"That's right." She had to marvel at how his speech had developed. His father had had a silver tongue when professing his passion for her. She had tried to put him from her mind, but now, looking at Billy as his child rather than a monster, she saw that processes of thought went on in his brain, love and hate tangled in his heart, impulses to good and evil warred in his soul. Maybe I can love him, she pondered.

And then there came a shout. "Hey there, Dee Heron!"

It was a voice from the past. She stood up and saw – beyond the waggonway and the tall summer grasses – a bonnet perched on yellow hair and an arm waving.

"Jenny! Jenny Coxon!" She must be sitting up in some sort of vehicle on the track to Burn Cottage and had spotted them by the river.

Dee wanted to leap up the bank to greet her but there was a cry from Francis. Billy had pushed him down into a pool. She snatched him into her arms. "Bad Billy!"

Scrambling up with the baby soaking her skirt she clambered over the rails and could now see the pony and trap and Jenny jumping down to embrace her.

"Oh Jenny, I am glad to see you but don't spoil your dress. I'm all wet."

She glanced back to see if Billy had followed her. Fortunately his curiosity was enough to bring him. He stared at Jenny and then at the pony and trap.

"That's a very little horse," he declared. "What's his name?"

Jenny laughed. "Ben, and he can pull the family. Show yourselves, girls!"

Two heads rose over the trap side, cherubic faces framed with golden curls.

"Jenny Coxon, you had twins!"

"Nay, there's twenty months between them and I'm not Coxon now, I'm Batey. You know me, Dee, I need a man. I saw one wandering about North Shields and fancied him so I found he'd been pressed into the navy and let go after Trafalgar. So I says, 'Are you without work or a woman?' 'Ay, neither,' he says. 'Can you read, write and add up?' I asks him. 'Tolerably,' he says. 'Then come and work in our shop. We need a man for the lifting and reaching down. Me da's bad with his chest and Ma's even shorter than me. If you work hard and we're suited we can wed so you can share me room above the shop.' And we was suited so here I am with another bairn."

Jenny had talked so fast that her two girls hadn't moved yet. Francis was gurgling at them and Billy stroking the pony. Dee was out of breath listening to her.

Jenny rattled on, "And here *you* are with two lads."

"I did write and tell you when Francis was born."

"Ay, and I didn't reply. Letter writing never seemed to fit me life after that first one but I promised Ally I'd take her to see where her da worked and where he died. So we been to the mine first and then I came on to see you."

"Come to the house then. I'll have to change Francis's clothes. I'm expecting an important messenger this week and I shouldn't be away from the house too long."

Billy took hold of the rein. "I'll lead Ben."

Jenny patted his head. "Good lad." But she was laughing again. "Important messenger! Bless you, Dee! *I'm* the messenger." She patted her skirt. "It's in me pocket under there."

In the hundred yards back to Burn Cottage she told the tale.

"This funny little man comes into the shop and fetches out of his knapsack a pack o' wee books. 'You sell most things as well as pies,' says he. 'A shelf o' these 'ud look canny.' I laughed in his face. 'Half our customers cannot read.' 'Then show them to the other half,' and he holds one out. I feel odd then, looking at the title. 'How do you say that name?' 'Dione Sharon,' he says, 'a north-country ma like you, but see the lovely pictures she can draw.' 'Where is she living?' I asks him. 'Up the Tyne in Wylam,' says he, and I'm leaping about like a crazy thing. 'I know her. I'm minded to go and see her soon. I'll take half a dozen for a start.' Next day solemn Joe comes in and says you write under a special name and am I really going to Wylam and will I give you a package which he won't trust to the mail? My, how well dressed he is now and talking like a gent. But eh, Dee, our girls just love *Susie the Sparrow*."

Dee was hot with excitement so as soon as they were in the house and the pony tethered she set Francis down on the floor, wet as he was, and held out her hand for the package. Jenny hitched up her skirt and took it from her hanging pocket.

"There's accounts of *Susie the Sparrow*'s sales so far, Joe telt me. *Freddy the Fish* is just out, now Mr Brandling sees how *Susie* is selling."

Little Ally squeaked, "I want to see *Freddy the Fish*." They were the first words either of the girls had spoken but Dee was fumbling to find a paper which would turn out to be a banker's draft. She opened up what was obviously Joe's letter and a gold sovereign fell out. Billy pounced on it.

"Hey there. Give it to your ma," cried Jenny. "That's a fortune that is."

"Mine," he shouted.

Dee was standing, hands flopped by her sides, the letter dangling from her fingers. "That's it? That's all?"

"All! It takes your Jack four weeks to earn that much."

Dee stared at her. She was right of course but it was a shock. She had been momentarily in the world of her childhood where sums in their hundreds and even thousands were spoken of. "How much do the books cost, Jenny?"

"Fourpence each. Some of my customers looks at them and says, 'Pretty little things but I cannot afford that.'"

Dee said, "And I am to have twenty-five per cent on each one. So he has sold two hundred and forty books." She looked at the elaborately set out accounts stating the sales week by week. "I suppose that's good."

"Ay, and Joseph said this is only the start. You're to get busy on the next one."

Dee clasped her hands to her mouth, smiling over the top of them at Jenny. She said in a whisper, "I have a new one of *Sandy the Horse*."

"Well, there you are. You're made. I told everyone in the village that you were on the way to being a great writer."

"Oh Jenny, no!"

"Yes, I did. Now where's that boy put your gold sovereign?"

"He threw it in the fire," said Ally.

"What!" Dee snatched up the tongs. Luckily the fire had died down to a few embers while they were out and stirring the ash she found it at once and, lifting it out, laid it on the table. "You are a wicked boy."

Jenny laughed. "Nay, he'll not know the value of it."

But she didn't laugh when Billy pushed Ally over, shouting, "Telltale."

Ally howled, though she obviously wasn't hurt, and Jenny said, "He *is* a bad boy. Where has he learnt that? Telltale?"

"At school, I'm afraid. He's getting lessons on his own but he plays with the older ones sometimes. Mr Hurst says the four-year-olds are scared of him because he's now as big as some of them."

Jenny, comforting Ally, said, "I'm going to teach Ally and Lily myself. I shan't let them be pushed around."

Dee dared not try to get Billy to apologise so she said herself, "I'm sorry Billy's been a bad boy," and then and there she made up her mind to teach Francis herself. How could she let him face the brutality of a schoolroom, or worse – and here she went cold thinking of it – the horrors of a coal mine.

She saw that he and little Lily were sitting on the rush-mat, pulling bits out of it and feeding each other with them. She sprang to them and found they were spitting them out but she inserted her finger to make sure Francis had swallowed nothing.

She looked up at Jenny. "Oh Jenny, we have to have eyes everywhere."

Jenny picked up Lily, took a kerchief from her sleeve and wiped her mouth out. "Ay, Ma says they'll be grown before we know it but I reckon it's a long time happening. Mind, I love them as babies and I don't care how many more I have."

Dee thought about this too. Francis was her whole satisfaction. She couldn't imagine how she could ever love another as much.

She looked doubtfully at Jenny. "I don't know that I want any more."

"Ay, well, you'll produce books not babies. Now, have you anything to eat in the house? If not, never fret yourself for I brought a whole basket of our pies."

"I'll ask Mother Jane to join us. She's been making blackberry jam this morning." As she spoke, Jane came in with a jar of it.

"Well I never! It's Jenny Coxon! You came in that smart little pony trap?"

"It's your Joe's. Me and the bairns came in a fishmonger's cart as far as Newcastle yesterday and Joe and Sarah put us up for the night in their new place."

Jane had to hear all about 'their new place' then and why Joe hadn't come if he'd got himself a vehicle like that.

"'Cos Sarah drives him like a termagant. She put us in the attic for she said we smelt o' fish but Joe was hammering away at cupboards in the floor below. He works in his shirtsleeves indoors but outside he's dressed like a gentleman and talks like one too. She hated to lend us the pony and trap and we must get it back before evening."

Dee saw that Billy was missing. Jane hadn't bolted the door when she came in.

"Ay, I forgot," she said. "He's always dashing off. He's a handful that one."

They all went out to look for him but soon spotted he had untethered Ben and walked him to the lush grass next to the stream.

"Leave them be," Jenny said. Then she laughed. "Joe wants to know how his godson goes on. What should I say?"

Jane said with pride, "Tell him he's getting schooling for all he's not four yet and he knows his letters and numbers. My man says the devil will be knocked out of him when he goes down the pit."

Jenny threw up her hands. "Dee won't send him down the pit. She's going to be a rich woman soon." And she told Jane the tale while Dee seethed with fury that the whole village would know it now and be shocked if she let Billy work in the mine. She had been longing for time alone with Francis, to love and nurture him, for if he was in the same mould as Jack he would need all the help she could give him.

She was glad when Jenny, who had never stopped talking, gathered up her little girls and said they must go, but now Jane wanted to know more about Joe and Sarah.

"Are there no signs of a bairn yet?"

"Nay." Jenny laughed heartily. "I reckon Sarah lied about her age. Joe knew she'd had a canny bit schooling and her family was set on rising up in life."

Jane sighed. "They didn't like her going for a miner, I could tell. That's why they let Joe have the wedding here. They didn't want us among their fine friends."

"Ay," Jenny said, "but Sarah knew what she was doing when she went for your Joe. She was lucky to get anyone and she saw Joe was a good hulk of a man with brains in his head too. She reckoned she could manage him and she does. If he has to write to lawyers and such she helps him. I saw her making him write a letter over again. Don't fret yourself, Jane Heron, Joe and Sarah will do mighty well together."

At last Jenny called for Billy to bring back Ben and as the little party climbed into the trap, Dee hoped Jane would be so eager to tell William news of Joe that the reason for Jenny's visit would be forgotten. But the moment they were out of sight Jane turned to Dee and said, "So let's see this gold sovereign, pet. I never had one in my hand before. What a day this is!"

Chapter 10

March 1809–Summer 1811

Billy

Billy Heron knew what was to happen when he was six and he was glad. His grandfather patted him on the head and constantly repeated, "Ay lad, ye'll be doon the pit wi' your grandda and ye'll be a man then." He had seen that those who went 'doon the pit' were a clan apart. His father, he realised now, was not one of them. He was in a surface job. Billy had supposed that having charge of Sandy and the wagon was very special but a boy at school said, "Everyone knows your da screamed so on his first day doon they had to pull him up and make him a wagon driver."

It was one more revelation to weaken his admiration for his father, who had been upset when the wooden waggonway was replaced with metal tracks. He pleaded, "Dee, I cannot get used to the different sound." The discovery that his father could barely read a word had been another blow, and that he deferred in everything to his mother. "She is a wonder, your mother," he would say and Billy, who knew only that she feared his own defiance, was muddled in his head between them.

He heard talk too at school. "My ma says your ma is making money but she wants rid o' you doon the pit."

"I *want* to be doon the pit," he would yell, "not stuck in school wi' you dunces or with her and her pet lamb, Francis."

He fought them all till he heard Mr Hurst tell his mother, "Maybe he *needs* the pit. Billy will school himself in life but first he must learn discipline."

Only with Grandfather William could he talk about his longing to start work.

"Do they give me a pick the first day?" he asked.

"Nay, lad, you'll not be a hewer straight off."

"But I want to be a hewer like you," he said, stamping his foot.

"You'll be called for work when there is any and most likely you'll start as a trapper boy. Very important that. Gets the air into the passages. That's how a lad started that lived not far from here, George Stephenson, and they tell me he's a banksman at Killingworth now and so clever with his hands he's trusted to repair engines. Start as a trapper and when you're bigger you may be a coupler or a driver. And then like young Stephenson you may go on to great things."

That sounded exciting, but what was this? '*When* there is any work'? Could he not go down the pit on his sixth birthday? Grandfather said he must be patient which was a word he loathed.

It was an autumn evening of 1809, when Billy was nearly six and a half, that his grandfather put his head round their door and said, "They want you in the morn, Billy. We'll walk there together, three generations. I'm mighty glad to have lived to see it. I'll be that proud o' ye if ye do a good job."

Billy drew himself up and squared his shoulders. "I will, Grandda." He looked up at his mother and pointed his finger at Francis with his mop of silly curls. "You'll never let *him* doon the pit. He's a baby and he always will be."

His mother said, "He may not grow as strong as you but he's no baby."

"Ay, Dee," said Grandfather, "but mind you don't turn him into one. He's a healthy lad is Francis and don't need coddling."

Billy saw his mother didn't look pleased at that and Francis had tears in his eyes. That was what made it so easy to tease him and such a pleasure.

But the first day 'doon the pit' killed all Billy's joy of anticipation. He came home at the end of the day, black of face and black at heart. It was not man's work to crouch in darkness by a wooden door and open it when he heard the putters coming, pushing the corves, hour after dragging hour. They carried a candle on their heads and he could see their straining muscles. That was *work*. But when they had passed along blackness fell about him again. Anger consumed him. Who could he tell? Grandfather took it for granted that trapper boy was the first job you were given 'doon the pit'. His father? His father had screamed at being confined in dark walls. *He* wasn't going to scream. Nothing would frighten *him*. His mother? She was the last one he would tell. Grandmother Jane? She would say, with smile lines at her eyes, "Eh, Billy, life's never easy. Just be glad you're bringing a wage in." But it wasn't the money he could earn but the work he could do that had driven his eagerness to 'be doon the pit'.

He learnt that the other trapper boys found it tedious but bearable compared with back-breaking tasks. But for him activity was everything. He must be doing, not thinking. They spoke of struggling to stay awake; he had to fight thoughts that burnt him up – his loathing of Francis, the creeping scorn he was beginning to feel for his father, his sneaking admiration for his mother which warred with his bitterness at her lack of love. But why should she love me? he demanded of the long dark hours. I am bad, especially with her. Everyone knows I am bad. Mr Hurst says I am. Uncle Joe and Aunt Sarah, on their rare visits, shake their heads over me. Oh, to be hewing coal or pulling corves so that I am not alone in the darkness with nothing to do but think!

The family wondered why he stopped talking. Grandfather told him the Overman was pleased with him. He'd never missed the door once and the putters said he was the most reliable boy on the levels. He just nodded. Any leisure moment in his week he went running as fast as he could by the river, gulping the cool air, bringing life to his muscles. He ignored Francis as if he didn't exist and when Francis began tentatively to address him, he made no sign that he had heard anything at all.

"Leave him be," his mother told her baby. "He's worn out with hard work."

Francis said, "Will I work hard when I'm older?"

"You do now," she said. "You help me all you can with the chores and you learn your letters and numbers."

It was all Billy could do to stop himself from smashing that fair curly head against the wall and battering its features into pulp.

To make things worse, it soon became obvious that Francis took after their father only in looks. Billy had heard people say "Jack Heron's a canny lad but slow-witted. The boys take after Dee." Billy saw that Francis was dreamy but intelligent. He already knew words from their mother's books. He will read harder things, Billy told himself, while I sit in the dark, opening and closing doors for twelve hours at a time.

So Billy went to work with rebellion in his soul, countered by a fierce sense that he must endure this thing because nothing more horrible could ever be asked of him. He spoke when necessary in the pit but scarcely at all in the family.

When he had passed his seventh birthday in the spring of 1810, he was on his way home between his grandfather and his father one cold April evening. He shook with hunger as he always did at the end of a shift. That day he had been gobbling his bait while opening the trap and had dropped a big piece of cheese. Reaching for it in the dark, he had felt the tail of a rat slip between his fingers as it scurried off with his dinner. Now all he could think of was the big pan of stew that awaited them at home.

He didn't sense that Grandfather, plodding beside him, was working up to a speech.

"Well Billy." The words burst out suddenly. "You don't care for being a trapper boy, do you?" Billy looked up at him and saw a grin of white teeth in the black of his face. "And ye know, Billy," he ploughed on, "that the army has taken a mighty lot of horses from the mines because we're fighting them Frenchies on land and we need them to pull the guns."

Billy nodded. He'd heard that the price of a horse was soaring. He wondered where Grandfather's ponderous speech was leading.

"So there's more for two-legged creatures to do, eh?" This sounded hopeful. "And Tommy Robson got his foot crushed yesterday so John Gibson needs a mate to heave the corves."

A spring came into Billy's feet. "A job for me, Grandda!"

Grandfather stopped and looked down at him solemnly. "Gibson is nine years old. Reckon you can do it?"

"'Course I can, Grandfather. He's just a shrimp."

"So you're speaking to us again, are you? It'll be hard work."

"All I want is hard work."

"Ay ay, that's my boy. See, Jack. He's been hiding his feelings. I telt ye how it must be. A man must do the work he's suited for. We've got our Billy back at last."

And so Billy's life became unending physical labour. At first there was agony in his thighs, knees and shoulders till they grew into the work. He fought the pain as he fought the exhaustion which left him just able to eat his supper before falling into bed. Talking was superfluous and, thankfully, thinking was crowded away.

There were glimmers of satisfaction in the looks of awe that he received from Francis, which helped him to hide his weariness and walk in with his head up, a sudden, alien, soot-stained presence in the neat room his mother always kept. Her writing and sewing materials would have been put away, the floor swept, the mats shaken and the dinner would be steaming on a good fire. It was a moment to savour.

"Here he is," she would say brightly and Francis would look up from his writing or his drawing and gaze in wonder at this apparition. No words were spoken.

When he watched his father hug his mother his stomach seemed to knot itself. Was it really such joy for him to find her still there after his day's work? And she responded. It was one more puzzle among the sparse experiences of his life, this bond between two such different people. *She* loved books. *He* couldn't read. *She* was seething with ideas; *he* had none. *He* met everyone with the same smiling trust, unless he heard them speak ill of her, when he looked big and glared at them. *She* judged people on their merits, wary with some, charming with others, warm and kindly to the old, fearful for Francis. Mr Hurst had persuaded her to send Francis to school, but the trial didn't last. Billy heard he was teased for his name, his fair curls and his shyness.

"He knows the answers but won't speak up," a lad told him, "so Old Hurst put him in the corner – 'Till you find your voice,' he says. That was too much for your ma. She hasn't let him come back. How is it you and your brother are so different?"

Billy had no answer to that, but there was comfort in the scorn Francis received and the reputation he had himself as tough and aggressive.

There was a day that summer when the boys were sent home early because of suspected fire damp. Running by the wagonway, Billy saw that the Tyne was hustling along in its central bed after overnight rain with a wide shore on each side and little pools among the shingle into which the river made swirling forays as it passed.

Then he caught a glimpse of his mother and Francis further along. He checked himself, puzzled by the absorbed stillness of their poses, the two bent heads at a small distance apart, against the background of the hurrying water. He forced himself to approach softly till he could see their whole figures. She was sitting on a rug on the bank, making a drawing in her sketchbook, while beyond her on the gravelly shore Francis was kneeling beside a garden he had made, surrounded by a wall of stones and marked out with paths of small pebbles. Between the paths he was carefully placing flower heads from a little pile he had collected. His stillness came from the difficult choices he had to make about which flower to pick next.

He is five and a half, Billy told himself, could soon be a trapper boy and those baby fingers are selecting daisy heads as if it wers the most important job in the world.

With a leap and a roar he was upon him, rolling him over onto his back and kicking the little garden to pieces. His mother jumped up, spilling her book and pencils and screaming at him, "You monster, where have you come from?"

She clasped sobbing Francis into her arms. Billy spun round and sprang up the bank to where she had been sitting. He snatched up her sketchbook and threw it so hard it reached the main current of the river and was swept quickly out of sight.

She stared at him, appalled. Francis, whose eyes had followed the arc of the throw in disbelief, pulled away from her arms and, grabbing a stone, hurled it at Billy. He missed but it was the first act of retaliation he had ever committed and Billy, astonished and delighted, jumped down from the bank, laughing aloud.

"That's it! You want a fight, baby brother."

He began pummelling him with his fists as his mother tried to protect him with her arms. Once started, Billy put all his strength into every punch, hitting her or Francis indifferently. She tried to retreat but, stepping on one of the stones of Francis's garden, she fell backwards, Francis with her, and Billy dropped his hands, panting, and looked at them sprawled on the rough ground. Francis's outflung hand lay among the scattered flower petals. He was emitting hysterical gasps and made no effort to get up.

Billy was suddenly alarmed for his mother. She was not getting up either. Her head had cracked on a stone as Francis's weight had pushed her backwards.

"Get off her." He hauled Francis to one side where he sat bowed over his knees, still struggling to get his breath. "Ma?" Billy knelt down and lifted her head. Her eyes opened and colour came back into her cheeks.

"What? What? You wicked boy, what did you do?" She put her hand to her head and sat up.

He drew a slow relieved breath. Life was normal again.

"You slipped on one of his silly garden walls."

He held out a hand to help her up but she ignored it and rolled onto her front and pushed herself upright, grunting with pain and clutching her back. Her first thought then of course was for Francis, who was still heaving with tears but managed to choke out, "Your lovely book" – gulp, gulp – "it's gone."

She took his hand. "We'll go home. Our peaceful happy day has gone too but we are alive."

She began painfully to climb the bank. Billy saw her pencils scattered in the grass and gathered them up. He held them out to her. She took them without a word and continued on the trodden path to the waggonway, which she stepped across, wincing as she lifted her feet over the runners. Francis trotted beside her, looking anxiously up into her face. Neither looked back to see if he was following.

Was this to be all his punishment, that he no longer existed for them? There was little new in that. When they reached Burn Cottage he hung back to see if his mother would turn to notice him but now she was clutching her hands round the front of her skirt and tottered in to flop in the basket chair. It was Francis who turned in the open doorway, briefly met his eyes and then slammed the door shut in his face. He heard the latch drop down but Francis was too short to reach the bolt so he could easily walk in if he wished. He decided he did not wish.

He galloped back across the waggonway and down to the edge of the river. It was still only early afternoon, he guessed by the sun. He was hot and the water looked inviting. He could swim after a fashion, a sort of dog paddle, but if he turned on his back in the centre of the stream and just lay there outstretched, surely this powerful body of moving water would carry him quite quickly to the sea. There he could swim to shore and enlist on a ship as a cabin boy. He could show them what a worker he was and how strong, and no one would know him as a wicked person, He would be an orphan whose family had all died from the smallpox.

The thought of a new identity lit his whole being like a burst of sun through cloud. He didn't hesitate. Clad as he was in his working clothes and shoes, he stepped across the gravel, splashed through a pool and walked into the river. For a few yards it swirled only round his ankles and then his knees. It was cold but refreshing. Then all at once he was floundering out of his depth. He swallowed a mouthful but flapped arms and legs and rose to the surface. He could feel the pull of the current. This was what he wanted. He managed to kick his legs and press his shoulders back and look up at the sky and breathe. He was doing it. In a short time at this speed he would reach the sea. Trees on the bank were gliding swiftly past against the blue sky.

A voice shouted, startling him. His head dipped back and a wave flowed into his mouth. He flipped over, choking, flailing his arms. The voice came again.

"A child in the river!"

Cursed, interfering humans! He had been in control. Now his limbs were just scrabbling at the water and seeking to escape the current. There were more shouts, different voices. He went under again and a hand gripped his hair and pulled him up. He was hauled, angry and spluttering, to the bank. Arms grabbed his legs and he was dangled shamefully upside down while someone pounded his back. Then he was set on his feet and unknown faces bent down and peered at him.

"What were you doing in the river then?"

"Where did you fall in?"

He shook his head. "I was going to the sea to be a cabin boy."

There was a laugh. "Did ye not think ye might need a boat then?"

"Where are you from? What's your name, boy?"

He hadn't planned the answers to those questions and stood, shivering, wishing they would move away so that he could feel the warmth of the sun.

A woman came up with a grubby blanket. "For heaven's sakes, stop pestering the child with questions. Stand back and let me wrap him up." She had a towel dangling round her neck too and proceeded to rub his head when she had enfolded him in the blanket which smelt of tobacco. He had a sudden bewildering memory of being clasped in something else, thick and smelly, when he was wet and cold. But the memory slipped away as she exclaimed, peering into his face, "Why, I believe it's William Heron's grandson. I took me man's bait along and Jane Heron and I used to have a chat some days till he got laid off with his chest."

Billy couldn't believe his ears. He had only been carried a mile or so downstream. Home, shame and punishment closed round him like an iron cage.

"How did you fall in the river then?" she asked.

"I didn't fall. My mother's notebook blew away and I went in after it."

"Did you find it?"

He spread out his empty hands.

"Hey, that must be Dee Heron of Wylam, the one that writes the stories," one of the men said.

Billy felt the cage close more tightly. He looked at the men and saw there were three of them, two wizened and old, one young and hefty and steaming in the sun. He was the one who had pulled him out. He spoke now.

"If this is her boy she might give me a reward. I reckon I'll take him home. They'll be out looking for him surely?"

"I can run home," Billy said quickly. "I'm all right, I'm dry." And he pushed the blanket into the woman's arms.

"And how about a thank you?" she said. "If it hadn't been for Luke here you'd be drownded by now."

"Nay, I'm taking him." The hefty man put a huge hand on Billy's shoulder.

"Is it not time for milking?" the woman asked.

"The cows'll wait till I'm back. Come on, lad, we'll run."

So Luke is a farmer, Billy thought, as he was propelled up a path churned by cows coming down for water. It turned away to his right where he saw a gate and a farmyard and cows lowing and shuffling. But he was dragged on up over rough grass till they reached the familiar waggonway and on to the track which would take him home to whatever fate awaited him. Farmer Luke spoke only to ask his name. The word "Billy" came out reluctantly. He had hoped to leave Billy behind for ever. Farmer Luke had such a grip on his arm and ran with such huge strides that his feet seemed to skim along and Burn Cottage was all too quickly in sight. He tried to dig in his heels and shrink into the shrubbery by the track to bring Farmer Luke to a stop.

"That's home. Just leave me here. Our door's at the back."

Farmer Luke was peering ahead. "Ay, well, there's plenty comings and goings. Must be for you missing. Come on."

Billy looked round the man's bulky frame. Grandmother Jane was scurrying out of Emmy Charlton's door at the front and behind her came the bent figure of old Emmy Charlton herself, bustling round the house to the back. Then Nan Slater appeared and his own da half carried a struggling Francis round to hand him over to her. Even from this point yards away Billy could hear him wailing. Then Da ran back and they heard the doors shut.

Farmer Luke pulled him forward. "They think you're drownded and they're all weeping for you."

But Billy was sure that wasn't the case. Farmer Luke was dragging him there and making him walk the pebble path round to the back.

"This your door?"

Billy nodded.

"What's up with you? You'll be the hero when they set eyes on ye." He lifted his hand and knocked.

Billy hid behind his legs as the door opened and his father's distraught face appeared.

"Go away. This is no time for strangers calling. My wife has just lost her child and she's terrible ill."

"Oh!" Luke stepped back, almost knocking Billy off his feet. "But here, I've brought him home."

He pulled Billy round by his hair just as he had dragged him from the river.

"What – you!" his father said.

Billy lifted his eyes and couldn't believe the look of agony he saw in his father's face.

"You. You must be the devil himself. Do you know you have just killed your baby sister and are like to have killed your mother too?"

"God in heaven!" the farmer cried, pushing him away, and taking to his heels.

Billy stared at his father.

Another voice spoke. Grandfather William had opened their door.

"Nay, Jack," he said, "that's a terrible burden to lay on a lad his age. Come in here, Billy." And he took him into their room and shut the door.

Chapter 11

October–November 1811

Jane

On a day in early October Jane was chopping onions for the stew-pot when Dee put her head round the door.

"I'm just away to that farm to offer the man Luke ten shillings' reward for rescuing Billy. I'll take Francis."

Jane looked up. "Eh, well, take it slow, Dee. You've not walked that far since you lost the bairn."

Dee nodded and went.

Jane stood idle for a moment, gazing into the fire, thinking what she could never have told a soul. Dee would gladly have lost Billy if she could have kept the little girl. Shaking her head, she resumed her chopping more vigorously.

She told William that evening what Dee had done. "Luke was mighty pleased, she telt me."

"He should be," William said. "It'll take Jack two weeks to earn that much."

"Nay, she puts money away that she's earning. I reckon Jack found a good 'un when he got her. She's made him happy. She's a strong lass with a good heart but losing a wee girl has hurt her deep down. She don't say much but *I know*."

She was scrubbing his back and he became thoughtful and talkative as he sometimes did sitting in the tin bath after his hours at the coal face.

"Ay, she's a canny lass but I wish she'd managed Billy better when Francis was born. It was too plain she liked the wee one best. You weren't like that with our lads."

Jane sighed. "Ay, I tried to be fair wi' 'em, but Joe did bully Jack. They are good friends now. Maybe Joe could help with Billy. He's his godfather after all. Should we get him to come over and talk to the boy? I see Billy all the time with a dark cloud round his head. He's never managed to say sorry for what he did but I reckon he's sorry inside. It was a mighty big shock for him when he knew about the bairn."

She poured the last of the water over William's balding head. He shook himself like a dog and, pushing himself upright, stepped out onto the mat before the fire. She wrapped the towel round him and asked, "What do you think to that then? Get Joe to speak to him?"

He rubbed himself for a few moments and then peered out at her with the towel round his head. She loved these moments of him looking at her and thinking hard. "Dee would have to write the letter. Do you reckon she would?"

"Ay, he writes to her about them books and she writes back. She could put in that we'd like to see him. I suppose he'd have to bring Sarah in the pony trap. Dee told me they know about her miscarrying and Sarah has writ a kindly letter herself."

"Well then." He wriggled his feet into his slippers. "It'll ha' to be a Sunday when we're all here but we could get Joe alone wi' Billy if we put our minds to it."

A few weeks later, Joe and Sarah both came and Sarah talked so much of how difficult it was to get away with her aged parents being ill and all the work they were doing in their three houses that Jane wondered why she had come at all, unless it was to show off her new bonnet and shawl.

When they had eaten dinner William fell asleep as he always did, so Jane took Joe outside on the pretence of showing him how they had expanded their vegetable plot, linking theirs with Jack's and Dee's to grow more food. But as soon as they were outside she faced him with her palms on his chest.

"Joe," she said, "your father and I asked you here for a purpose. Will you take Billy a walk and talk to him as his godfather? You see how it is with him."

He lifted her hands from his best Sunday coat as if they might be greasy from the dishes and stepped back. "Indeed, Mother, I don't see anything since Billy has scarce spoken a word. Only he has a sullen, hang-dog look. Never raises his eyes."

"Did Dee tell you he was to blame for her miscarrying?"

Frowning heavily, he shook his head. "How could that be?"

"He knocked her over on the riverbank in one of his fits of temper. Course he didn't know she was with child, but eh, she lost what could ha' been a lovely little girl and it fair broke my heart. She doesn't speak of it to Billy but I reckon he's brooding on it and cannot forgive himself. He's that jealous o' Francis too. He knows she'll never let Francis go down the pit but he works there like a maniac your da tells me."

Joe shook his head again. "I don't know why he's not at school. I'll ask him if he's missing that. Jack and Dee can't need what little he brings in. She's earning from her books now they're selling more widely – which is mainly Sarah's doing."

Jane's head jerked up. "Sarah's?"

"Ay, Mother, but don't say anything yet. Sarah has an eye for business. She calls herself House of Heron publishers, and writes to newspapers to promote Dee's books. Dee wrote that she lost a new one through an accident before she was ill."

Jane sighed. "That was Billy's doing too. Come now Joe, you must speak with the lad. Jack cannot bring himself to chastise him. He is just upset that there seems to be a badness in him. You took on being his godfather so it's your rightful duty."

Joe nodded his head several times like a confused bull. Then he took a deep breath, looked up at the sky, charged back into the house and grabbed Billy by his collar. Jane trotted after him, full of curiosity. Her elder son could still surprise her.

Joe said, "We're having a walk, you and me, Godson. I need to know you better. Come along."

Billy stared at him, open-mouthed, with what looked to Jane like rising rebellion in his eyes. But he had no choice. Joe marched him out and shut the door.

Sarah, who had been listening to Francis picking out words in *Susie the Sparrow*, looked up, chuckling. "*I* told Joe he should take the chance to question Billy about his progress, but he need not be quite so abrupt about it. Men have no subtlety, do they, my dear?" she added to Dee.

Dee just smiled. Ay, thought Jane, *she's* taken up wi' showing off Francis.

And of course Sarah would have to make it *her* idea for Joe to act the godfather.

She set the kettle on the trivet and pushed it over the fire with the poker. William would be wanting tea when he woke up.

It had only begun steaming when Joe and Billy were back.

"Coming on a shower," Joe said, "but Billy and I understand each other now. So what are you going to say, Billy?"

Billy's face was puckered up, eyes and lips compressed. He's got words stuck in his throat, Jane thought. He'll be lucky if they don't choke him.

But he stepped up to his mother, who had Francis on her lap and the book on the table. She turned her head and looked at him and he didn't lower his eyes.

The words burst out like an explosion. "Ma, I'm very sorry I made you lose my little sister and threw your book in the river and spoilt your garden, Francis."

There was a silence so sudden that William woke up.

"What's to do then?"

Jane was thinking, I never heard Billy use his brother's proper name before. Has Joe bewitched the boy?

Sarah said, lifting her hands heavenward, "You were asleep, Father, but Billy's just confessed to crimes *I* never knew he'd committed."

"Well, I did do them things, Aunt," Billy said, stamping his foot. "I was bad but I'm good now. You'll see. You'll all see. And Ma, you must tell Uncle Joe I'm being good. Every time you send him a new book you must tell him."

Jane was willing Dee to make a hearty response. She felt Billy's manner was hardly that of true contrition but surely he needed his mother's encouragement at this moment of good resolution.

Instead it was Jack who leapt from the window seat where he often retreated in company, while Dee stared in a sort of wonder at Billy.

"That's my boy." Jack clasped him and lifted him to the ceiling. "No more badness. I couldn't bear it when you were bad. I thought I'd lost you down a terrible path, that awful wide road that leads to destruction, like Parson Birkett was saying last Sunday. It stuck in my mind all the way down the waggonway every day since."

He set him on the ground and, keeping his hands on his shoulders, said to Joe, "You was always cleverer than me. What did you say to him?"

Jane, watching Billy's face, thought a second of alarm showed in his eyes before Joe answered, "Nay, that's between him and me."

A grin split Billy's face. "Well, Ma?" he said, looking up at her.

"Billy," she said, "nothing would please me more than to have you showing me and your brother little acts of kindness, thoughtfulness, being a cheerful soul about the place. Is that how you're resolved to be from now on?"

His face was compressed again, his eyebrows drawn together, but he nodded.

Oh Dee, give him a hug for God's sake, Jane cried in her heart. Reach out, kiss him.

But Dee only said, "Well, that is so good to hear, isn't it?" And she looked round at them all.

William was shaking his head, Jane saw, having missed the first part of the drama. "Nay, I don't know what's going on but Billy's a canny lad wi' me. He has a temper and silent moods but he's a worker and I reckon he'll turn out a fine man."

Billy pulled away from his father's grasp and rushed to his grandfather, pushing between his knees and burying his head on his chest. His shoulders heaved.

Jane, with tears blurring her eyes, got up to make the tea.

Sarah exclaimed, "Ee, Mother, not for us. Look at the clock, Joe. I promised my father we'd be back long before their supper time." She stood up and grabbed her shawl from the back of her chair. "I'm sure we've done a power of good coming but we must be away now."

Dee rose and graciously embraced her. "Thank you for hearing Francis read. He's so shy and that was a great help to him."

Jack, awkward as he always was with goodbyes, hurried out to hitch up the pony. It was something he could do.

Joe had taken his hat from the peg. Dee stepped up to him and gave him a sisterly kiss on the cheek and one of her dimpled smiles. "I thank you, Joe, for whatever you said to Billy. God will bless you for it if he is truly a new creature."

Billy had not looked round yet from William, whose arms were tight round him, Jane could see.

Joe was looking in his direction. He said sharply, "Billy, we have to leave. Remember everything I said."

Billy briefly showed a very red face. He waved a hand.

William gave him a little push. "Nay lad, say goodbye to your uncle and aunt like a wee gentleman."

Billy stood up. "Goodbye and thank you," he said, looking pointedly at Joe.

Dee set Francis down. In his piping voice, cocking his curly head, he rattled off, "Thank you for hearing me read, Aunt. Goodbye Uncle. Come again soon."

Sarah patted him on the head and whispered to Dee so everyone could hear, "Such a pretty boy he is."

Jane felt a spasm of nausea.

William had started to heave himself from his chair but Joe and Sarah both waved him down.

"We'll be back, Father," Joe said.

And Sarah added, "You must make *us* a visit when the better weather is here and we can show you all we've been doing."

Jane hustled them out into the cool air and thinly falling drizzle. Sarah quickly stepped up into the trap as Jane squeezed Joe's hand and murmured, "You can tell *me* how you did it."

He just shook his head and gave her one of his rare bright smiles. Jack passed him Ben's rein. He sprang into the driver's seat and they were off.

Jane trailed back into the house, unsatisfied. Francis was begging Dee to read from her book, *Lenny the Lamb*, which she had rewritten after it was lost in the river. "Aunt Sarah has taken it away to be printed," she told him, "but I can tell you the story and you shall see the pictures when it comes in the postboy's bag."

Billy was standing by his grandfather's chair, talking into his good ear. "Uncle Joe asked if I wanted to go back to school. I said I can read and write and the Viewer at the pit gives me sums to do but he knows head work isn't enough for me. I have to feel the corf fighting me when I'm pushing it uphill. *You* understand."

William was nodding. "Ay, lad. I'm happy when I gets the pick in me hands of a morning. It's a good feeling."

Jane sighed. She wondered how much longer her man would be wielding a pick. She herself was still sturdy at nearly fifty but she had already heard the telltale croaking in his throat. The years of coal dust in his lungs were beginning to take their toll. She dreaded the drawn-out wasting she had seen so many miners suffer.

She picked up the heavy kettle and began to fill the teapot, hoping to hear more from Billy about his walk with Joe, but that was it. He had said his say and when she questioned William later in bed he could add no more.

"Ay, Joe cleared the lad's head I reckon, but I know no more what he said to him than you do. He'll be all right, will our Billy, if Dee starts to take kindly notice of him and Jack stops acting like he was afeared o' the lad."

"Happen you're right," she said and snuggled close to him, wishing she could share his cheerfulness.

Chapter 12

October 1812–June 1813

Dee

It was a raw October day nearly a year later when Dee looked out to see her menfolk coming from the pit, Jack in a flurried state with Billy grinning beside him and William plodding along in his steady way, saying little.

"Oh Dee," cried Jack as he came up. "They're going to pension off Sandy."

William shook his head. "Nay, don't let him fret, Dee. The word is flying round that engines is coming and horses will be put out to grass but it'll not happen tomorrow." He turned in to his home where Jane would be ready with his bath.

Jack said as they opened their own door, "Dee, I saw them push this engine on a length of rail. I don't know why but it was a great frightening monster!"

Billy put on the scornful voice of a nine-year-old who knows more than an adult. "Da doesn't understand. They were testing smooth metal wheels on smooth metal rails and they gripped well. Of *course* engines will replace horses. One was tried in Gateshead but George Stephenson will make a better one. We have engines now, Ma, to drive the pumps and winding gear, but soon they'll pull the wagons. You won't understand because you're a woman and Francis won't because he's a baby."

He said this in his ringing voice as he marched into the house where Francis was sitting at the table reading.

Dee said, "Billy! Do you want me to report *that* remark to your Uncle Joe?"

He laughed and shrugged his shoulders.

Jack said, "Engines are horrid noisy things, Dee. Give Sandy hay and he'll go quietly on for ever."

"No he won't," Billy said. "He's too old *now*."

Jack looked frightened. "*I* could never drive an engine."

Dee sat him at the table and put a steaming bowl of broth in front of him. "They'll find you something else to do." She was thinking, Here am I longing for change and he dreads it. How could I have foreseen that incompatibility when I chose him by the churchyard wall? She kissed the top of his fair curls and saw Billy lift his eyes to the ceiling. Francis said nothing but she knew he noticed everything and kept his own counsel.

She served the boys, wondering as she often did how a baby girl might have changed their lives. She thought, If I mention her to Jack he weeps so I don't speak of her any more, but if I could have seen Billy love a little sister I might have warmed to him. I believe his 'goodness' is a clever act. He fetches water and makes the fire in the morning so I can write to Joe that he is helpful and has not assaulted anyone since their visit. But I seek in vain for warmth in my heart. His sturdy pugnacious body simply will not attract my loving arms as Francis does.

She laid down her spoon and drew a long sigh.

"Oh, *you* mustn't be sad," Jack cried at once. "Don't *think* of engines."

She gave him her best smile. "We will not think of engines till they are really here and then I will help you to love them."

They were not long in coming. That winter one was constructed at their own Wylam pit but when it was tried out in the new year it was not a success, much to Jack's relief. But the news was full of the progress being made all over the north-east and George Stephenson's name was always in the papers, which Billy read avidly.

In the spring Dee was impatient for a change, any change, and at last a letter came from Joseph at the end of May that they wished the family to make a visit to them in early June. *Sarah and I would like you all to get leave to come but if my father and Jack cannot, then you and my mother and the boys must come and I will send my man, James, with the pony trap to fetch you. I would beg you to stay a few nights. We can show you some of the sights of Newcastle, which is a fine town, and we may visit the seaside if the weather is clement.*

Dee took the letter in to her mother-in-law.

"A few nights!" Jane cried. "He thinks our men would manage without us for a few nights! You go with the boys. I saw the sea once and it was a deal of grey water with a cold wind churning it up and I wondered how anyone dared venture upon it."

"But would you not like to see Joe's home and the other houses?"

"I would fine, but you can describe them to me. No, I'll stop here and Joe knows I will for we couldn't all get in the pony trap. The man James would be walking!" Then she giggled. "Eh, fancy our Joe having a servant to send."

Dee nodded but her heart quailed when she realised this would be the first time she and her two sons had been away anywhere together. Could she trust Billy to maintain his efforts at good behaviour?

She had not expected Jack's agony. He couldn't bear her going but at least he was still leading Sandy with wagons of coal to Lemington. If he asked for time off they might bring in the dreaded engine. Such a dilemma as this had never confronted him before. He wrung his hands and wept.

"Your father and mother will be here," she said, "as they were before I came into your life. I will only go for two nights." He was inconsolable.

Francis made his own small objection when he heard Billy was coming too.

"But he can't. He has to go down the pit."

"He's been given leave – without pay of course."

"He won't like that. Does he *want* to come?"

"He wants to see the sea very much."

"So do I!"

"Good. You'll enjoy it together then."

Francis stuck out his bottom lip but said no more.

When the day came and the man James arrived, an elderly taciturn individual, Dee was thankful that Jack had already gone to work. His tears had flowed when he kissed her goodbye, begging her in a choking voice to come back safely.

Billy had looked at his father with a sneer on his lips.

She had dressed the boys in their Sunday suits and Jane came out to admire them and give them both a kiss. She stowed a basket of hot stotty cakes under the seat and said, "Don't eat them till your ma says and wipe your hands on the clean cloth I put on top."

As they drove away from the immediate familiar surroundings, Dee found herself light-headed at this sudden freedom apart from Jane and home and even from Jack. She drew deep gulps of the fresh June morning and looked down at her boys, one each side of her, heads turning on stretched necks, bodies tense with the novelty of this adventure. For the first time, she thought, I am happy and carefree in the presence of Billy. Her hands itched to creep round the shoulders of them both to share their excitement, but she held back. I will not intrude myself on them. I had wider horizons in my first eighteen years. Aged ten and seven, they are taking in so many new things.

The strangeness of everything when they reached Newcastle seemed to overwhelm Francis while Billy opened up his senses to absorb every new sight and sound as his rightful due. It was a shock to Dee when she suddenly saw Ralph in the confident turn of his head as he gazed up at the brick terrace of tall houses, three of which his Uncle Joe was telling him he now owned. Sarah lost no time explaining to Dee that her father had put two of *his* houses in Joe's name.

"And people pay you to live in them?" Billy wanted to know.

Joe, she could tell, was delighted with his interest. "Indeed they do. When we have eaten I will show you all over them."

Sarah, however, made a great fuss over Francis, much to his confusion. "Look at his smiley dimples. Dee, he favours you but he gets his fair curls from Jack."

When two ancient grey beings joined their party for the meal, Francis clung even closer to Dee. She knew Sarah's parents were not yet seventy but their faces had a frail papery look and their voices came out with a struggle.

"So we meet the great authoress," croaked Mr Simpson, holding out a skeletal hand.

"I don't know how you think of your ideas," his wife echoed.

Dee thought, They are both wasting away and Joe will inherit everything. He and Sarah have worked hard to make the houses habitable and are on the way to wealth while Jack and I still live in one room. They keep a maid as well as the man James. They have put silver on the table for us and their best china plates. I will tell Jane and she will be proud of her son but she and William have no ambition to change anything in *their* way of life. But I – oh surely! – *I* must break out one day.

The bedroom she had been given was small and dimly lit by a narrow window overlooking roofs and chimney stacks. The boys had another small one across the passage. Francis had never slept apart from her since the day he was born and, tired as he was after a walk along the quayside to look at the ships and a session with Uncle Joe to test both the boys' progress, he had energy left to beg to be let into her bed.

"Oh, go," Billy said. "I'd rather be on my own. Babies must be with their mothers."

Dee held up a warning finger. "Uncle Joe wouldn't like to hear you say that."

"Well, he's not here, is he? He told me he goes round the houses checking doors have not been left unlocked and window bars are all in place. Is he feared o' thieves now he's got so many possessions? I told him our doors are left unlocked all day but of course he knew that because he used to live there." Billy chuckled and snuggled under the blankets. "I like it here," he added, as she led Francis out, musing that Billy had never shared his thoughts with her at such length in his whole life.

She murmured a "Goodnight" but his eyes had shut already.

Curled against her body, Francis was soon asleep too, but she lay awake listening to the sounds of feet on the stairs and voices as Joe and Sarah prepared to settle in the adjoining room. It was only a partition wall and she heard their bed creak as they climbed in and then clearly she heard Sarah say, "I could swear they're a different breed. One small and fair, the other big and dark."

Joseph made dissenting grunts, sounding just like his father. "Jack's a big man. Dee is dark-haired."

Sarah's reply was shrill. "And what about Billy being born in March instead of April and yet a heavy baby? I thought Dee got Jack into bed before the wedding but now Billy's turning out so different I can't help wondering what had happened before they met. Why was the wedding so quick, and her a Sheradon too?"

Joseph was grumbling. "Stow it, Sarah. Let me sleep."

There were some more mumbled noises from Sarah and then silence.

Dee lay straight and tense, her heart pounding. Her fearful secret had leapt into the present moment, hovering on the verge of discovery. But no, no, no, she thought, nothing can be proved. I will deny and deny again and Jack will never believe it. But did Sarah speak out deliberately, hoping I could hear? Did she want to frighten me?

Francis stirred against her but didn't wake. She put a protective arm round him. My precious, she said in her heart, you have bewitched your Aunt Sarah and she will try to persuade Joe that you only are his nephew. Sarah is capable of anything. She could hire lawyers to question me. She broke into a sweat and shivered at the same time. I will not let her beat me. I am a match for Sarah. I am forewarned now.

Francis wriggled. She released her grip and let one arm flop out from the bedclothes. It was a mild night and Francis's body was warm against her nightgown. She thought briefly of Jack and hoped his pillow was not wet with tears. It was a privilege to be loved as he loved her and she must never find it stultifying. She resolved to be very easy and friendly with Sarah in the morning and at last she slept.

Sarah did not appear at breakfast. Joe said she had gone next door to attend to her parents. "Her mother will keep to her bed today. Company tires her. But we must make time to talk, Dee," he added, "for you will be gone tomorrow." Dee found this ominous yet his manner was gentle, almost wistful. "But first we will walk up to Mr Septimus Brandling's place as he has expressed a desire to meet the author of the Moral Tales, and then I believe the boys wish to see the sea." He looked at them benignly and Billy delighted her by speaking up for them both.

"Yes please, Uncle Joe."

Dee had already resolved to visit Jenny Batey if their way took them by North Shields. After the shock of Sarah's suspicions she was even more determined.

"Joe," she asked, "may we call upon Mistress Batey, Jenny Coxon that was?"

"Indeed," he said. "I will tell James to bring the pony trap to the print shop at ten. I have papers to attend to and will come back here, but James knows the pie shop in North Shields and then he can take you to the sands at Tynemouth."

She saw that the day was falling into place as she hoped, and Billy had not disgraced himself.

At the print shop, Septimus Brandling, as small and soft-spoken as his press was large and noisy, showed them how the cover of *Lenny the Lamb* was set up and printed. Francis was enthralled but Billy wanted the seaside. At five minutes before ten they stepped onto the sunny pavement to look out for James with the pony trap.

Francis studied the placards in the window illustrating the different prints that were offered inside while Billy, unable to stand still, said he would run round and round the block of buildings till James appeared.

Dee asked Joe about the health of Sarah's parents. "They both seem so frail."

"They have a weakness of the heart," he said, and then, lowering his voice, added, "I meant to tell you, Dee, that I fear I have a similar weakness."

"You, Joe!" She looked up at his solid frame.

"Ay, it's true. I built all the partitions when we made extra rooms and felt pains in my chest after wielding a hammer for too long. That's why I hired James. He can turn a hand to any task and though he is older than I he seems indestructible. Pray do not tell Father or Mother. I will do no more heavy work myself and am minded to take up a quiet occupation such as fishing. But do keep sending your books to us. Sarah enjoys writing pieces to promote them before taking them to the printer."

"Well!" Dee was taken aback. "How kind of her!" she added quickly, not sure if she wanted Sarah's assistance at all.

He nodded gravely. "She likes to be busy."

"But Joe, I am distressed to hear of your—"

He held up his hand. Billy had come running back.

"Been round six times while you talked," he announced, hardly panting. "At the pit I would be pushing the corf to the shaft foot. *That's* hard work."

"How much longer do you want to do that?" Joe asked him. "I had in mind that you should have more schooling, fitting you to help me as I get older."

Billy screwed up his mouth. "What sort of help?"

"Keeping the rent books in order. Buying and selling property. The work of a businessman." Dee saw that Joe was smiling at Billy's expression. "There might be physical work too if I bought land with derelict houses. You could demolish them."

Billy displayed his arm muscles. "That's better."

James had now appeared with the pony trap and the seaside trip could get underway.

Dee wondered if his health was all Joe wanted to speak of. If that were the case she had nothing to fear except Sarah's suspicions.

Joe saw them installed in the trap and, touching his hat, turned and walked briskly away. A sick man, she thought, watching him. Surely not?

When they drew up at the pie shop in North Shields there came shrieks of delight. Jenny, in a white cap and apron, rushed out, with a baby on her hip.

"Dee Heron! Why did you not let me know you were coming, you wicked girl? How wonderful to see you! And look at these great lads of yours. Why, Billy's as tall as you, and wee Francis! His curls are as fine as my lasses'." Her two girls, Ally and Lily, also dressed as bakers, came trotting out. "See, I can only keep girls. I lost a wee boy."

"And I a girl," Dee said.

Jenny hugged her. "Is it not dreadful? But one recovers somehow."

"We were going to the sands. I suppose you can't come too."

"Oh, but we will. Ma!" She ran back into the shop. "Tell Tom to come in and help. He's only mending the rocker on Susie's cradle. We can't all get in the trap. We'll walk."

"*I* thought of walking from here," Dee said. "How far is it to the sea?"

"A bare mile."

Dee told James to feed the pony and refresh himself at the inn across the way and they would return later in the afternoon. She would carry the basket of provisions the maid had put up for them. He touched the brim of his hat in acknowledgement.

Jenny ran inside, plucking off her white cap and apron, the girls following.

Billy stamped his feet. "Why do we have to wait for *them*? Why are *they* coming?"

"They are friends. It's good to have friends."

"Not girls."

Francis said, "I'll be shy."

Billy laughed. "*I* won't. I'll just push them over. I pushed Ally over before."

"You remember that? That was in your bad days."

He wrinkled his face and stuck his hands on his hips which Dee feared was an ominous sign. But when they emerged with shawls round their shoulders and a basket of steaming pies he stalked beside them, saying nothing, but with an eye on the basket, which Ally was carrying since her mother had Susie in her arms.

Ally was eleven now and as tall as Billy. She seemed determined to draw him into conversation and before they reached the sea Dee could hear him boasting to her about his work in the pit.

Jenny laughed. "She's like me, with an eye for the lads."

Dee said, "And Billy has never spoken to a girl in his life. Wylam pit employs no women or girls and that's all the life he knows."

"Why, Dee? You can't need his earnings."

"He relishes it." Dee sensed Jenny's disbelief and changed the subject.

The ruins of Tynemouth Priory lay ahead on its cliff with the sea horizon beyond, a hazy line against the summer sky. She had seen it herself long ago but now saw it through Francis's eyes and was glad when he stared up at her and exclaimed, "Is all that water the sea? Where does it stop? Is anything on the other side of it?"

Billy, seeing his excitement, pretended to be unimpressed, but when they began to descend a steep path to the beach, he ran ahead, raced across the sand and spread out his arms to the little waves. Dee exulted with him. Her artist's eye was thrilled by the sight of the rugged cliffs, burnt umber in colour, the azure water paling to duck-egg blue and streaked with wrinkled lines of white breaking over yellow sand.

"I should have brought my paints!" she exclaimed to Jenny.

Susie was starting to wail so they found a nook among the rocks on the north side of the bay where they could have shelter from the sea breeze and Jenny could suckle the baby in comfort.

It came back into Dee's mind why she had particularly wanted to see Jenny after what she had overheard last night. She took a good look at Susie.

"Your girls all favour you, Jenny, fair and rosy. I wish my boys were more alike."

"Why?"

"It's Sarah. I heard her talking last night. She seemed to be telling Joe that Billy can't be his nephew – just because Francis is so like Jack and Billy isn't."

Jenny snorted. "Billy's got Jack's shoulders and your colouring. What a silly woman!"

"Yes, but she has calculated from our wedding day and thinks Billy came too early to be such a big baby."

Jenny laughed. "Ah, well we know about that, don't we?"

"But she might try to shame me and hint that I had known a man before Jack."

Jenny laughed even more heartily. "You! The most innocent greenhorn I ever saw, the pair of you too! I reckon you owe Billy to me for all the advice I gave you."

It was just what Dee hoped Jenny would say. She felt she had laid the ground for a robust defence if she ever needed one.

Jenny transferred Susie to her other breast and said, "They change as they grow up. My Ally's changed. She was a timid little thing when we came to you but she's shed that now. She may not look much like her father, Sam, but she has his boldness." She sighed. "Tom's different. Meek and mild like your Jack." She pointed across the sand. "Look at Ally now."

Dee saw that Ally had the others organised into throwing stones at a rock. She made Billy stand further away than Francis or Lily and the game was to see if they could hit the rock with each throw. Dee watched, astonished that Billy was submitting to her leadership, but she could see that he hurled each stone with all his might. Was there venom in the throws because he felt under restraint?

She drew a long sigh. "Things *can* change, can't they? If Jack has to give up Sandy and the wagon he may still be happy, as long as he has me."

Billy missed the rock with his next throw and came running over to them.

"Time to eat now," he announced. The others followed him.

Two hours later, they climbed the path out of the bay with empty baskets. Billy walked by Ally with a belligerent swagger and Francis and Lily trailed behind, tired and silent. Jenny tied her shawl into a bag for Susie and carried her on her back. Dee was weary of Jenny's chatter but envious of her easy attitude to life, in which a few fixed notions stood out like rocks. Her girls must be taught at home, work hard, marry and produce children. "If they keep on the pie shop, good, but I don't mind as long as they and their men are honest and faithful. Openness is all. I abhor secrets."

This last remark as they reached the pie shop stabbed at Dee even as she smiled and nodded her agreement. They parted affectionately. Seeing his mother kissing her friend, Billy grabbed Ally and planted a kiss on her cheek.

"Ee, you forward boy," she cried, flapping her hand at him, but her laughter was just like her mother's.

Francis glanced at Lily, as quiet and shy as himself, and hid behind Dee's skirt. James appeared with the pony trap and he was saved further embarrassment.

At the house – the whole block was grandly named The Heron Mansions – Joe gave Billy a logbook of the progress of the renovations and for Francis he found a *Boys' Book of Heroes* open at the story of Sir Francis Drake. Then he took Dee into the parlour to drink tea and have some serious talk.

"Say nothing at home about my health," he began. "If I am wise I am sure I will be spared. But I wish to tell you now that I plan to make Billy my heir. He knows it depends on his progress as a good son to you and Jack. I like his devotion to hard work and he has shown me he can calculate and write a fair hand which pleased me."

Dee was much relieved at this revelation. This accounted for the change in Billy and explained his interest in houses and furnishings so unnatural in a boy of ten. If Joe could now adopt him, if she could leave him here…but Sarah would never agree to that. In their childless state it would be Francis she wanted.

Sarah reappeared at supper time and Dee asked solicitously after her parents.

She shook her head. "In a poor way, but," she added brightly, "Joe and I are in excellent health so you can tell that to the dear old folk at home."

Dee, avoiding a glance at Joe, assured her she would. So is he imagining illness or is that what Sarah believes? She is certainly anxious to contradict anything he might have said. Does she know he planned to tell me he was making Billy his heir and she wants to indicate that day is a long way off?

That night she heard only low voices from their bedroom which convinced her that Sarah had meant to send her a message the previous night.

I will not fret about her, she determined. Today has been full of sea air and bright colours. Change is afoot. Life must open up for us. Francis needs new horizons. And Billy is a being in my life and I must learn to live with him.

Chapter 13

Billy

Next day as they neared Wylam, Billy felt a few pangs of shame at his behaviour on the way. It had been tedious to sit for so long and Francis-baiting was all he could think of to pass the time. He had taunted him about his shyness and his pretty dimples, but softly so that James would not hear and report back to Uncle Joe. When his mother tried to stop him he said, "You've made him a 'Ma's boy', that's what Grandfather William says. He'll never do anything in life because he always has to be with you."

"Francis will do great things in life," she hissed back at him. "He's read about his famous namesake, Sir Francis Drake, haven't you, my pet?"

Francis nodded, but Billy could see tears were flowing.

"As soon as we're home," Billy said then, "I shall run to the pit and meet Grandfather William coming off his shift. He's a real man. Uncle Joe is all right but he was out of breath when we climbed to the attic in the tallest house."

His mother looked interested in that but now he could glimpse the towers and winding gear ahead. He gave a "Whoopee" and as James reined in the pony he leapt down and ran. The pit had a sort of magnetism for him, and Grandfather, he knew, was the only family member who understood him.

His steps slowed as he approached. Something was wrong. Men were scurrying about and a cage was being prepared for lowering with the Overman and a doctor stepping inside with grave faces. He put on a spurt and reached it before the word was given.

"What's up?" A sickening premonition gripped him.

The Overman looked him in the eye and then turned to the doctor. "'Tis his grandson. He mustn't come."

"What? What's happened to Grandfather?"

The Overman shook his head and gave the word to lower away.

Billy leapt in and the cage began its descent.

The Overman's brows drew together in a dark frown. "Have you not learnt to obey orders, Billy Heron? There's been a fall of rock. Your grandfather is trapped."

"I'll dig him out."

"You'll not move from the shaft foot."

Billy clenched his jaw. It would be he and he alone who cleared the fall. Grandfather would crawl out without a scratch on his body and say, "Thank you, Billy. Fancy you coming in the nick of time like that."

At the foot of the shaft, which was lit by lanterns on wall brackets, several men with their candles lit were preparing to head along the level, but one boy was huddled against the wall with his hands round his head. The posture spoke grief and shame. Billy, stepping from the cage, recognised him as the lad who had been brought in to take his place during his three-day absence.

Billy gave him a shove with his foot. "What happened, Charlie?"

Charlie just shook his head from side to side.

"Don't ask him," the Overman said. "He allowed a run-back of the corf. It dislodged a prop and caused a roof fall."

Billy knew the slope well where the corf must have escaped its putters. He tried to squeeze past the doctor and follow the men.

His way was firmly blocked as the Overman detailed two men to hold him there. "He is not to come. It's Heron's grandson."

Billy struggled in their grip but power drained from his limbs as his fear rose. Waiting, gripped so, was an agony. He listened for the sound of shovels.

Minutes later, which lasted an age, he heard activity from down the level. The points of candlelight appeared. The heads bearing them were low down and they were accompanied by a well-known rumbling sound. They were pulling something on a rolley.

The arms holding him relaxed slightly. He burst from them and ran to meet the group. The Overman shouted after him but he was there, alongside the rolley, as the men checked at the sudden rush of running footsteps. Even in the dim candlelight he could tell that the shape on the rolley was covered. No face was showing.

"My grandfather!" he choked out. But it could be anyone! Grandfather was trapped. This one was dead. He reached to pull aside the covering.

The man at the front gave him a push and he fell against the wall. The rolley trundled on. Were there other men further back clearing the rock fall? He could hear nothing.

Sick with dread, he followed the rolley.

When it reached the foot of the shaft the doctor lifted the cover, shook his head, and dropped it again. As Billy came up they both looked at him with eyes that said everything.

"No, no, please no." He stood before them, every muscle of him trembling. Then he sprang forward and snatched at the cover before they could stop him.

"God in heaven!" cried the doctor. "He shouldn't see that."

There wasn't a face. It wasn't Grandda. That mess was not a face. But there was a soot-black ear and a wisp of grey hair curled behind it and then the baldness began but the back of the head was underneath.

Billy emitted a scream that pierced his own ears. He heard nothing of the murmuring of voices about him. He saw nothing but the face that wasn't a face glaring out of a black mist. Someone took hold of his shoulders but he wrenched away, flinging himself against the wall and beating his fists on it.

Vision was coming back and from the corner of his eye he saw the shape of Charlie, hunched into a ball, trying to edge away from him.

"You," he screamed at him. "How dare you let the corf go? You killed my grandda." He was hauling him to his feet, his hands were round his neck, he was squeezing with all his strength.

He was pulled back and his own face slapped hard. Charlie dropped to the floor and the doctor bent over him.

Words from the Overman came to Billy's ears. "Get him out of here. You two take him up and if Jack Heron is back from his last run, hand him over to him. You'll have to tell Jack what's happened so he can tell his mother. It's a bad business but not all Charlie's fault. The lead rope broke and Charlie at the rear leapt aside or he'd have been knocked underneath. Go on, take him up."

He heard the signal to haul given and realised he was in the cage with the two miners who had held him before.

One said, "A hazard o' the job, Billy. You've seen many an accident before."

"Not so many fatalities," the other said. "Wylam pits have been lucky."

"Ay, careful too."

"But 'tis the lad's own kin."

Billy was still shaking and his stomach heaving, but his brain took in their words. Yes, he had seen men and boys maimed – here a foot crushed, there an arm or leg broken – but the sights had aroused in him only curiosity. Now he was in the cage making its clanking way up to daylight and down there was what was left of Grandfather William… Better by far if Charlie had been underneath. Charlie was expendable. His body would have braked the corf long enough for someone to come to the rescue.

So it had truly happened. Time was not going to go back and Grandfather would not come smiling out to greet him in his undramatic way. "Well, here we go, home again, Billy." It was all he would say; a man of few words. And now he would never utter another one.

Unbelievably bright, warm sunlight was all about him. That wasn't right. Better to hide in darkness. He was in his smart clothes and people were looking at him. No one came up the shaft that was not black with coal dust. As he stepped out he wasn't sure if his legs would hold him.

One of the men who had come up with him had his hand on his shoulder, guiding him to the mine office and sitting him on the bench that ran down one wall.

"Your father's due with the wagon. Sit ye there till he comes."

Sitting still was impossible but the banksman was watching him from behind the table strewn with ledgers and documents. Billy fixed his eyes on him and saw him lower his to the list he had in front of him and select a pen.

He's going to cross Grandda off the list, Billy thought. He's going to write 'killed by rockfall'. When it's there in black and white it'll be fixed. Grandda will be in the past. The end of William Heron.

He shivered. This was a cold place. He had been icy cold here once with that threadbare mat round him, which he could see in front of the empty fireplace. It was a hot day now outside. It was June but he was trembling with the cold. His mother had come then and he had rejected her arms till he heard the wagon and rushed to his father. He could see his little hands pushing her away. She was to blame now for him not being here for Grandfather. She had taken him away to the sea when he should have been pushing the corf. If the rope had broken he would have held the corf for the second it would have taken for the lead boy to grab the ripped end. Thinking of it, he could feel the strain in his shoulders and legs. He wouldn't have jumped aside and let it run. Grandfather would still be here. Grandfather would be sitting beside him now saying, "Ay, we'll wait a wee moment for Jack and walk back together like we sometimes do." He could hear his voice.

Grief welled up so fast an explosion of tears burst out of him and, trying to hide it from the banksman, he jumped up and rushed outside to lean against the timber fence with his hands about his head, shaking and sobbing.

He hadn't heard the wagon but suddenly his father was beside him, in a panic.

"Billy, Billy, what's up? Your knuckles are bleeding. Has there been an accident on the way back from Newcastle? Dear God, tell me Dee is all right?"

Billy looked up at him, rubbing his hands over his face. The last time he had seen his father was when he had walked off to work three days before with tears running down his cheeks because he had had to say goodbye to his precious Dee.

"Billy, *please*." His face was twisted with pain.

"Of course she's all right. She's at home with Francis." He drew a gasping breath. "Grandfather is smashed to bits, that's all."

His father stood and stared at him with the puzzled frown he hated. "Your grandfather? You mean – my father?"

One of the miners came up and slapped him on the back. "Ay, Jack, I'm mighty sorry, but your poor old da's gone. Worked nigh on fifty years with scarce a scratch on him. But it was quick. I'd rather go like that than linger on, a cripple or coughing me lungs out."

Billy listened in disbelief. It was Grandfather he was speaking of. Grandfather had been alive and now he wasn't. Was the vanishing of life so slight a thing?

His father said, "Are you saying my father's dead?"

"Ay, a rockfall. You'd best tell your ma before she hears from someone else."

"I can't believe it. My father?" He was looking about him. "But where is he? Sometimes – don't they bring – bodies – back to the house?" Billy saw that he was crinkling his forehead and biting the end of his thumb.

"Not this time I guess. They'll coffin him first. You get off home and take young Billy here. He's mighty upset."

"Ay, I'll do that."

His father put an arm round Billy's shoulders and walked him out of the pit yard. He can do that, Billy thought, now he's been given his orders.

But on the familiar track home his father's steps kept slowing and he looked down at Billy several times to say, "Is your grandda really dead? When did you – how did you – but you just came back – does your mother know?"

Billy shook his head. He couldn't speak. He couldn't explain anything. If he kept his silence he thought he might just be able to hold himself together.

A few yards from Burn Cottage his father came to an absolute stop. "My mother – how can I – what can I say?"

He was spared by Dee waving to him from the window and then running out to greet him. "Jack dearest, I've missed you so much."

She stopped, seeing their faces.

"What?"

But to Billy's astonishment, his father ran into her arms and, hugging her with passion, burst into tears. "Oh Dee, to have you back! It's been hell without you. Don't ever leave me again."

Billy strode up to them with furious steps and beat his fists on his father's back. "Tell her about Grandfather. Ma, Grandfather is dead. He'd be alive if you hadn't taken me away from the pit. Charlie let the corf run back. I would never, ever have let that happen. I wish you were all dead rather than Grandfather." He turned aside to the field gate and, flinging himself against it, gripped the top rail and bowed his head over his hands.

He didn't see his grandmother emerge from the house. He didn't see Francis follow. What he heard was an unearthly cry that chilled his heart. He couldn't look. He had given Grandmother not one thought but that agonised wail echoed the one that had been screaming inside him since he had lifted that cover.

No one came to him. They must be getting Grandmother inside. He could hear Francis's sobs. When the footsteps were receding he tore himself from the gate and followed. They were not to forget him. He mustn't be shut out. He slid in behind his mother who had her arms about Francis, comforting him.

His father, shoulders still shaking with sobs, was helping his grandmother into the rocking chair. Billy could see she was quivering all over and strangely that made his own trembling stop. He stood with his back to the closed door.

They were in her room and the absence of Grandfather was palpable. A pan of stew was already heating up for his return from the pit.

His mother set it on one side and filled the kettle. Of course she would make Grandmother tea. As she moved about, putting the fat brown teapot and a mug on a tray, she was muttering to herself. Billy with his sharp ears heard every word.

"Dear Lord, I knew changes were coming, but not this, not this. What will this bring? Oh, what indeed?"

Billy couldn't have answered that but he noticed that Francis had flopped onto a stool with his elbows on the table and was sniffing into his clasped hands. That left the way to his grandmother clear. He jerked away from the door, took two strides towards her, flung his arms round her neck and buried his head against her bosom. At once her own hands clutched him in a convulsive movement and held him tight.

"Eh, Billy lad, they're telling me your grandda's gone. I cannot believe it."

He lifted his head as a thought struck him. "I'm William Heron. I shall be a hewer like Grandda."

She gazed into his eyes with a puzzled frown. "Ay, you are. But you'll have to wait till you're bigger. Grandda will tell you the right time. He'll be here shortly."

Billy looked up at his father, still standing by her chair and still quietly weeping. There was no help there. His mother approached with the tea tray and set it on the table. There were mugs for them all.

"Come now, Mother Jane, you're going to have a cup of tea. We all are." Out of the corner of her mouth, she said to Billy, "It'll take time, Billy. It'll take time for all of us."

He nodded. She was giving Grandmother her best dimpled smile. He saw she was wearing a pale blue dress with a matching ribbon in her dark curls. She had dressed for Father and he had to admit she looked beautiful.

I can't love her, he thought, but at least she takes charge of things. Maybe she never cared for Grandfather because he always stood up for me.

That thought wrenched the tears from him again. He drew away into a corner to hide them and found himself by the bed where his grandparents had slept all their married life. He saw Grandfather's smashed face again as if it lay on the pillow and he stifled a howl. That would haunt his dreams for ever.

He felt a touch on his shoulder. His father's voice said, "Come back to your grandma, Billy. She's asking where you've gone."

So she needed him. That was important. One day when Uncle Joe and Aunt Sarah died he would have houses and money and he could make her life comfortable. He was after all William Heron and it was his duty to look after her.

He choked back his sobs and went to stand by her chair.

"Ay," she said, gripping his hand, "that's better. I don't rightly know what's going on but I know you've been away to Newcastle and your grandda and I want to know what you did." She looked about. "Is his shift not finished yet?"

A knock came at the door, making them all jump.

Billy saw his mother open it to find the Viewer from the pit standing there.

His grandmother screamed out, "Go away, you. I know what it means when *you* come darkening folks' doors. What have you done with my man?"

Of course he came in and spoke kindly words and sat at the table and left a paper with Dee as the only adult who could read. It was the start of the procedures that always followed a fatal accident, Billy knew.

When he had gone his mother gazed at the paper and seemed to speak to herself. "There it is in writing. A changed life without him. God help us all!"

It *is* a new life, Billy told himself. I am the man in Grandma's house. I will hack those walls that killed Grandda. I fear nothing nor no one.

Part Two

Reaping Whirlwinds

(Seven Years Later)

Chapter 14

September 1820

Francis

Francis waited in the line of boys before the headmaster's desk. Looking over their heads, he was staring into a gilded mirror on the wall above the desk and seeing a face he scarcely recognised as his own. Instead of the crown of curls that made his face look small and cherubic, his hair had been trimmed and flattened and scraped back into a black ribbon, where he knew it must spring out into an ugly tuft at his neck because he had felt it with his fingers after Aunt Sarah's administrations.

"There now," she had said, "your sweet babyhood has gone but you will not be bullied and teased by the other lads. Keep a straight, serious face and don't let them see your dimples and you'll have no need to be anxious."

He was holding that face now and thought it looked long and lugubrious in the mirror. He was sure Mr Hurst would not remember him.

His turn came as the boy in front reported himself and moved away to the rows of desks behind them.

The headmaster didn't look up. "Name?"

"Francis Heron, sir."

"Age?"

"Fourteen, sir."

"Eh! Did you say Francis Heron?" Now he did look up and stared. "Well, bless my soul, it is! Somewhere in there is that pretty wee boy that sat close to his mother in Ovingham Church of a Sunday morning, keeping as far as he could from his big brother. So what happened to Billy? He's not still hewing in Wylam pit, is he?"

"Yes, sir."

"But your mother's changed her mind about you, has she?"

"No, sir. I persuaded her." Always be completely truthful, she had exhorted him, when she said goodbye.

"Well done. Dee Heron was always a stubborn one. You know I wrote to her four years ago when I was setting up this school and suggested you and Billy could be among my first pupils?"

"Yes, sir."

Francis could see his mother's face when she opened the letter. She had said, "Well! Billy won't leave the pit. He has to hew coal like his grandfather and Mr Hurst's not getting my Francis when he stood you in the corner the only time I let him have you. Besides, Newcastle is beset with riots. You are safer here."

"So it's taken you four years to decide you want a bit of education?" Mr Hurst cocked his head at him. Francis could see a streak of grey in his flowing hair and there were deep lines around his mouth that suggested severity, but his eyes were twinkling.

"Mother has kept me studying at home, sir."

"Latin and Greek?"

"I have a Latin Primer but I'm afraid—"

"Don't be. I am not pushing Latin or Greek. This northern area is humming with new industry. Science and mathematics are needed here."

Francis felt his face smiling but hoped the dimples were not evident. "I am very interested in science, sir. My father built me a shed where I did experiments. I knew candles were dangerous in mines so I tried to make a safe lantern but George Stephenson succeeded first."

Mr Hurst laughed. "Shame! But you tried. Well done. I see you have your mother's spirit in you. And your father? Still driving coals to Lemington Staithes?"

"No sir. Engines have replaced horses. He is working in the mine farm now."

The boys behind were shuffling.

Mr Hurst held up his hands. "Enough. To your desk, Heron. I am pleased to have you."

Francis retreated to the place the usher had assigned him. It was that gentleman, a stooped, elderly assistant called Kirkley, who had seen Uncle Joe when he went with Francis at the end of the summer holiday to The Hurst School for Young Gentlemen in the village of Jesmond on the northern edge of Newcastle. Uncle Joe had looked very much the prosperous businessman and there had been no hesitation on Mr Kirkley's part in adding Francis to the roll of pupils.

"Mr Hurst is abroad," they were told, "but is expected back for the autumn term."

Francis had seen the spacious schoolroom, four times the size of their own home, with the dais and headmaster's desk at one end and on the polished floor individual desks with inkwells. There were some fine pictures on the walls as well as maps and charts and stained glass panels at the tops of the windows. His fears had melted away. Wylam School had bare brick walls and rough benches and slates and chalks. Here were shelves of books down both sides and an air of learning about the place. The handsome mirror over the dais had caught his eye then too. His mother had often mentioned her dreams of seeing him in grand surroundings, always laughing at herself when she said it, but it had implanted in him a longing for an expansion of his world, which had intensified in recent months since he had turned fourteen.

It had been a battle to get her consent for this move. "You should come home every day," she said. "It is not a boarding school but you cannot because it is too far."

"Uncle Joe would let me stay and I could have Saturday and Sunday at home. Uncle's always asking if Billy can live with them and learn his business but maybe he won't mind me. I'll learn anything I can, anywhere. I need – I need – space, Ma!"

At that he remembered she had looked on the verge of tears and muttered, "I know, I know." Then she had changed the argument. "Aunt Sarah would grab hold of you, body and soul. You would begin to think of her as a mother."

"I would never do that," he said. "I do not even like her. She fidgets and fusses over me but now I am older I can endure that and laugh about it."

The Reverend Birkett and Mr Hammond had both told her she must give way. Even his father had said, "I want no changes but if he comes on

Friday evenings and goes to the Lord's House with us on Sundays, that would be good, Dee."

Grandmother Jane had roused herself from her habitual torpor and said, "What? Is our little Francis wanting schooling after all this time?" She had looked up at him from her rocking chair which she hardly ever left. "Eh, he's not so little now. He's grown long and leggy. Ay, he should be out earning a good wage to help us all."

He had felt guilty then because he knew Mr Hurst would have to be paid and the days of his own earnings were still in the future. Billy's wage was good now he was a hewer and by living at Grandmother's he enabled her to stay in her own home which was all she wanted. Joseph sent her regular money but she refused to go and live in his house. "I've got William Heron with me," she said.

Billy had laughed at Francis's failure to make a safety lamp. "What did baby Cis ever know about mines and lamps and fire damp and explosions?" Then his laughter had died and he went on in a rage, "Or hacking coal or running corves or falling rocks and smashed faces?" And he stormed out and slammed the door. When he was in Grandmother's room they never heard him shout so it was a blessing when he retreated there.

Mr Hurst had now registered all the boys present and Francis saw that the round-shouldered assistant, Mr Kirkley, was taking charge of the eleven- and twelve-year-olds at the far end of the room while Mr Hurst had the rest, including one or two who looked sixteen or seventeen. He had hoped to be put with Mr Kirkley since he had never had proper schooling and Mr Kirkley had a gentle manner and had been quite obsequious to Uncle Joe when they met.

Mr Hurst, however, began briskly shooting questions at the older boys under headings like 'Recent History'.

"What happened on the eighteenth of June five years ago?"

There was a chorus of "Waterloo" and "We won."

"Where is Napoleon – Heron?" He suddenly pointed at him.

"Saint Helena, sir."

"Ah, glad to see you can speak up now. And where is Saint Helena?"

"An island in the Atlantic Ocean, sir."

"This is our rapid-fire question time so we dispense with 'sir'. Now, modern mining inventions. What is the difference between the Davy lamp and George Stephenson's safety lamp? Robinson?"

Robinson had no idea.

"Anyone?"

Francis, hot with excitement, embarked on the explanation, his words falling over each other. "Well, sir, I mean, sorry sir, the Davy protects the flame with a sort of gauze cage round it. The light can get out but little heat, while the Stephenson lets in air at the base through a tiny hole and if there's gas outside there can be a whoosh up, which blows out the flame and prevents a big explosion."

Mr Hurst held up his hand as Francis drew breath to add more.

"Thank you, Heron. I seldom ask questions to which I do not know the answers but that was the case here and I am grateful. Take note everyone. Throughout your life, learn from those who know. For most of your next few years that will be from me, but if any of you have special skills or knowledge, ask for a time to present it to the rest in clear language. Though we are not a classical grammar school in the ancient sense of the term, that will be our version of the reciting of Latin or Greek orations and it will be very much more useful."

Francis felt himself redden under the stares of the other boys, but inside he was exulting at the thought of recounting all this to his mother, only a little dashed at remembering that he would not see her for five more days. He would have to share it with Uncle Joe and Aunt Sarah, who would not appreciate, as she would, how much it meant to him. Mr Hurst had gained a devoted pupil and Francis, gazing up at him, surprised a wink in his direction and knew that he knew it too.

As the week progressed Francis was delighted to find that he could keep up with the older boys and he blessed his mother for his home education. She had asked Mr Hammond for old school books his sons had used and they studied them together. Sometimes he saw sooty marks where Billy had dipped into them, but if he asked him, Billy's answer was always, "Real men hew coal like Grandfather. *He* never needed to read a book in his life."

In the evenings at his uncle's, Francis began to fear that his presence was causing tension between his uncle and aunt. Uncle Joe was delighted to be consulted about the mathematics of investment, gross and net interest, profit and loss. "Ah, to open a young mind to these things!"

His aunt expected him to be useful about the house. "Dear Francis, could you just run up to Room Six in Number Two? Miss Jordan wants to rearrange her furniture. She's such a helpless creature but always prompt with her rent." Once she said to him, alone, "After all, you occupy a room where we could charge rent but of course it would not enter our minds to do so to a member of the family!"

Since her sickly parents had both died, their house had been turned into another rented-out property and his uncle told Francis, "We are hiring a new maid. I won't have you cleaning stairs and passages when you should be at your studies."

Francis was still only in his third week when he glimpsed the new girl leaving as he returned from school. She passed him without a glance but next day was waiting for him on the doorstep.

"They said you were living here. Well! Francis Heron, I can just see in you the wee shy boy with the curls – now I take a good look at you – but how you've grown! Your ma's been to see my ma a couple of times but she never brought you boys again. Is your Billy still heaving corves about?"

Francis could feel how hotly he was blushing. As she had talked he realised this must be Ally Batey, but she was a well-developed handsome young woman now with her golden hair twisted up in a knot. He reckoned she must be eighteen and his complete inexperience of such a category of the female species left him speechless.

She laughed the ringing laugh of her mother. "Oh, you're still shy, but you need not be. We are old friends. Tell me about the tough lad, your brother."

"He's a hewer now, the one that digs at the coal face, the most dangerous job in the pit." It was after all possible to speak with her and exciting to notice that her expressive eyebrows were darker than her hair and she had startlingly blue eyes.

But further conversation was interrupted by the door opening behind her and Aunt Sarah snapping, "You still here, Ally? You'll miss your lift home in the fish cart, won't you?"

"I'm away, Mrs Heron." She waved her hand at Francis and ran up the street.

"Come along in," his aunt admonished him. "You're not expected to talk to the maids, you know. I was not sure if it was wise to take on that girl but your uncle said he knew the Bateys would have brought her up honest and a hard worker. She seems somewhat irrepressible, just like her mother."

"I thought she and Lily both worked in the pie shop."

"She did, but they needed her to earn her living now little Susie is old enough to help in the shop. I make Ally change her clothes when she comes for I can't abide the smell of fish. I'm afraid she's sweet on the fish man too so I may not have her long. Such a trial finding suitable servants these days! You might just take the brush at the back door and sweep the yards before your meal. Smuts and dust, you know."

"Yes, certainly, Aunt."

"I shall put Ally in charge of Number Four, as far away as possible. I can still smell fish in her hair."

Francis had not smelt fish and he suspected his aunt of trying to keep them apart. For himself, the few words they had exchanged had given another spurt to his confidence. He was not obliged to be 'the wee shy boy' all his life. The growing up he had achieved in such a short time was an astonishment.

He knew it was an astonishment to his mother too.

"I have lost my wee boy," she said, "but gained a tall, upstanding man."

Even Grandmother took notice. "He used to creep about as if he was afraid of his own shadow but he looks at me now and tells me about Joe and all the houses."

"That's Mr Hurst's doing," he told her. "He believes in bold deportment and not being afraid to talk when you have something worth saying."

"Then I forgive him for putting you in the corner when you were little," his mother said.

His father now seemed in awe of him, and as for Billy, he glowered at him under his strong brows and could scarcely stay in the same room with him.

One Sunday, when they were all eating together after morning church, Francis mentioned that Ally Batey now left very promptly to meet him in the street and exchange a laugh about Aunt Sarah's 'little ways'.

Billy, who seldom spoke at family gatherings, broke in, "If I ever wanted a woman it would be Ally Batey, so you can keep out of her way. She has a bold free way about her but don't you be deceived. She'll only think of *you* as a schoolboy."

Their mother laughed. "Oh Billy, you haven't seen her since she was eleven. I didn't know you ever gave her a thought, or any young woman for that matter."

"Of course I think of women," he snapped out. "What do you imagine we hewers think of when we're down there for hours at a time?"

Francis was shocked into silence. Billy had the same thoughts that he had lately been plagued with. Billy was a human being with emotions hiding behind his habitual surliness. He pondered this for several minutes, his spoon idle in his beef stew, which he had been enjoying.

His father grasped his mother's hand across the table and said something about having dreams till they came true when he met her.

Billy was staring belligerently at him, so Francis found himself blurting out, "Anyway, she's sweet on the fish man who gives her a lift."

Billy flung down his spoon and leapt to his feet. "Of course, she would be."

"Nay, sit down. There's steamed blackberry pudding," his mother said, "and if you hadn't kept turning down your uncle's invitations to come and visit you might have met Ally again before she got sweet on the fish man."

Billy scowled and sat down again. "I was going to go in the summer when the shifts were reduced for the surplus of coal. Then it was settled *he* was going to be their pet lamb and of course I couldn't stomach that."

Their mother put the boiled pudding on the table. "Why 'of course', I ask you? An uncle can be happy to see *both* his nephews."

Francis saw a blush rise up her cheeks the moment she said the words. It was odd, he thought, but he supposed she was hot, leaning over the steaming bowl.

Billy just grunted and no more was said on the subject.

When they had eaten, Billy helped Grandmother up to take her next door for her afternoon sleep in her rocking chair.

They heard her say, "Ay, William knows what I need. All my life he has."

When they had gone, his father said, "What made Billy cross this time? I didn't rightly understand."

His mother said, with a mischievous twinkle, "Our Billy would like to marry Jenny Batey's eldest but it seems she's spoken for."

His father's mouth hung open as he looked from one to the other and Francis shared a smile with her. She often teased her Jack fondly but never in a conspiracy with anyone else. Francis rejoiced that, since leaving home, he had become her companion as well as her son. It was another milestone in his growing up.

Chapter 15

Dee

On the Monday, when Francis had returned to Newcastle for his school week, Dee woke to find Jack bending over her with his lips pursed for a kiss.

"Oh!" He stepped back. "I had no wish to wake you. You looked beautiful."

She sat up and hugged him. "Have I slept late?"

"The mine bell just rang but I should be at the farm to feed the new pigs. Billy will be off and Mother's alone."

She put her feet to the ground. "Go, my darling. I'll see to Mother Jane. Billy will have got her fire going before he left. I'll make her tea."

She slid her arms into her bedgown and her feet into her slippers. He gave her the kiss she loved and was gone, happy, to his animals.

She stretched and yawned. For the first time since Francis had started school she had overslept and missed the early morning she loved to spend alone with Jack. To her surprise, she had not missed Francis as much as she had feared. She found Jack's tenderness in that dawn hour like a peaceful balm on the frustrations of her life. He was contented in his work so there were no bemused frowns on his brow.

When she opened the door to step to Mother Jane's door, she realised why she had slept late. A leaden sky sagged low over the fields. There would surely be rain soon. She sighed and, lifting Mother Jane's latch, went softly in.

The room was dark and chilly. The curtain was still drawn over the window and no fire blazed in the hearth. Billy must have slept late too and scrambled to work, for once neglecting his grandmother's comfort.

Dee peered at the bed in the recess to her left. Jane's crumpled face was peaceful, her breathing slow and steady. She looked at the hearth. Yesterday's embers were not cleared. It would be hard to make a fire without the clattering of the irons waking her but the early October day was raw and Jane felt the cold as she had never done in her younger, bustling days. Dee's compassion was beginning to fragment. She had never supposed Jane would give up on life so completely when the shock of bereavement had worn off. She asked Joe once, "Did you not think your mother would recover her old stalwart self?"

He nodded, then shook his head. "She was already relying on your youth and vigour while she still had my father. But they were like one tower together and when he fell away she collapsed too. Billy has tried to be a bulwark and I praise him for it but a bulwark can't hold up a tumbled wall."

Dee was struck by his perceptiveness.

While her thoughts roamed over them, Joe's health, Sarah's dominance and their temporary charge of her precious Francis, she was gently stirring the cinders and letting the ash fall through the grate. She managed to build and light the fire before Jane lifted her head at the crackle of the kindling and the glow in the dim room.

"That you there, William?" She had called Billy that since her husband's death and seemed to find comfort in it.

Dee straightened up. "He's gone to work, Mother Jane. It's a dark morning. We'll have our tea as soon as the fire's hot. You just rest there till the room's warmer. I'll fill up your buckets for there'll be a rainstorm soon I wager and it'll be mud, mud, mud round the spring."

"Ay, you're a good lass, Dee. Has William not done the buckets?" She sat up with her hands to her head. "Eh, I forget. He's gone. I was dreaming of our wedding day." She looked at Dee with her eyes moistening and her lips trembling.

Dee said, "Now, Mother Jane, it's your grandson Billy does the buckets. He must have slept late and had to run to work." She hurried out into the darkening day.

The first big drops began to fall as she came back, half running and slopping water, and heard a shout of "Hey, Missus!" from the path to the pit.

A lad who ran messages for the Viewer was waving to her. Her heart thumped. An accident! Billy! Oddly her first thought was, Dear God, Jane can't lose another William.

He panted up. "They wants to know why Heron's not come to work today," he gasped out just as the black sky emptied itself over their heads.

"What? What are you saying? Oh, come inside. You'll be drowned."

She motioned him ahead as she struggled in with the buckets.

"Mother Jane, you stay where you are. Don't be alarmed, this is—" She looked at the boy, a skinny lad with a face like a ferret.

"Timmy, ma'am."

"Timmy from the pit has something to say but the rain's pelting down now."

Jane looked at him. "Ay, I can see he's wet. But there's never good news comes from the pit. It's not about my William, is it?" Her face had paled and there was a wild look in her eye.

Dee gave the boy a peremptory gesture to speak up. He had his back to the fire and was steaming. He looked up at Dee.

"They thought Heron must be ill."

She repeated, "Heron, Billy?" The men were called by their surnames. Billy, whatever had happened to him, was a grown man. She must remember that.

"Ay, Billy Heron." He was warily watching the old woman in the bed.

Dee said, "But he went to work as usual. He's not here." Had he fallen down a disused shaft and nobody knew? Her mouth went dry.

The boy said, "He never signed in. We all has to sign in."

She was thinking, He couldn't vanish between here and the pit. It's not half a mile. What dangers were there on an early morning with only pitmen about? In a flash the river came into her mind and the day he had walked into it as a boy. Surely he couldn't have drowned himself!

Jane was babbling, "It's my William and you're not telling me!"

She shouted at her, "It's *not*. It's my *son*." She snapped at the boy, "Are you telling me no one has seen him today at all?"

"Ay, he just never turned up."

"Have they searched the pit?"

He grinned. "No one gets down without they've signed in."

She put her hands on the boy's shoulders and turned him to the door. "Well, get back and tell them he's not here and they'd better search above ground. Maybe someone had a grudge against him and killed him in a fight and hid his body."

The boy opened his eyes wide. "Like murdered him!"

She opened the door on a curtain of rain. He seemed reluctant to leave.

"Go on. There'll be a fire in the mine office." She remembered little Billy crouched in the hearth rug beside it.

He nodded and plunged out, muttering, "Murdered!" The idea seemed to have excited him.

She shut the door quickly. The rain was churning the gravel path into mud and splattering it over the threshold. The same thing seemed to be happening to her brain. How could she make sense of it to Jane, whose eyes were blazing with fear and fury?

"You're not telling me, girl. There's someone dead, isn't there?"

Dee pulled out a chair from the kitchen table and turned it to face her. She had sat up, her face poked forward like the beak of an anxious hen.

Dee sat down and said in a level voice, "Billy has not turned up for work, that's all." All! she thought. When he could be carried downriver in this torrent and never seen again.

Jane was shaking her head. "Not gone to work? But he always goes to work. William Heron never missed a day's work in his life."

Dee wanted to scream at her, "Which William Heron are you thinking of now?" Husband or grandson? But he is *not* your grandson. His father was evil and he is evil too. He has been trouble from birth, to me at least. And I have no one to lean upon in this trouble. If I go and tell Jack at the farm he will say, "What should we do, Dee?" One day I can lean on Francis, only he is not here and he is still a mere boy, and how can he be experienced when I kept him close too long?

To Jane she said, "I am trying to think what might have upset him on Sunday when Francis was talking about Jennie's daughter."

She could see from Jane's expression that she had lost her now. The days flowed together for Jane and she would have a clearer memory of her own wedding than she would of yesterday's conversation.

Dee stood up and added coal to the fire and filled the kettle. Practical action and the following of routine would quickly soothe Jane and help her own mind to probe into what might have driven Billy to go off somewhere on his own, for suicide seemed utterly out of keeping with his stubborn nature.

He had been angry that no one believed him capable of thinking upon women. He had been angry that Ally fancied the fish man who gave her lifts to work. He had been angry that Francis was now living at Uncle Joe's and he felt shut out. He hadn't spoken to Francis when he left for Newcastle on Sunday evening but then a brotherly 'goodbye' never passed his lips. Jack for once had rebuked him. "Nay, Billy, speak fair." He had scowled at his father and no more was said.

Surely none of that was enough to make him wantonly miss work? He had recently been named 'best hewer' for the quantity of coal he had dug in a day. "I did it for Grandfather," he had told Jane, receiving a bewildered look in return. Now he would lose the bonus he had been given and a day's pay too.

Her hand paused as she stirred Jane's porridge. So had he been attacked by someone jealous of his success? Was her almost comical word to Timmy that he had been murdered – was it – could it possibly be true? Or beaten senseless and lying in some corner of the pit buildings behind a pile of slag perhaps? Would they search for him? She should go and see.

Mechanically she put her hands to work again. She laid a tray on the table with a mug of tea and the porridge bowl.

"Will you have it in bed, Mother Jane?"

"Nay, I'd likely spill it. I always gets up. Was there something wrong just now? Did someone come?"

"The rain. You're hearing the rain. It's splashing off the gutter and churning the gravel into mud."

Jane nodded and got herself out of bed; her feet, in the white bed stockings she always wore, wriggled into her slippers. Dee tucked her shawl round her shoulders and watched her settle to eating and drinking. She still relished having food put before her after the years of being the one who served her menfolk.

Dare I leave her and run to the pit? Dee wondered. She would think me mad in this rain. Or to the farm for Jack when I know he can't take charge of the situation?

She remembered hunting for Billy when he was two and how the Slater girls had run to and fro shouting, "Billee! Billee!" They were grown up and in service now and their mother went out cleaning too. Their father was working in a newly opened shaft and would probably know nothing of Billy's disappearance. Emma Charlton's room had been taken by the steam engine driver, of whom Jack was abjectly in awe. So she and Jane were alone in Burn Cottage.

Dee stayed where she was, her imagination conjuring up visions of Billy running away to join the navy, while she scuttled between their two rooms finishing off the chores in each and wondering why no knock came on their door with news.

Towards midday the door opened without a knock and Jack stood there, his hat brim dripping rain.

"They telt me Billy's gone missing, Dee. What can we do?"

She put her finger to her lips and looked at his mother. "Have they searched at all?" she whispered. "I couldn't leave her."

Jane, who had been nodding by the fire, looked up. "Is that our Jack? Is it end-of-shift time? Where's my William?"

"We don't know, Mother," Jack blurted out.

Dee tut-tutted in exasperation. "He'll be here presently. The rain's easing off at last. Jack's come in to share our dinner 'cos it's quiet at the farm."

Jack sat down, a little surprised, and ate what she put before him, leaving her a mere spoonful of the broth.

Dee asked softly, "How did you find out?"

"They sent the lad Timmy to the farm to see if Billy might have come to me for something. I couldn't rightly grasp what they were saying at first. Then I got leave to come and see if he'd turned up at home."

"Well, he hasn't."

"What are you talking about?" Jane's bowl was empty so she began to take notice again.

"The horses took refuge from the rain in the barn," Dee said quickly.

Jack grinned at her, eyebrows raised. "Ay, they did that. How did you know?"

She got up and looked out of the door and up at the sky. "They'll be trotting out again." The clouds were shredding and blue sky was appearing through the holes. She could see where the stream had expanded into a lake round Jack's little waterfall. Sunshine burst out, turning the scene into a blaze of colour. Steam began to rise from the hedgerows. Where, she thought, is Billy?

She beckoned Jack to come out to her. "See, the sun is shining," she said loudly, and then at his ear, "Go straight to the mine office and say he's still missing and find out if they've searched the pit surface area." She was tempted to add, "And ask if they have alerted the constabulary," but too much would only confuse him.

He nodded, repeating, "Pit surface area," and loped off.

She went back in to Jane and had begun washing the pots when she heard the sound of horses' hooves and voices. Surely that was Joe's! She dashed out and stood, astonished. The pony trap was coming with Jack running beside it, all smiles, Joe at the reins and sitting beside him with a twisted grin on his face, Billy! And he and Joe were not wet at all. Had they descended from another planet?

She shook her head at Billy. "God in heaven, you turn up – as always!"

He jumped down. "Did you not want me to, Ma?"

She saw he was wearing his Sunday suit. Why had she not checked his clothes' chest? He wouldn't drown himself in that. She felt his sleeve. It was dry. Was it real that they were actually here?

"Now Billy," Joe said, clambering out and handing the reins to Jack. "Sorry first for all the anxiety you must have caused. Remember all I have said."

"Ay, I'm sorry, Ma. I'll change out of this and report for the afternoon shift."

He brushed past her and went in to his grandmother. Dee heard him say, "I had a free morning, Grandmother, but I'm away to work in a minute."

Dee looked at Joe and shook her head. "I cannot believe this is happening. How did you escape the rain?"

"Ah, that! We saw this great cloud ahead of us all the way but we were in sunshine." He chuckled uneasily.

"Well!" Dee said. "Come into my place and tell me the tale."

Jack hitched the pony's reins on a post and followed them in.

"No Jack," she said. "Run to the mine and say Billy is here and is coming to work directly. He'll have to explain himself when he gets there."

"Do I come back here when I've done that?"

"No, you'd best go to work too."

"Oh." He looked disappointed but hurried away at once.

Joe sank down on one of the kitchen chairs. "Have you any ale in the larder, Dee? I'm parched."

She poured him a mug and waited for him to take a long drink.

"That's better. I thank you. Will Mother want to hear this? How are her wits today?"

She gave a snort of a laugh. "Her wits, as you call them, come and go. She'll accept what Billy said. I'll go in and settle her for her afternoon sleep. When she's wakened later we'll just say you called to see her and she'll be delighted."

"Dee, you manage everyone."

She slipped next door and bumped into Billy in his pit clothes dashing out, his Sunday clothes in a heap on the floor.

He gave her a cursory nod and was gone.

She found Jane ensconced in her rocking chair. Her increasing deafness could be a blessing. She must not have heard the horse or she would have been curious.

She said, "Pull the wee curtain across, Dee. That sun is shining right in my eyes. William was on late shift so he's gone, but he dropped his things on the ground. He never used to be so untidy."

Dee picked them up and folded them on the clothes chest and drew the curtain over the small south-facing window. Then she bent and gave Jane a kiss on her forehead. "Sleep tight. I'm only next door."

At last she could hear what she feared would be an infuriating story. She sat down opposite Joe. "Will I give you some refreshment first?"

He pointed to the mug of ale. "That will do very well for now." He drew a long sigh. "Well, he's a strange lad, my godson. Good and bad mixed in him and I cannot tell which will win in the end."

It had started, he said, with a hammering on the front door at six o'clock. Billy stood there and his first thought had been that someone had died. But no, Billy said he had walked from Wylam to find out if he was still his uncle's heir.

"What!" cried Dee. "He woke you at that hour to...! Oh, he is mad. I am so sorry. You must have been very angry!"

"Sarah was. She told him he would be so no longer if *she* had anything to do with it. I was more curious, once I had recovered from the shock of seeing him. It seems he could not sleep at all on Sunday night – he told me this over some breakfast, for he was very hungry – and he said he was burning up at the thought that his brother had replaced him and at last he was driven to rise and come. He had no idea of the time. He was sorry he had roused me from sleep but he had to know. I asked him if he had left word and would he not be in trouble at work? He said he had to come because he was burning up – he kept using that phrase – so I rebuked him severely, knowing how anxious you would be. It was at that point that we heard Francis coming down and I asked Sarah to see him off to school without telling him his brother was come. After she had left the room Billy became quite passionate."

Dee gasped. "Oh! Not violent, I hope."

"On the contrary, almost sobbing. Pleading with me not to cast him off. He had vowed when my father died that he would be a hewer all his life to honour his memory. That was why he hadn't come to work with me here as I hoped he might. He hews coal faster than anyone and won a bonus for it just lately, he said."

"Oh, he did," Dee broke in. "I told him I was proud of him, but he seemed not to care what *I* said. He had done it for his grandfather. Joe, I never told you or Jack that he saw your father's smashed face. One of the miners came later to tell me. I think he gets nightmares but your mother is deaf and doesn't hear. He never speaks of it and I find him unapproachable – on that subject above all."

Joe nodded his heavy head, his bristly eyebrows meeting in a sad frown. "I am sorry he saw that. Yes, I did grieve for him when he spoke to me of my father but when he began to speak of Francis I am afraid my heart hardened. Francis was now learning all my business, he said, and last night he had become possessed with the thought that I must have altered my will in his favour, so he had to know. I told him I had thought of it but had taken no action yet. To tell you the truth, Dee" – and now he lifted his head and solemnly met her gaze – "Sarah has pestered me since Francis came to stay to make *him* my heir. Of course I know not how long I may have to live and Francis is too young to run a business like ours. But Billy? Would he ever be able to?"

"Not if he is to be a hewer all his life."

"Well, I must finish the tale." He drained the mug of ale. "I made it clear to him then that as Francis had sought the path of education and shown an interest in my desire to provide good housing for the less fortunate, it was logical for him to pursue that work. Billy was beginning to 'burn up' at that so I put a stop to the talk and, mindful of your ignorance of his whereabouts, I said we would leave at once. Sarah rejoined us when Francis had gone to school and to my surprise Billy asked her if he could speak to Ally Batey. She absolutely forbade it and was then so alarmed by his scowling face that she feared I would not be safe with him and wanted me to send him with James, but I had to come to explain it all to you. Does he *know* Ally Batey?"

"Not since they were on Tynemouth beach. I fear this is a new passion of his – to know a woman, *any* woman. But, oh Joe, what a trouble he has been to you! And he hardly seemed ashamed of himself when he arrived."

"Ah, yes, I was sorry to hear him speak to you as he did, but we had time to talk on the way and out in the fresh air he was quieter and more rational. He spoke fondly of my mother, reminding me that though I help with her rent, she would lose her home if he ceased to work at the pit and she needs her familiar surroundings. I hope time will heal his grief for my father and when my mother dies he might give up mining. So I promised him that, for the present as my godson and elder nephew, he would remain my heir."

Dee shivered. The long-buried sin reared up to cut her to the quick. Joe was acting upon a lie.

He went on unawares, "Well, Billy thanked me heartily. Of course if I go Sarah could manage the houses, as she does the publishing side of your little books. She's a clever woman."

He has to speak up for her, she thought. He's a good man and I am deceiving him. She asked, "Do I owe her for her help? I am afraid I simply write and illustrate and send them without further thought."

"If she deducts postage she keeps a ledger of every transaction to show you."

Dee nodded. "I am grateful." She knew you had to have a publisher promoting your work and House of Heron sounded well. It was a pity it was Sarah but her own life was too full to allow her to do more than create the books and send them.

Joe was studying her solemnly. "Whatever Billy or Francis do in life, I can't see *you* wishing to live here much longer." He glanced round the room with a smile. "But Jack? How does someone with your talents and upbringing tolerate the sort of life with which *he* is contented?"

Dee felt her face softening and her eyes moistening. "He loves me, Joe. That's enough."

"Ah." He nodded slowly and there was an uncomfortable pause. Then he went briskly on. "I have put Billy on probation again. He must never act impulsively as he did last night. He must show respect to you and Jack. He must not display jealousy to Francis, but brotherly affection. That will be the hardest, I fear." Then, with his head on one side and his eyes searching hers, he finished, "Have I done right, Dee?"

She was deeply moved by his humility and her own duplicity. She swallowed and answered huskily, "Yes, Joe." When she had first known him she had thought him austere and remote but life had moulded them both and now they had achieved an intimacy she could never have imagined. How hurt he would be if he knew her secret!

At least she must feed him. "Will you eat something now, Joe?" She was trying to remember what she had in the larder.

"A crust of bread and a piece of cheese if you have some, for I must be on my way when I have spoken with my mother. Sarah will fret till I am home."

"You cannot stay till Jack and Billy are back?"

"I fear not."

"Then we will go in to her now and she will wish you to eat with her."

Mother Jane was overjoyed to see Joe and roused herself to search her own larder for a great feast. Finding only two eggs and a turnip, and hearing that he had no time for cooking, she had to be content with three slices off a ham and some bread and watercress that Dee brought in. She made him tea with her own hands while Dee led the pony to the shrinking lake for a drink and Jack, seeing her from the farm, came running with a bundle of hay and an apple and helped her hitch him to the trap again.

Of course he had to come in then and embrace Joe as he got up to leave.

Joe muttered, "Mother thinks I had business in the country and called on my way home. She has forgotten this morning's anxiety. Dee will tell you everything."

Dee stood watching the brothers as they parted. Smiles and a manly hug. Why could her sons not do that? She wept in her heart. They came from my womb yet there is no bond between them.

She returned to Jane and found her tearful at the shortness of Joe's visit. And I, she thought, feel only dread when I anticipate the return of *my* elder son. Dear God, wherein have I failed so grievously?

Chapter 16

September–Christmas 1820

Billy

At the end of his shift, the Overman told Billy, "Mr Burns wants to see you. You'll lose a day's pay of course and the badge of 'best hewer' I reckon. A pity for he gives you books to study and fancies you for Overman when you're twenty-one."

Billy stiffened. "Nay, I won the badge last week. That stands in the records."

The Overman had the stunted, wiry shape of many miners and Billy had to bend to look him in the eye. He read astonishment there and reluctant admiration.

"Ay, Heron. You had a clean slate before this. Well, off you go to him."

"I should go home for my bath."

"Nay, he wants you now."

Billy walked over to the mine office where there was a good fire in the hearth. The Viewer, grey-haired and sombre, looked up from his desk.

"Ah, Heron. Sit down."

Billy was surprised. The wooden bench could be wiped clean of course but sitting in the presence of the principal authority in the pit was unheard of.

Mr Burns went on, "I have heard no excuse given for your absence today. A reputation for reliability is forged over years but can be lost in hours."

Uncle Joe had said much the same: "You build character brick by brick and if you insert a bad one, discard it quickly or it weakens the whole structure."

Billy had thought of an excuse while he was working. It had elements of truth and would have to do. The Viewer was regarding him steadily.

He looked down at the stone floor and focussed on his own sooty footmarks.

"It's hard to talk about, sir, but I get nightmares since my grandfather was crushed." There, he had brought those words out and the rest would not be so difficult. That much at least was true. "Last night's was bad, sir, very bad."

The Viewer nodded as if to say, *Let's have it*.

"Well sir, this time I dreamt of my uncle who left mining and now lives in Newcastle. In the dream he was creeping to the coalface and I saw the roof begin to crumble above him but he went on regardless. I tried to warn him but no sound came out. Then he seemed to hear the rocks move and twisted his head to look up so I knew his face would be smashed – just as Grandfather's was." He rushed that out with a glance at Mr Burns. Seeing sympathy in his eyes, he added, "I never speak of that."

"I can see it's hard for you. But what happened then?"

"I woke in a sweat as the roof fell. But the dream was so real, sir, I just had to get up and go and look upon my uncle to see that nothing had happened to him."

"You walked to Newcastle?"

"Yes, sir. It was dark and I had no notion of the time. I thought I'd be back for the shift but it was already morning. We returned in his pony trap. I was happy to see his face unmarked and I trust now I won't have those nightmares any more."

Mr Burns sat stroking his chin. "So strange a tale has to be true. Tell me, do you think of your grandfather's accident when you are at work yourself?"

Billy bit his lip. Why had he spoken of Grandfather? Could he tell the Viewer of the fierce anger that made him hack so hard and fiercely? Could he tell him how he had lately tried to quell those thoughts by thinking of girls, picturing them naked, and then cursing himself for defiling Grandfather's memory?

He shook his head. "I cannot speak of it, sir."

"Then I will not ask. I inquired this morning when your absence was reported and it seems you have a reputation for toughness and courage and, though you are admired, the younger boys are afraid of you and the men see you as a safe man to work with but hardly a mate. No one knew why you would disappear. Your Overman said you were a 'private' lad. I take it you would not want this story to get out?"

Billy looked up sharply. "No, never sir. They can guess what they like."

Secretly he was rather pleased with this portrait of himself.

"Very well, Heron, I will report that you should be fined for your absence a half day's pay but you will not lose the bonus you won last week."

Billy stood up. "Thank you, sir."

"And remember, if you wish to speak to me on any matter, knock on my door."

Mightily relieved, Billy ran home to his grandmother who had entirely forgotten the morning and welcomed him with her usual delight. She loved him sitting in the tin bath before her fire so she could scrub his back for him. He understood how that helped her to keep a fragile grip on reality.

As he sat while Grandmother soaped him and his flesh whitened under her hands, he wondered, Who am I inside this body? He looked at his scratched legs as if they were a stranger's. No, they encase *me*, he told himself. But who am *I*?

When he and his uncle had left the house and climbed into the pony trap he had thought how easy it would be to fake some sort of accident on the way. The road was well-rutted ahead of them from the rain that preceded them as they travelled westward. The trap could overturn and he, young and nimble, could leap out as it rolled, but his uncle would land heavily and it would be his business to see that he never got up again. That would prevent any change of his will in favour of Francis.

Am I capable of such a deed? he wondered. What do I want in life that could put such a thought into my head? That would indeed be a bad brick. But two minds warred within him. One had dedicated his life as a hewer to his grandfather's memory and to the care of his grandmother, and the other demanded wealth, ease and deference to compensate for all that was lacking in his present day-to-day existence. Could he ever leave hacking at the coal face? Would he diminish himself if he inherited wealth? What was this clean, well-muscled body destined for?

"There you are, William." She held out the towel she had warmed at the fire.

He couldn't talk to her. She viewed him as the husband she had begun to bathe when they were first married. What experience had she of miners then, or men for that matter? She had been in service. She had never before washed a man's body, but in her practical way, she had got on with it as she had the business of loving him and producing his children. That was all her life. And then an idiot of a boy had let a corf run back and the roof had fallen and she had her man no more. That wouldn't have happened if *he* had been there. Was that at the back of his nightmares? He had failed his grandfather. But he had also caused his mother to miscarry so the death of his baby sister was laid at his door. He hardly ever thought of that. But is that who I am? Is that why I could think of killing my uncle, because I am an embodiment of death?

He rubbed himself hard. Mr Burns said people feared him. He wondered why that gave him so much satisfaction. And yet when he was dressed and his father and mother came in with a pan of stew and said they would all eat together, he saw only disapproval or wariness in their eyes as they looked at him and that gave him no satisfaction at all. It was all he could do to stop his own filling with tears.

They made no allusion to his escapade of the morning, so he said, when they had sat down and begun eating, "I shall try to see Uncle Joe more often."

His father beamed. "Good, good. That's good, is it not, Dee? Families happy together."

"Was Joe not here just now?" Grandmother Jane said. "Or was I dreaming? He was eating a slice of ham."

"He called on his way home, Mother Jane," Dee said, and to Billy, "Will they give you a few days' leave, after…?" And she raised her eyebrows at him.

"Ay, if I take it without pay. I wouldn't go when Francis is there so it must be in his Christmas holidays."

"Why not travel back with him on the stage one Sunday evening before the nights are dark?"

"Because I couldn't bear it, Ma, and well you know it. Besides, they have but the one room untenanted."

The subject was left there but Billy fixed it in his mind that he would go and find out if Ally Batey had grown into the girl he imagined, and he would show Uncle Joe there were no tasks Francis could do that he could not do as well or better.

On one matter only he wished he could consult his father but he knew he never would. Had his father been with a woman before he met his mother? Other lads at the pit boasted of a particular village girl who would initiate you if you asked her. Billy, aloof from them in most things, could not bring himself to join them in this. As the Viewer had rightly discovered, he was a private person.

Mr Burns granted leave at Christmas and Billy wrote to his uncle and invited himself. Whether his mother wrote too he didn't know but Uncle Joe agreed. When the time came he was apprehensive. Uncle Joe wrote that Aunt Sarah was planning a luncheon party on Christmas Eve as she believed Billy had no experience of society, but they would invite only the Batey family, whom he already knew, and Septimus Brandling, the printer, and his wife. This was not how Billy had hoped to meet Ally Batey. He had imagined bumping into her on the stairs with a duster in her hand.

Francis, home for the holidays, told him how fussy Aunt Sarah was about table manners. "I've learnt the different pieces of cutlery and not to sit down till ladies are seated and all manner of things."

Billy made no reply. Francis would be at home here with the family and without him he knew they would all enjoy Christmas, which was a bitter thought.

His mother had altered a suit of clothes passed on by Mr Hammond to fit him and stitched him two new shirts and said he could take Francis's portmanteau.

"No, I can bundle my things up and carry them on my back when I set off."

"Nay," his father said. "A seat is reserved for you on the Carlisle to Newcastle stage. You are to travel like a gentleman."

The night before the visit Billy lay awake in his grandmother's room, fearful of being drawn away from the single-hearted hewing of coal where, ironically, he felt safe, to something alien and complicated where he might flounder. He clung to the thought that in four days he would be back in the pit and need never leave it again.

His Uncle Joe greeted him warmly which compensated for the coolness of Sarah's, "Well, Billy, so we are to have the pleasure of *your* company for a change?"

She showed him to Francis's room. "I have given him little things for his comfort but he is so generous he won't mind you making yourself at home here."

He noticed a silver-handled brush and comb on the mantelpiece under a round silver-framed mirror. There were some of Francis's clothes hanging up and schoolbooks on the shelf above the bed. He wished he had been shown a bare cell.

Aunt Sarah was saying, "You can fill your water jug yourself. I don't ask the maids to look after this room. Francis keeps it clean himself."

"So Ally Batey doesn't come up here?"

"Certainly not. She is employed mainly in Number Four." She faced him with her arms tight across her chest. "I trust you are not here to see *her*. You will in any case see her tomorrow. I must say I am not happy to sit down with the Bateys since Ally is our servant but your uncle felt you would be uneasy with strangers. We dine with the best people in town. However, you must start somewhere, only pray do not entertain amorous hopes about Ally. She is courted by a person in the fish trade."

"I know," Billy said. He struggled to add something she could pass on to Uncle Joe. "It's good of you to let me come and I'll try not to disgrace you at all."

She smiled faintly. "Scrub your hands well before we eat." She looked at his scratched and bitten nails from which he could never eradicate a black rim. "And wine will be served tomorrow but partake very sparingly as you are not used to it."

Billy lay between Francis's sheets, cursing himself for coming. Had he done it to remain Uncle Joe's heir or to meet a girl who had briefly impressed him years ago?

He woke to hear his uncle and aunt getting up and presently the gap under his door showed the light of their candle passing to the stairs.

"No, no, he's young. Let him sleep," he heard his uncle say.

Of course he had to get up then. At home he would have been up, ready for his shift. This day would be impossibly different, but there might be a little excitement in the difference. Could he manage anything so far outside his experience?

He dressed and crept downstairs. From behind the closed dining-room door he heard his aunt's voice. "He is so uncouth. I dread what he'll say to them."

His uncle said, "I warrant he'll be tongue-tied. Think what his life has been."

He crept halfway back up the stairs and then stumped noisily down and rapped on their door.

"That you, Billy? Come in, come in."

His aunt made an excuse to leave when he was halfway through a substantial breakfast. "So much to attend to. As soon as you've finished I'll set out the table for the luncheon party. There are two leaves to pull out. You can do that for me." And she disappeared to the kitchen.

"Leaves?" Billy looked round at the foliage of several sombre plants on the windowsill.

His uncle laughed. "The table. It extends. I'll show you when you've finished. And I wish to expand your horizons too. We'll do a tour of my office this morning."

Billy, angry at being called uncouth and tongue-tied, was trying not to revolt at all this arranging of his time. At the mine he was an experienced man. Now he felt a child again, to be moulded and instructed.

He tried to listen as his uncle talked his way through the property ledger with the cost of repairs and furniture set against the rent brought in. There were lists of every tenant with their records of payment, suitability or otherwise and reasons for eviction. There was a list of servants, James first and extending to their live-in maid and three daily maids. Billy noticed the word 'cook' did not appear.

"Is Aunt Sarah preparing today's luncheon?" he asked.

"She is, and a fine meal it will be. Of course, the kitchen maid works under her instruction but your aunt would trust no one but herself when there are guests."

Billy tried to see what was written against Ally's name, her earnings and remarks on her progress, but his uncle kept his hand over that. By the time he had closed the last book Billy was weary of the lack of physical activity.

"What do you think of it all then, Billy?" Uncle Joe asked.

Billy was not sure what he should say. "You keep it writ small and very neat."

"Ah, but could you carry on with it? Would it engage your mind?"

He had to agree or Francis would grab it. There was certainly money in it.

"I reckon it's common sense, sir. When you have made a profit you can buy what will bring you in more profit." It wasn't an answer but Uncle Joe was pleased.

"You put your finger on it, lad. But you must also buy at the right moment which requires a certain aptitude. Your aunt has it and I have learnt from experience."

"Then I daresay I could too." He felt a pang of hunger. "When are the people coming?"

Uncle Joe took out his pocket watch. "Ah yes, a timely reminder. In a few minutes. We will go down to the dining-room and see if all is ready."

Aunt Sarah was looking cross. "You should have been here to set out the glasses, Joe. And Billy can carry in the heavy water jug from the kitchen."

He was there in four long strides and to his surprise found a colourful young woman with a highly rosy face stirring a pan of soup on the fire.

She burst out at him, "Why, it's Billy, the coal hewer!"

Her yellow curls and bright blue dress were partly hidden by a cap and apron but the impression was still dazzling.

He stumbled to a halt with what he felt was a silly grin on his face.

"You must be Ally? I thought you were a guest today." He couldn't keep his eyes from her large mobile breasts as she stirred the soup.

"Poor old Sarah was getting hot and bothered so I had to help. I only have to throw off cap and apron to turn into a guest when my folks come. I brought my best dress when I came to work this morning. Do you like it? It matches my eyes."

She poked her head towards him and opened her eyes wide.

"Ay, they're certainly" – he fumbled for a word – "vivid."

"Good word for a hewer of coal."

He allowed one of his heavy frowns to form. "I tell you, there is no higher task in the world than hewing coal. How could you do without that fire?"

"Very nicely. I'm roasted to bits."

Aunt Sarah bustled in. "Where is that jug, Billy? It must be placed on the side table. Ally, that's enough stirring. Draw the pan to the side and put the lid on or it will be all boiled away. Your people are late. The Brandlings have just arrived."

She was gone again. As Billy looked about the kitchen for the water jug Ally pulled aside the pan and covered it. Then she took off her cap and popped it on Billy's head so it fell over his eyes.

"Hell!" He snatched it off and flung it to the floor. She was laughing and there came echoing giggles from the scullery beyond. He could see now that there were two maids there laying out dishes on a marble bench. One was Gertie, who came forward holding out the water jug.

Ally said, "Ooh, wouldn't I love to pour it over you when you come home from the pit!"

He stalked out with it to the dining-room. Ally, he decided, had not improved with the years.

Voices came from the front parlour, Aunt Sarah's raised in what he supposed was her high-society tone. He glanced at himself in the mirror over the fireplace, dipped his fingers in the jug and smoothed down his lank dark hair where Ally's cap had ruffled it. He knew he was uncomfortably ruffled himself now that the moment had come when he must join the company.

The front door bell clanged as he was hesitating. Ally scampered past him and flung it open. Billy stepped back into the dining-room while Uncle Joe came out to greet the rest of his guests. Hats, coats and shawls were hung up and Billy managed to slip into the parlour behind the group as they were ushered in. Keeping his eyes down, he backed into the dim corner between the door and the window while greetings were exchanged, but Aunt Sarah spotted him and announced, "And we have staying with us for Christmas our nephew, William Heron. Pray come forward, Billy, and be introduced to Mrs Brandling whom you have not met before, though Mr Brandling is gracious enough to remember your visit to his printing works as a young boy."

Billy held out his hand to a large lady towering over the little printer, who was rounder and smaller than he remembered. She grasped his hand and boomed, "Your mother is Dione Sharon, the writer. You must be so proud of her."

Billy, who had ignored this side of his home life for years, could think of nothing to say in reply. He had resolved to be neither uncouth nor tongue-tied but seemed likely to be both. He mumbled something and the little printer shook hands with him too. From his right side Jenny Batey was pressing forward to embrace him fondly and from the left her husband Tom was reaching to pat him on the back with a "Good to meet you, lad. Heard from Francis about your prowess at the coalface. Well done."

Aunt Sarah visibly trembled with horror at this and hustled them all into the dining-room, saying, "We must sit down for everything is ready to serve."

Uncle Joe directed Billy to the side, away from the fire between Ally and her mother. He sat at once, wanting to obliterate himself from view, and then remembered he had to wait for all the ladies to be seated. Hot-faced, he stood up again as Mrs Brandling edged round to the fireside. There were four chairs his side and only three chairs opposite but she spread some way over hers and Tom, who was quite broad, was beside her. But who was going to the other? He had the little printer on his side beyond Ally. And his uncle and aunt were to be at the head and foot of the table.

Then from behind Uncle Joe emerged a figure he had not yet noticed, slight in a pale-green dress with a moss-green wrap round her shoulders so that she merged into the plants behind her. Billy stared in wonder. She was perfection.

Uncle Joe was patting the remaining chair. "Now, Miss Lily, you sit here next to me." No one seemed to be aware that she had not been brought forward to greet Billy. But Billy was very aware and knew at once that she was too. She gave him a shy smile across the table and mouthed, "Billy."

He smiled back, unable to frame any words with his lips. She had been nine years old when he had played with her on Tynemouth beach. Absorbed in competition with Ally he had hardly noticed her. She was only a little thing with fair curls, a nondescript copy of Ally. Now Ally's hair was a coarser yellow like her mother's, while Lily's had softened to a pale honey. Her face was smaller too and her eyes a gentler blue, but it was the neat symmetry of her features that amazed him – the smooth rounds of her cheeks, the curve of her chin, the precision of her nose and the way three curls dangled over her forehead, the middle one precisely in the centre.

Occasionally by the river at home he would pick a flower, seeking perfection, the petals absolutely equal, not a blemish anywhere. Then he would sit and enjoy it till his restlessness got the better of him. He had never seen it in a human being.

The arrival of the soup forced him to lower his eyes so that he didn't make a mess round his plate by sloppily drinking. At home soup or broth was in a bowl you could pick up. Using a spoon was tedious especially when he only wanted to watch Lily having hers. Each mouthful was popped centrally between those lips. No drop fell from the spoon. How did she do it?

Ally was speaking. "My ambition is to get you and Francis together. He says you have nothing in common so you don't talk much. Not like Lily and me."

Jenny laughed. "And Lily seldom gets a word in the rate you go at it."

Billy didn't think Lily had spoken a word at the table since they sat down. Uncle Joe had made a few remarks and she had smiled up at him and nodded. Her father was the other side of her and was in conversation with Mrs Brandling about customers wanting credit. It was a topic common to pie shops and printing works and produced a flow of anecdotes. Aunt Sarah joined in to entertain Septimus Brandling with tales of tenants' excuses for not paying their rent on time.

Uncle Joe poured the wine and Jenny and Ally partook freely, but when Tom refused Billy did too. Wine was not a man's drink. Uncle Joe fetched stout and Tom had a swig at that but Billy asked for water from the jug. He was thrilled then to see that Lily nodded at him with her little smile and asked for water too.

The two maids came and went with the different courses and Aunt Sarah was not required to leave the table herself, though there were many hissed instructions in their ears. At any other time Billy's concentration would have been entirely on the food, which was good, but he could not keep his eyes from Lily. When she poured cream on the apple pie, which concluded the meal, the flow was into the centre of her bowl and she managed the jug so that nothing trickled onto its saucer when she finished. He had run his finger round and licked it because it was good cream and Ally had nudged his arm and grinned. He scowled back at her. Ally was nothing. If Francis fancied her he was welcome to her. Lily was all neatness and precision.

He was determined to get into conversation with Lily in the parlour where Aunt Sarah had said they would all drink tea after their meal, but instead, Tom announced that they must be back by three at the inn where he had left their horse and cart so they must leave at once.

Jenny said, "Ma and the young ones can manage just so long but it gets busy later with folks wanting pies for their suppers."

Aunt Sarah didn't attempt to stop them but begged the Brandlings to stay for a leisurely afternoon.

Billy managed to take hold of Lily's hand as goodbyes were said.

"Will I see you again this visit?"

"I doubt it. I'm sorry." She was looking up into his face with what he knew was admiration. From her he would have respect, from Ally only teasing. He held her hand longer than necessary, his own engulfing hers completely, and squeezed it meaningfully before they were parted. She gave him another quick glance, her perfect arcs of pale eyebrows raised, and smiled – such a sweet smile.

"Bye, Billy." The three syllables conveyed wonder, delight and regret.

They were gone and he sat a painful hour more with the Brandlings while his whole being was engrossed with Lily Batey. The rest of the visit crept by with his mind half-engaged. A Christmas Day service was stretched out with a long sermon which even Aunt Sarah agreed was "Trying in those hard pews." Christmas dinner was hardly festive as Aunt Sarah warmed up the leftovers and he had to wash the dishes, all the maids having been given the day off to spend with their families.

Next day he was to go home and the thought came to him that he should rise very early and walk to North Shields and see Lily before he left. He had no doubt of the meaning of her smile. It was her reply to his squeezing of her hand. She was smitten with him, as he was with her. He lay awake thinking of it and was only held back by the fear that everyone, particularly Uncle Joe, would be convinced that he was as wild and impulsive as he had always been.

At least he had a great secret in his life of which he would say not a word to anyone. Lily Batey was to be his and no one and nothing would stand in his way.

Chapter 17

January–May 1821

Francis

Francis woke early on a bitter January Saturday. He could hear Billy at his grandmother's next door filling her bucket from the coal box outside. He rose and dressed in the dark and crept past his parents' bed. He hoped the shock of icy air when he opened the door would not wake them. He slipped out quickly, gasping at the cold, and bumped into Billy as he was lifting the bucket to take it inside.

Billy swore. "What? Oh, it's you! What's up?"

"Nothing. But you always avoid me and I have to tell you something."

"Not out here. Come inside and be sharp about it. I go to the pit, remember?"

Inside, there was one candle lit and the fire was beginning to burn up. Grandmother was so swathed in blankets she was invisible.

"Well, what is it?" Billy took the tongs and put more coal on the fire and set the bucket down by the hearth.

Francis, feeling the incongruity of the moment, gave his message in a hissed whisper. "Aunt Sarah says I must tell you Ally Batey is engaged to her fish man."

Billy gave him a glare that was plain even in the dim light. "That's not news."

"She didn't want you to be hurt. Gertie told her you and Ally were flirting in the kitchen before the meal on Christmas Eve. She said Ally's a tease."

"Me, hurt! Nothing touches me. What an oaf you are to get up and tell me this! Can't you see Sarah is a meddling old crow?"

"I thought it was kindly meant."

Billy straightened his back and glowered down at him. "You see people through a rosy mist. Well, you need not see *me* like that. It would mean nothing to me to kill you if it suited me. Go back to bed."

Francis crept out, quivering with shock, and heard Billy go off a few minutes later as the mine bell sounded. Safe in the warmth of his bed, sleep was impossible. His thoughts flew back over life with Billy. When they were young he had felt him leave the bed in the mornings, but mostly he was the dark being that erupted from the bowels of the earth to mar family evenings. Sundays, there was a wariness in the air. How would it be with Billy at home? When Billy moved in with Grandmother the relief was so great he could still enjoy it. Billy's disdain for him had always been obvious, but hatred to the point of killing! It happened in the Bible with Cain and Abel. Jealousy? he wondered. Billy's too proud and confident ever to be jealous of *me*.

After his father had gone to the farm and he and his mother were working at the table, he blurted out, "Billy would like to kill me."

She was writing below a drawing of an elephant and he could see by the smile on her lips that a clever idea had just occurred to her. All the same he repeated it.

She looked up, still smiling from her flash of inspiration, and her eyes were laughing. "Eh, my pet, that's nonsense. Billy hacks coal not people."

"He could kill me in my sleep."

"But *why*?"

"He hates me. And didn't he knock you over and kill my baby sister?"

"But he didn't *mean* to kill anyone."

"So why is he always in a rage?"

She drew a long sigh and her eyes lost their sparkle. Then she shook her head several times and applied herself to her writing. "I have a good thought for the plot of this elephant story. Let me get back to it. Have you no lessons to do?"

"Oh, yes." Hurt not to be taken seriously, he tried to settle to a mathematical problem but the shock of Billy's words would not go away.

When he went back to Newcastle on Sunday night he told his aunt that Billy's response was only, "That's not news," to which she replied with a snort of a laugh, "He *would* say that to hide his disappointment." Then she took his arm and murmured, "If he comes again to see Ally I shall tell your uncle he's only welcome if he spends the time with *us* as a family member should, and helps about the place as you do. Otherwise there are going to be *changes*." To her penetrating look she added a wink and a squeeze of his arm which made him very uncomfortable. If she boasted to Billy that she could make Uncle Joe change his will Billy would have good reason to murder him. And Billy planned to visit Newcastle again at Easter when he, Francis, would have a week's holiday at home. When he returned he could have devised some way to make it look like an accident.

On the morning Billy was setting off Francis shrank onto the window seat when Billy walked in to borrow his father's coat brush for his Sunday suit. He had scrubbed his nails and dampened and combed his unruly dark hair. He drew himself up to his full height and gazed at his image in the mirror over the fireplace. There was an air of tense excitement about him but he showed no hostility to any of them.

His mother looked at him for a moment with new eyes, in which – was it possible? – there was a hint of pride. The look gave Francis strange and unsettling sensations in his stomach.

After the peaceful two nights of his absence, Billy returned and resumed his work clothes, saying nothing to anyone but taking up again the duties he performed for his grandmother, who had said constantly, "Where's my William?" to each of them in turn while he was away.

Francis found it impossible to guess what he was feeling – frustration, anger, or perhaps elation? There was something certainly but it was battened down inside him. At least it did not seem directed at him as he had feared, but he must be wary.

Two days later, a letter arrived inscribed to Mistress Dee Heron. Francis recognised Uncle Joe's handwriting as his mother broke the seal. Father was at work on the farm so, as his mother's confidant, he expected her to share the contents.

She glanced down the page and quickly folded it, popping it into a book on the bookshelf. Then she got up briskly and rubbed her hands together.

"I shall clean Mother Jane's pantry shelves today. It's not a task Billy would think of and she always kept them spic and span. When I have her settled in her chair I'll call you and you can come and lend me a hand to do the top shelf I can't reach."

The moment she'd gone he picked out the book, for it was not fully pushed back into place. Am I doing wrong? he asked himself. She didn't tell me not to look.

He had the letter unfolded as he convinced himself and, kneeling on the window seat for the best light on this showery April morning, he devoured it rapidly.

My dear Dee,

I regret having to write this but trust you will have had some suspicions of what was in my mind. Billy has made it impossible for me to continue my special favour towards him and I have reluctantly instructed my lawyer to make out a new will in which Francis will be my heir.

Francis put his hand over his mouth and dropped the letter on the table.

Oh God! Billy must never see this! And I should not be reading it. But he snatched it up and read on, guilt and dread growing inside him like twin cancers.

Billy's visit at Easter was to his aunt and myself but he had barely greeted us before he declared that he was walking to North Shields to visit the Batey family. He knew we had given all the maids but Gertie time off for Easter so Sarah was sure he was trying to supplant the fish vendor in Ally Batey's affections.

I protested to Billy that it would be too late for visiting as the walk would consume so much of the evening and I had laid out the stock market reports for him to study after an early supper, which was actually on the table. He simply turned round and walked out and did not return till after midnight in a sullen mood. We were kept from our beds as I had to lock up safely and Sarah would not retire until he returned. He must have been told that his attentions were not wanted, but he said nothing of his reception, indeed nothing at all but perfunctory thanks for the meal kept for him. He went to bed and did not rise till noon when it was too late to join us at the Easter service. I advised Sarah not to question him for I quite feared an outburst of temper.
I assure you, my dear Dee, that I could forgive much to a young man

disappointed in love but his behaviour was so discourteous to his aunt from the moment of his arrival that I fear I have no alternative.

Francis thought, I wager she stood over him and dictated the letter.
He was too engrossed now not to finish the last paragraph.

I would beg you to say nothing to Billy at present as I hope he may be in the grip of a passing infatuation. If he is left in ignorance he will still have an incentive to learn how to conduct himself in a more seemly manner in society. I do not know if he will still cling to hewing coal when my dear mother departs this life, but I trust he finds opportunities to put to good use the talents God has undoubtedly given him.

Francis ran a quivering finger down the letter, then inserted it into the book and replaced it on the shelf. He was thinking, Thank God Billy is not to know. But I? Will Uncle tell me? If he does I'll admit to Mother that I read the letter.

He heard her open the door and call him. As he went out he looked back at the bookshelf, feeling a bomb lurked there.

When he went back to school his uncle said nothing of his intentions, only Aunt Sarah had a special smile for him which made his secret knowledge lie on his conscience like an undigested crust on his stomach, and he lived in dread that next time she saw Billy she would crow about his fall from favour. Then surely – he gulped as he thought of it – my life will be in danger.

Billy

Billy gave not a second's thought to the words he had said to Francis back in January. In fact, after his Easter visit he hoped to use Francis to further his plans to see Lily. To his fury, she had not been at home when he went and the day after his return, as he hacked at the coal seam in a confined space, it was Jenny Batey's laughter that rang in his brain, mocking him, and he hacked harder to drive it away.

The family had greeted him pleasantly enough despite the unusual hour of his calling but he could see at once that Lily was missing. Tom poured him a mug of ale and before he had taken a drink Jenny burst out, "Eh, Billy man, it ain't a bit of good you coming after our Ally for she's bespoke already."

Ally just looked up and grinned at him.

He set down the mug with a shaking hand and managed to gulp out, faking a chuckle, "Oh, well, where's Lily then?"

They all laughed but when it subsided Jenny said, still chortling, "Nay, ye cannot run through my girls like that. You'll be looking at Susie next. They've all to earn their bread before they starts wedding and bedding and child-bearing."

More laughter made his insides squirm with shame and fury.

Tom said, "Ay, Lily's got a good post in a titled lady's house. They asked for a quiet neat girl and Lily was just what they were looking for."

Billy had the question, "Where is the house?" hovering on his lips but just managed not to say it.

No one must know that Lily was secretly his now but when she was older he would make it happen in the sight of them all. Lily knew it herself and would be ready when the time was right, but he must not raise suspicions now.

What rankled with him as he hacked at the coal was being made to feel a fool. His journey had been fruitless and he had lost the goodwill of his uncle and aunt. He clenched his teeth. He would not be mocked by anyone. He would win again the best miner's bonus and Uncle Joe would hear of it and forgive him.

Meanwhile he must find out where Lily was and get there somehow to satisfy his urge to look upon that perfection again and show her his heart was unchanged.

But for this he needed Francis's help. Could he question his brother next time he was home about Lily's whereabouts? Impossible. But Francis would know the answer. Ally would be sure to tell him all about her sister's new position.

He hacked harder, longing for the power to hack the information out of Francis without him suspecting anything. No, somehow the subject must come up in family conversation over Sunday dinner and he would assume his usual air of not listening. He rarely sat long at Sunday dinners, which were held in his parents' room to give Grandmother Jane a change of scene. If she grew sleepy afterwards he always helped her up and said, "You like your rocking chair, don't you?" and then he could escape too. And Father, Mother and Francis would sit longer, chatting in his absence.

He must not appear to act out of character and he must let a little time pass so that whatever they had heard about his visit to North Shields would seem unconnected to any new gossip about the Batey family that Francis might bring home.

Some weeks passed and the tangles of bushes on the banks of the river became a vibrant green, daisies speckled the field beyond the stream and Dee received a letter in Jenny Batey's childlike writing. She shared it with Grandmother at Sunday dinner and so, inadvertently, with Billy.

She did glance up at him, he noticed, before she turned to her mother-in-law.

"Mother Jane, you remember Jenny Coxon who used to be next door?"

"Ay, she had a great mat o' yellow hair, like straw it was."

"Well her eldest, Alice – Ally as they call her – is to be wed next week. She'd like to ask us all and have a wedding feast on the beach at Tynemouth but times are not so good and the pie shop is not bringing in a fortune – these are her words – so she's just letting us know as old friends and neighbours."

"Hoping for a present," Grandmother said with a hint of her old sharpness.

"Maybe. The young couple are to live at Cullercoats where his folks have a coble."

Billy was scrabbling in his mind for how to bring Lily into the conversation without saying a word himself when his Grandmother said, "You telt me they've a string o' girls. Don't you be starting with presents."

His mother laughed. "They are still young. No, Lily must be about seventeen. There was not so much between her and Ally though they have different fathers. Jenny lost no time in marrying Tom Batey."

Billy prayed that the flush of heat that rose in him at the mention of her name would go unnoticed, but he felt Francis observing him. Let him think it was for Ally, but now they must go on speaking of Lily. He willed his mother to do it.

She was looking down at the letter. "Jenny says Lily is doing well, caring for a sick old titled lady who might leave her a fortune."

"Are there folks in North Shields with titles?" his father asked. "I thought they were in grand houses in the country, like what you came from, my lovely."

"We were not titled, though my father would have liked to be."

"Nay, we mustn't mention that sad time. Forgive me, Dee."

She reached across the table and squeezed his hand. "Long past."

Billy clenched his teeth. The talk was slipping away, then Francis said, "I don't think Lily is in North Shields. The house is in the country somewhere but I don't know where."

Billy wanted to scream, "Find out, you dolt," but he sat rigid on his stool till he could bear it no longer and jumped up. "Ready for your sleep, Grandmamma?"

"Nay, I'm not so dozy today."

"Well, I'm off for a walk. I get enough of being confined inside, this fine weather." He strode to the door.

He had barely got himself outside when he heard Francis hiss, "Aunt was right. He *was* sweet on Ally."

He plunged away down to the river and stood staring at the endless flowing of the water to the sea. He remembered the day he had walked out into it. Time never flowed like this. It went in cruel jerks and long periods of stagnation. But Lily was still his. No talk of a lover. She would be bridesmaid to Ally and he could go to the wedding and see her. But he could not. He would not get leave and in any case Jenny's mirth would choke him. When he saw Lily he must be alone with her. It would happen because he would make it happen.

The sun came from behind a cloud and its late May heat fell about him. For a moment he thought of casting off his clothes and plunging in for a swim. But if they came looking for him they would think he had planned to drown himself for sorrow. No such thought must ever enter their heads. The only thought anyone but Lily should have of him was fearful admiration, never pity.

He climbed the bank and began to stride along it, keeping pace with a small branch drifting down the river. It was the only thing on the surface and looked very alone, like himself. One tiny wish tapped at his brain that sometime they *might* come looking for him, and then round the bend came a family of ducks, two parents and a happy flotilla of young. He walked on, faster.

Chapter 18

October 1821

Billy

The news of an explosion in Wallsend pit flew to the other pits in the area as fast as a man could ride. Certainly it reached Wylam the same day that it happened and was the talk of the levels just as Billy's shift finished.

"Over fifty dead."

"Crushed?"

"Nay, suffocated some say."

"That's worse. Kill me quick, say I."

"It blew a corf up the shaft."

"Shook the earth for miles."

Billy, with his grandfather's face in his mind's eye, burst into anger. "Some idiot with an open flame!"

"Nay, we don't know that."

Billy rounded on the speaker. "It doesn't happen if care is taken. Nothing need ever go wrong if every man does his duty. Some little thing, a door left ajar, a man quitting his post for a few seconds. It has to be something." He railed all the way up in the cage and was heard by the Viewer still raging about it as he crossed the yard.

"Come here, Heron," Mr Burns called. "So you think there's no such thing as an accident? An act of God?"

"No sir. A mine is as safe a place as any on earth if no one makes a mistake."

"You think you need to defend the Almighty?"

"No sir. He leaves us free to be wise or foolish. And fifty men are dead because someone was foolish."

"Well, I'm minded to go myself to Wallsend to find out what happened and see if we can learn from it. I'll take you with me. You write a fair hand and I know you have studied the science of mining. We'll give them two days to make their own inquiries and go on Friday. Be ready at my office at eight."

Billy went home with his mind in confusion. His initial clean anger at the waste of life was now fuzzed by excitement and anxiety at a new role thrust upon him. This could lead to a promotion. But he needed the physical action of hacking at a coalface to work out his bitterness and longing and be left with nothing but eating, sleeping and caring for his grandmother.

At one time he would have told her that the Viewer wanted him for a special task. He might even have told his mother and father but since his secret yearning for Lily he was more closed up than ever.

On Friday morning, his grandmother sat up in bed and exclaimed, "Is it Sunday?"

He shook his head.

"Why are you in your church coat then?"

"Getting my reward for best hewer."

On many mornings she wouldn't lift her head from the pillow till she saw a mug of tea by the bed and the fire lit. Why today was she curious? But she only said, "Ah, ye're a good 'un, William," and lay down again. Would she tell his mother when she brought her porridge in? He hated to feel his movements known and commented on. It was already the talk of the pit that he had been singled out, but that was his world and he held his peculiar place there as one you approached with caution.

He was a little anxious that he might be expected to ride to Wallsend and display his lack of horsemanship. Uncle Joseph had given Francis a horse for his birthday and he was now a competent rider. Mr Hammond had offered stabling, so Billy had to add riding to the accomplishments to be scorned and derided. He was relieved then to see a small carriage drawn up ready at the pit gates.

How he was to make conversation with Mr Burns over a journey of fifteen miles, for Wallsend was further east than Newcastle, he could not imagine, but it turned out to be simple enough. Mr Burns took the opportunity to question him on the latest developments of deep mines and the problems already encountered. When he had given satisfactory answers, Mr Burns looked at him with his sharp eyes, a luminous grey Billy saw now he was close to him, and said, "What improvements would *you* make in mine construction, Heron?"

"No pit should ever be sunk with one shaft only, sir."

"However limited the workings are going to be?"

"That is not usually known. Good seams are found and the mine extends and soon there are fifty or a hundred men at work and no second escape route has been provided. There must be an extra source of ventilation, sir, and everyone below ground should be provided with a safety lamp, even the trapper boys."

Jacob Burns smiled. "Your pit would be costly, Heron."

"And I would employ no boy younger than twelve."

"Twelve! You were not yet seven."

Billy thought, He has looked up my records. "I know, sir, but I was ready for hard work. Some of them fall asleep."

"But the families are thankful for their pennies."

"And lives are put at risk. If the owners make so much profit that they can ride in carriages the men should be paid more and the children need not work so young."

"You sound like a revolutionary. The owners make money to make more pits because the country needs more coal and that means more work for more people. If coal owners had to walk everywhere they would not have time to plan for all that."

Billy was growing hotter but the Viewer suddenly laughed. "Nay, Heron, I am leading you on. I grant there is much wrong. I see it and endeavour within my own powers to run a safe pit. That is why I wish to find out the cause of this tragedy at Wallsend. But just remember from your own mother's experience that businessmen with money work hard to create new businesses, bringing employment and prosperity to a region, but if they also make mistakes they can bring disaster on themselves as well as on others. The higher you are the harder you fall."

Billy sat up. "My mother's experience?"

"Surely you know what happened? I enquired about her because she is so obviously an educated lady. If she has not told you her story, did you never wonder why she speaks differently from the other miner's wives and has given you and your brother a grounding of education?"

Billy had heard Francis as a young boy ask about their 'other grandparents' and their father told him it was all very sad and not to bother their mother about it, but Francis would certainly have found out her story by now. It angered Billy to find that the Viewer knew more about his ancestry than he did himself.

"I heard talk," he mumbled.

In his early days in the pit boys would say, "Your ma thinks she's a fine lady but she's no better than my ma." If he could have loved her he would have been proud of her, but what business had she to be different from the rest? Sometimes he admired her capability, her quickness of mind – such a contrast to his father – and sometimes, grudgingly, her face and figure, especially the smiles she would give his father, but so rarely himself.

"It was her father who lost the business her grandfather had built," the Viewer went on, "and she lost her titled betrothed who had believed her to be an heiress. So, brave woman, she married your father and with every skill she had she augmented his income and raised you two lads."

"She was *betrothed* to someone?"

"Justice Hammond told me it was arranged by the family against her wishes. I should not be telling you this if she has never spoken of it."

Billy held back the words that rose to his lips: 'she never talks to me'. Mr Burns should confine himself to mining matters. He was invading his home life and Billy decided he would have none of it.

He looked at the window and, seeing a vast rolling field with cows grazing, he asked, "Are we not in Newcastle yet?"

"That is the Town Moor. We are passing to the south of it and will see more terraced streets presently."

They went through a small place called Heaton which Billy remembered from his walk to North Shields. The bitterness he had felt at Lily's absence from home flooded back at him.

He said nothing more and after a while Mr Burns remarked, "I have made you thoughtful, Heron, which I regret for your mind must be on our purpose today. We are approaching Wallsend Colliery. There are the gates standing open, but much bustle is going on so we will alight here."

Billy straightened his back and looked him in the eye. "I am ready, sir."

But he was *not* ready, for the first creature he saw as he jumped down from the carriage was Lily Batey.

He scarcely believed his eyes; he knew that slight figure emerging from a door marked 'Mine Office', stepping swiftly across towards him. Her bonnet was awry, her shawl slipping from one shoulder, and she was crying.

Oblivious of everything else, he planted himself in her way and uttered her name. "Lily!"

She started violently and looked up, bewildered, before recognition came into her eyes. "Billy Heron!"

But this was not his Lily. She was not perfection; she was not symmetry. He reached his hands to her bonnet and put it straight. He drew the shawl neatly across her shoulders so that the two points met evenly. Touching her between her small breasts roused him alarmingly.

"You mustn't cry," he said, but there was one teardrop in the centre of each cheek so he let them be. "Why are you crying?"

"Oh Billy," she said, "they were so burnt. It was horrible. Pray, give up mining." She seemed to take in his smart clothes. "Have you given it up? Oh! You are wanted. I must go."

Mr Burns was calling sharply, "Heron!"

Billy could see only Lily before him.

"Why are you here? Where are you going now? I will come with you."

She was nodding her head in the direction of Mr Burns. "See, the gentleman calls you. You can't come with me. I am going back to my lady."

"Where? Where is she? Why did you come here?"

"Our gardener. His two sons. We heard the explosion on Tuesday. She sent me to find out and they were bringing men up. Oh, the faces, scorched and twisted! But not his boys. So she sent me again today and they've reached them but of course they are dead. Now let me go."

He was gripping her arm. "Tell me where."

"Heron! Come here."

She shook her head. Then looked up into his face. "Oh Billy, don't go down a mine again. They are evil places." She pulled away and ran from him.

Mr Burns had stepped up and grabbed his other arm or he would have followed her.

"What are you doing, lad? If you see an acquaintance you raise your hat, say you are engaged in business and continue with your duties."

"I must find out where she lives." He was still looking after her but she was lost among crowds outside. He could catch her up. His feet itched to run.

"You must *not* find out where she lives. If the young woman does not wish to tell you, you must not pester her. Come to business. They await us in the office."

He sounded severe but there was a twinkle in his eye. In the midst of his disappointment Billy was aware of it.

"Perhaps more than an acquaintance, eh Heron?"

Billy began to take in the mine buildings and winding gear. He couldn't believe Lily had been standing here a moment ago and was now gone. He tried to gather his wits and find something to say. "She knew two of the dead miners, sir."

"And did not wish you in the same state. I trust you will not heed her words. This" – he waved his hand at the men scrubbing stains from the paved yard – "was, thankfully, a rare occurrence."

They walked into the mine office and the Viewer there introduced himself to Mr Burns as John Buddle. Billy took his notebook and stub of pencil from his pocket but he was recalling the pleading look on Lily's face. She had indeed said that – "Billy, don't go down a mine again." She cared with passion. Of course she would. She had understood the squeezing of her hand at their last meeting. Their lives were to be one and he was not to endanger his. His heart lifted. He found himself smiling round at the bare walls and the few tattered notices. Over the Viewer's desk a new one hung with a list of names. He composed his face. It was still maddening that he had not learnt where she lived but it could not be so far away. He would find out.

Mr Burns said, "Have you noted that, Heron? The pit had only been reopened eight weeks."

He jumped to attention and wrote the words down and then ventured to comment.

"More likelihood of gas, sir."

Mr Buddle bristled.

Mr Burns said, "We are assembling facts. You are not asked for your conclusions, Heron."

"Sir." But he would make them to himself all the same. He was jolted into the matter now and, with an effort, slid Lily into his inner mind to bring out later with secret delight that he had seen her and she was still his.

They were not allowed down into the pit and had to return to Wylam with little accomplished. All they could learn with any certainty was that the most senior Overman in the whole colliery had been in charge, with two younger Overmen. Had the older man been too sure of himself and failed to order the extinguishing of lights in time when gas was detected? No one could tell because all three had perished.

"I say there was an error," Billy pronounced. "If all had been done by the book, what could have gone wrong?"

"That may be" – Mr Burns studied his face – "but are we to see our best hewer quit his post or not?"

"No sir." He could not yield to Lily's pleading and she would on reflection exult in his courage.

Mr Burns surprised him with his next question. "When will you be twenty-one, Heron?"

"March the thirty-first, 1824, sir."

"Two and a half years. I will see that you have some experience of other work by then, such as helping the furnace-man and banksman, and I will expect to make you an Overman after that."

"Thank you, sir."

"But you must rein in your sometimes wayward and impulsive behaviour." The sharp grey eyes were probing his.

"Never in the mine, sir."

"Except as a boy you leapt into the cage when you had been forbidden and attacked the lad who let the corf slip. I know all about you, though I was not Viewer then."

"I was a child, desperate. My grandfather had been crushed."

"But only a few days ago you were raging at the loss of life we have just been investigating. Emotions are dangerous. There is no place for them in a mine."

Billy nodded. It was true. Emotions could distract from extreme carefulness. He must remember that, but only in the pit. There would be a time for passion when he could approach Lily to make her his own. It would be hard if years had to pass first but they were young yet. He must await promotion. He must have money. It would behove him to be on good terms with his uncle which was a nuisance. Relationships were troublesome, apart from himself and Lily. That was the sure thing. Fixed.

He peered from the carriage window and saw the buildings of Wylam

Colliery ahead. He would change into his work clothes and go back to the thing he loved and hated, that demanded care, experience and physical effort. There was relief in that.

Chapter 19

November 1821–Summer 1822

Dee

Dee abstracted from the plump packet which the post boy had brought a first copy of *Edwin the Elephant*, several welcome bank notes and a letter from Joseph.

My dear Dee, she read, taking it under the window for the little light there was on this November morning, *I wonder if you know that Billy has written me a letter asking to come and pay his respects to his aunt and myself at Christmas to make reparation for his discourteous conduct at his last visit at Easter by helping us with any tasks about our various properties.*

No, she thought, I didn't know. He tells me nothing. I learn from others that he is 'Mr Burns's favourite' and has 'prospects'. She sighed and read on.

I regret that I have had to write and tell him that we plan to spend Christmas quietly at home but I hope to see him myself soon. My physician has advised me to take outdoor exercise and the dealer from whom I purchased the mount for Francis has a quiet mare which I propose to buy for myself. As soon as I am comfortable with her I will pay you a visit and spend more time with my mother whom I fear pressure of business has caused me to neglect of late. I will then also renew my acquaintance with my godson and trust to find further evidence of a new spirit at work in him.

I know of no new spirit, Dee thought, frowning at the window as the steam engine clattered by, a prolonged noise since it drew ten coal wagons. To her it was a troublesome intrusion since Jack no longer led Sandy and gave her his joyful wave. When silence fell again she could think. Perhaps, she mused, Billy has a more quiet spirit, a little flame of self-congratulation, but it is inward, held back from all of us.

It still troubles me, Joseph's letter rambled on, *that I altered my will hastily after his last visit. He is not aware of this and in my uncertainty I will say nothing to either boy for Billy may yet prove a fine man. You have told me he is highly thought of by the authorities at Wylam Colliery which pleases me. I trust Sarah to be equally discreet.*

"I don't trust her an inch," Dee said aloud, "but *I* will not tell them. There is enough bad blood there, certainly on Billy's side, without adding further cause."

There was not much more in Joseph's letter. He said they enjoyed Francis's company during the week. Ally Batey, now Ally Ward, was expecting a child so they must appoint a new maid. Sarah, as energetic as ever, sent her loving greetings.

Dee put down the letter and examined *Edwin the Elephant* to see there were no printing errors. There was still pleasure in looking at her work but it was muted, like so much else in her life. Even the stab of pain she once felt if Joe referred to Billy as his elder godson was a faint qualm, no longer impinging on her consciousness.

Day followed day. She was stirred into active pleasure only by Jack's hug at seeing her still there, the pivot of his life, on his daily return from work. But being held close was enough. The doctor had told her to expect no more children after her miscarriage. With Francis away during the week and Billy sleeping at Mother Jane's, they had privacy, but Jack had learnt no subtlety in his love-making. He approached her with his habitual respect and she was content to restrict him to once or twice a week for which he invariably expressed his loving thanks in the most tender words.

Perhaps, she thought, Joseph coming more often will break into the pattern of our lives. But what can he do? Neither Mother Jane nor Jack wish for change, Francis already has his horizons widened by his studies and for him home is just home, there when required. As for Billy, God only knows what *he* wants.

She rose, shivering from sitting too long, and put more coal on the fire.

Her eyes turned instinctively to the clock on the mantelshelf. In the larder was a leg of mutton Mrs Hammond had sent the day before in payment for some lace she had mended for her. Boiled slowly, it would be ready when Jack came in. There would be plenty for Billy and Mother Jane and it might even stretch to two days for them all with vegetables from their own plot, stored on the larder shelf. We eat well, she thought. Why can I not be content? She sighed and began to peel some onions.

Joseph rode over in March as the days lengthened. Billy had remarked several times during the winter, "Uncle said he would visit. Why has he not done so?"

"He'll come for your birthday, maybe," Dee replied blandly and she was right.

He came on the quiet mare with two saddle bags and a long bundle tied to one of them. After greeting his mother, he turned to Billy.

"Nineteen!" He rubbed his hands. "You're a man, William Heron."

"Ay, and I've been doing a man's work for years."

Oh Billy, Dee thought. Show humility. But Joe was in a genial mood.

"I've brought my own fishing tackle and a fine rod for you. As it's mild for the time of year I thought we'd take a walk along the riverbank and maybe bring your mother something for supper. I'll sleep at the inn in the village. Shall we go, lad?"

Dee watched them cross the waggonway and head east along the riverbank. Billy was hung about with much of Joseph's paraphernalia including a folding wooden stool. He did not look pleased. Fishing would be too tame for a hewer of coal. But their absence allowed her time to prepare a suet pudding for later.

It was not part of her plan for Mother Jane to come in and watch her but she was far too excited at Joseph's coming to stay in her own home.

"Will that basin be big enough, Dee?" "How long have you had them apples stored?" "What's that you're adding now?"

Dee's patience was now habitual. To Jane's bursts of liveliness she replied in her usual level voice. Once, in front of Jack, she had snapped at his mother and his face had shown such shock and hurt that she had never done it again. He had said later, holding her close, "That was not my angel speaking. I must make sure she is not wearied to death. I must do more to help. It is all my fault."

Her mind, though, was not on Jane now but on Billy and Joseph by the river and on Francis and Sarah back in Newcastle. Francis had told her on his last return home, "If Uncle is out, she uses me like a hired man." It was the first signs of rebellion Dee had ever seen in her younger son. He was becoming his own person now that he saw less of Billy but when they were in the same room, he was still wary of him. On his own he read and made voluminous notes. He was studying steam traction and planned to write a paper on the feasibility of rail travel for human passengers. Billy would have been scornful of his work so he kept it hidden from him.

When Joseph and Billy returned two hours later they had nothing to show her.

"Well, we had good conversation and fishes prefer silence," Joseph said.

"I must change my clothes," Billy said, "for the late shift. I thank you, Uncle, for the lesson in casting a line." He gobbled his dinner and disappeared next door.

"You had conversation – with *Billy*?" Dee asked.

Joseph smiled. "I asked him about his hopes for the future and he gave brief, contradictory answers. He hews coal, but reckons he will be an Overman at twenty-one and in charge of a whole level. He will be obeyed, he says. He also wants wealth, which is hardly compatible, and imagines himself as owner of a great country estate with a wife and family, but was vehement that he had no lady in mind. Does he court any village girls? I sensed that he was too quick to quash that notion."

"No indeed. In his life he is a puritan of the puritans – as far as I can tell. He is married only to the Tyne, taking long walks by its banks when he is not down the pit."

"And his brother? Are they reconciled at all? I asked him if he and Francis discuss the future of steam traction."

"Ah," Dee said. "Francis was keeping that from him for fear of ridicule."

"Indeed, I thought Billy showed some surprise. Well, Francis may be at fault there. It is a topic that should bring them together."

Dee held back her scepticism. "And tell me, Joe, did he take to fishing?"

"Nay, he wanted only to keep casting his line, but when he had mastered the skill, sitting and watching his bait was not for him. No wonder the fish did not bite. But he is young and vigorous and unaccustomed to stillness. Guided aright, he may yet be a success in life. I am minded to come and fish here often now I have permission from Mr Blackett who owns the rights. Maybe I will not ask Billy to join me again unless of course he is willing. Ah, there is a good smell from that pot."

"And there is a dish of ham and eggs in the larder to eat first. I see Jack coming across the field." She felt warmth flooding through her.

Jack took her in his arms and held her tight before he turned to Joseph, exclaiming, "By, it's right good to see you, Brother."

Tears of bitter regret that her sons would never say such a thing filled her eyes. She hid it by bustling them through to Mother Jane, who held out her arms wide and cried out, "My boys! Eh, what fine men they are. I just want my William here too."

No one was sure if she meant her husband or grandson.

After this visit, Joseph began to come to Wylam every five or six weeks, and twice in the months before Francis's summer holiday Billy consented to go fishing with his uncle but Dee had no doubt it was not for pleasure but to ensure his inheritance. Would Joseph change his will again? She couldn't guess. He kept his counsel but looked well and at ease which she attributed to time away from Sarah.

The day Francis returned home for the summer holiday was so balmy and still that she suggested taking the stotty cakes she had baked for him to the riverbank as soon as Mother Jane was settled for her afternoon nap. As they walked down she asked Francis how his uncle's health seemed to be at home these days.

Francis shook his head, with a rueful chuckle. "He is well enough but I grieve for him. Aunt Sarah rules The Heron Mansions now like a dictator."

"Ah," she said, "as I thought."

The bankside here was a grassy slope among wild flowers. They sat down and gazed at the river beyond a strip of stony shore. The sun was warm on their faces.

Francis took a stotty cake from the basket and talked between mouthfuls.

"Yes, Aunt Sarah frightens the maids, which Uncle finds distressing. The girl she took on when Ally left departed in tears. But Aunt heard that Lily's old lady had died so she has taken her on."

Dee looked up from the grasses she was idly plucking. "I'm surprised Jenny will let her. Ally could laugh about Sarah but Lily is a meek little thing and will be crushed to bits."

"She needs work to keep her mind occupied. She still has nightmares from that Wallsend mine disaster. She told me she was sent to find out if men were still trapped and on her second visit she saw Billy and begged him not to go down a mine again."

"Billy!"

"Yes, he was with an official from Wylam come to investigate."

"Mr Burns, the Viewer, I suppose, whose favourite he is. He never told us of course. How did Lily speak of him? You don't think she is sweet on Billy, do you?"

Francis laughed and shook his head. Then his usually pale cheeks reddened and he lowered his eyes.

"Is it that way?" Dee was laughing too.

"It's both ways, Ma." He looked up, smiling. "She fancies me and that's why she came, so we can see each other often. Oh Ma, she's so pretty and so good."

"Good is more important than pretty, but both are certainly to be welcomed. But you are very young."

He popped in the last bite and lay back, chewing. He seemed happy to confide in her which gave Dee a thrill of joy.

"Does it matter that she is a little older than I? She has just had her eighteenth birthday and I am not seventeen till January. But it's quite proper for us to have an understanding, is it not?"

She patted his knee. How long his legs were now! He would not reach Billy's six-feet height but he would certainly dominate Lily. And he was handsome, with good clean-cut features, a little like his father's but with a firmer jaw, and the fair curls he had inherited he kept tied back in a black ribbon which was quite alluring. Jack's locks she cut herself to keep them tamed, loving him, caressing his head as she did so and evoking a kiss and profuse admiration for her skill.

Francis knew she was studying him and repeated his question.

"Oh yes, yes, have an understanding with Lily," she said, "as long as the years and absences do not change your minds."

He sat up. "But I am not going to be absent. I want to be apprenticed to an engineer and the north-east is where everything is happening."

"But Mr Hurst destined you for the university if you could win a scholarship."

"Ah, but he has looked into the progress of experimental science at Oxford and found that the old stuck-in-the-mud traditionalists will not allocate the space and resources to such studies. He has given me good grounding in physics and chemistry himself and I feel more than ready to leave school."

"What? You are not going back after the holidays? Is this because you are in love and that is not suitable for a schoolboy?"

He flushed again. "I've been wanting to talk with you about it, Ma. It's so lovely here, surrounded by flowers and watching the river drifting by."

"A day for dreams. Talk away, my boy." She lay back with her hands behind her head. This was the fulfilment of all it meant to be a parent. She knew she would remember it if there were darker days to come.

He lay back too, mimicking her pose, and began to speak of his awe at the rate of change in the world. "When you were young you thought a man could never travel faster than a horse. But the steam engine is changing all that and then there are iron and steel. There's no limit to what we can build with them. My generation will see much change but it must all be good. If I ever own a mine or a factory I will make it a happy place. Poor Lily was dreadfully affected by the faces she saw scorched and twisted at Wallsend. I was angry that her old lady sent her there the day it happened but she says the gardener's leg was swollen from an insect bite and he could scarcely walk. Lily darts about like a wee elf. Anyway, the old lady is dead now and that upset Lily because she grew fond of her though she was a bit of a battleaxe. Lily even speaks well of Aunt Sarah. There is no one she doesn't love. That is her nature."

"Like your father," Dee murmured.

Francis turned his head to look at her. "I hadn't thought of that but it's true. He would love even Billy if he could. But I don't want to speak or think of Billy on this blissful day. You've never told him he's no longer Uncle's heir, have you?"

The words were scarcely out of his mouth when he clapped his hand over it and, raising himself on his elbows, looked down at her with eyes of shame. Dee could tell at once that Joe had not revealed it. She had to pretend to be angry. She sat up too and faced him. "You read your uncle's letter?"

"Oh Mother, I shouldn't have but I couldn't help it. I wanted to confess at the time but somehow I didn't. You were cleaning Grandmother's pantry."

"I remember. I never suspect *you* of *any* wrongdoing. But Joe believes neither you nor Billy know and so it must remain. Put it out of your head if you can."

"I'm truly sorry, Mother. I know it was wrong."

She had forgiven him before he said the words. He was so easy to forgive. But she couldn't leave it there. She feared Joe's vacillating ways. "I don't want you or Billy building your lives on the hope of your uncle's wealth."

"He won't put Billy in again, will he? He told me he has taken Billy fishing a few times. I was a little worried to hear that."

"Oh, Francis, that is not worthy of you. Uncle Joe still finds Billy abrupt and difficult, but *you* should be above jealousy for his attention."

He was instantly contrite again. "Yes, of course. I hope Uncle's kindness can make up for Billy missing Grandfather."

She smiled, reassured. "You are right, he misses his grandfather. I want *you* to be good to him too. You once said he wanted to kill you. That was nonsense. But none of us know what lies in wait for us. Your uncle and aunt may live to a ripe old age or lose their money as my parents did. I have told you something of that."

"I know, I know." He nodded and lay back again, closing his eyes as if the warm sun were too much for him. He murmured, "I *would* be good to Billy but he hates me so. I won't think of him today." He opened his eyes. "Ma, I really want to be older but time is so slow. I'd like to know what I'll be doing in two or three years' time. I want to know when I can be married to Lily and where we will live and how many children we will have."

She lay back too, chuckling to cover her sudden fears of the unknown future. Billy was at the centre of it like a lit fuse. She must live this present moment and be thankful for the companionship of one son.

There came a sudden flapping of wings as a heron flew over. They both looked up and watched it as it swooped and settled on the far bank. They exchanged a smile. Silence followed except for the whispering of the water caressing the gravel as it passed. The day resumed its peace.

Chapter 20

January 1824

Dee

"We must let Joseph know," Dee said.

"I'll ride there," Francis croaked and was then taken with a fit of coughing.

"In that state? Never." She looked at Jack, hunched on the window seat, sobbing with his arms about his head. There was no help there.

Billy, freshly scrubbed by Mother Jane in her last act, declared in a voice that brooked no argument, "I am going now. I will be halfway there before a horse could be fetched and saddled."

Dee saw his coat was buttoned, his boots laced up and his hat in his hand. There were no tears in his eyes though it was he who had seen his grandmother, after the exertion of rubbing his back, slump down onto her bed and gasp her life away.

"Very well, Billy. Go. It will be late in the evening when you get there so you must stay the night. But I warrant your uncle will come back with you tomorrow in the pony trap and put up in the village."

"It's not my fault that she died," he said as he turned to the door. "She *would* get up as usual when I came from the pit. I tried to stop her."

"I know that. She could be very obstinate."

Then Billy spoilt it by pointing to Francis. "It was *his* fault for kissing her when he had that cold. Her cough racked her to bits."

Francis, still struggling for breath, looked piteously at Dee. She pushed the mug of water towards him and reached across the table to press his hand. She heard the click of the latch and when she looked round Billy had gone.

She sighed, shaking her head. "No one is to blame. Last winter took its toll on her. Those long months of snow right into spring. I never thought she would see *this* winter through. Her time had come, that's all. She hadn't reached three-score years and ten but she was not far off and that is more than most of the folks round here."

She turned her attention to Jack, putting her arms round his heaving body, and nuzzling the top of his head. His arms flew round her at once.

"I have you," he cried. "Oh, I still have you. But death comes so suddenly. I can't believe she's gone. My mother! I have no parents left."

"You still have me," she echoed.

"Ay, I thank the good Lord, but life is so uncertain. It plods on and then all of a sudden…!" He clung to her as if he could hold her from slipping away too.

He's not built to cope with shocks, she thought. Changes should come upon him gently. I am already seeing consequences. Joe paid his mother's rent. She was the tenant. The colliery still have Billy registered as living with us. In two months he may be an Overman and could afford it himself but the colliery have sunk a new shaft and taken on more men. They may want that place for a family. Dear Lord, Billy mustn't sleep here again. Francis couldn't bear to share his bed with him when he comes home.

The woman who had come to lay out the body tapped at their door and called out, "I am here, Mistress Heron."

Dee went next door with her and saw Billy had covered up his grandmother before coming to tell them in that level voice and with dead eyes what had happened.

"Ay, well, you can leave her to me," the woman said. She looked round the room. "I mind laying out her husband. That would be some years gone."

Dee nodded. "About ten I reckon."

She went back into her own room where Jack had set off Francis's tears.

"How could Billy be so calm?" he asked.

"He can't bear us to know his feelings," she said. "That's all."

Billy

Billy had wiped his face several times as he ran, stopping sometimes to take deep gulps of the evening air to quell the overwhelming sense of desolation that was crushing him. The only two people close to him were gone from his life – Grandfather, whom he had needed as a boy, and Grandmother, who had needed him as a man. He had held her, willing her not to die, demanding of God that she would live. But he had had small hope of that. God, if He was there at all, had assigned him to the devil's kingdom. His grandparents had just managed to keep him from the brink but now!

He stopped still in his tracks. *He had Lily.*

He shouted her name out loud. He was on the moonlit highway and not a soul was within hearing. So he shouted it again and began running. Today, tonight, somehow he would find her, even if he had to brave a visit to her mocking mother.

He had resolved to present himself to her family once he was made Overman. That would be the time for him to declare his love. The previous appalling winter had prevented any visits between Wylam and Newcastle and the following cold summer had deterred his uncle from coming fishing.

But now all had changed. He panted out the words "I must have her," over and over again in time with his pounding feet. It was imperative that he find her quickly even if he had to ask for Aunt Sarah's help. I must carry her off, he told himself, and be married to her so that we can be together for ever. She cannot leave me. She is young and healthy and perfect in beauty. She will never need to weep as she did at the pit gates. She looked up at me, loving me. She pleaded for me to leave mining. I knew in the meeting of our eyes how much she loved me.

The moon went behind a cloud but he could feel the grass verge of the highway crisping with frost beneath his feet and he kept running.

At last he began to see points of light and knew he was approaching the town. His thoughts jerked back to his mission. He must deliver his news to Uncle Joe before he did anything else. Uncle Joe would be grateful for his trouble. Uncle Joe was solid and steady and could be very useful to him now.

As he passed from the suburb, dimly lit with oil lamps, and entered the brighter gas-lit town within the walls, his wild thoughts of Lily slowed with his tired legs. He must curb impulses as Mr Burns had warned him. Uncle Joe would not condone a hasty marriage. Nor did he want his bond with Lily to be bandied about yet in talk among the family. As long as he could find her and meet her eyes again and know that their day would come he could wait. There were matters to be thought on. As an Overman he could support a wife and pay the rent for the one room in Burn Cottage but he could not bear to take Lily there. Once together they must be far from the family. With her he would need no one else, but he could imagine, as he had once told Uncle Joe, a time of prosperity and himself as a comfortable family man. Indeed, when he and Lily were 'one flesh' as the Bible put it, he might be able to look outward to the rest of humankind as other people did. But for marriage he must have money.

Heading towards The Heron Mansions, which marched downhill in a stately terrace, he struggled to think what words to use to convey his message. Would he have to rouse them from sleep as he had madly done once before? There were still people on the streets and he stopped to listen as the clock of Saint Nicholas's Church began to chime. He counted nine solemn clangs, and with relief that it was no later, he hurried forward to Number One just as the door opened and a female figure, muffled in a shawl against the cold, descended the steps onto the pavement.

There was no mistaking that swift precise movement. He gasped with astonishment and a sense at last of a benign fate. Lily!

She was shrinking against the wall to let this tall male figure pass by when he seized her arm, pulling her hand from under her cloak.

She gave a small shriek.

"No, no," he cried. "You know me. It's me, Billy."

The gas lamp was just above them. She looked up, meeting his eye, and he saw that relieved look of recognition and, it must be, delight.

"Oh, Billy, you startled me. Are they expecting you? I must hurry. My father is waiting at the church with his cart."

She was not going to escape this time. He held onto her hand.

"No, they're not expecting me. I have to tell my uncle his mother has died."

"Oh! Oh, I'm so sorry." He saw she was taking in what that meant. Her eyes, brimming with sympathy, still looked into his. She withdrew her other hand from her cloak and pressed both over his and held them there, a precious moment. "That is your grandmother to whom you have been so devoted. Oh, you will feel bereft!"

He nodded, tears welling up. They were so at one with each other that she had used the exact word.

She loosed his hand and, shivering, pulled her cloak round her.

"But I am so sorry, I must go. I am late already and Father will be waiting in the cold. He doesn't come to the door because he can't turn the cart on the hill. She kept me longer than usual."

"Who? What are you doing here?"

"I work here. Didn't you know?"

"I knew your old lady died."

"Yes, and they needed a new maid. Sorry Billy." She tried to edge past him.

"You are always running away. You know we are to be united one day."

It was a statement, not a question.

"United?" Her startled frown gave way to an understanding smile which brightened her whole face. "Oh, I see! Of course. I didn't realise that you knew."

The last word was murmured so low he was not sure he had heard it and then she finally slipped from him with "I must go. I promise I won't always be running away. Sorry, Billy."

He watched her run, so light, so easily, making nothing of the steepness.

What had she meant? "I didn't realise that you knew." Had she doubted him? Doubted his certainty that they were meant to be together? *She* had known it from that first squeeze of his hand but time had passed and she had, perhaps, feared the fickleness of men. Now she did know. It had been put into words and she had promised that the running away would cease.

He drew several breaths of the cold air before bounding up the steps and banging the brass door knocker.

When his uncle, holding a candle, peered out warily he found himself unable to speak. Light-headed with joy, he had to tell this man his mother was dead.

"What? Is that you, Billy? My word, you choose some strange hours to come calling. Your aunt and I were just having a nightcap, this new drink of chocolate, before bed. But come in, come in. I don't let Gertie, the live-in maid, answer the door as late as this."

Billy got himself into the hallway and when he heard his uncle closing and bolting the door behind him he managed to blurt out the words, "Your mother's died."

Uncle Joe pulled him round to face him. "*What* did you say?"

He repeated the words but this time he added, "I'm very sorry."

In the kitchen before Aunt Sarah and a glowing fire and with a glass of chocolate in his hand, he had to endure an interrogation to extract every detail.

"Dee should have told us she was ill," his aunt snapped. "We would have fetched her here where she would be comfortable. What? The doctor only gave her a cordial for her cough!"

Uncle Joe intervened after more of these tart comments. "Sarah, Billy has walked here on a bitter January evening to bring us this news. We are mighty beholden to him and I'd like you to prepare him some supper for, by his own admission, he left before he had had anything."

She got up, muttering that she had sent the girl to bed early out of the kindness of her heart and with Lily rushing off she had made their chocolate with her own hands already. She did, however, spend two minutes placing on the table before Billy a bowl of warm broth from the stew-pot by the hearth, and the heel of a loaf on a plate with a small pat of butter and knob of cheese.

Billy saw Uncle Joe about to protest so he took it quickly, saying, "Thank you, Aunt, that's just what I need." He gobbled in it five minutes. Then he asked Uncle Joe for a bed for the night and asked if he would be coming with him to Wylam in the morning.

"Ay, there will be a funeral to plan and much more. You go up, Billy. You know the room your brother had when he was at school. We have not let that one."

Aunt Sarah snapped, "And we won't be letting it. I want Lily to live in. She can't get here from North Shields early enough for all the work there is." She explained to Billy, "She has to wait for her father to come in with the pies for their market stall so she is never here before nine in the morning which is no use at all. Anyway, the bed is there, so off you go if you're tired. I'll clear your supper things." She said it as if it were a great favour.

Billy didn't hesitate. He mumbled a goodnight and took the jug of warm water his uncle offered and a candle in his other hand and made his way up to the little room where he had last felt Francis's presence and hated it. Now it was swept bare, no books on the shelves, no clothes in the closet and it was bitterly cold. But it might be a room Lily would soon occupy. He would sleep in the bed where her small perfect body would lie. The thought made him hot with desire. He paced about till his legs protested with weariness. He used the chamber pot under the bed, poured water into the bowl on the washstand and barely splashed his face. Seeing some towels on an upper shelf, he snatched one down and, finding it large and thick, he took off only his coat and boots and, wrapping the towel round him, slid under the chilly covers.

Wanting to think only of Lily, he found himself building up anger that he had never been told she was at his uncle's. He hadn't even realised Francis was no longer living here. He had heard talk of an apprenticeship to an engineer who built bridges for the new waggonways that were sprouting everywhere. But how dare he conceal Lily's whereabouts when he, Billy, had been desperate to find her?

It was a fruitless line of thought and he abandoned it to relive the brief time with Lily, going over every word and seeing again the sympathy in her eyes when she clasped his hands. She had felt at once his pain at Grandmother's death. And that had happened only hours ago! The pain of it stabbed him again, but grieving wouldn't bring her back. She was already the past. Life was going to change. He couldn't see how yet and in puzzling over what the next few days would bring he drifted into an exhausted sleep.

Chapter 21

Dee

Trying to warm up, Dee set a fast pace back from the funeral. Jack, who had broken down again at the graveside, choked out a small protest.

"My angel, aren't we to be in a slow procession?"

"Well, we are not a procession. Joe is settling Sarah in at The Black Bull before he comes here for a family conference. He has plans to tell us. Billy ran ahead to tell Mr Burns he would work the late shift. Do you call three of us a procession?"

"Where have the village folk gone that came to the church?" Francis asked.

"To the alehouse of course."

"Should we not have invited them all to a feast at home?"

"No, we should not. We are to settle today what is to be done as your uncle wants to take your aunt home tomorrow."

Jack said, "Your ma has everything in hand. She is always a marvel."

They were silent until Francis, stepping closer to Dee, whispered, "Mother, I have to ask you, did you tell Billy that Lily and I have an understanding?"

She had been thinking it would be a relief *not* to be a marvel and to have a husband with some plans of his own. The question startled her.

"Tell Billy? Of course not. Why would you think such a thing?"

"That letter that came today was from Lily. She met Billy on the doorstep when he took the news to Uncle and she said he seemed to know he would be her brother-in-law one day. He spoke of them being 'united' and told her she wouldn't have to keep running away from him then. So she wanted to know if she was allowed to ask her parents if they were agreeable for us to be betrothed."

Dee, with her mind pondering what Joe was going to propose, was not ready for a new problem. "I told you you're too young. You have an apprenticeship to complete. She must have misheard what Billy said. He would be thinking how to break the news to his uncle."

"She says she felt sorry for him because he was good to our grandmother and I know she wants me and Billy to get along together. But of course she doesn't *know* Billy. And I can't possibly ask *him* what he said to her."

"Why not? It's time you started talking to each other. But not tonight. We don't want any bad temper and he's so unpredictable." The square shape of Burn Cottage loomed before them. "Thank goodness we're here."

All she wanted was to be warm. The chill by the graveside had bitten her to the bone. The fire had sunk down in their absence.

"More coal, quickly," she said to Francis, aware that he was dissatisfied with her answers, but for the moment indifferent to that.

A few minutes later, Billy marched in, demanding, "Where's Uncle Joe then?" and the chance to talk intimately was gone.

He stalked over to the window seat and sat down, moving a copy of *Edwin the Elephant* to do so. Dee saw him flip the pages and a slip of paper fell out. She knew it was the note Sarah always put in the parcel to say what royalties had been paid. Billy picked it up and studied it.

"Put it back in the book," she said. "I use it as a marker." It was odd to see him handling her work. He obeyed with a shrug and laid the book down. Despises it, I expect, she thought.

As soon as a good blaze was reaching up the chimney and the kettle had produced boiling water for a mug of tea, she took heart.

She smiled at Francis and murmured, "We'll speak of it later when your uncle has revealed his plans and gone back to the inn."

Joe hurried in and had barely sat down before he burst out, "Well now, big changes. You must all come and live in Number Four Heron Mansions."

There were startled gasps. Dee guessed immediately from his breathlessness and anxious look round that Sarah had not sanctioned this.

"You will give up both rooms in Burn Cottage and spread yourselves over the first two floors. You would have lodgers in the attics to bring in an income and of course I wouldn't charge my own brother rent. If you found work in the town, Jack, you might contribute to repairs and such."

For a mere second the thought of having separate rooms for eating, sitting and sleeping tempted Dee but no, she told herself, the proximity of Sarah, the loss of independence, the enclosing streets, the grime, the absence of fields and trees would kill her spirit. She was planning a tactful answer when Jack said, "But Joe, how would I get to my animals?"

Joe smiled and asked Francis what *he* thought.

Francis shifted uncomfortably. "Well, Uncle, as you know I am lodging with Mr Trace, the engineer, in the village of Heaton while I serve my apprenticeship. The workplace is next door which is so convenient. Of course if home was in Heron Mansions I could walk there on a Sunday and save the expense of a horse. It is a most generous offer, Uncle, but my father and mother will have to decide."

"Joe," she said, "you see how it is with Jack. What work could he do there to satisfy him?" She looked very fixedly at Joe and noted his face was very red. He would be shocked if she said "Thank you very much, we'll come tomorrow." She went on, "You are goodness itself but I see us eventually being able to rent a small house of our own, when my books pay a little better."

Joe looked relieved but crinkled his forehead. "I thought your books were doing very well, Dee. Of course you would be nearer Septimus Blanding, the printer, and could deal with him direct, but if Jack—" He was looking at his brother, who gave him a wide grin, hearing his name mentioned.

Francis said, "I think machines will replace animals soon and the farm may close." Dee saw that Francis wanted her to accept so that he could be close to Lily, but she saw the alarm in Jack's eyes.

She said, "Don't worry, Jack, with your experience you could get work on another farm. We might be offered a farm cottage then and be happy in a more country place away from the pit."

"Away from the pit? Away from my waggonway?" He could not imagine such a thing.

It was at that moment that Billy, who had been sitting silently on the window seat, suddenly spoke up. "Uncle, *I'll* come to Number Four."

"You, Billy, on your own!"

Dee could see Joe struggling to hide the consternation on his face.

"Yes," Billy said in his emphatic way. "I would want only the ground floor and I would look after myself and keep things in order. The rest of the house could be rented out."

"But the pit," Joe protested. "Your promotion to Overman?"

"Did you not expect me to give up mining if we all came to live in Number Four or was I not included in the family?"

"Of course you were. Naturally, I wanted to know your views on finding work as an Overman in another pit."

"No, I would give up mining altogether. I would be coming to help you with your business. After all, as your heir—"

He stopped because Joe's mouth opened in a gasp and his hands clutched at his chest. He was in pain.

Dee jumped up. "It's a seizure. Help me to lie him down."

They were all on their feet but Joe took a great breath and shook his head. He withdrew his hands and held them up in a calming gesture. As soon as he could speak he said, "A spasm only. The pain has passed."

"Francis could run to Ovingham for the doctor," Dee said.

Billy glared down at her. "*I* would be quicker."

"No, no," Joe said, his speech quite steady. "It happens from time to time. I never know when. My physician says a severe one may be my last but I tell him to be quiet. I keep living, don't I?"

He was half laughing to cover his embarrassment but Dee knew that the boys, though not Jack, would have noted what had triggered the spasm.

She poured Joe a glass of water and watched him anxiously as he sipped it.

Then he pointed a finger at Billy. "You do well, lad, to want to be of service to your old godfather, but to live on your own as you suggest is not suitable for a young man. What? Cooking and cleaning! Your aunt couldn't undertake that for you—"

"I looked after your mother," Billy almost shouted at him, but he was vehemently hushed by both Dee and Jack.

"I made her morning porridge," Dee said to Joe, "and sent in the other meals."

"As I thought," Joe said. "I appreciate you were a companion to her, Billy, and made her confused years happier, but you must not exaggerate or show that spirit of anger you are too prone to."

"I'm sorry," Billy said, and Dee saw a look of astonishment in Francis's eyes, but she knew of Billy's desperation to keep his uncle's favour.

Joe went on, "And you must know that my business, as you call it, does not yet warrant the hiring of an assistant. Your aunt is so good at keeping all records. If my health fails she could no doubt run Heron Mansions on her own. I respect your parents' decision not to accept my proposal and as my mother's sad death relieves me of the expense of her premises, I presume you will move back with them. Francis will not often be there but when he is it will be as it was when you were boys growing up."

Heaven forefend, thought Dee, and heard a gasp of "No!" from Francis.

Billy would certainly have heard it too. His face darkened with rage. "I will never do that, Uncle. The tenancy of your mother's place passes to me. I have checked that with the colliery manager already, as long as I pay the rent myself. I'm in charge of my own life and will stay there if I am not to come to you. If I wish to leave I will leave. I am my own man."

"Well spoken," Joseph said, and began to rise from his chair. "I must return to Sarah. The accommodation at The Black Bull is not what she is used to but she couldn't fancy the cold walk here after the funeral. She said she would lie down in the bedchamber they gave us and begged me not to be late."

Dee jumped up. "But the walk back, Joe, are you fit to do it?"

Jack said at once, "I'll go with him."

Joe patted Dee's arm. "The air will do me good, my dear. You have had such a splendid fire in here that I am quite roasted."

"I have to do the late shift, Uncle," Billy said, "or I would walk your other side."

"I'll do that," Francis said. "Two of us can hold you up."

"Nay, I am not so helpless. But I accept your company gladly. And Billy, I trust you will pay us a visit in the warmer weather if you get a few days' leave."

"Ay, I will do that." A semblance of a smile appeared.

"And maybe we can do some more fishing together. I am better in the summer days," he added to Dee. "I like that spot at the curve of the river along the bank from you. Very peaceful."

When they had all gone Dee sat down at the table with a great sigh. Joe must not be upset or another seizure might be fatal. He had wanted to make a grand gesture to his brother's family and, but for Sarah, might have been happy to have them close by. Now he would jog on in his own way, coming to visit them occasionally to escape her dominance. Jack too would be happy at the outcome. She was sure the mine farm would continue even if the horses became redundant. It made a profit for the owner, selling produce from the pigs and the crops.

As for herself, these four walls would still encompass her and the small irritations from Mother Jane had ceased. But those, she thought, gazing into the glowing coals, made me a better woman. Not snapping at her gave me my small daily triumphs. But what will it be like if Billy stays next door? *I* won't scrub his back. I would be afraid to touch him and I am just as sure that he would loathe me to do so. He'll buy himself a loofah.

Jack and Francis would return presently and she must address the matter Francis had raised before. What happened on that doorstep? Had Billy guessed Francis was in love with Lily? He could try to separate them out of sheer malice.

We know from Milton, she thought, that the sight of love infuriates the devil.

When they returned they said Joe seemed well and had begged them to say nothing to Sarah. Then he had slipped two sovereigns into Francis's hand, saying, "You will be seventeen shortly, my boy, and though you may not show the interest your brother seems to have in my affairs, you are learning useful skills. So stick at it."

"I fear he now favours Billy more," Francis said, "and may change his will again. Billy still believes he is the heir. He'll kill me if he finds out he isn't."

Dee frowned at him, a rare thing. "You promised me you would not set your heart on your uncle's wealth. Billy pleased him with his stout declaration that he was his own man. That is what you must do. But listen to me, you had better not ask Billy what he said to Lily. It will rouse his curiosity and if he suspects your feelings he will try to make discord between you."

"He'd never succeed."

Jack asked what they were talking about.

"Why, Joe of course," she said quickly.

"Ay, I was mighty frightened when he had that turn. It's terrible when folks about you die. I still can't believe Mother's not there to go and kiss her goodnight."

Fearing there would be more tears, she said, "Come, let us get to our beds. I'm weary. We may hear Billy come in next door but he'll be late."

Jack put on his rueful face. "He's all alone there."

"And that suits him fine," Dee said. "Come, darling."

But when Jack was asleep her imagination saw Billy as a dark cloud about to break over their heads in a storm. Joe's wealth was a hill of coins reaching up to the cloud. The cloud would engulf it soon. Francis was trying to climb up the hill and she was yelling at him to stop but no sound came. She remembered the dream all too plainly next day.

Reality was more prosaic and she put away her fears.

In the next few weeks Billy came and went silently, eating the dinners she took in for him and leaving the plate for her to collect. He didn't come to Ovingham Church with them on Sundays but at least he was quiet.

One weekday morning, she heard a horse's hooves outside and, looking out, found Mr Hurst tethering his animal to the gatepost.

She hadn't seen him for a long time and his flowing hair was grey and his face lined, but he was his old ebullient self. "Ah, Mistress Heron, I thought I would visit old haunts. You are as young and blooming as ever. May I come in for a few moments?"

"Of course, sir." She gestured him in, not too pleased at his familiarity.

He sat at the table and picked up the manuscript of *Urwin the Unicorn*. "Into mythical animals now, are we?" He laid it down and looked brightly up at her. "Pray sit down. I need no refreshment. It's young Francis I've come about. My good friend, Gordon Trace, the engineer, will be writing you a letter so I thought I would come ahead of it and prepare you."

Her throat went dry. She had a premonition. "Francis! Oh, what's happened to him?"

"Only what happens to a thousand young men every day. A heady dose of unwonted freedom. Unruliness, drunkenness!"

"Francis! No, never."

"Oh come, no one is a saint. This is the first time he has lived outside family supervision and in the company of other young men. He had a few sovereigns on his birthday from his uncle and, wanting to be seen as a young buck about town, took his friends out for the night. Unused to strong beer, they all went wild and climbed on the church roof and dislodged a few slates."

Wild and drunk! Francis! Dee's imagination could not compass it, but as Mr Hurst talked she had to be convinced it was true and that a sum of money from the parents of the culprits was likely to be demanded. It would not be much but Mr Trace warned that any repetition might lead to the ending of the apprenticeships.

"I doubt Trace means that," Mr Hurst said cheerfully. "Apprentices have been notorious for their antics since medieval times and he is in fact quite impressed with Francis so far. He likes to keep his young men up to the mark and will give them each a special task before the end of their first year with threats of dismissal hanging over them, but to my knowledge he always keeps them on."

Dee rose when Mr Hurst rose and thanked him for coming but when he left she sank down with her head on the table and sobbed. Life had turned a somersault. Francis, a source of worry! Fallen from grace. She was shaken to the core.

But when she told Jack, which she did reluctantly, he was not much perturbed.

"I am sorry he's upset, my angel, but he'll have learnt his lesson. I was plied with strong beer once about his age and fell down and bruised my head. I didn't like that so I never tried it again."

She hugged him for his sweet simple logic but feared that Francis had been the ringleader in this case. When he came home on the Sunday, however, all she realised was how young he still was. A year ago she had begun to think of him as her intellectual companion, a tall, sophisticated young man, when really he was still a child who had been naughty because he had forgotten about consequences.

"We have our punishment," he told her as they ate Sunday lunch. "Three days at home at the end of March working out some problems without any help."

"And if you don't succeed?"

"Maybe Mr Trace won't want to see us again."

"You will succeed."

"I'm surprised you've still got any faith in me."

Billy walked in at that point to ask if there was any food for him. Unexpectedly, he was at home for once.

Jack, with a great smile, cried out, "Sit down with us."

Billy looked at Francis. "*He's* here."

Dee saw a struggle going on in Francis's face. Then he lifted his eyes to his brother's and said, "Come and sit beside me. And when it's your birthday

I'll be at home. I'll have three days to work on some engineering problems. Maybe we could look at them together."

Billy stared, his eyebrows drawn into one line. "End of March? I'll be visiting Uncle Joe. I have three days' leave and come back as Overman. Your problems are *your* problems."

Dee had piled his plate with the last of the stewed beef and vegetables while he was speaking. He took it and walked out.

Jack's face fell. "I wanted him to stay. Oh, I *did* want him to stay."

Dee pressed his hand. "One day perhaps. You did well, Francis."

She got up to clear the plates. Life had righted itself but her premonition of danger had not gone away.

Chapter 22

March 1824

Billy

Uncle Joe, with an apologetic grin, showed Billy into the first floor back at Number Four Heron Mansions.

"Your aunt has given Lily and Gertie Francis's old room which freed one for Sam, our live-in manservant. So this is the only vacant one in the whole block at present. Of course, we would have cleared out all Number Four's tenants except the attics, if your family had agreed to come here, but I understood. I quite understood."

Billy, alight with the news that Lily was only three doors away, answered heartily, "This is a grand room." It was dark with a high yard wall outside and roofs rising to a small square of sky. There was a bed, a chair, a chipped marble washstand and some hooks to hang clothes. He asked, "Do I come to Number One for meals?"

His uncle laughed. "My dear boy, of course. Tonight there will be a supper at eight but we like our main meal in the middle of the day. For your birthday tomorrow I have a fine Burgundy laid up in the cellar. I regret you can only stay two nights but you go back to new responsibilities so we will celebrate your promotion."

"Thank you, Uncle." Billy had been studying his face for signs of illness but his complexion was sallow, not red, and his manner jovial.

Billy was disappointed not to see Lily that evening. She should surely have been asked to sit down with them, but Sarah had made an exception when she had invited the Batey family many Christmases ago and she was evidently not going to repeat it.

Conversation was a trial since he was so used to eating alone but he observed everything in the dining-room, from the ferns in ornate pots to a narrow door he didn't remember on the same side as the window.

"Where does that go?" he asked his uncle.

Aunt Sarah broke in, "Such a clever idea of your uncle's! When we extended the kitchen premises to make a larger scullery he made me a little private room adjoining it and a way in from here. I keep my needlework in it and a few books."

"And that's where she makes up your mother's accounts for the Moral Tales," Uncle Joe added.

Billy saw Aunt Sarah flush and dismiss this with a flapping of hands. "Just to be downstairs – nearer to catch the post boy. I call it my sewing-room."

Billy was surprised by her unease. Then he recalled the slip of paper he had seen in *Edwin the Elephant* in her writing. And why had his uncle said on the day of the funeral, "I thought the books were selling well," when Mother had hinted at a modest return? A tiny seed of suspicion settled in his mind. Was Aunt up to no good?

By ten o'clock, wearied at being shown stock market figures, he was glad to walk down to Number Four and retire to his bleak room, but being on an upper floor with strangers about was unsettling. Used to solitude and a glimpse of river and trees from the window, he wanted to step outside and walk in the fresh air as he did at home if he couldn't sleep. He lay wondering at his aunt's uncharacteristic discomfort. What role did she really play in his mother's work? But finally he gave himself to the joyful thought of seeing Lily tomorrow.

He was awake early with the chiming of Saint Nicholas's clock. It struck six and at the half hour he dressed and crept downstairs and out into the street.

At Number One Gertie was polishing the brass door knocker. He said, "Good morning," and walked in past her and thrust his hat onto the hall stand.

She gave him a startled look. "Oh, of course you are Mr William Heron?"

He nodded, liking the sound of that, but as soon as he was inside the hallway his spine tingled and he had to put a hand on the wall to steady himself.

Lily had appeared at the top of the stairs, clutching some garment in her hands and answering someone above, "Yes, ma'am, I'm sorry, as quick as I can." He heard a door close on the landing. She came running down and was almost at the bottom before she saw him in the dark corner by the door.

"Oh Billy, what a fright! I have to run and put Madam's apron to soak. I spilt coffee on it and she's so cross."

"Let me help. You're always running away."

He put out his hand for the apron. There was something hard in the pocket.

"What's this?" She was trying to pull the apron away. "Nay, if it's some trinket she'll be even angrier if it's lost in the laundry."

She stopped then and looked in the pocket. "Oh my, it's her sewing-room key. She carries it everywhere. I'll have to take it back. She never lets it out of her sight."

He put his hand in and drew it out. "I'll take it to her. You put the apron to soak."

"Oh Billy, thank you. She won't be cross with *you* since your uncle is there."

She scampered along the passage and down the steps to the kitchen. The moment she shut the door he looked at the key in his hand. His uncle and aunt were upstairs and Lily would be scrubbing the apron. It was no business of Gertie's if he went into the dining-room. The chance had been handed to him to pry into the mystery – if there was one.

He slipped into the dining-room, dodged round the table and inserted the key into the narrow door. His throat dry, he stepped inside and immediately locked the door behind him. With his back against it he quickly assessed the little room. No needlework was on display anywhere, just one easy chair and a desk and chair under the window with pens and ink, but below the desk was a small basket which might contain sewing materials. The lid was slightly askew and he glimpsed a white corner of what looked more like paper than cloth. Instantly suspicious, he pulled out the basket and opened it. It was full of slips of paper headed 'Septimus Brandling, Printers'. He took out the top one and held it to the window.

One glance showed him it was the printed version of the handwritten one he'd seen in *Edwin the Elephant*, but after the number of books sold, a figure showing a lesser number was pencilled in. He looked at the others in the basket. Some showed as much as ten less if sales had been good. He could scarcely believe his eyes.

"The thieving old witch! She has kept back money each month!" For a second he thought of taking one slip as evidence but she might notice and he needed time to think how he could use his discovery. Whatever happened, he mustn't be caught here.

Listening for any sound, he pushed the basket under the desk again and backed away, checking that all was as before, and with his heart pounding he unlocked the door and peeped into the dining-room. No one was there. His hand quivered as he relocked the door, dropped the key in his pocket and, breathing deeply with relief, walked casually out and up the stairs.

He hesitated outside the bedroom door where presumably his uncle and aunt had an early cup of coffee, a drink not known at home. Then he lifted his hand and rapped once.

"Lily?" came his aunt's voice.

"No, it's me, Billy."

His uncle called, "By the Lord, you're early, but come in, lad," and he heard his aunt say, "I knew that wasn't Lily's knock."

He opened the door and peered round. They were seated in their long morning gowns either side of a small table at the foot of the bed.

He put on an apologetic smile. "The church clock wouldn't let me sleep. Gertie was polishing the knocker so I walked in and then…" Turning to his aunt, he added as lightly as he could, "Lily came out of the kitchen to bring you what she said she'd found in some pocket or other so I said I'd save her the trouble. Was that all right?" He handed her the key.

Sarah looked at it in horror, dropped both her hands to feel in her gown pockets, and then snatched it from him.

Uncle Joe was chuckling a little. "Oh, Sal, you'd only just taken it from under the pillow and popped it in your apron pocket when in came Lily and joggled the coffee pot as she set it down. I think you frighten her sometimes."

"Nonsense. She was careless. If I hadn't been standing up the coffee would have been through the apron and ruined my morning robe and no doubt scalded me badly. If you saw everything, why didn't you say?"

Billy saw she had put the key into the left-hand pocket of her gown as she spoke and kept her hand over it. So at night it was under her pillow, was it? No wonder, since behind that locked door was evidence of a crime that could send her to gaol if his mother chose to bring charges against her. She wouldn't, of course, for the sake of his uncle who knew nothing of it, but she would want her rightful money. He was surprised by her gullibility. She had blithely sent off her little books and never questioned handwritten notes from Sarah about the sales. "Your aunt calls herself House of Heron as my publisher," she would chuckle. "It's the way things are done. I told Joe she must take her expenses." A small sum for postage perhaps but not large-scale fraud, Billy thought.

He couldn't put his mind to it now. His uncle was talking of plans for the day while he was yearning for time with Lily alone. He wouldn't burden *her* with his discovery. All he wanted was to be with her when she was not hurried but sitting by him, hearing his thoughts for their life together, deciding when they could bring this about, sweetly and privately. And she must be as neat and perfectly symmetrical as the day he first noticed her, the only young woman he would ever want.

"Well, it is your birthday," his uncle was saying. "Would you care to see some entertainment? We have a theatre, you know, in the town."

"Nay, that's not much to my taste," Billy admitted, never having seen a play in his life and not impressed by the travelling showmen that passed through the villages on their way from Newcastle to Carlisle. "A walk by the river to see the ships would be pleasant." If Lily came too, he was thinking. That, however, was unattainable.

He and his uncle walked down to the quayside and he had not even glimpsed Lily before they left. It was a fresh March day and Billy took pleasure in the tumult that was the River Tyne at full tide, with vessels of all sizes jostling for the open sea.

They returned for the main meal of the day and it was Gertie who waited at table. Billy found himself watching his aunt as she gave her orders. It was strange to think of her as a criminal, so precise, controlled and dignified, sitting there with her buttoned-up bodice and little lacy cap perched on her tightly wound grey hair.

His uncle was saying, "And you think you are ready, Billy, to have miners under your supervision when you are made Overman?"

"Oh yes, sir. They respect authority, just as your servants do. You and Aunt give the maids their duties and make rules for them. Of course in a pit the rules are for the miners' safety which helps to keep discipline."

"You'll have some discretion too in allotting work. Knowing your men."

Billy beamed at his aunt. "As you do with your maids. Gertie polishes brass and Lily brings your morning coffee. I suppose they have different days off, too."

Aunt Sarah lifted her eyebrows. "Hardly a subject for your interest?"

"Oh no," he said quickly. "I meant as employers you really have complete control more than I will have as an Overman answerable to the Viewer."

"I daresay," she said. "And we are generous employers, aren't we, Joseph? But of course my maids do every task except the heavy work our handyman does."

"Do they clean all the other houses?"

"You are very curious. In fact I now have two dailies who come in to do the tenants' rooms. Is there anything else you would like to ask?"

Billy laughed. "Oh no. You see, my parents have never had servants so this is new to me. They have one room and you have four houses. You *need* servants."

Uncle Joe, he could see, was looking uncomfortable. "It was my brother's choice to stay there and your mother is wonderfully loyal to him. And you, Billy, will you stay in mining much longer? Look at George Stephenson whose family lived in a cottage not far from yours. He is now building engines and railways and has become a great man. I think your brother is studying to emulate him."

Billy had just taken his last bite of apple pie. It instantly became dust in his mouth. He could say nothing to that and the conversation died, without him answering his uncle's question.

"If we have all finished I shall have my afternoon rest," his aunt said, rising.

His uncle rose too. "Now if we were in charming Wylam I would fancy a stroll along the river and a little fishing. I will make a point of riding over soon to enjoy that. But today I will imitate your aunt and have a nap. You are a fast walker, Billy, and I am a little weary from our exertions this morning."

"I am sorry, Uncle. I was going to suggest walking west along the river to view the staithes where our wagons discharge their coal but I will do it on my own."

"Very well. I'll fetch the Burgundy up and we will break it open this evening and drink to your health."

Billy watched his aunt mount the stairs to their bedroom and then, picking up his hat from the hall stand, he strode out of the front door and up the street. His intention was to get round to the back of the house and find a way to the kitchen door where he hoped to find Lily.

He had noticed an alleyway between Number One and the next terrace rising up the street. Glancing round to see there was no one about, he slipped into it. The house wall was on his right, the parlour first and then the dining-room with its small window. No wonder it was a dark room. He peered in but could see no one at work there. Now came the 'sewing-room', jutting into the passage, but leaving room to walk round past the new scullery. There was a window there too but no one at the sink behind. Then the alleyway joined a wider one serving the backs of the houses and reaching down the hill towards the jungle of masts marking the river. He tried what must be the door leading into Number One's yard but it was bolted on the inside.

He listened and could hear voices and a swishing sound that could be a broom. Putting his ear to the door, he heard a voice, not Lily's. "You say he's a coal miner. I thought he was a gentleman. He took his hat off to me and walked in like he owned the place. But he hardly spoke at the table. I'd say he's the tough, quiet type. But ooh, he's mighty handsome. I wouldn't mind a romp with him!"

Then came Lily's voice, raised as he had never heard it before. "Don't speak of him like that. He's going to be – well, he is a friend. My family knows him."

"Sorry, I'm sure."

Billy, tingling from head to foot at what she had nearly said, lifted his hand to knock at the door. Then he checked it and, holding himself in, counted to twenty. He heard a door close. Had he missed his chance? Then the swishing sound began again quite near. At once he gave two sharp raps.

A little gasp, "Oh, goodness me!" in Lily's voice and then just behind the door, "Who is that please?"

"Billy. Open up."

"Oh!" Pause. "Did you get locked out at the front?"

"Yes. Let me in."

He heard the sound of a bolt being drawn back and pushing on the door he nearly knocked her to the ground. He caught her and she gave a little laugh.

"You're so vigorous. I dropped my broom." He had his hands on her waist and would have clasped her to him only he glimpsed Gertie at the kitchen window. He released Lily and picked up her broom. Taking it, she backed across the yard to open the kitchen door. "Just walk straight through and you're in the hallway," she said.

"No, no, we need time together."

"Time? What for? I'm working."

He looked round the yard. "It looks clean enough."

"Not for Madam it isn't."

Gertie had gone from the window so he followed Lily and said, "Here. Face me, let me look at you. Your apron is not straight. And that little cap you wear, it shows more hair on this side."

"It doesn't matter. She wouldn't notice anything like that. Let me get on."

"You have to be perfect, symmetrical." He adjusted cap and apron and stood back to study her. "That's better."

"I tell you, she isn't as fussy as that." She moved away and went on sweeping. He followed her again.

"You know you won't be doing this sort of thing for ever."

"I know, but I am now, so off you go, Billy."

He took hold of her arm. "You're not to run away again."

"No, *you* run away. We shouldn't be here together."

She's frightened in this place, he thought. She feels watched.

She looked up at the kitchen window and gave a little shriek.

"It's Madam! Let go of me."

He saw his aunt's face twisted with outrage. He had nothing to lose now.

"You are mine, Lily. Just say yes." He didn't realise how tightly he was gripping her arm till she squealed, "Yes, yes."

He released her and she flung her broom against the wall and ran to the kitchen door where Sarah now appeared like a vengeful angel barring her way.

"Lily, you let him in! I can see the bolt is pulled back. Go to your room and stay there till I send for you."

She moved to let Lily past and then came down the step to Billy.

"As for you—" She stalked by him and shot the bolt into place. Then she faced him. He squared his shoulders and returned her look with defiance. All preened up like an angry bird, ready for grovelling submission, she was speechless for a moment.

He said, "You'll not lay a finger on Lily. She let me in because I was locked out. She and Gertie were both in the yard and wouldn't have heard the bell."

The bird ruffled its feathers and regained its pose with beak raised. "I'll deal with her as I choose fit. But you! Wait till I tell Joseph what his own nephew has been up to! You'll suffer for it. What! Not to be trusted with the maids! His godson!"

Billy knew she was hinting that Joseph would cross him out of his will and she was right, he would. She would pester him till he did.

He tried a little light-heartedness. "There's nothing to tell, Aunt. Lily's a pretty girl. I fancied a kiss but she wouldn't let me. Uncle was a young man once and he won't look on that as a great sin."

"Indeed he will. What! You, a guest in our house, to be assaulting a young woman, not a mere kitchen maid but of a family your uncle knew from childhood, whom we took in to nurture and help when she was without work. I shall go and tell him now. He may not want you to stay a minute more under his roof."

She made a move to return to the kitchen but he stepped in front of her. He held an ace and he was going to have to play it now before his uncle woke up. There was no time to think of consequences or even what words to say.

"You won't be telling him, Aunt. Don't think of it. Or I will tell him and my parents and all the world that you have been defrauding my mother of her rightful earnings for many years."

The colour flew from her cheeks. She would have fallen to the ground if he hadn't caught her and held her up. She did not faint away but her legs were unable to bear her. She clung to him, gasping. He lifted her into his arms, hissing in her ear, "No one knows but me and I will tell no one as long as I am still my uncle's heir and you will pay the money back to me. You will treat Lily well because I'll hear about it if you don't."

The kitchen door was standing open. He began to carry her towards it and it occurred to him that Gertie must have fetched her from her bedroom to get Lily into trouble. Gertie had a face marked from smallpox. Was she jealous of Lily?

"Tell Uncle you had a little faint," he whispered to his aunt. "Gertie woke you suddenly saying there was a man in the yard and you hurried down half asleep. But it was me. Do you hear? It was all nothing. Nothing at all. Have you understood that?"

He carried her through the kitchen to the hallway where Gertie was anxiously hovering. And there coming out of the dining-room was his uncle, jovially brandishing the bottle of Burgundy. The laughter died on his face.

"Eh! Eh! What's this? Sarah! What's happened?"

She was looking up into Billy's eyes as if she could read words there.

"Nothing, it was all nothing," she muttered.

"Lay her on the couch in the parlour," his uncle said. "She never faints. I must send for the doctor."

She went on, babbling, "No, no doctor. It was nothing at all." Keeping her eyes fixed on Billy's face as he lowered her to the couch, she brought out the words, "Gertie woke me suddenly saying there was a man in the yard. I was half asleep. I hurried down too quickly. It was only Billy. And Lily let him in because he was locked out – where *is* Lily?" She looked frightened.

"Gertie can fetch her," Billy said. She ran up at once. "And Uncle, I think a glass of that is what Aunt needs." He pointed to the Burgundy.

"Well thought on." A tray of glasses was ready on a side table. He poured a glass and brought it to Sarah who was still trembling as she sat up to drink. Billy had the impression Uncle Joe was pleased with her weakness and glad to minister to her.

Gertie came down with Lily, who gave him a reproachful glance.

He said under his breath, "Don't worry. All will be well."

Both the girls' faces registered amazement as they peered into the parlour and saw their mistress sipping wine and no tirades of fury coming in their direction. The master ordered them back to work. "And Gertie, never wake anyone suddenly."

Gertie bobbed. "Yes sir," and they both scuttled away to the kitchen.

Billy's mind galloped – extract money from Sarah, keep friendly with Joe and marry Lily! He hadn't meant to be rough with her but she could never be her perfect self till she was free from here. He saw them by the sea together and she finishing her words to Gertie – "He is going to be my husband." She would be still, calm, lovely.

His uncle said, "Your aunt seems well enough now. It was an odd business. Did you change your mind about the walk and then couldn't get back in?"

"Ay, I felt a drop of rain and didn't want to pull the bell and wake everyone."

"Why did Gertie think it was a stranger in the yard?"

Sarah reared up. "Oh, leave it, Joe. He had a hat on and his back to her. Come, let us drink to Billy's health on his birthday and toast his promotion to Overman." She held out her glass for more. Billy watched her but she kept her eyes on his uncle, all smiles. He had to marvel how quickly she had regained her composure.

His uncle handed him a glass. He pretended to like the drink but would not take a second glass when he felt a fuzziness in his head after only one.

"Would you like me to tell you some of my ideas for the future before we have our supper?" Uncle Joe asked Billy, but Aunt Sarah held up her hand.

"No, Joseph. It is my turn to have Billy's attention. I want to show him all my work for House of Heron and how I promote the great writer, Dione Sharon."

Billy couldn't prevent a sharp intake of breath. He had wondered how to make time with her on her own and here she was brazenly inviting him into her sanctum.

"By all means," said his uncle, "if you feel well enough, my love."

She got up at once and, ramrod-straight, preceded Billy into the dining-room, took the key from a small pouch that hung at her waist and unlocked the 'sewing-room' door. As soon as they were inside she locked it again and turned to face him.

"Did Lily direct you here this morning?"

Shocked, he gave an emphatic no. "It was exactly as I told you. She said she had to run up and give you the key so I saved her the trouble."

"After looking in the room?"

"When she had gone into the kitchen and shut the door."

"And what interest had you in a sewing-room?"

"I had been suspicious of your activity under the title of House of Heron for a long time. I took my chance and found the evidence."

"Suspicious? Why? Who else was suspicious?"

She looked shaken and sat down in the easy chair, motioning him to the chair by the desk. He turned it round and leant on the back, looming over her.

"No one," he said. "They are all innocently trusting. My mother expected you to take small expenses but never thought she needed a formal contract with family."

"*You* are neither innocent *nor* trusting. I took expenses. That is not fraud."

"Why did you collapse when I used the word in the yard? Because you knew the scale of what you did was fraud. Now we settle the terms on which I keep silent."

Her eyes narrowed with fury. "You know nothing of my trials. I was caring for my aged parents. There were expenses, doctors, medicines and I was worn out but I got your mother's books printed and wrote to newspapers and booksellers and—"

"And your parents died and left you their house which you and Uncle could rent out and make more and more money. Well, that's what *I* want. Money now to give back to my mother little by little so she suspects nothing and money when Uncle dies. You are to tell him only good of me and make sure he never changes his will."

She was biting her lip. "You will have to please him mightily yourself to make up for past sins then for you are not in his will at all."

"What?" He clenched his fists and thumped them on the back of the chair. "I *was* in his will. He told me." And then he remembered his uncle being taken ill when he had said, "I am your heir."

She gave a tight-lipped grin. "It goes to Francis."

The name cut him worse than a knife wound. When he could speak he hissed at her, "Then I will tell Uncle what you did and make him change it again or he will find his wife in the town gaol."

She heaved herself out of the chair and for a second he thought she might produce a knife from her sleeve and stab him to death. But all she did was lay her hands on his chest and say, "You won't do that, Billy, because I shall persuade him to put you in. He always said it should be you as his godson but I made him change it when you were rude and insulting. I can make him do anything."

His body relaxed a little. "I believe you can. I believe you are a witch. But you must do it at once or I tell."

"Then you must ask him about his plans over supper and listen to him and converse with him. That's what he likes. You were so glum at supper yesterday."

"I shall tell him I was tired for I walked here to save the coach fare. But you must act at once and I must know that you have for he must tell me himself."

"Sometimes it takes a little while," she said, stroking his arm, "but I will try."

"You must do it tonight so he tells me in the morning before I go."

"I'll do it. You'll see." She drew herself up and tossed her head. "You'll see what power I have."

He didn't know whether to loathe or admire her. "And now," he said, "you can give me fifty pounds as a start."

She flopped back in the chair. "Fifty! Why do you think I have fifty pounds?"

"I am quite sure you have more, but that will do for the moment."

"But this is blackmail! That is a crime."

"And you have committed robbery."

They heard the clink of cutlery from the next room.

She put her finger to her lips. "Lily is laying the table for supper."

"Good. I'm hungry and that's another thing I demand. Time with Lily alone before I go tomorrow."

"What? So you can have your evil way with her? That I cannot allow."

"Evil way – with Lily! I want to apologise to her. She's a sweet little thing and I didn't mean to frighten her. Give me the money and I will go and speak with her openly in the dining-room while you stay here."

"You're not going to give *her* the money?"

"I told you, it goes back to my mother. And remember, no scolding Lily or Gertie about anything. You and I will have no more private talk at this visit but if Uncle does not tell me tomorrow that I am his heir you know what will happen."

He turned the chair round to the desk and in a swift movement bent down and abstracted a few slips of paper from the basket and stuffed them in his pocket.

"You'll know I can use this evidence at any time?"

She looked old suddenly. "How can I trust you to be silent?"

"I have to trust Uncle that he will change his will if he promises to do so. I know he'll want to send for his lawyer."

"Your uncle is a man of integrity."

"And *I* keep *my* word. Now give me the money and I will leave you."

"Turn your back then."

"You have a secret drawer, eh?" He went and faced the door. He could still hear Lily moving about in the dining-room. In a moment he would be with her.

There were some clicking sounds and rustling of paper from the desk but he didn't look round. Then she tapped his arm and put a roll of bank notes into his hand.

He nodded at her and put them in his pocket without counting them.

"Unlock the door," he said, and she did so.

As he passed through he said, "Well, thank you, Aunt. Mother will be so grateful for all you do for her Moral Tales. I will see you at supper. Here is Lily making preparations."

He shut the door behind him. Lily looked up and smiled warily. She was placing a silver saltcellar on the table.

He stepped up close and whispered, "Now listen. We have the means to go away together when we are ready."

"Go away?" she repeated.

"I may serve as Overman for a few months and you continue here but then we can be together and go where we please."

"I don't know what you mean. I'm not going anywhere with you, Billy."

"Nonsense. You've known we were meant to be one from the day I squeezed your hand and you smiled back. We can't be one unless we're together, can we?"

"But Billy—" Her eyes showed consternation. Why? Surely she had expected this sometime?

"Why are you surprised? You agreed we'd be united one day. You begged me not to risk my life down a coal mine. Today you rebuked Gertie and said I was to be your – husband? What's the matter with you? Is it too sudden? You were thinking it was still a long way in the future. Well, it doesn't have to be."

She was looking apprehensively at the sewing-room door. That was it. She was still fearful.

"Don't worry about her. She can't hear us when we're talking low."

"I've finished in here. I must get on." She made a move towards the hall.

He caught at her hand but she pulled it away.

"No, Billy. It's all a mistake. 'United'? That puzzled me and then I supposed you meant 'connected'."

"How connected?"

"Related. I never said 'husband'. And of course I didn't want you crushed in a pit like those poor men."

"Yes, you pleaded with me. You cared about me."

"Well yes. You are Francis's brother."

Francis! That word coming from her lips was an outrage. He planted his hand over her mouth. "No, not *him*." She struggled and he thrust her from him. "Not *him*."

She backed to the door, murmuring, "Yes, we have an understanding. I thought you knew."

'I thought you knew'. She had said that as well.

"I'm sorry, Billy. I must see to the supper."

"You said 'yes, yes' in the yard?"

"You were hurting me."

He looked at her, still unable to believe what was happening. He had built a great marble tower on nothing and it had crashed to the ground.

Her face was all crumpled. It was not beautiful, not symmetrical. Her cap was awry, her hair tousled. He lifted his hands and for one horrible moment he could imagine them around her throat.

She was watching him as she fumbled at the door handle.

He bent towards her and hissed at her ear, "If you've gone after him because he's the heir you're wrong. Uncle is changing his will again. *I* am the heir."

She had managed to turn the knob and pulled the door towards her. In the opening she said, "That doesn't matter. Francis and I love each other." And she fled down the passage to the kitchen.

He turned round to see his aunt standing at the sewing-room door.

"Were you frightening her again?" She had achieved her old imperious look.

He couldn't reply. He left the room and turned right to the front door. Before he could reach it his uncle appeared from the parlour.

"Ah, Billy, has your aunt shown you everything? We have ten minutes to supper time. I think it's my turn for your company."

Billy never knew how he managed a smile but he said, "I fancied a little fresh air, sir, but I'd be delighted to hear of all your plans over supper."

"You shall, lad. I'll watch for your return so you won't need to pull the bell."

He was out in the darkening street. A chill wind had got up and was blowing dust about and sending plumes of chimney smoke horizontal. People were hurrying home to their hearths. He wanted still cold darkness. He strode up the street and sought St Nicholas's Church.

He found an unlit corner and braced his back against the stone wall of the building. His jaw was clenched. If I had Francis in my sights now, he was thinking, I would kill him. He will still be at home when I get back. God preserve me from killing him – he looked up at the church spire reaching into the dusky sky – for if I kill him they will hang me and I will not inherit my uncle's money. I must have wealth. *She* was nothing. Perfection? Symmetry?

He summoned anger to quench grief. He had vowed to have Lily. Lily had done the unforgiveable. She had made a fool of him. No, it was Francis, living in their uncle's house when Lily was working there, seeing her day after day and insinuating himself into her favour. A mere boy, a fair pretty boy! Even Gertie had seen that he, Billy, was a fine, handsome man. How could Lily…?

For a few seconds he pressed his clenched fists against his eyes and ground his teeth together. Then he took a long breath, shook himself and began to walk back with big fast strides. Wealth. That was where he was going.

Gertie waited at the table for which he was thankful. He hoped he would never see Lily again in his whole life. Intensely proud of himself, he responded to everything his uncle said about plans to invest in more houses, to branch into industry now that new steelworks were being set up for the proposed railways.

"But I will proceed with caution," Uncle Joe added. "I bear in mind what I learnt of your maternal grandfather's mistakes. His example has sometimes been cited to me as a warning by people who had no knowledge of my connection with him."

Billy listened, and made intelligent comments. Out of the corner of his eye he saw his aunt with a smug smile on her face, giving little nods from time to time.

At the end of the meal she rose with a pointed look at him and said, "Your uncle has something to say to you, Billy. You might call it a birthday present. So I will just see the girls clear up properly and then I will retire. If I don't see you in the morning before you go I wish you great success in the post of Overman. I know you will fulfil the trust *everyone* places in you in *all* respects. Goodnight, Billy."

He rose and gave her a meaningful bow. "Indeed I will, Aunt." He had to wonder at her. She was indeed a witch. He sat down again and saw that his uncle had the Burgundy bottle out again. This he must treat with caution.

"Only a little, Uncle, for I am not used to it. It is almost too good for me."

Fortunately his words seemed to please his uncle. "You are right to be careful. I admire self-restraint in a young man. You would hear about Francis getting into trouble with his friends over drink. It was the first and last time, he told me, and I hope it will be, but *you* seem to me to have grown into a man of maturity while still young."

It was lucky that his uncle kept on talking and missed Billy's astonished reaction to the news about Francis. If the saintly Francis had misbehaved, he thought, that must have helped Aunt Sarah's task of persuasion.

His uncle poured him a very small glass while he took a generous one himself.

"Yes, you have improved like this good wine with age, Billy. I judged you a rather difficult boy and, very reluctantly, for you are my godson, I changed my will in Francis's favour. I felt uncomfortable about it, as I told your mother at the time."

Ah, Mother knew, Billy thought, and she would be delighted to tell Francis, her pet lamb. No wonder he has ignored me so contemptuously these last months.

"So now," his uncle continued, "I am minded to come with you tomorrow and tell your mother I propose to make a new will. She knows I gave money for Francis's apprenticeship and Mr Trace speaks well of him – apart from his small lapse – so I see him on the way to a successful career in engineering. That leaves me free to place you, after my dear wife of course, as sole heir to all my property and also to provide you with three hundred pounds at my death. Now, what do you say to that, Billy?"

Billy got up and shook his hand. He was adjusting his mind to the idea of his uncle travelling with him tomorrow. That was unexpected. He had hoped to hear he would send for his lawyer tomorrow.

"The next day I will send for my lawyer."

"Uncle, I don't know how to thank you. I can only study to deserve your generosity. Will you tell Francis?"

"I leave that to your mother's judgment. Now try your wee drink and I will toast your birthday again and your future prospects." He drained his glass.

Billy watched anxiously as his face grew redder, but he remained benign.

Billy said, "I need to take the early stage tomorrow, Uncle, for I report to the Viewer to be given my shifts for the week."

"I will be up and ready. It will be a pleasant break and I might try some fishing in this mild spell of weather."

They said goodnight and Billy hurried down to Number Four. The thought that Lily would tell Francis what had passed between them seared him like a hot iron. He took the stairs two at a time to escape the pain of it. He must think only of his own brilliance with his aunt and uncle. Pride would sustain him now. But, as soon as he put his head on the pillow, he appalled himself with a great rush of sobbing at what he had lost.

Chapter 23

Dee

Dee sat in Jane's rocking chair which Jack had brought into their home after his mother's death. Billy had said, "Take it. I never sit in it."

It was half an hour since Francis had jumped up and thrown his hands in the air with a triumphant shout. "I've got it. I can see how to work it out. I must finish the writing of it before Billy comes back."

"He won't trouble you," Dee said. "He'll go straight to the pit to see Mr Burns about his new duties."

"I know, but it unsettles me knowing he's around. These few days have been so calm. I could *think*." And he cut a fresh quill and began to write.

Dee had some mending in her hands but her fingers flopped loosely in her lap. The day was mild and she had let the fire sink low. It mustn't go out but the effort of rising was for the moment too much for her.

Watching Francis's pen, she thought, He will be a fine engineer one day. When he explains his work it opens for me a new world. He has enthusiasm and a delight in sharing it. He is full of love too, for me, for Jack, for Lily, even for his horse which has taken him down to North Shields to see Lily at home on her days off. He tells me he has confided to his uncle his hopes of marrying her one day but Sarah has no inkling yet. I think she and Billy are the only people of whom he is wary and that makes him uncomfortable for his nature is to be open and free.

The door opened and Billy's head looked round.

Dee shuddered as if an icy draught had chilled her spine.

Without preliminary, he said, "Uncle's come with me. He's leaving his bag at The Black Bull. I'll report to Mr Burns. Oh, and Uncle wants some fishing. I'll be back to see him after my shift."

He gave not one glance at Francis, who had looked round startled at his voice, and he withdrew as suddenly as he had appeared.

Francis put down his pen and slapped both hands on the table. "That's it then. I cannot finish the work now and I have to be back tomorrow with it all complete."

Dee had leapt up the moment she heard Joe was coming. She made up the fire and looked in the larder but she came back to Francis when she heard his lament.

"You think Uncle Joe will want you to accompany him fishing?"

"He always does if I'm here."

"Well, I shall tell him nay. You have work to do. And you'll see, Billy won't disturb you." She filled the kettle and set it to heat up while she laid out mugs and plates on the uncluttered end of the table. "No, you must greet your uncle but ask his leave to carry on while he is here."

"Will that not seem impolite?"

"Will what not seem impolite?"

They looked round to see Joe standing in the doorway beaming at them both.

"I did tap first," he said, "but you were talking and didn't hear."

Dee went up to him, truly pleased to see him, and he bent to give her a peck on the forehead. Francis rose, blushing at being overheard, and shook his hand.

"You are most welcome, Uncle, but Mother was saying I must tell you I have some study to finish and I feared that would be unmannerly."

"Nay, carry on, lad. Your mother and I have things to speak of and might even go next door to leave you in peace when Billy has gone to the pit."

"You will have some refreshment first," Dee said. "Sit ye down. Francis only needs so much room for his books."

Joe reached inside his coat. "But first he will want to see this." He produced a sealed letter. "A missive from his lady-love. She slipped it into my hand as she gave me my stick, careful not to let my dear wife see. I'm afraid she has witnessed Sarah's dismissal of a maid who had 'followers'."

Francis took the letter, the colour very high in his cheeks. He exchanged a look with Dee, who couldn't help a little laugh at his embarrassment. He squared his shoulders, drawing himself up, and very pointedly put the letter in his pocket.

"I will read it when my work is done," he said.

They heard Billy's door shut and his footsteps crunch on the gravel. Dee was curious now about Joe's wish to talk to her privately. Was it about Billy? What had happened in the last couple of days that had brought Joe back with him? She watched Joe as he tucked into the ham and eggs she had set before him with bread and butter and a mug of ale. He seemed to be stuffing it down quickly and there was an air of excitement about him which made her anxious for his health.

As soon as he had cleared his plate he rose and held out his mug for more ale, saying, "Let us go next door so Francis can work undisturbed."

Francis began to protest but Joe moved to the door and Dee had to follow.

Billy's room was bleakly tidy and the fire, as Dee had expected, was unlit. She would have reached for the tinder box but Joe said, "Nay, it's a mild day for March and we will not be long for I fancy a walk to my fishing spot and maybe cast a line."

There were only two kitchen chairs so they sat down on opposite sides of the table and Joe rested his clasped hands on it and looked earnestly at Dee.

"Well, Joe?" she said.

"Well, Dee, I'm minded to put Billy back in my will as my heir."

She sat very still and then nodded. She had sensed this coming. Billy had noted his uncle's shock of guilt when he had said, "I am your heir." So he had decided to visit him and show himself as a mature man. His coming of age and being made Overman was the perfect opportunity.

Joe chewed at his top lip. "You are not upset?"

"It's *your* will, Joe. You are free to do as you please. You have been very generous to Francis already."

He took out his handkerchief and wiped his forehead. "I am relieved to hear you say that. Billy was a troublesome boy but he has changed out of all recognition."

"Have you told Sarah? She always favoured Francis."

"Nay, she has come round to Billy too. She reminded me I always felt it was my duty as a godfather to remember him in my will."

What spell, Dee asked herself, has Billy cast that he has caught Sarah in his web too? There is more behind this than Joe is saying. She thought wistfully of Francis working away in the next room, oblivious of the change.

Joe said, "Sarah will of course have all the property at my death and Billy thereafter when she is taken, but I can afford to set three hundred pounds aside for him when I go. He could build up a business of his own if he wishes to leave the pit. He is intelligent, hard-working and sober. There is no youthful wildness about him."

Ah, Francis, Dee thought. Your drunken prank is known. It is village gossip too for they have nothing else in their lives. Our family is a curiosity. Jack Heron they love but the wife and sons he has brought into their midst are beyond their experience.

"I shall not tell Francis," she said. "He is only eighteen and all his hopes are in the future."

Again Joe looked relieved. He gulped his ale and got to his feet, swaying a little. "Good spring air is what I need. You store my fishing tackle next door I think."

"Francis could carry your gear along," Dee said.

"Nay, I can manage that." He paused at the door. "Dee, I am so grateful for the way you have taken this. When I go home tomorrow I will talk to my lawyer. I have arranged for him to come and see me in the evening and set the change in motion."

"Very well," she said and followed him into her room.

When he had collected his fishing tackle and small stool, he patted Francis on the shoulder. "That's the way. Stick at it, lad. I won't be more than an hour or so, Dee. Maybe Billy will have returned then and we can have a cosy time together before I seek my bed at the inn and catch the stage in the morning."

She walked with him across the roadway and the waggonway to see him safely onto the riverside path.

"You will find it dry, Joe, for this south-west wind blew all night, but watch your footing for the river is not far below the path. It must have rained in the hills for the past few days."

"Ah, but this air is good," he said, moving off.

She looked after him with apprehension. His cheeks had been very rosy indoors before their fire but it had been cool in Billy's place, yet he had wiped perspiration from his face. She watched him till the path following the river bend was hidden by the willows and alders on the bank.

She heaved a great sigh and began to retrace her steps to Burn Cottage. Money is a curse, she was thinking, pushed this way and that way between brothers. Joe has made money but is no happier than Jack. Still, without children of his own, he is thankful to be able to keep it in the family and Billy has persuaded him that *he* will manage Heron Mansions when Francis is building railways.

She stopped with a foot on the rail of the waggonway. "Did I mean *family*?" she said aloud. "Joe is deceived. Billy is no kin to him at all." The rattle of the empty train returning penetrated her brain and she stepped quickly back and stood among the dead winter grasses till it passed. She had grown used to banishing Billy's origin to the forbidden part of her memory. When Joe spoke of his nephews that was what they were. As she walked back with heavy steps the old guilt was stabbing her unbearably.

In the house she sank down into the rocking chair and was thankful that Francis just looked round and smiled and went on writing. She could see he had made a drawing with lines and angles and was now providing a written explanation. There was some solace in pondering how God's universe was there to be probed but cared not for man's success or failure. But she shrank from the thought of God.

She put her head back and closed her eyes.

The scraping of Francis's chair on the floor and his shout of "Finished" woke her with a start. She blinked and looked about. The day had darkened and the wind had risen. Francis had lit a candle.

"What? Is your uncle not back?" She scrambled out of the chair.

"He has not been gone so very long. It's light outside still."

"He said an hour. Oh Francis, go and seek him. Carry his gear back."

Hearing the anxiety in her voice, Francis didn't hesitate to put on his coat which hung on the back of his chair. Dee thought for a second of Lily's letter, perhaps still unread, but she urged him outside and watched him run towards the river.

Then she froze with horror. From the other direction came the black apparition of Billy from his first shift as an Overman.

"Where's *he* going?" Billy yelled as he came up.

"Just to fetch Uncle Joe." The words were out and couldn't be recalled.

"That's *my* task." Billy set off in pursuit.

Dee shouted, "No, Billy, no."

There was such malevolence in his eyes that the sight of him chasing

Francis brought sharply back her own premonitions and Francis's fears of him. Without thought she began to run after them. Her foot caught the rails she knew so well and she fell to the ground. Shaken, she got to her feet and scrambled back off the waggonway, feeling blood trickling down her leg. Her shin must be badly cut. How stupid! Billy only wanted to be the one to help his uncle. He would loathe Francis seizing the chance. She limped back to the house and, fumbling in her odds and ends drawer, she tore a piece of linen into strips and sat down on a hard chair. She was almost sobbing with the pain and her own impulsiveness. Lifting her skirt, she saw how her torn stocking clung to the gash on her shin in a mess of blood.

"You imbecile," she said aloud and, gritting her teeth, peeled the stocking down to her shoe. The kettle still held enough water to bathe the wound using some of the linen. It bled copiously but she bound the rest of the linen strips round it and tied them. They were reddened at once but she drew the stocking over them and tucked it under her garter and pulled down her skirt. Jack would find out later and would be all anxious care and solicitude. Joe, she hoped, would notice nothing when he came back.

But where were they? She felt panic rising. They had had more than enough time to come back here. She clasped her face in her hands.

"God in heaven," she breathed aloud. "What has happened to them?" Painfully she got to her feet. I must go and see.

Chapter 24

Billy

Billy had one thought in his mind. Uncle is mine. Francis has taken Lily. He is not to have Uncle too.

He took to the bank side in a series of leaps, just saving himself from landing in the river when he reached the path. A glance along showed him Francis about to round the bend. He galloped after him. Reaching that point, he could see his uncle fifty yards away gathering together his fishing tackle. There was another fisherman walking away at a little distance beyond him.

His uncle had now heard Francis coming and swung round quickly. Billy could guess at the smile of greeting on his face and saw his hands raised in welcome. Next second they clutched his chest. He staggered and uttered a cry which made Billy shudder. In his heart he shrieked, No, you great fool. Not that. Not now!

He broke into a hopeless run to stop the awful thing he could see about to happen. Francis was one stride away from his uncle and made a desperate grab at his arm and the back of his coat as he tottered. It was not enough. Uncle Joe, a big, ponderous, helpless shape, swivelled away from him and fell forwards into the river.

The other man had turned at the cry and, casting aside his own fishing tackle, came running back as Billy, in a few bounds, arrived at the spot.

Francis had dropped to his knees and was scrabbling at his uncle's legs.

The other man was yelling, "You needn't pretend to save him now, you villain. I saw you push him in."

Billy, unheeding of his words, was so desperate to get his uncle out that he thrust Francis aside with such force that he fell against the toppled stool and gasped in pain.

The other man cried, "Well done," and bent down too to help. Billy managed to haul on his uncle's legs and, putting out all his strength, backed across the path to yank the rest of his body free of the water.

The other man said, "Pound his back. Get the water from his lungs."

Francis had stood up, one hand against his ribs, unable to speak, when the other man gave him a blow that knocked him sideways again.

He repeated what he had uttered before. "I saw you push him. If he's dead you're a murderer."

Billy dragged the body over his knees, screaming in his mind, Don't die, you great fool, don't die.

But the head dangled down, and there was no reaction to being slapped hard across the shoulders. With his other hand Billy scoured out the slack mouth, aware already that his uncle was dead. Perhaps he was dead before he fell. He had risen suddenly from long sitting and his heart had seized up.

He looked at the great heavy shape pressing across his thighs, forcing him to believe that this thing had happened. It was a mere moment of time but complete and irrevocable. This was the man he had travelled and talked with that morning who had complained of the bouncing on the rough road, and had seemed both excited and apprehensive about the purpose of his trip. How could he have become this mere lump of flesh?

The fisherman was peering at him. "It's no good, is it? He's gone, hasn't he? What a dreadful thing! But how were you, a miner, happening by at that moment?"

Billy remembered his soot-blackened face.

"He is my uncle. I came off shift to fetch him home."

"Eh, I'm sorry. But we've got the villain who did this and he's in our power for I believe I knocked him senseless. Leastways he's winded."

Fury gripped Billy. Francis had been slow, feeble. I'd have saved him if I'd been closer, he told himself. Uncle is never going to change his will now.

With disgust he rolled the body off his knees and took two steps to Francis, who was gasping where he had fallen. The kick he landed on his body was good and inspired another on his head and another. That was for Lily.

"Nay" – the fisherman was plucking at his arm – "let the law deal with him. I'll testify. I saw him push him in."

The man's words finally struck into Billy's brain. From where he had been standing that was what the man had seen. He had heard a cry, looked round and saw a stout, heavy man fall into the river, a young man right behind him, touching him.

The word 'murderer' had been uttered at some point. A great light flashed like an explosion in Billy's head. This man has seen my brother commit murder. The law hangs murderers. *I* am not to kill Francis. But I can be rid of him.

Like one jumping across stepping stones that thought leapt to another. A murderer cannot inherit from his victim. Again a leap. Did Mother tell Francis he was to be put out of the will? Was he trying *not* to save Uncle when he fell? Was he seizing the moment fate had thrust into his hands? No, never. Francis couldn't – but that was a motive.

He clutched his head in his hands as the thoughts galloped. The law would need a motive.

"I know you are shocked and grief-stricken," the man said, peering again into his face, "but we have to take action now. We need to report this crime but we need help to move your poor uncle, and as for *him* I don't think he can stand."

Billy's thoughts moved even faster. Mother will wonder why we haven't returned. This man wants to be involved. He's a lonely little fellow excited to be in an adventure. I can leave him here in charge. Francis is not dead. His eyes opened when I kicked him and he stared into mine, but he will go nowhere as he is. I can run into the village and get some of my men together to carry Uncle's body, and I will run on to Ovingham for the constable to come and arrest Francis. The plan was no sooner formed than he stood up and spoke it out loud to the fisherman, who nodded eagerly.

Billy asked him, "Is anyone waiting for you at home who will be anxious?"

"Nay, I live alone since the cholera took my poor wife. This is a dreadful thing. Your uncle was a pleasant fellow. We had quite a conversation together. I had just left him when I heard him shout and this villain rushed up and shoved him in the river. What grudge had he got?"

Billy was impatient to be off. "Tell me your name."

"Harry Allthorp from Newburn."

"And I am Billy Heron. I will be very quick and I thank you heartily for your help."

Billy set off, determined *not* to call at Burn Cottage. Let Mother find Harry and learn what account he gave. But as he reached the path up to the waggonway he saw her stepping carefully over the rails. There was no avoiding her.

As soon as she was safely across, she looked up and saw him. "Billy! What's happened?"

"Uncle Joe is dead. I'm going for help. There's a fisherman called Harry Allthorp guarding the body." He brushed past her and ran on, hearing only her cry, "Joe, dead! Oh no!"

At the roadway he hesitated. There might be something in the cottage to implicate Francis. He went in. The light was dim but he saw Francis's books on the table and his coat on the back of the chair. He felt in the pockets. A letter! He took it to the window. The writing was small and feminine. Lily's! The seal was broken so he opened it and read it.

Dearest Francis.

Bitter anger nearly choked him at the words but he cast his eyes rapidly down the few sentences.

Billy came on at me a bit strong yesterday and I had to tell him of our love. I never meant to encourage him but, what is worse, your uncle and aunt seem to have switched their favour to him and he is to be put in your uncle's will in your place. I don't care about the money but I do wish you and he could be friends. I am writing this in haste because I didn't know till this morning that your uncle was going to Wylam too, so I can give it to him for you.

Ever your Lily.

Billy clenched his teeth at 'Ever your Lily'. "Lily was mine," he growled in his throat, but the stupid girl never grasped it. Well, she will lose her precious boy now. Fate is with me at last.

Controlling himself, he folded the letter carefully and replaced it in the jacket pocket. It was vital evidence that Francis knew of the change of will. He must not display any knowledge of the letter himself but he would make sure the authorities found it. He closed the cottage door and set off to the village at top speed.

Chapter 25

Dee

Dee reached the riverbank and, limping round the bend in the footpath, saw a group of figures ahead: a body lying flat, Francis propped against the bankside and a man of short stature fussily arranging fishing gear. Billy of course had not thought Francis's presence worthy of a mention. But she knew that Francis, shocked as he must be, would not leave his uncle's body with a stranger.

She hurried painfully towards them, scarcely believing that the prone shape could be Joe. "We were talking together," she sobbed aloud. "It cannot be!"

The river moved by, full and flowing, indifferent to life or death. She came up to the group and Francis and the man both looked round.

"Oh, thank God!" she heard Francis cry in a weak, choking voice.

When she was close she was thankful to see that the body was face down, no twisted mouth and staring eyes. But she wanted to cover him with something. It was indecent that he should be lying there inert, and his clothes wet, she noticed. Tears bubbled up. You're not there, Joe, I know it, but it's not right you should be flopped here on the path like this. Poor dear man, you overexerted yourself today.

She removed her apron. It was only enough to cover his head and torso but she laid it down and spread it as far as she could. She stepped round the body then and said to Francis, "Did you find him floating in the river?"

He shook his head and lifted his hands. They were tied with a bit of twine; so were his feet. She saw now that he had bruises on his face and blood on his shirt. His eyes met hers and he broke into gasping sobs.

"Oh God," she cried. "Billy did this? Why? What has been going on? Is it not enough that your uncle is dead?"

The fisherman had been practically bouncing up and down in his eagerness to speak. "Harry Allthorp at your service, Lady. I saw it all. *I* tied him up when I thought he might make away. Do you know this villain, Lady? Is he from your village? Did you pass the poor gentleman's nephew who's gone for help?"

Dee stared at him. "*You* tied these knots?" She pulled at the twine but it was strong.

Francis struggled to speak. "He thinks I – oh Ma—" And then his head slid sideways and he fainted away.

Dee dropped on her knees beside him. "My lamb!" She cradled his head in her hands. "What have they done to you?"

"Did he say Ma?" Harry Allthorp gaped at her. "Surely *he* is not your son?"

Dee turned on him. "He is and so is the other. You have mixed them up. Billy must have attacked *him*. But how did Joe…? Oh, what has been going on? I must get my boy to a doctor. Untie him this minute."

The man was flapping his hands before his face. "No, no, they are coming to arrest him. He's just had a bump or two. The other one – Billy – gave him a blow when he saw what he did but I stopped him. I said, 'Let the law deal with him.' I know he was angry. He pulled his uncle out – what strength he had – and tried so hard to save him but he couldn't. I wanted to help but what could *I* do? He's gone for the constable and some men. I'm not as young as I was but he's a mighty strong lad. Are you saying *he* is also your son? They are *brothers*?"

Dee shrieked at him, "Yes, yes, brothers. Billy has half killed him. If anyone is arrested it will be Billy. Get this binding off Francis. He is as innocent as the day."

She pulled the kerchief from her neck and dabbed at Francis's head. She looked up at Allthorp and saw in his eyes uncertainty giving way to stubbornness.

"I know what I saw," he said.

"What did you see?"

Then the man sat down on Joe's stool close to her, peering into her face. A weasel, Dee thought, with instant dislike. From his wide-brimmed hat, sallow face tapering to a weak chin, dun-coloured coat and breeches sagging about a skinny body.

"It's as clear as day what I saw and mighty shocking it was," he said. There was relish in his light voice. "I was talking with this poor gentleman" – pointing to the body – "and had only just left him. In truth I hadn't gone fifty yards when I heard him shout and I swung round and there was this young villain with his hand on his back giving him a shove that made him tumble face down into the river."

Dee cried, "No, no, not this one. You saw the other one, Billy."

"Ay, I did see him, the sooty-faced one, come running from the other direction, from the pit. Ay, I saw him, but he was too far away to do anything. I could see his face as he came up, horror writ all over it, black as he was. The fair lad made as if to grab the poor man's legs when he saw the other fellow – his brother if I'm to believe you – but the force o' the water would have took the body away if the big man – Billy – hadn't pushed this one aside and got a hold o' the legs himself."

"You are grossly mistaken." Dee was feeling in the pocket hanging from her waist for her sewing scissors to cut Francis's bonds but they were not there. They must be in her workbox. "*You* tied these. *You* take them off," she demanded of Harry Allthorp.

"Nay, he's my prisoner. I'm guarding him for Billy Heron when he brings the constable. Ah, here's someone coming."

Dee looked but it was not Billy. Trampling along the riverside path came four miners carrying between them two stretchers.

"Ay, here they are," said one. "Heron said we'd find them here."

"Well, Mistress Heron," said another as they came up, "this is a bad business."

She stood up and faced them. "It is indeed. I don't know what Billy's told you but his brother is grievously hurt and needs a doctor at once. Lift him gently onto that stretcher and carry him home to Burn Cottage. If you have a pocket knife about you, cut this twine round his hands and feet."

"Nay," piped up the little fisherman. "He's my prisoner till the law comes. He sat up before and might have made away if I hadn't tied him up."

"He don't look as if he's going anywhere. This is his mother so I'll just be doing what she says." And the man, whom Dee recognised as Jim Porter, old Elsie's grandson, stepped up and cut the twine.

Harry Allthorp looked outraged but Jim and another man lifted Francis onto the stretcher with Dee hovering by. He winced and opened his eyes.

"It's all right now, my lamb," she said. "You'll be cared for and your hurts seen to."

"Oh Ma, I'm thirsty."

She saw a flask among the fishing gear which was stacked in two piles. This was Harry Allthorp's. She picked up the flask and put it to Francis's lips, lifting his head so he wouldn't choke. He drank greedily and seemed to revive. He's not going to die, my baby, she told herself. Then she handed the flask back to Harry who had watched open-mouthed.

"That's good ale, missus."

"You might have offered him some sooner then."

The other two men had rolled Joe's body onto the spare stretcher. She didn't look at it till they had covered the face. Then she laid his fishing tackle alongside his slack right hand, shuddering as she touched it. She picked up his stool herself and waved the four men forward, following close behind the two carrying Francis. The path was not wide enough for her to walk beside them. Harry, with his own gear over his shoulder, stepped up next to her, with an eye to his prisoner she supposed, but he was of no consequence now. She wanted only to see Francis laid on his own bed so she could tend to him herself. Maybe a doctor was not needed. She feared he had many bruises but perhaps his fainting was due to a bump on the side of his head, made she was sure by Billy's boot, for it had left a sooty mark.

When they had left the river behind and crossed the waggonway Dee expected the bearers to turn towards Burn Cottage.

"What are you doing? His home is that way," she shouted.

Jim Porter looked round. "Heron – your Billy – told us to head to the village. He's coming from Ovingham with the constable and expects to meet us on the way."

"That's right," Harry said, pushing forwards. "He's my prisoner till he's handed over to the law."

"The law!" Dee mocked. "He's never broken a law in his life."

"Oh no?" said one of the men. "There was talk about Holy Francis in a drunken brawl in Newcastle a while back, damaging a church. We have to do what we were told."

Francis lifted his head. "Ma, that will come back to haunt me. You know I wouldn't hurt Uncle for the world. Let me down, fellows. I can walk. I'll face them, Ma."

They readily set the stretcher down and he tried to stand but staggered and clutched at Dee, who had stepped at once to his side. Jim Porter put a hand under his arm to hold him but he cringed in pain.

"I think a rib is broken," he said, "but I can walk with help."

"Then you can walk home," Dee said, "and Jim Porter and I will support you. It's just there, you fool," she told Harry, pointing to the cottage a mere thirty yards away. "Your prisoner!" she scoffed at him. "I'll send word to his godfather, Justice Hammond, and see what *he* has to say to this nonsense."

"Hammond's not the magistrate now," one of the men said. "Got too old to do the work, they say."

Dee stamped her foot, forgetting the pain of her shin. "I know that." She could see beyond the men to groups of people now coming from the village, chattering and pointing. The bearers of Joe's body seemed uncertain where they were to take him.

"To the cottage," she urged therm. "All of you if you must. The gossip vultures are gathering."

The light was fading too. Jack would be home soon. Would he have heard anything at the farm? Somehow she must keep control of this terrible day.

They obeyed her, Harry Allthorp evidently contented as long as he was keeping an eye on 'his prisoner'.

She directed the men with Joe's body to lay it on the bed in Billy's home and cover it decently. Jim Porter told her Billy had said the coroner and a doctor would have to view it and it should be taken to The Black Bull by cart if they could get one.

"All in good time," she told him. "My concern is with Francis."

"A mug o' ale would be welcome, missus," said one of the other men.

She pointed to the larder. "Get it yourself. There are mugs on hooks on the back of the door and a jug of ale on the shelf. Take anything you want."

So while she tended to Francis resting on the box-bed, a bustle of eating and drinking and chatter between five men went on behind her.

When she eased Francis's shirt off his body she saw where he had been kicked, the skin broken in several places. Feeling his side with her fingertips, she found a spot where he squealed with pain.

"Yes," she said, "your rib is cracked. I will bind some strips of cloth round so it won't move."

She was so engrossed with this that she didn't hear Jack come in till he was standing beside her, horror-struck, pleading, "Dee, Dee, my angel, what's to do? Jim says Joe is dead and there's folk gathering outside talking of a murder. And my boy here is hurt. How is it with you, lad?"

"I'll live, Father. Mother's bound me up but my head's throbbing like hell."

"Ay, that's a terrible bruise you have there."

Dee was helping Francis into a clean shirt and before she could begin to explain anything to Jack there was shouting from the men now standing in the doorway.

"Heron's here with the constable and a horse and cart. Now we'll get some action."

Dee looked round. Billy appeared at the door. She saw only a cruel vengeful monster till her eyes cleared and she saw he had washed his face somewhere and stood quietly composed, ushering Constable Brown in front of him. The men were looking to *him* though. He was taller than all of them and had an air of command. He has contrived all this, she thought, the work of the devil.

Constable Brown, a stolid character who valued his dignity, Dee knew, looked about him.

Billy said, almost apologetically, to him, "They have not done as I asked. They should have come direct to you but I trust no harm has been done. Harry Allthorp here is the one who wishes to bring charges."

"Ay," said the little fisherman. "I saw it happen. There is the murderer." He pointed to Francis, sitting up on the side of the bed.

Dee pushed her way through the now crowded room. "And I," she told the constable, "accuse *this* man of viciously attacking his brother."

She looked Billy in the eye. He returned the look steadily. "You yourself, Mother, may be the cause of all this. Did you tell Francis my uncle intended to make me his heir instead of him?"

Heads went up and there was a general gasp of excited interest.

Dee saw at once all the implications of his question. "No, I did not." She looked round at Francis, whose face spoke astonishment.

"Did anyone else then?" Billy asked. "Did Uncle himself tell him?"

Francis rose from the bed and took two steps towards him as the men parted to give room for what looked like an explosive confrontation. "No, he did not. I had barely two words with him."

"Did anyone send you a message?"

Dee reached for the jacket on the back of Francis's chair. "Yes, but here is proof that he never saw it. The seal is unbroken." And she plunged her hand into the pocket.

Francis was urgently calling, "No, Mother," as she drew out her hand and saw to her horror that the seal *was* broken.

Constable Brown took two strides across the room and seized jacket and letter from Dee's limp hand. "These here could be items of evidence. What does it say now?" And he read it through to himself, placed it carefully back in the pocket and tucked the jacket over his arm.

Dee was looking at Francis with disbelief, her mind leaping to the day Mr Hurst had told her about the drunken escapade and she had cried, "Francis! Never!" But it was! Now Joe had had a seizure and Francis had tried to save him from falling in the river. Did he give up trying? No! It was *not* possible. She knew him.

Francis was speaking, desperately searching her eyes with his. "Mother, I was at a problem in my work and I thought of Lily's letter which I had vowed not to look at till I'd finished. I was tempted and took it out and broke the seal and then I thought, I promised Mother and Uncle, but more importantly myself, that I wouldn't, so I put it back. Pray let me see the letter. It is *my* letter but I swear I have not read it."

Dee heard the truth in his voice. How had she dared to doubt him for even a second?

Billy said, "So he had a letter in his hand from his lady-love" – he spat the words out – "and didn't read it. Who would believe that?"

Harry Allthorp was jumping up and down again. "*I* wouldn't. But there's your motive, Constable. I lay my accusation. I did wonder why a young man would kill his own uncle. There's the answer – money! It was ever thus." And he shook his weasel head sadly.

Dee wanted to swipe her hand across his smirking mouth. Even more she would liked to have strangled Billy but she caught sight of Jack sitting on the window seat with his head in his hands. She went to him at once, though Francis's frantic protestations were bombarding her ears.

"Jack, look at me."

He raised his head. There were tears of bewilderment in his eyes. "I don't understand any of it, Dee. What are they all shouting about? Is Joe really dead?"

She said slowly and clearly, "Joe had another seizure – like that other one we saw – but he had been fishing and this time he overbalanced and fell into the river."

Harry broke in, "*She* wasn't there. She didn't see he was pushed. I know what *I* saw."

"Enough of all this," Constable Brown said, stepping forward and laying his hand on Francis's shoulder. "Is your name Francis Heron?"

Francis, silent now and white-faced, nodded.

"Francis Heron, in the name of the king I arrest you for the murder of Joseph Heron. Now come along with me."

Jack jumped to his feet. "What are you doing? He's not well. Murder! You can't suppose *Francis* would murder anyone."

Dee was proud of him as he loomed over the constable, who was solidly built but not tall. Jack's face, though, still showed bewilderment rather than anger.

"Nay, Jack Heron," Brown said. "I've always knowed you as a law-abiding citizen. If the lad here is not guilty he'll be able to show it to the magistrate and to a jury if it comes to the crown court. You'll not interfere with me in the execution of my duty, now will you? As for his well-being, we are not savages. It's a snug wee gaol at my house and if he needs care Doctor Ransom will be sent for. I have a horse and cart outside but he'll have to travel with the body for it needs to be looked at quickly."

He glanced round the room then and asked with some agitation, "Where *is* the body?"

The two who had carried Joe came forward and reassured him that the body was safe and sound next door and no one had interfered with it.

Dee could see that Jack, hearing only a voice of gentle reason, would offer no physical resistance now. He was right too. Unbelievable as it was, the law was going to take its course and anger or violence would not help Francis at all.

"You won't let them, Pa? Ma!"

Dee snatched down her shawl from its peg and the pillow from Francis' bed. "My darling, I'll come with you."

"I too," Jack said.

"I'm the witness," piped up Harry Allthorp.

"Ay, he's got to come, and Billy Heron," the constable said. "You men bring the body to the cart and then get off home to your suppers. The law thanks you for your help as good citizens."

Outside they found half the village, or so it looked to Dee. Voices began yelling when they saw her. "What's your pet lamb been up to then?"

"Learnt bad ways in the town, didn't he? *Saint* Francis!"

"You brought death again, Dee Heron. Two suicides and now a murder."

There were groans of "Aah" and a push forward to look as Joe's body was carried out. Constable Brown tried to make way for the men carrying him.

Dee, shaking, clung close to Jack.

"Is it really Joseph Heron dead?" asked one man. "I served with him in the pit when we was youngsters. A good man."

"Ay, a miner like his father William."

"He got on and made money but see where that's brought him."

Jack was making no effort to hide his tears and Dee was astonished to see a grimace of suffering on Billy's face as he helped to lift the body onto the cart. He turned on the more vociferous voices. "Nay, hold your noise. Show some respect."

They quietened at once and one of the bearers said, "Ay, listen to him. It's his uncle murdered on the very day he's become our Overman."

Some voices murmured then, "We're right sorry, Billy."

A man close to Dee said, "Ay, Billy's a miner. He's one of us."

Francis, held between Harry Allthorp and Jim Porter, was helped into the cart. Dee pushed the cushion at him. "Lie down against the side. Put that under your head." He did so, gritting his teeth with pain.

"Ma, you believe me. I didn't read Lily's letter."

"Yes, yes."

"And wasn't I right that Billy wanted to kill me?"

"Oh yes."

"I feel like death."

"No, it will all come right. You'll be home in no time. They won't let us in the cart but we're following"

There was no room as Harry had climbed up and perched at Francis's feet and Billy had taken his seat next to the constable who held the reins. The crowd followed the cart, so for a moment Dee and Jack clung together unseen. Then she looked up.

"God in heaven! Who is to tell Sarah?"

He shook his head.

"No matter," she said. "Francis is our concern. Come, Jack."

Unheeding of her painful leg, she put her arm through his and they set off on the three miles to Ovingham.

Chapter 26

Jack

When they got home hours later, Jack was as bewildered as ever about what was going on but he was more concerned with Dee's painful limp. He had half carried her most of the way back.

She flopped into the rocking chair and pulled up her skirt. "I hurt my leg."

He looked in horror at the swollen, purple flesh and mess of dried blood marring his perfect Dee.

"It will heal," she said, "but not before Francis comes to trial." There was a shrill edge in her voice which he didn't like to hear. She rushed on, "I cannot believe that the law can act so fast. I cannot believe this fearful day has happened at all."

Jack stood aghast, hands by his sides. What could he do to mend such a wound? She directed him to a basin, cloths and soap. Then he began cautiously to wipe away the blood. The action released his questions. "Why could Francis not come home with us?" "Where's poor Joe's body?" "I never knew why he was here or how he got drownded."

"You heard Harry Allthorp accuse Francis of pushing him into the river."

"Francis would never do that."

"We know that, Jack" – he sensed she was holding back impatience

– "but we weren't *there*, so our word goes for nothing. Billy was there and he backs the man's story. So they will send Francis for trial quite soon and keep him till then in that cell we saw in the constable's basement."

Jack recalled Francis's anger which had upset him more than anything. He had shouted at the magistrate, "You'll regret treating an innocent man like this." He had even seemed angry with them, his parents, for not insisting on taking him home. But Dee had been firm and warned Francis to be quiet and obedient. It was now, enduring his clumsy bathing of her leg, that she seemed tense and fragile. He longed for her to be well and strong!

He dared to ask again, "But what did they *do* with *Joe*?"

She sighed. "They have to find out how he died. Then the coroner will let Sarah have his body for burial."

"But she doesn't even know he's dead yet."

"She will soon. Billy is going to tell her."

"Billy! That's good of him. He'll have to miss his shift."

"Billy – good! He's at the root of all this evil. I can't speak of him. There, that will do. A clean dish-clout can go round my leg. That wee drawer in the dresser."

"Ay, and you must rest it in bed. I'll set the fire for the morning. Can I get you any supper?"

She shook her head. He wasn't hungry either. Mistress Hammond, the former justice's wife, had given them a right good meal, though it had been sad to see the old gentleman hardly recognising them and repeating the name Francis as if he'd never heard it before. Mrs Hammond said, "He can't help you but fear nothing. In a day or two you will have your boy home. We believe in English justice, don't we, Godfrey?"

He had repeated, "English justice," with nods and smiles.

Jack was thankful now for tasks to do. He helped Dee to bed, cleared the grate and laid the fire. He washed the mugs the men had used and swept up their crumbs. As soon as he was in his night shift he brought his candle to the bracket above their bed, hoping Dee was asleep, but he was shocked to find her silently weeping. She clung to him as he slid in beside her and her sobs grew more frantic.

"My angel, what is it?"

"Francis is lying in that tiny prison cell," she choked out.

"Ah, but we mustn't be anxious. Mistress Hammond said all will be well."

"She was trying to soothe us." Her sobbing went on as if it would never stop.

He held her tight, desperate for her to find relief. He hadn't heard her so heartbroken since the moment of their first meeting. The pain he had felt then came pouring back with all that he had promised her. His tears welled up.

"Oh Dee, my angel. You are as sad as you were by the churchyard wall. I was to bring you only joy and gladness." How had he dared to think that was in his power! In his early life he had failed at almost everything he had tried to do. Yet he had put behind him his years of shame when Dee became his wife. She had made him a new man. But here she was, more wretched than ever, and he had no idea how to comfort her. Where did I go wrong, he asked himself, in all those years of marriage?

"Dee, my angel, how has it come to this? I have failed you." Dimly he could see that he had not been a husband or father as he should have been. She had been *his* rock. She had carried the burdens.

She was murmuring, "No, no, no," but the weeping went on, rising as if from a bottomless well. How could he quench it?

"My darling, I am so ashamed," he said. "I brought you to this place when you were used to grand dinners and silk beds and maids and such and you never grumbled. We had children but they seem to have brought only trouble. I haven't been a father as I should. Billy was too clever for me and I never knew how to manage him."

She put her hand over his mouth. "Stop it. Stop it, Jack. It's all the other way about." She sat up and her face was flushed and her eyes wild. She spread out her arms to encompass the room. "Here was your honest family who worked on weekdays and worshipped on Sundays, and into it I came and threw a monster among you, a beast called Billy who has brought us nothing but evil. You have been all love to all of us. It is *my* fault. I should have stayed out of your lives."

"What!" he cried. "You are everything perfect. You brought me all the joy I thought I could never have. A wonderful wife to love and who loves me – that's the miracle – loves me in spite of all my stupidity."

She shook her head. "I tell you, I threw Billy into your midst. That's *my* sin and he is taking a horrible revenge on me, on you, on Joe and on Francis." Her voice cracked on his name and she put her face in her hands and her shoulders heaved.

"My angel, what do you mean? Threw Billy? You gave birth, which was cruelly tough I remember, but if he has grown up wrong that is all *my* fault. I hadn't had a son before and I didn't know how to deal with him."

She withdrew her hands and looked up. Her eyes pierced his. What was coming now? If she said she would leave him it would be the end of life.

"Jack," she said, and the words seemed to be torn out of her, "Billy is *not* your son. You are *not* his father. Billy is my *sin* and if I confess it now before God He may let Francis live."

He swallowed hard and shook his head several times. Her words were making no sense. The word 'sin' linked to his angel was impossible.

"I don't know what you mean," he said.

"Blow out the candle and lie down by me, for this will be the last time you want me here."

"Last time? I cannot do without you. You are my life, my everything."

"Don't talk," she said. "Just listen. But blow out the candle first."

He did so and lay down, frightened of words beyond his understanding.

'Last time' convulsed his mind. He wanted to hold her tight but she eased away from him, lying flat on her back and speaking it seemed to the rafters.

"When you saw me by the churchyard wall I was desolate for many reasons. Everything I had known, a fine house – as you call it – pretty clothes, parties, had been snatched away in a moment."

"You said you were weary of those things," he pleaded.

"Don't interrupt. It's true. They were tedious but losing them was a shock. Finding my parents broken people was a shock too. Finding my betrothed didn't love me was a worse shock."

"You told me you hated him."

"Pray, keep silence. This is hard enough. I *did* hate him – when he deserted me. Worst of all I feared he had left me with child."

He let his mouth hang open. Words should be spoken but he could frame none.

She hurried on after a pause. "I had no one. My mother turned me out and my father was a drunkard. I felt God had deserted me. And then he sent you. My saviour."

"*I* your saviour!" He rolled closer to her. "If I was ever your saviour you won't let it stop, will you?" He was desperate to feel her in his arms. His one dread was that she would turn away from him.

"Do you realise what I am saying?" Was she exasperated by his slowness? "I deceived you. I let you and your family believe the child was yours. I did evil."

"Never, you couldn't." He hesitated, unsure if he had grasped her meaning. "Are you saying Billy is the other man's child? Is that right?"

"Yes, yes, yes, but it was not right, it was wrong. I made you be the father."

It was growing upon him that Billy had not come from him and that was a strange kind of relief. Billy had never had any likeness to him. He had always seemed a strange being and now he was confirmed as such.

"But it doesn't change anything between you and me?" he pleaded.

"Doesn't change anything! What! You are not hurt, not angry?"

"Angry with you? Oh Dee! I was so frightened just now that you were going to leave me."

She was silent for what seemed to him a long moment, then she was in his arms, clutching at him, squeezing him to her breast, feeling for his face and kissing him with passion. Her tears had gone. She was almost laughing. All his joy and confidence flowed back. He still had Dee's love. With that he could face whatever other trials they were to go through.

He could not hold back and they made love, she with a sort of desperate enthusiasm that was new and wonderful to him. He forgot her poor leg till they both sank back on the pillows and she said, "Bother, it's bleeding again."

When he would have risen to fetch more cloths she held him back.

"No matter. I am too tired. I must sleep. Let God take care of the morrow."

He was asleep himself in another minute.

Every morning he had his routine – rise, light the fire, fill up the coal bucket, fetch water. Dee got up then and prepared their porridge when the fire was hot enough. This morning she had performed all his tasks and her own while he slept. He leapt up.

"Have I slept late?"

"Nay, I was early." She read the mantelshelf clock. "You have plenty of time. Sit and eat your porridge." She sat too and placed her clasped hands on the table and compelled his attention. "Do you remember what I told you last night?"

"Ay, I do that. Billy is not mine. He's the bad man's son."

"And was not I bad too? I need you to understand so you can forgive me."

He scratched his head. "*I* forgive *you*? You – bad? Nay, you and he were betrothed so it was not a sin. After all you and I – I mind Jenny Coxon saying it was right to do it." All the same the thought of her and a strange man must be blotted out. He blustered on, "He was a bad man so he likely forced you. If I had him here I'd knock him down."

"Oh Jack!" She was smiling. That was a lovely sight. "But I loved you and I didn't tell you, all these years. Can you forgive *that*?" The smile had gone and her eyes were glistening.

He scratched his head again. "I reckon you'd want to forget all about the bad man and want me to be a father to Billy. I didn't do it well but maybe if I'd thought he was someone else's I'd ha' been no good at all." He didn't want this talk. He wanted only to go off to work thinking of how last night had ended.

She got up and kissed the top of his head. That was good and was perhaps the end of the matter. But his mind switched to the loss of his brother and he thought of Joe's domination and how small and despised he had felt as a boy. That prompted another thought which he spoke out loud as she sat and resumed her porridge.

"Dee, if you'd told everyone about Billy he would have felt left out, like not part of the family." That was a good point and he was proud to have thought of it.

She was very quiet after that so he supposed there need be no more talk of the past. When she next spoke it was about the present.

"I ought to take Francis's work to Mr Trace and tell him what's happened."

"That's in Newcastle. What about your poor leg?" He was chewing his thumbnail when they began to hear voices outside and a rush of footsteps.

"Dee Heron! Are you at home?"

Jack saw Dee jump up to shoot the bolt but she was too late. The door burst open. He scrambled round the table to protect her.

The foremost man was Jim Porter. "I came ahead to warn you."

Faces appeared behind him. "There's newspaper men all over the village. They'll be here in a jiffy."

"You can't all come in," Jack said. "Go away. We're having breakfast." He made shooing motions.

"What newspaper men?" Dee demanded. "Where have they come from?"

"From Newcastle."

Jim said, "You can't hide from them, Jack. It's known all over now that there's been a murder. They went to Newburn and roused the fisherman to tell his tale. Then they came on to Ovingham and saw the constable but they weren't let in to see the prisoner so they soon found out where his home was. Here they come."

Voices in the crowd were shouting, "Let's see where the body was laid," and some went into Billy's place to look.

Others said, "Where was he pushed in the river?"

"I'll show you." Jim took several away with him across the waggonway.

"Eh Jack," said their neighbour the engine driver, "it's a terrible thing to have your lad in gaol for murder. And Billy cannot lie about it in court for another fellow saw it too. Your Joe was going to change his will, eh? And Francis got wind of it."

Jack stared at him but Dee screamed at them all hanging around the door, "Get out of our house. Francis is innocent. He knew nothing of any change of will. Don't you dare spread that round. Who is going to print such a tale?"

"My paper will, missus." A young man in city dress pushed his way in, followed by another, older and grey-haired. "From the *Chronicle*," said the first.

"From the *Courant*, ma'am" said the other. "*I* would like to hear *your* story."

"I cannot leave you with these strangers," Jack said, with his arm round Dee, while his other hand, still grasping his spoon, reached for his porridge bowl and scraped out the rest of it. "I must get to work. You won't go to Newcastle?"

Dee shook her head. "Mr Trace will know. The news is there already."

"A local murder," the *Chronicle* reporter said with a grin, "travels like wildfire. It was known last night. Your magistrate wants it heard at the Assizes coming up next week. If your boy is the accused he's lucky. Some prisoners wait months in prison for the Assizes. They only come twice a year, you know."

Jack had no idea what Assizes were. They seemed to be a place and yet they could move about, presumably in pairs.

Dee said, "I will go and comfort Francis if one of these gentlemen on returning to town will take this package to Mr Trace, the engineer at Heaton.

It is the work my son had to hand in today. He finished it yesterday and went to help his uncle home with his fishing tackle. He ends up being accused of murdering him."

Jack marvelled at the way Dee could talk to these people, though her chin trembled on the last words. The older man held out his hand for the package.

"I will be pleased to deliver it and talk with Mr Trace. I only wish to report all that I learn, not to speculate or prejudge." He glanced at the *Chronicle* reporter.

Dee thanked him and Jack thought, He's a kind man. She's safe with him.

Then she said, "Go to work, Jack. We have to earn our bread if we are to help Francis." Yes, he thought, that is what I can do. I can go to work.

As he took his hat from its peg Dee whispered, "What I told you last night is our secret. Remember!"

He nodded solemnly several times. It was a huge privilege to share something with Dee that no one else knew. All the same as he set off across the field to the farm buildings he was a little sorry that the truth must remain hidden. He still wasn't clear what Billy had done. Maybe he had pushed Joe into the river and was blaming it on Francis, but certainly Dee was sure that Billy was at the bottom of all this trouble and it would have been good to be able to tell people, "Well, Billy is not *my* son."

The farm manager met him at the gate. "This is a bad business, Heron. I'm very sorry you have lost your brother. I wondered if you would be at work today. Don't mind what folks say, at least the animals know nothing." He gave an uneasy smile. "Too many rumours. The truth will come out in court."

Jack nodded. It hadn't struck him before but he had now lost his father, mother and brother. I am all that is left of my childhood family, he told himself. I would be desolate but that I have Dee.

He lifted his head, thinking of her passion last night. Nothing could stop that happening again and again. As long as I have Dee I am all right, he thought, and he went to feed the pigs.

Chapter 27

Lily

Lily was awakened by a loud banging on the front door. She prodded Gertie whose head was buried beneath the covers.

They both sat up and listened. It was pitch dark.

"Why doesn't Sammy go?" whispered Gertie.

At Sarah's insistence, when Joseph was away, Sammy, the handyman, slept on a truckle bed in the hallway.

"He was drunk last night," Lily said. They heard stirring below. "Madam has risen. We must get up and attend her."

"I shan't." Gertie stayed resolutely in bed.

Lily flung her shawl round her shoulders and felt her way out of the room to see the dim shape of her mistress on the landing below, lit by the candle in her hand. The knocking continued.

"Sammy!" she heard Sarah call down, and finally Sammy must have reared up because she heard the front door bolts being drawn back.

"Oh, Mr Heron!" Lily heard him exclaim. Goodness, she thought, the master's back in the dead of the night, and then with a shiver of fright she heard Billy's voice.

"I have to speak with your mistress."

Her first instinct was to get back into her room and into bed with Gertie where he would surely not come but she must hear what had brought him. She leant over the banister.

Sarah was descending to the hall, exclaiming, "Billy! What is this? It's the middle of the night! Sammy, go to the kitchen and stir up the fire and light candles."

The street gaslight coming through the window showed Lily the tall figure of Billy take Sarah by the shoulders. His voice came up strong and clear.

"Be brave, Aunt. Your husband is dead and my brother has been accused of his murder."

He had to hold her or she would have fallen. Lily stood frozen for a second before she found herself plunging down the stairs in a wild run.

"Billy! Billy! What are you saying?"

He turned to her, grim-faced. "You up, Lily? You chose badly. Your Francis will surely hang."

She recoiled from him. "Hang! Oh no, never. This is *your* work. This is your *revenge*. You are a devil."

"It may be *your* work, Lily. *You* told him his uncle was to change his will."

"What! What are you saying?" She clasped her face in her hands. "My letter!"

"Should you not see to your mistress?" He was supporting Sarah in a complete state of collapse.

Sammy came from the kitchen with a candle in each hand. Lily was so overwhelmed with fear and horror herself that she could hardly stand but she managed to think of smelling-salts and the warmth of the kitchen.

"Sammy, take Madam in by the fire. Her salts are on the mantelshelf." She was desperate to question Billy alone but he kept hold of his aunt till she was in the rocking chair by the kitchen fire and Sammy was fiddling with the salts. She had to follow and took the salts bottle from him. Her hands shook so much that Billy snatched it from her and, removing the stopper, shoved it under Sarah's nose.

She gasped and struggled to stand up. Billy repeated the same words he had said in the hallway. She sank back but her eyes were now fully alert. "What are you telling me? Was it not yesterday that you and Joseph went to Wylam?"

"Yes, and Francis was there and this silly girl must have sent a letter to him saying Uncle was to change his will in my favour, so he took him fishing, shoved him in the river and he drowned."

The face Sarah turned to Lily was a sight she would never forget.

Lily fell on her knees at her feet. "Oh ma'am, I did, but Francis would never – you can't think – we never wanted anyone's money – you *know* Francis."

Sarah was shaking her head. "People do strange things for wealth." She looked up at Billy and an odd look passed between them. "So I am a widow, am I? I can't believe that without seeing him. Where is he?"

"His body is in the care of the coroner in Ovingham."

"And were you there when this happened and couldn't stop it?"

Lily jumped up and shrieked at her, "*He* did it and is trying to blame Francis."

Billy said in a level voice as if she hadn't spoken, "I was going to bring Uncle home to Mother's and when I came in sight of them there was another man there too, a fisherman further on. He was nearer than I when Francis just gave Uncle a small push, enough to overbalance him, and in he fell."

"Joe can't swim," Sarah said. "Could you not get him out?"

"Of course. I ran to him but he was face down. I hauled on his legs and got him onto the bank and worked to get the water from his lungs but it was to no avail."

Sarah sat, nodding, with her hands folded in her lap. "I thought to be widowed one day. He had these seizures. Murder I did *not* expect and certainly not by a member of the family."

Lily took up her words. "But of course it was a seizure. I've seen the master totter about when he had suffered one."

Sarah looked coldly up at her. "You don't want to be the cause, do you? You sent that message to Francis! What about the fisherman – the independent witness?"

Billy remarked almost casually, "He is the trouble of course. Whatever *I* saw I could have covered up to save my brother. But it is the fisherman who has brought charges. He will be called upon as chief witness when it comes to court."

"So there will be a trial?" his aunt said.

Lily grabbed hold of Billy's arm. "Oh, where is Francis now? What have they done with him?"

He shook off her hand. "Locked up of course. Murderers are not allowed to wander the streets."

"I'll go to him. Oh ma'am, you must give me leave. Where is he locked up?"

"In the gaol in Ovingham but today he is likely to be moved here to Newcastle in readiness for the Assizes."

"Oh, then I can visit him easily. Where is the gaol?"

Her mistress rose and glowered down at her. "You forget yourself, girl. You go nowhere today. Is this a time for you to go gallivanting when the master of the house has just died?"

For a second Lily was appalled at her own thoughtlessness but the picture of Francis under sentence of death reared up before her eyes.

"I'm sorry, ma'am," she said. "If I make you a cordial would you return to bed now and try to sleep?" She resolved that as soon as her mistress was resting and it was broad daylight she would go out and find the gaol whatever the consequences.

The grandfather clock in the hall struck four.

"I want nothing but to have speech alone with my nephew," Sarah said. "Go back to bed yourself, and you, Sammy."

Lily realised with a start that Sammy, having placed the candles in their wall brackets, had been standing by the door listening to everything.

"Have I to stay down here, ma'am?" he asked.

"No, get to your own bed. Be off with you, both of you." Her voice for the first time quivered with emotion.

Sammy grabbed one of the candles to light their way upstairs. Lily longed to vent her fury with Billy in words but the enormity of what had happened bereft her of speech. She followed Sammy and heard Billy shut the door firmly behind them.

Gertie had pulled the covers to her side and was fast asleep, completely enveloped. Lily drew close to her for warmth but sleep was out of the question.

Billy

"So, Billy, what *really* happened?" His aunt waved him to the three-legged stool at the other side of the fire. "If my Joseph has gone I have a right to know."

He perched his big frame on the stool and felt at a disadvantage. He could see her eyes were brimming but she was trying not to let one tear fall.

"It was all just as I told you," he said. "I cannot stay long. I will be given time off to attend court if needed but I must return to the pit now."

"No, you must give me the whole story. Then I can judge for myself what is true."

He gave her an account of yesterday afternoon with the scene in Justice Harker's house in Ovingham where the constable made his report and produced Lily's letter. The magistrate read it, interrogated the fisherman and decided there was a case to answer. Francis was charged with murder and would be tried at the coming Assizes.

"And did he not interrogate you?" she asked.

"Briefly. But the fisherman was much closer than I."

"And were your parents at this hearing?"

"They arrived late."

"And what did they think of the outcome?"

"They are very upset, naturally."

"Naturally." She repeated the word with scorn. "And just as naturally they don't believe for a moment in Francis's guilt. Any more than I do. Lily spoke a true word just now when she said I know Francis. It is plain to me what happened. My poor Joe had a seizure and tumbled into the river. You saw it happen and you knew he had had no time to change his will in your favour so—"

Billy leapt up, overturning the stool. "That is a terrible line of thought, Aunt Sarah. It was not I that got Francis charged but this fisherman—"

"Whom you bribed with my fifty pounds."

He stared at her, horrified. "I did *not*." He reached into the inner pocket of his great coat. "There's your money."

She held up her hand for it and he put it away at once.

"If you spread such a tale," he said, "you know what I can do. I have had no chance to speak to my mother but when all this is over I will tell her and the law what you were up to all those years."

She sat very still, her brows drawn together in a deep frown. He thought, She knows what a hold I have over her and that I'll use it if she thwarts me in any way. Uncle's will still stands but if there is no Francis it is she now who must make me her heir. I'll see that she does.

She looked up at him at last, meeting his eye. "I believe you are the devil incarnate. Leave me. I must see my Joe's body. I must go to Ovingham or wherever it is. I won't travel with you. I will hire a post-chaise. Go away. Get out of my sight."

He set the stool on its legs and backed to the hall door.

At the door he said, "I grieve for Uncle Joe and for you in his loss but you do not need to go anywhere. They will come and tell you the coroner's findings and bring him to you, possibly today, so that you can make arrangements for the funeral."

She inclined her head and he left, letting himself out. The new March day was just showing a flicker of light in the east. He climbed the hill with difficulty, for his legs were shaking. There was too much of the witch about Aunt Sarah and when she had stared at him so piercingly and called him a devil, it was as if she had put a curse upon him. He was angry with himself for letting her affect him for he had always scorned the superstitions of the miners and their wives.

The walk to Wylam will put me right and clear my head for what comes next, he reassured himself.

Looking back towards the river he saw the shimmering snake of it as it slid under the bridge towards the sea. The shapes of colliers waiting for the days' coal showed up beyond the bridge. One day it would be his own boats heading for London with the coal from his own pits.

The thought renewed him and he strode on.

Chapter 28

Dee

It was mid-morning and Dee was on her way to the new Moot Hall in Newcastle where she had learnt Francis had already been taken. Mrs Hammond had lent her her own carriage and groom.

"Will Jack go with you?" she had asked, "for I cannot leave Godfrey so long."

Dee told her he was at the farm. "This horror is all too much for him. He is better working. I will do well alone but how can I ever thank you?"

As she leant back in the carriage she felt her painful leg blessedly rested but her brain pulsated with a mass of horrible images. She had sworn a thousand times to herself in the early hours of the morning that this was all a ridiculous mistake which would be swiftly resolved, but the impassive face and cold eyes of Justice Harker when he committed Francis for trial kept coming back to her. A trial led to a verdict and a guilty verdict led to the gallows. Her imagination put her boy there, so young, so sweet, so innocent and she could scarcely stop herself from screaming aloud.

Behind it all the image of her other son loomed, a black shadow, but a human being that surely she could work on to prevent this awful culmination. Jack's words, spoken so slowly and weightily at breakfast, hung in her mind. "If you'd told everyone about Billy he would have felt left out, like not one of the family."

But I did leave him out, she thought now with fearful clarity. From the very beginning I wanted none of him. Newborn, I hated the look of him. Toddling, he went to Jack to be played with. When he was so ill I fought for him to stay alive for I feared in my heart that I wished him dead. And that would have made *me* a monster. But I *was* a monster to him. I was no mother. Oh God, what have I done? I have reared a fiend to bring misery and destruction upon us all. Is it too late? It must not be too late. I hoped last night that by confessing my sin all would be well. But there has been no penance done, for Jack cannot blame me for anything. He would not have it as a confession. My punishment is still to come.

She sat with her hands pressed over her eyes and tried silently to speak words of contrition. She found no ease. Soon she would see Francis and what hope or comfort could she bring him?

The carriage stopped and she peeped round the window curtain. They were in a wide square with people scurrying to a newsstand where a boy of about ten waved a printed sheet with 'WYLAM MURDER' at the top of the page. He broke into a shrill shout. "Horrid murder at Wylam. Buy your newssheet here. Only one penny. Nephew drowns uncle. Murder on the River Tyne. Only a penny. Thank 'e sir. Thank 'e miss."

Dee sank back. Dear God, he is condemned already!

Mrs Hammond's groom came round to the window.

"We're here, Misses Heron. I'll need to find an inn stable to feed the horse and brush him down. Will I come back for you in an hour?" He handed her down.

"If you please." She gaped as she looked up at the grand entrance to the Moot Hall, starkly new in pale shiny stone. There were wide steps up to a portico with four great columns. It's a palace, she thought. I cannot be allowed in there.

As the groom climbed back onto his perch it came to her that he must believe she was a murderer's mother. If I were a lady he would have gone forward and made inquiries himself and escorted me to the right door. Now, heaven help me, Francis is in here somewhere and how I am to find him I know not.

She looked all round the cobbled area and saw on the opposite side the ancient castle of blackened stone that gave the town its name. That is more like a prison, she thought. As the carriage rattled away she felt lost and desolate.

But people were about, some dressed in black coats – court officials perhaps –and also ordinary members of the public like herself. Shunning the magnificent entrance she walked round the side. The ground sloped down and there were small windows lower than the front of the building. Perhaps those were the cells. An inconspicuous door opened and the slight figure of a girl emerged, shawl pulled close over her bowed head and obviously weeping.

Some instinct made her stop in front of her and say, "Lily?"

The girl lifted her head and her hands went to her mouth in a gesture of dismay. "Oh, Mistress Heron!" She seemed to cringe before her. "Oh, forgive me. It is all my fault. That wretched letter."

"You have seen him? Take me to him."

"I have had my few minutes. It was all I was allowed. He is so distressed. He cannot believe it is happening. I wish I had died rather than writ that letter."

"But he never read it."

"So he tells me but they found it and they believe that's why—" She couldn't go on.

Dee was shaking her head and putting out her arms to enclose her in a desperate embrace. "I was the one who drew their attention to it, fool that I was, believing the seal was unbroken and it would exonerate him. They might not have found it else." Although, she remembered now, Billy had said, "Did you receive any message?" Billy! It was all his plot. He must have known of Lily's letter. It all comes back to Billy, she thought, and Billy, God help me, is all *my* fault.

She released Lily. "Go home, my child. Tell your mother what has happened. We must gather all that know Francis to testify that he could not have done this thing."

Lily murmured, "I will, but first I have to go back to Madam. I'll be in trouble for coming out. But thank you. I feared you would be so angry with me."

"Madam?" Dee repeated. "Oh heavens, Sarah! God forgive me, I had forgotten her. How has she taken it?"

"Very shocked. Billy just told it straight out but she's a brave woman. I do admire her."

Dee nodded. "Go back to her but don't tell her you saw me. I cannot call upon her now." Nothing must keep her from Francis.

"We will save him, won't we, Mistress Heron?"

"Of course, of course."

They went their ways. An official of some sort stood in the doorway observing their meeting. She approached him.

"To see Francis Heron?" he barked.

"I am his mother."

Without a word he led the way down a flight of stairs. At the foot he unlocked a door.

"I can give you the quarter hour. If that basket is provisions for him, give it to me. He'll get it when it's been searched. But they are all well fed and cared for and *he's* even had a medical man look at him. You speak through the bars. No touching – you'll be slipping him something so he can foil the hangman."

She was in a stone vaulted passage from which rooms led off. The upper half of each door was open with bars across.

"He's in Number Three," the man said. "I'll be watching ye."

Dee, shivering and shaking, barely glanced in the first two cells but was just aware that there was more than one inmate in each and that shouts came at her, either raucous or pleading, as she passed. Then she was looking into Number Three and there was her own boy alone, curled on his bed with his back to her. Was he asleep? She glanced round the room. It was clean with a fireplace but no fire and a small high up window through which the bright day could just be seen.

"Francis!" she called.

He rolled over. "Mother!" He got to his feet with a grimace of pain and staggered to the bars, clutching them convulsively. "How did you find me? Did you see Lily? Oh, have you come to take me home?"

He was reaching for her hand but she shrank back.

"He said no touching. No, I cannot take you home today but we will have you free soon. And I have sent your work to Mr Trace and he and Mr Hurst will speak up for you." She hardly knew what she was saying. His appearance shocked her. He was not pale but flushed and bore a strong resemblance to Jack when distressed at something. Jack would run his hands through his hair, making his fair curls unkempt, as Francis's were now. His cheeks would go red and his eyes frightened like their poor boy's.

Oh, how she longed to take Francis into her arms as she would Jack at those times and hold him till he was reassured by her love. This was a situation a thousand times more desperate and she must not even squeeze his hand.

"My precious," she breathed. "How are your hurts – your sore rib?"

"Oh, a man claiming to be a doctor saw me when they brought me here. He said I would be well enough for mounting the gallows."

His casual tone was belied by the trembling of his lips.

"How dare he! That will never happen. Mistress Hammond – she lent me their carriage – has absolute faith in English justice."

"But Billy – did I not always say I feared he would kill me one day?" Now all his pent-up thoughts began to pour from him. "This is how he'll do it. But I can't die, Ma. I am going to be an engineer and marry Lily. Did you meet her? She only just left me. God couldn't let Billy win over me, surely? I've been trying to pray but it's so unjust. I couldn't find words."

"No words," she said. "God knows you and He will raise up everyone on this earth who knows you to testify to your character. Yes, I met Lily. She will tell all her family, and Sarah too loves you, the widow of your supposed victim. She knows you could not have done such a thing."

"But did she not persuade Uncle to change his will? They will make so much of that, though I never knew of it, but they don't believe me because I broke the seal. You believe me, don't you?"

Dee spoke through her tears. "Of course I do, and curse myself for taking the letter from your pocket in front of the constable."

"They searched everything I had with me. They would have found it. But Uncle must have told Billy of his plan. Why? Had I offended him? I have been racking my brains. Was it that wretched drunken spree? Oh Ma, that was not a hanging crime. I've gone over and over it all. What had that fisherman against me? Billy has him in his pocket. He saw me push Uncle. That's what he is sticking to. Of course he may have seen my hand. I was trying to grab his arm or coat or something when I saw him totter. Billy must know he had a seizure. Uncle was facing towards him when his hands went to his chest. I was behind but he made a noise and I knew what was happening. I thought he would sink back onto the bank but as I put my hands up to support him he seemed to twirl round in pain. His feet tangled up I think. It all happened so quickly. He's a big heavy man. I couldn't stop his fall."

Dee broke in. "Nay, my darling, I know, I know. And if you tell it all like that to a jury they will know you are speaking the truth."

He looked aghast. "You think it will come to a trial then? Can they not be convinced before that?"

"Oh, I am sure they can." Dee spoke vehemently but doubted in her heart who *they* were. Justice Harker had swiftly decided there was a case to answer and the processes of the law must now be followed. That was why Francis was locked up here and had she not heard it said that the Assize judges were coming next week and this case would go forward with others that had been awaiting their visit? Mrs Hammond had told her the Assizes were held only twice a year in the provinces and they came to Newcastle during Lent and in the summer. It was Lent now.

Francis, still holding the bars, was protesting that Billy must have known their uncle was dying when he fell. "So he made his plan when the fisherman said I pushed him. Was that not the devil's work – to think all this out so fast? Lily believes he hates me because of her and that upsets her terribly. I told her he has always hated me. Is that not true, Mother?"

She nodded, speechless. She had nearly burst out with a confession of her own guilt but she held herself back. It was not the time to crowd Francis's mind with more disturbing thoughts. He needed to trust her to save him and she must be the rock he had always believed her to be.

The gaoler was approaching. "Time, missus."

Her fingers itched to grip Francis's as he tried to reach her through the bars.

"I am going to talk to Billy," she said urgently. "Think no more of him. Think of the life you will have when this is all over. I can love Lily as the daughter I lost. She is a sweet child and loves you dearly."

"I know," he gulped. "Oh Ma, don't go. When can you come again? Will Father come?"

"I don't know. Perhaps it would be too bewildering. You understand?"

He inclined his head, biting his lower lip.

The gaoler was pulling on her arm.

"My darling one," she said, desperately holding back tears, "be brave. All will be well."

He pressed his face to the bars to see her to the last moment. She felt it like a physical tear in her heart when she could no longer see him.

Blindly she climbed the stairs to the open air, convulsed with sobs, and had to lean against the wall outside till she had recovered enough to retrace her steps to where she had been set down by the surly groom. He was not there yet.

There was a bench against the wall of the Castle Keep and she sank down on it. She had promised to speak to Billy and though the thought of it filled her with dread it also put steel into her. It was something she could do to save Francis. She would do it and succeed. The determination helped her to dry her eyes and get up steadily when the Hammond carriage drew up.

Chapter 29

Billy

Billy was awakened from a profound sleep by somebody shaking him. He saw he was lying fully-clothed on his own bed and it was broad daylight but sleep was tugging him back. His eyes would have closed again but he heard his father's voice repeating over and over, "Where's your mother, Billy?"

"Not my business. Let me alone," he mumbled.

"She went to see Francis but she should be home. She may have collapsed. Her leg was painful. Why are you not at the pit? Everything is out of order and I don't know where she is."

Billy had now sat up but longed to lie down again. He could only get rid of his father by answering his questions.

"Francis is in prison in Newcastle. She'll be home later. I walked there and back overnight and went to work. At midday the Viewer sent me home to sleep. So will you go away now? Surely *you* should be at work."

"Ay, but I got leave too. Are you telling me she went all the way to town?"

Billy turned his head to read his grandmother's clock on the mantelshelf. He had only been asleep ten minutes. He glared at his father. The round, weather-beaten face and troubled eyes infuriated him.

He said in a loud voice, "She'll come home later. Now go back to work."

He lay down facing the wall and heard his father move away, murmuring,

"Yes, go back to work. If you're sure, Billy." Then the latch clicked and he was asleep again at once.

The next time he woke he could hear voices outside. His father's *and* his mother's. His father was saying, "He didn't like me waking him."

His mother said, "You told me that was hours ago."

"Ay, but we must eat first."

"Nay, you eat. I cannot eat till I have spoken with him. I thought he would be at work. Now you come home and tell me he has been next door all this time."

Billy swung his legs off the bed. Looking at the clock he saw he had had at least five good hours of sleep. He strode to the door and opened it.

"If you've something to say, Ma, come in and say it."

He held the door open for her, noting her red eyes and pale drawn look. She has aged in a couple of days, he thought, but felt no pity for her.

She lifted her head, braced her back and came in.

"I have no comfortable chair," he said. "If you are staying more than two minutes there is the bed."

"I am staying long enough to turn you aside from the path you are on, Billy."

"What path?"

"The path that may lead to the death of your brother."

"Huh! That is not *my* path. *I* am not the prosecutor. If that's all you've come to say you'd better go and eat with Da and leave me alone. Your boy is in the hands of the law. If he gets clear well and good, if not…" He shrugged his shoulders and turned from her to see what was in his larder for he suddenly felt ravenously hungry.

She came after him and plucked at his arm. "I knew you might take that line but it will not do. You call Francis my boy. You are also my boy."

"Am I?" He looked round at her briefly and saw her eyes were startled. "It has not always seemed so," he added.

The startled look went and her face began to crumple. She put a hand over her mouth and retreated to the bed and flopped down onto it. He shut the larder door and stood staring at this phenomenon of his tough mother disintegrating before his eyes.

"Oh Billy," she moaned. "I haven't loved you as a mother should."

He gave a harsh laugh. "I was a bad boy so you couldn't love me."

She shook her head vehemently. "Oh, no, no. It was because I never loved you that you were a bad boy." Her wet eyes pleaded with him at this confession. He was struck by it but he would not ponder it now.

"Well," he said, "I am a man now and you are too late with such notions. You had better go back to Da. You always had enough love for him and baby Francis."

He stepped to the outer door and opened it.

"Oh Billy, no. It can never be too late to do right. It is in your power to stop this trial. You could not live with the thought that you let your brother die."

He stamped his foot. "You keep saying that. *I* am not the witness who may convict him. That fisherman saw him push our uncle."

"You were there. Francis knows he had a seizure and you saw it too."

"I was fifty yards away. I know no such thing."

"But you know Francis could never deliberately harm anyone."

"No, I don't. I don't know him at all. He was tempted by anger that Uncle would change his will. So he gave him a shove. He may regret it now but it's too late." He still stood holding the door for her to go.

Then his father opened their door and called, "Are you coming, Dee? I won't eat till you come and I'm hungry."

Billy smelt a savoury aroma and yearned for his mother's beef stew.

She had risen from the bed. Her face was distraught. "Have I really failed to move you, Billy? How will you answer *God* at the day of judgment?"

"Maybe God was invented by priests to frighten us. Go. Father is hungry too."

"Oh Billy, you speak blasphemy." She peered up at him. How small she was! She seemed to have shrunk. "If *you* are hungry, will you not come and eat with us?"

He was tempted but she would work on him and he would not beg for some dinner to eat here. "I have plenty." He drove her out and bolted the door after her.

Immediately he knew he had made a horrible mistake. He was left with nothing but his own thoughts which he dare not let loose. God's wrath. Mother's confession. His own childhood. He brought shutters down upon them all. Pulling on his coat, checking he still had his aunt's money in the inner pocket, he softly unlatched his door and set off at a fast pace to the village inn.

When he pushed open the inn door he heard shouts of "Why, it's Billy Heron! He'll know all the answers." Good, he thought, I can sway opinion here.

He called to the drawer, "A mug of ale and one of your pork pies."

The innkeeper's wife beckoned him to a bench near the fire and the men there made room for him. She leaned over his shoulder and cooed, "Come on, Billy, tell us truly. Is your brother guilty or no?"

"I hoped not to speak of it," he began to a chorus of protest. "It's horrible. My own brother. I would lie in court to save him but it is not I who brings the charge."

"Folks are saying he did it for the money," said one.

"Nay, I know not," Billy said. "There was nothing planned for he had only just had word that our uncle was leaving him out of his will. I suppose he went along the river path to find him and ask him why. Maybe our uncle angered him in his answer. I was not there. I was not privy to any words that passed between them."

"Ay, but when did you come on the scene?" another asked.

Billy shrugged. "I had just come off shift and my mother said my uncle had been fishing and Francis had gone to help him carry his tackle. I felt uneasy. My uncle had told me about the will so I went along too to keep the peace."

The innkeeper's wife pushed her face, red and perspiring from the fire, close to his ear. "Now, tell us what you saw, exactly, for we have all heard different tales."

"I saw my uncle fall."

"Ah, but was he pushed? The judge'll make you speak out. They call it purgation if you tell a lie you know."

"Perjury, you silly woman," said her husband.

"That's what I said. And 'tis a hanging matter."

"Nay, it's not," several voices said, "but the courts don't like it."

There was an argument then but the innkeeper's wife pressed on. "You saw your brother push him, didn't you, but you don't like to say?"

Billy was rehearsing the words he would use in court. "I saw his hand was behind my uncle's back and then he fell forward. If I'd been on the other side where the fisherman was and so much closer I could be clearer. I won't *swear* it was a push."

"That'll be good enough for a jury to convict him," she said, "with Harry's testimony. Eh, fancy a murder in our own village! I tell you, Billy, I never took to your Francis. Our Len was at Mr Hurst's school the short time Francis was there. He always said he was a spoilt brat. And then your ma taught him at home so he never played with the village lads. Then he was sent to town and got town airs and talked like gentry. He wouldn't go down the pit like you. He'd want your uncle's money to be a real gent without working for it. Eh, I can see it all. He thought one little push and Uncle'll not be changing his will. He didn't know Harry Allthorp was watching."

Everyone had fallen silent to hear this conversation but the chatter buzzed out again in a general discussion about Francis's character. All had heard about his drunken spree and greatly exaggerated the damage his 'gang' had caused in the town.

One old miner said thoughtfully, "Ay, when a lad as quiet as Francis breaks out with these idle Newcastle lads ye cannot tell what'll happen."

Billy let the talk flow along these lines till the innkeeper's wife said, "Mind, your ma may have spoilt him but I'm right sorry for her now. If our Len was lying in prison and likely to be hanged I think I'd go mad." Dee then became the subject of talk with scant regard for Billy's presence. He listened uncomfortably but the men agreed she had worked hard to help Jack but she could never truly fit in.

The innkeeper's wife said, "You'll not remember, Billy, when you were a wee bairn and got the pneumonia? I mind your gran, Jane Heron, telling me Dee fought for you, day and night, and pulled you through. Ay, she's a tough woman your ma and may get over this in time but you and your da will need to stand by her. I hope you can get the lad off but it's doubtful from what ye've telt us."

"Oh, shut your mouth, woman," said her husband. "We none of us want a hanging. We don't need the village famous for that."

"Why not, man? It'll bring the crowds. You'll make your fortune." There was a general laugh at the innkeeper's expense. Billy got up to go.

"Nay," said Ed Porter, who had been keeping quiet, Billy noticed. "Don't be running away. You come in little enough. We're not heartless. It's just that nothing ever happens here and it's got us all jabbering like monkeys."

"I'll be getting home," Billy said. "It was good to get away for a wee while." He looked round the room, spotting the men on his level. "Usual shifts tomorrow."

He went out into the sharp night air. Had it been a good idea to go there? He didn't know. The light and noise from the inn faded away behind him. He ran the half mile to Burn Cottage, slipped in and bolted his door, saw that his water buckets were nearly empty and went out again to the spring, returning speedily and locking up again as silently as he could. His larder was rather bare but there was the heel of a loaf and some cheese. He ate up every scrap, put his porridge bowl on the table ready for the morning and prepared himself for bed. All the time he thought only of doing the task in hand as fast and as neatly as possible. Once in bed and safe from a visit from next door he blew out his candle and pulled the blanket and coverlet over his ears.

Even then he would not allow thoughts to come. He told himself in plain words, This thing is underway now and must run its course. Nothing I have heard tonight will make any difference. I have rehearsed my part and I will think no more and speak no more of it. He drifted into sleep.

Chapter 30

Dee

"Oh Jack, my leg is on fire." Dee set her foot to the ground and squealed.

Jack was just placing the kettle on the trivet but was so startled that he knocked it over and the fire went out with a hiss of steam.

Exasperation and exhaustion from a wretched night reduced Dee to a flood of tears. He was by her side in an instant.

"My angel! Forgive me. I am so clumsy."

She shook her head and drew up her nightgown to show a leg all swollen and purple. "I thought to go to Francis again and see Sarah and Mr Hurst and Mr Trace and anyone else who can speak to Francis's good character."

"You can't, Dee. I must run to the village for the doctor."

"No, get the fire going and make a cup of tea. Mistress Hammond may lend her carriage again."

There was a tap at the door and it opened before Dee could slip back into bed.

Billy walked in and straight up to his mother, without a glance elsewhere. He handed her a bank note, saying, "If you need it for the coach fare," and walked out again.

"Oh Billy—" she began but he was gone. He was in his pit clothes so he would be going to work. She looked at Jack, who came over and peered at the note.

"It's for ten pounds," she said. "Where could he have got such a sum?"

Jack had no idea but he could lay a fire so he went back to that.

"We will just be grateful and use it," she said, wondering if her words last night had moved Billy after all, but how could she go to Newcastle if she couldn't walk? Painfully she dressed herself and bound round her leg the clean rags she had boiled ready for a new dressing.

She saw Jack had set the porridge to heat on the fire and was now pulling on his work boots without stirring it first. She tried to reach the three-legged stool by the hearth but collapsed on the floor in pain.

"My angel, you mustn't move." He lifted her up and carried her to the bed, gently raising her legs so she could recline on the pillow.

"The porridge," she said, half laughing to ease his distress. "It'll be lumpy."

They managed some breakfast before it was time for him to go to work but he said he would send the doctor before he reported to the farm. Because all his anxiety was for her she said nothing more about Francis.

"I will return when the beasts have been fed and watered," he said at the door.

Alone, she lay fighting despair. She had failed with Billy. The ten pounds was a sop to his conscience. God had struck her down so that she could do nothing for Francis. It was her punishment. But why should it be his – the innocent one?

She sat up. God had given her the ability to write. She reached for her writing materials on the shelf above her. She would write letters and when Jack or the doctor came she would have something for the post. First was Sarah. She must express her sorrow for the death of Joseph and go on to beg her to attest to Francis's good character and attend his trial however painful it might be for her. Her testimony on Joe's state of health could save Francis. This was done and sealed ready when she heard horse's hooves. The doctor had responded swiftly.

But it was not the doctor who knocked and entered at her summons. It was Mr Hurst, fresh and vigorous after a ride from Newcastle with his mop of hair tousled as he pulled off his hat. Seeing her in bed, he was about to retreat, apologising for the early hour, but she called him in.

"No, no, I am fully dressed and so glad to see you. You save me a letter.

Pray sit down. God bless you for coming to us in our distress. Have you some news?"

He laid his hat and riding crop on the table and sat down, observing her intently.

"Are you ill, Mrs Heron?"

"No, no, I fell and injured my leg or I would have been early to the prison today to see my poor Francis."

"You saw him yesterday."

"How did you know?"

"I visited him last evening."

"Oh, thank you, sir! How was he?"

"Bitter at the injustice of the charge but I trust I left him more hopeful."

"Bless you for going to him. What could you say?"

"That in less than a week he would be free and glad of this experience to toughen his character."

She repeated, "Free in less than a week!" Her heart soared.

"Yes," he said. "I inquired of the clerk to the court and he said that the Assize judge from London arrived by the night coach and has been informed of the cases before him. He read the committal report from Justice Harker. This fisherman fellow, whom they call the prosecutor, is bound over to appear at the Assizes along with your Billy as a witness. The story interested the judge so he said he would take the murder charge first which means the trial is set for Monday next."

"Oh, I must be fit to go! I can refute everything Billy may say."

"Billy will witness *against* his brother? Francis told me he feared that, but surely when it comes to court—"

Dee's eyes filled with tears. "He will not *help* him, I am ashamed to say, but *I* will speak. They cannot stop me."

"But you were not there at the death," he said gently. "There is however the matter of the motive and you can testify to his ignorance of his uncle's plans for his will. The clerk, who was very voluble since the newspapers have made much of the story, told me it is likely that 'the lady-love' as he put it will be called to testify and also the widow if she is in a state to do so."

Dee showed him the letter addressed to Sarah. "I have begged her to be there. Surely if she had believed Francis guilty *she* would have brought the prosecution. What has this man Harry to gain by it? If I had been fit I would have been at his house already urging him to withdraw."

He smiled. "And that is where I have been this morning on the way through Newburn. I hardly needed to inquire after his dwelling for he was holding court on his doorstep to a crowd of villagers and newspaper men. You ask what he will gain by this prosecution. It is just that – fame. He is a little man in every sense and now he is somebody, sought after, talked about, marvelled at."

"Could you not persuade him to withdraw then?"

"Alas, no. This is the pinnacle of his life, playing the central role in the court of our splendid new Moot Hall. 'What a setting for a great drama!' he said to me."

Dee, biting on her thumb, worried over this. "You still seem confident that Francis will be freed."

"I believe the judge will interrogate Harry vigorously and reduce him to pulp. An inflated bladder is soon pricked."

Would Billy succumb so easily? she wondered. She must work on him again.

Mr Hurst stood up and unrolled a sheet of paper. "Time is short, Mrs Heron. I am collecting signatures of people who will testify to Francis's character. I have Mr Trace and myself and the other teachers who knew him and the vicar of Heaton, despite the damage to his church roof. I am relying on you to direct me to the Ovingham vicar and anyone else of note in this area whom I can approach."

"*I* will sign, of course, though I am of no account."

He smiled, ruefully. "Nay, it is too obvious that you would be biased."

"Well then, his godfather is the former Justice Hammond but I fear he has lost his wits in recent years. His wife will sign your paper, I am sure."

"And put his name too, I trust. A justice's name will look well."

Dee was doubtful about the forging of any signature but she said nothing. Mr Hurst looked so confident, standing very straight and businesslike. For her, the relief of knowing action was being taken when she herself felt so helpless was quite overwhelming. She directed him to the Hammond house and told him the name of the vicar and a few of the gentry who attended in Ovingham, who had occasionally commented with a condescending air of surprise on Francis's polite manners.

"In some quarters I am looked down upon for marrying a pit worker," she finished. "Truly I belong nowhere and Francis too is between two worlds. There is hostility among the mining community. People remember Joseph as a miner and all liked his father and mother. Billy as an Overman has more respect than Francis."

"Indeed," he said. "I remember the community well when I had my little school. Do you think they will remember *me*? I will try to turn a few hearts and minds as I pass through."

She smiled. "You have scarcely changed at all. Grey hair among the brown but as profuse as ever. And you still have the bearing of a young man. Your former pupils will be in awe of you."

He laughed. "And you, when you smile, are the same Dee Heron who brought me Billy because he was too much for you and took away Francis because *I* was too much for *him*."

"Nay, I gave him back to you and you wrought wonders with him and now I cannot thank you enough for what you are doing for him."

He brushed this aside with a friendly gesture and held out his hand for her letter. "I will see Mrs Joseph Heron gets this. It was too early for me to call upon her when I set off but I intend to do so on my return. If I can see Lily Batey too I will advise her how to conduct herself if she is called upon."

Before she could add her thanks for that they both heard the sound of a horse and trap.

"You are expecting someone else?" He took up his hat and riding crop.

"The doctor," she said. "He must make my leg well for Monday. Oh, Mr Hurst, you have given me hope."

He bowed and took his leave. And a few moments later the doctor knocked and entered.

When Jack returned to see how she fared, she told him, "Doctor Ransom has lanced it and removed what he called the evil from it and says it will do very well now, for he has bound it up close. He will come himself to look at it on Sunday and change the dressings. If I rest he believes I will be fit to travel to Newcastle after that. But oh Jack, Mr Hurst has been here too and he is sure Francis will be set free."

Jack's relief at her cheerfulness was so palpable that she forgot the soreness of her leg and reached up her arms to hug him. He was overjoyed at the thought of waiting upon her and made up the fire and under her direction put the stew pan to cook with some vegetables and lamb bones.

"I can nurse my angel back to health," he declared. "I will try not to be clumsy for my days of shame are surely past history. The manager knows I am your nurse now and I will go to the farm only to feed the animals."

She beamed at him and leant back on the pillows and closed her eyes. Perhaps now she could dare to sleep.

Lily

In Number One Heron Mansions Lily was preparing her mistress's midday meal with tears flowing as she recalled everything Francis had said to her that morning. He had tried to be hopeful for her sake, she could tell, but his fears would rise to the surface and mirror her own. "I have a life to live with you," he said. "That *cannot* be taken from us." She had spent a wakeful night imagining just that terrible dark hole that the future might become for her. Would she ever be able to put away the bitterness of such a cruel injustice to her first and – she was sure – only love during the dreary years she might be required to live?

"I am praying," he told her, "but it is just a mass of words and brings little comfort."

She nodded. Her own prayers had felt like moths fluttering against a great black wall. She pleaded, "But you say Mr Hurst is so sure of British justice?"

"He says their case is weak and he will find so many to speak for me that the horrid little fisherman will be laughed out of court. I wish Aunt Sarah would come and see me so I could tell her how I grieve for Uncle Joe, but I suppose she is prostrated. God knows what I would feel if you and I had been married over twenty years and I lost you."

He had tried then to grasp her fingers through the bars only for the gaoler to shout, "None of that now. You've had your ten minutes."

Now she carried her mistress's meal into the parlour where she had chosen to eat from a tray rather than sit at the dining table. "I cannot bear to look at his empty place," she told Lily and Gertie.

As Lily set down the tray bearing a steaming bowl of broth and some thinly cut bread and butter which was all her mistress had asked for, she felt brave enough to say, "Ma'am, I do thank you for giving me time to go and see your poor nephew. He was asking after you and wondering if *you* might be able to visit him. He so grieves for Master and I know it would comfort him to tell you so."

Sarah looked up, startled. "See Francis! Oh no. I couldn't do it."

"It is barely five minutes' walk, ma'am, from the top of our street."

"No, girl, you are too bold!" Then it seemed to Lily that a good excuse jumped into her mistress's mind. "How could I? I may not stir out till they bring me the coffin with my poor husband's remains and I can bury him decently. Any gadding about before that would be unseemly."

"Oh, but ma'am, no one would call visiting an innocent man in prison gadding about. Didn't the good Lord say we should visit those sick or in prison?"

"Do you preach to me, girl? Get yourself to the kitchen and remember your place."

With murmured apologies Lily scuttled away. She knew Mrs Heron had received the same summons to appear in court next Monday that she had herself received by special messenger that morning. Sarah would have to go whether her husband had been buried or not and what would she say? There was a sick feeling in Lily's mind that her reluctance to see Francis was somehow linked to Billy's visit the day before and that his vindictiveness might have imparted itself to Sarah.

Her own guilt over her letter was still raw. Worse still was her fear that her rejection of Billy had provoked all this. Although the sight of the subpoena had turned her legs to water, she knew it gave her the chance to pour out the truth to a judge and jury. Maybe she could undo some of the harm she had unwittingly caused already. She had surprised herself just now with her boldness to her mistress. In a crowded courtroom she would need much greater courage but desperation would call it forth.

She was still in this frame of mind when later that day she opened the door to a tall man who doffed his hat to show a thick head of hair reaching to his shoulders. He asked if she was Lily Batey. She nodded nervously, fearing he must be a reporter, several of whom had called already and hung around outside trying to peer in. But when he introduced himself as Mr Hurst, she exclaimed, "Oh sir, you are Francis's schoolmaster who put such hope in him last night. I will tell Mrs Heron you are here."

"In a moment. I wished a word with you first. You may be questioned in court on Monday. Does that alarm you?"

She set her jaw. "No, sir. I will speak the truth."

He looked delighted with this answer. "Francis was mistaken then. He told me you might be overawed by the grand courtroom and the judge in his robes and all the officials. He was sad that you had to be put in such a situation for him."

"But because it is for him I will *not* be frightened at all."

"They will be after a motive for the crime, you understand that?"

"I know, and they think my letter gave him the motive. I shall admit I wrote it because I did and I'll tell them he loved his uncle and if he *had* read the letter, which he didn't, he would never ever have done a thing to harm him."

The parlour door clicked open behind them and Sarah's grim face appeared.

"I heard the doorbell, Lily. Do not talk with gentlemen callers in the hallway."

Mr Hurst handed Lily his hat and made a deep bow.

"Mrs Heron, I beg pardon. Edmund Hurst. We have met when your nephew was my pupil. I came to offer my sincere condolences on the death of your husband and to give you a letter from Mrs Jack Heron who is unable to travel to see you at present as she has injured her leg." She took the letter as if it might bite her. "I would also speak, if I may, about the coming trial which I fear will be an ordeal for you."

"I remember you, Mr Hurst," Sarah said. Lily, as she cowered in the corner unable to flee to the kitchen, thought her tone very stiff and formal. "I thank you for your condolences but I am not speaking to anyone about the trial. Lily, show Mr Hurst out." And she went back into the parlour and shut the door firmly.

Lily looked to see him somewhat abashed but he just smiled at her and shrugged his shoulders. "We are not dependent on her testimony. She was not at the river and may not be called. Possibly *you* will not be called but keep that good courage up and I am sure all will be well." He took his hat from her and she hastened to open the heavy outer door for him. He said, "I hoped his aunt would add to my list of signatures to Francis's good character but I have a fine collection already."

"Can I sign it?" Lily cried.

He shook his head. "They would discount your name and that might throw doubt on the others." Quick to understand, she inclined her head, and thanked him again for all he was doing. She watched him stride up the hill and the jauntiness of his steps was very comforting.

Chapter 31

Billy

Billy sat on top of the stage coach knowing his parents were inside and that they didn't know he was there. At the last moment he had slipped round the inn wall and climbed up to his reserved place. He had watched his father lift his mother into the coach and was angry that she needed help from such loving and protective arms. They had no business to look like a pathetic, tottering old couple at their age.

While looking about at the country and holding on to the rail when the coach jolted over potholes, he let himself ponder at last his mother's admission that she had never loved him. Why hadn't she? He thought his father had tried to but was always disappointed in him. He conjured up images of his childhood. The most painful stood out like thorn bushes on a grey desert plain.

In the earliest he was jumping on the rocker of a cradle and could see the tiny fair-haired baby bouncing. Then a sharp slap came across his face – from his father! The first and last but never forgotten. He had hated the baby from that moment.

In a later picture he saw the heads of his mother and Francis against the background of the river. Their closeness and absorption provoked his fury. With his fists he pummelled them both and when they went home Francis slammed the door in his face. That was a moment seared into his brain, how he stood there, resolving to run to the river and float to the sea and enlist as a cabin boy. That it ended in the humiliation of nearly drowning and finding he had caused his mother to miscarry was all the result of closed doors. He was hot with anger just thinking about it.

Why had she loved Francis from birth but not him? His memories couldn't explain that. But she had admitted it and deserved to suffer today. And Francis himself! His mind dwelt on many other pictures of the fair boy, loved and cosseted down the years, and finally daring to rear up and take his Lily from him. What has he left me? he asked himself. Why should he live to enjoy her? His blood boiled.

At Newburn, Harry Allthorp, his weedy frame smothered in a great coat and scarf, mounted to the remaining place on top of the coach, slapping him on the back.

"What a day this is going to be!" he cried. "Justice will be done for your poor uncle. I never dreamt I would have a leading part in such a thing. And you too, man."

Billy shivered and drew his coat closer round him. His hands clutched at suddenly cold knees.

"Ay," said Harry, "it's a raw day for early April."

Francis

Waiting to be taken up the special stair which he now knew led direct into the courtroom, Francis tried desperately to control his trembling. He had no idea of the layout of the court but if he could only see his mother's face he was sure he would take heart. From babyhood he had looked up at her loving gaze. Growing up, he had begun to look down at it, as she smiled up at him. She was his sworn ally in every vicissitude of his life and if she could not come today he would be utterly bereft. His father would not leave her if she was in bed and though he was no rock to lean upon Francis was sure of his love too. Their absence would be so conspicuous. Would it not be said, "His parents don't support him and his brother believes him guilty"?

And what would Aunt Sarah say? Lily on her Sunday visit had seemed to expect little help from her. "But she knows of Uncle's 'turns'?" he had protested.

"She denied them," Lily said. "She didn't want to face losing him I suppose."

"But now he's dead."

"Don't think of her. Mr Hurst said she might not be called. But you can be sure *I* will speak out." How he had loved her when she said that, but she would be kept in a separate witness room and her sweet face would not greet him when he had to appear as a criminal before all those eyes.

"Time," called the gaoler and suddenly he felt icy cold.

Dee

Dee avoided looking about her. They had managed the walk from the coaching inn but here were those stone steps between the great pillars. Jack almost carried her up. Then there were the wide doors and an usher standing, inquiring their business. Jack said they were visitors come to the trial. She had told him not to say their son was the accused. "I want no one nudging and staring."

An inner door opened and they crossed a floor and here were more stone steps with a railed gallery ahead. People were sitting there in tiers reaching towards the ornate ceiling. She lowered her eyes again and Jack managed to propel her up, step by step. Seeing her difficulty with walking, the people in the front row shuffled along to make room for them. She sat down and then dared to peep at the scene before her. An arm waved at her from the far side of the gallery. Jenny Batey – all smiles! She gave a tiny wave back but couldn't smile. Jenny, with her jollity and jokes, had no place here. She tried to forget her presence.

She looked into the courtroom. The judge's bench was directly opposite and slightly below but ranged to one side were the places for the jury. There, raised before them, was the prisoner's bar where shortly she would see her son accused of murder. How had it come to this? Could she hold herself together for this fearful ordeal? She clutched at Jack's hand and held it tight.

"We must smile at him when he is brought in," she whispered and he nodded, but his eyes showed only fright at these intimidating surroundings. He would give the world, she thought, to be back at the farm in the monotony of his day-to-day routine.

A hand tapped her shoulder from the row behind. It was Mr Hurst, leaning forward to say softly, "I am so glad you have managed to come. Francis will be much relieved. Last night I presented my list of names to the clerk of court so the judge will have seen it now." Then he indicated the gentleman beside him. "This is Mr Trace."

Dee saw a heavy-browed man with a rough-hewn face but sympathetic eyes. He gave her a little bow and mouthed "Have no fear."

She managed a small smile and a nod. It was heartening to have them so close.

She began to realise how noisy the courtroom was. Whispering was hardly necessary. Everyone else was talking loudly. There was even joking and laughter but presently a stentorian voice called, "Pray silence for His Honour Judge Milburn." The door behind the bench opened with a flourish and a figure came briskly in.

Dee was surprised to see that he was a small man, engulfed by his large wig and ponderous robes. He seemed to be walking on tiptoe as if struggling to achieve appropriate dignity as he ascended the two steps to his 'throne'.

Then the jury of twelve men was sworn in. Dee tried to spot some wise and kindly souls among them but their faces were an inscrutable mass. The judge addressed them briefly, in a thin high voice, telling them to try the case fairly and ignore any gossip or rumours they might already have heard. Then he called for the prisoner to be brought before him. Dee held her breath.

A solid-looking trapdoor was opened up in the floor and the head of the gaoler she remembered appeared. Handcuffed to him came Francis. At the first sight of the top of his fair head she felt Jack quiver beside her.

"Our boy!" he gasped, as if surprised to see him.

She was still holding her breath to see how he looked and if he would spot them in the crowd. He was very pale, his features thin and tense. Once installed at the bar with a guard each side of him he did look up and his eyes swept the room.

Dee couldn't help leaning forward and raising one hand. He saw her and a radiance transformed his whole face and body. He grew an inch and even turned a smile on his two warders as much as to say, 'She's here. All will be well now.'

Dee exhaled her breath and leant back on her seat again. It mattered nothing that her position had now been made public. Let the exchange of glances tell the whole court, 'There is my innocent boy. He will be free soon and we will take him home to a joyful celebration.'

The proceedings took off at once with a speed that alarmed her. Francis was asked his name and the charge was read by the clerk of court in a fast monotone.

"...did murder one Joseph Heron of Newcastle by wilfully and maliciously drowning him in the River Tyne..."

Jack turned to her and murmured, "Our Joe?"

She quelled him with a look and riveted her eyes again on Francis as he was asked if he pleaded guilty or not guilty. She clasped her hands tightly together.

"Not guilty," he answered, loud and clear, and she sighed and relaxed a little. How could they not believe that?

Straight away little Harry Allthorp appeared as the prosecutor and began to tell his tale in an excited voice.

The judge interrupted him. "Why are you prosecuting this man? What connection have you with the victim?"

Harry was not cowed. "He was my friend, Your Honour, and I clearly saw him pushed into the water by that man."

The judge nodded and he went blithely on, saying how he and Mr Heron had been chatting together and had just said goodbye and separated when he heard him shout and looked round to see a fair-haired young man give him a shove that pushed him into the river. "It was the accused and I arrested him as a good citizen should."

Dee was angry and sickened by his obvious relish in the role. She hoped the judge would not sympathise with him as one small man to another. He was asking him now, "How far away were you when you saw the push?"

"Oh, not more than twenty paces, Your Honour. Of course I ran back but I am neither big nor strong and Mr Heron was a heavily built man, face down in the water and like to have been carried away by the current for the Tyne was full that day. We had had quite a fall of rain."

"I want no irrelevant details," snapped the judge. "What happened then? What was the accused doing?"

That's right. Squash him, thought Dee.

"He was pretending to grab his legs but really pushing him further out."

"How do you know what was in his mind?"

"That's how it looked to me."

"Discount that," the judge told the jury. "Have you any more testimony?"

Dee was pleased to see Harry looking aggrieved.

"Why yes, Your Honour. Don't you want to know what happened next?"

There was giggling in the courtroom and the judge glared at him.

"Carry on, but don't be too long about it."

Still enjoying his audience, Harry related how a dark-haired young man had appeared, all black from the pit, and dragged out the man he said was his uncle and tried to revive him without success. "He was very angry with the murderer and would have hurt him but I restrained him and said the law would deal with him which I am glad to see Your Honour is now engaged upon."

"No comments, please," said the judge. "Did you ask the miner's name?"

"Oh yes. It was Billy Heron, the brother of the accused."

The court rippled with excitement as Dee shivered. She hadn't seen him since their words together. Did she dare to hope he was unable to face the court?

"He will be called presently," the judge said. "Is that the extent of your knowledge of the actual crime?"

"Oh no, Your Honour, for later on I learnt what could be the motive for it and a crime without a motive, as Your Honour knows, is not nearly so believable."

"Thank you, Mr Allthorp, I will spare the jury your guesses. I will be calling Constable Brown for the *facts* relating to that part of the case. The accused may now cross-examine you."

To Dee's delight Harry Allthorp shrivelled up with disappointment. This judge is no fool, she decided, and leant forward eagerly to see how Francis would conduct himself.

His first question, shot at the disconsolate little fisherman, was, "Did you see my uncle's face before he fell?"

"Yes," he murmured.

"Was it red or white?"

"Nay, I was not near enough to tell that."

"What? At less than the length of a cricket pitch? You would have seen he was taken ill. The truth is you were much further away than you said. Too far to see anything clearly."

The judge said, "Confine yourself to asking questions. You will have a chance to make your own statement presently."

"Did you see my hand on my uncle's back?"

"Plainly."

"Did you see him whirl about before he fell?"

"Yes, because you pushed him."

"He was ill. I was trying to catch hold of his coat and save him. Could you not see that?"

Dee, knowing Francis's voice so well, heard the anger in it. This one stupid little man held his life in his hands. But again the judge intervened. "You persist in wanting to tell him your version now. Have you any more questions for him?"

"Yes, Your Honour." He turned on Harry again. "Did you and my brother attack me viciously after my uncle was pulled out of the river?"

"Nay, *I* did not. In his anger he did knock you down but I held him back."

"Have you and he colluded together to bring this charge?"

"Colluded?"

The judge explained, "Agreed together, worked on it together."

"Nay." Dee felt Harry was reasserting himself. "I told your brother *I* would arrest you because it was *I* who saw you push your poor uncle. *I* tied you up with twine while he, shocked and grieving as he was, went to fetch help."

"You know I was too hurt to resist you or you could not have tied me up."

"You just had a wee bang when you fell over. You came round soon enough."

Francis looked up at the judge and Dee could see the exasperation in his face.

"Your Honour, I have nothing more to say to this man. He is twisting the truth at every turn. In the gaol here they know the injuries I sustained."

"Then let us press on. I have Justice Harker's report on the case and as a constable was quickly fetched I wish him to be called next."

Harry Allthorp subsided onto his prosecutor's seat. He looked unable to believe that his part in the play was over.

Constable Brown was called and sworn in at the witness stand. Dee listened intently as, in his solid matter-of-fact voice, he gave a truthful account of everything that had happened at Burn Cottage. He had remembered too well how Francis had not wanted her to bring out Lily's letter, how the seal was found to be broken and how Francis had denied that he had read it.

The judge let him finish and then looked to the jury. "You have followed this? You understand that this relates to the matter of motive for the crime? Did the accused read the letter? If he did he knew already that he was to be left out of his uncle's will before he went to the river to meet him."

Oh no, Dee thought, he is implanting the idea in their minds. I am beginning to hate this judge now. She looked round at Mr Hurst and Mr

Trace. Mr Trace gave a small shake of the head while Mr Hurst's more mobile features expressed strong disapproval. She wondered how much Jack was following and whether there were any Jacks among the jury. One smart young gentleman was making notes and she saw him underline something heavily.

Constable Brown did attest to Francis's injuries and when Francis had a chance to cross-examine him he admitted they could have been caused by heavy kicks. He was then dismissed and William Heron called for.

Jack whispered, "Don't they know my father's been dead for years?"

She mouthed, "Billy." And waited, taut as a bow string, to see if he would come.

The door opened and he was there. Tall, broad and, she had to admit, a fine-looking man. Suddenly she saw his father in him. It was when Sir Ralph Barnet was announced by the butler and stood in the doorway just like that, stiff and tense, scarcely knowing anyone at the party, and she had been devastated by his presence.

A shaft of sunlight lit Billy's face and Dee was back in the fearful present. Dare she draw hope from his pallor and rigid bearing? He took the oath in a low voice and the judge ordered him to speak up.

"According to Justice Harker's report, you went to meet your uncle by the river on the afternoon of the second of April. Is that correct?"

"It is." Dee saw that Billy had not once looked at Francis but only at the judge.

"Describe briefly, if you please, what happened."

"I saw my brother close to my uncle. Then my uncle turned round quickly and fell forward into the river. I ran, pushed my brother aside and got hold of my uncle's legs and pulled him out. I tried to get the water out of his lungs but failed. He died."

"Did you see your bother push him?"

There was a fraction of a pause and Dee found herself holding her breath.

She could almost hear Billy swallow before he answered, in a flat tone, "No."

She squeezed Jack's hand and sent smiles to the two gentlemen behind.

The judge said, "Justice Harker's report says you corroborated Mr Allthorp's account."

Billy didn't flinch. "I believed his account because I saw no other reason for my uncle to fall. Thinking it over carefully since, I realise I didn't actually see a push, just a movement from my brother close to my uncle. Mr Allthorp was the other side and nearer than I."

Dee despaired. He had undone all the goodness of that 'no'.

The judge asked, "Did you know your uncle intended to replace Francis as his heir and put you in his will?"

"Yes, he told me."

"And did he tell you his reason?"

"I am his godson and he had recently helped my brother into an engineering apprenticeship." His tone had now become easier, almost conversational.

"Did you tell Francis?"

"No, Your Honour."

"Constable Brown testified that you accused him of knowing and believed that was why he killed him."

"I couldn't help the suspicion entering my head when we learnt he had been informed in a letter that day."

Dee saw Francis was desperate to cry out, "I never read it," but he wisely held himself back. He would get his chance in a minute.

In fact the judge turned to him now. "Does the accused wish to question this witness?"

"Yes, Your Honour." Francis faced his brother but Billy kept his eyes down. "Billy, look at me. You know I never read the letter."

"That is not a question," the judge said.

Billy looked at the jury. "He says he never read the letter."

"Leave the letter," said the judge. "Ask him about your uncle's death."

"I intend to. Billy, do you recall an occasion when our uncle had a seizure?"

"Yes." Now he did look at Francis.

"Did he clutch his chest and give a cry of pain?"

"Yes, and recovered in a moment."

"Did you not see him do the same by the river before he fell in?"

"I was too far away."

"You must have heard a yell."

"I heard a noise certainly."

"Did you not see me try to grab him because he was tottering?"

"I saw you make a movement. Your two figures were close together." He looked up at the judge. "Your Honour, I am trying to be accurate because I am on oath. God knows I want to save my brother."

A wave of emotion swept over the crowd. Dee moaned inwardly, Hypocrite!

"Very commendable," the judge said, "but my task and the jury's is to get at the truth." He asked Francis, "Have you finished with this witness?"

"No, Your Honour. Billy, just tell me why you attacked me so cruelly. I was trying to pull Uncle out."

Billy looked at him then, very steadily. "I am sorry I hurt you. I suppose it was anger at that moment that I had not got there in time. If you were trying to pull him out you were not succeeding and I knew I could have done it and saved him. I am afraid too that even then the thought came into my mind that it was deliberate. The wretched business of the will was so new. I lashed out at you and I am sorry. It was only when Harry Allthorp said you had pushed him – he sounded so certain of it—"

"That's enough," the judge said. "You answered his question. We have a picture of the incident and the constable has described the arrest of the accused and his committal to this court for judgement. You may step down, William Heron."

Billy walked out. Dee was aghast at how cleverly he had led the jury.

The coroner was called next and testified to death by drowning. Francis asked him if he could tell that the deceased had had a seizure first.

"Medical skill has not advanced so far," he replied, "but it is not impossible."

"My uncle shouted in pain and clutched his chest and swayed about. Are they not signs of a seizure?"

The judge poked his head forward. "The witness cannot answer that. You are describing what you believe you saw but he did not. The witness may step down."

Dee felt a cold lump in her heart. But now the judge was saying, "Francis Heron, you may now speak in your own defence," and the clerk of the court was starting up and begging His Honour's pardon but he had asked for two more witnesses to attend, Mrs Sarah Heron and the maid, Lily Batey. "They are waiting."

The judge waved his hand. "We do not need to trouble the deceased's widow. We have heard how the change of will came about and as for the letter writer she cannot tell who broke the seal or who read or did not read the letter. Why she sent it is obvious. She heard about the change of will and wanted her lover to know. We will have the accused summarise his defence."

He nodded at the jury. "There are half a dozen more cases before me today and you gentlemen are to try them all. It is a heavy responsibility."

Francis stood amazed at how swiftly they had reached this point, a feeling, Dee could tell, shared by everyone. Mr Hurst muttered, "They feel their entertainment has been curtailed." Dee was frightened at the speed. She wanted to hear Sarah and Lily speak up for Francis. He had certainly been Sarah's favourite as a boy and Lily's sweetness would have enchanted the jury. But he will be eloquent, she thought, speaking for himself. No one could hear him without being sure of his innocence.

He looked round the court and then up at his parents and two masters. He must be in pain from standing so long, she thought, but he smiled at them and then turned to the jury and squared his shoulders at them and began, "Gentlemen, I loved my uncle. He was good to me all my life. He and my aunt let me bide with them on weekdays when I was at school in Newcastle. He encouraged me to take an interest in his business ventures, hoping I might follow in his footsteps."

"Is all this relevant?" cried the judge.

Francis frowned. Dee could see he had prepared a great deal more. "But Your Honour, I am trying to show these gentlemen I had no motive for killing my uncle."

"Is that so? But you *didn't* follow in his footsteps. We know you are training to be an engineer. So your uncle decided to switch his benevolence to your brother, a miner. Are you sure you are helping your defence?"

Francis shook his head in bewilderment. "But Uncle approved my being an engineer and helped me towards it."

"Unfortunately, we cannot know now what your uncle thought. It is what you *did* that concerns us. Just give us your version of what happened at the river."

Dee hissed to Mr Trace and Mr Hurst, "Can the judge put him off like this?"

Mr Hurst shook his head ruefully. "In his court a judge is king."

Dee looked back at Francis who began too hastily to explain how he only went to help his uncle with his fishing gear and had no idea of the change of will. He had to digress then and account for not reading Lily's letter although he had broken the seal.

The judge grew impatient with that. "Come to the river now."

Francis rushed into his uncle's state of health. "He jumped up too quickly when he saw me. He had been sitting a while. He cried out and clutched his chest. I knew it was a seizure, having seen one before, but this time he lost consciousness. He's a big man, I mean he *was* a big man, and I couldn't get hold of him as he spun round. Harry Allthorp says I pushed him. I was trying to grab his coat but he just toppled over and I couldn't stop him. It was horrible. I was on my knees at once trying to reach him and pull him out. Harry said I was pushing him away. Of course I wasn't. What business had *he* to accuse me? He claims to be a friend of my uncle but I believe they had only just met that afternoon."

The judge said, "One could say it is all the more credit to him if their acquaintanceship was slight that he took the time and trouble to lay an accusation against you when he believed a murder had been committed."

Dee looked round again and breathed, "Is this being impartial?"

She glanced at Jack to see if he was as troubled as she but he was only wearing a heavy frown of concentration. Behind her, Mr Hurst was muttering, "Disgraceful."

"My brother," Francis went on, "must have seen that our uncle was ill for he was facing that way but he does *not* say I pushed him, so you only have Harry Allthorp's word for that."

The judge held up his hand. "Enough! You have described the whole incident as you saw it and have had your chance to question the witnesses. It is now up to the jury to elucidate the truth." He turned to them. "That, gentlemen, is what you have to do. Is the accused speaking the truth when he says he did not read his sweetheart's letter when it lay at hand for hours? He even broke the seal and replaced the letter unread in his pocket. You have heard his account of his uncle's fall, alleging illness, which his own brother could not corroborate, much as he wished in his own words 'to save him'. And you have heard the prosecutor's very specific statement that he saw a push, a man who had no reason to invent something to disturb a quiet afternoon's fishing. You may now consider your verdict. You may confer here in court or leave if you wish for more time."

Dee's heart seemed to die within her. He was telling them to find her boy guilty! There was a sound behind her and Mr Hurst stood up and shouted out, "Your Honour, you have not shown the jury the petition of names speaking for Francis Heron's good character."

"Ushers, remove that man!" the judge ordered, and then seemed to relent and turned to the jury. "You should know that I am not obliged to receive such a petition for I am well aware with what bribery such names are usually collected."

"That is a slur on good men's characters," Mr Hurst shouted back. Dee could see an usher making his way to the foot of the steps.

The judge retorted, "One name at least should not be there, that of former Justice Hammond. I have learnt he is not capable of signing his name. For me that invalidates the whole list. Remove that man."

Dee saw Mr Hurst clap his hand to his head. "God forgive me. She *would* sign for him."

"I repeat," the judge said, his high-pitched voice sounding more shrill, "gentlemen of the jury, you will now consider your verdict."

In two minutes Francis would be condemned. Dee bit both her thumbs to stop a scream. This could not happen.

The usher was beckoning Mr Hurst but he wouldn't move.

The court was buzzing with talk.

Voices cried, "Not yet!" Others called, "Shame!" Others shouted, "Give the lad a chance!" and "Call the sweetheart! We want to hear the sweetheart!" A voice at the back yelled, "That was no trial. You condemned him yourself, Your *Dis*honour."

The usher looked bewildered. Officials yelled, "Silence in court."

Dee felt a huge inner compulsion to stand up and quell the din. She was on her feet and the scream burst from her.

"It is I. I am the guilty one." She shot out a quivering finger, pointing to the judge. "Find *me* guilty, not my innocent boy."

"Who is that woman? Remove her," the judge ordered.

Jack was tugging at her skirt to pull her back, but she shouted out, "I am mother to them both, Billy and Francis. Hang me if you like for I am guilty as hell."

The judge was standing on tiptoe. "Get rid of her. What are you ushers for?"

There was uproar. "Hear the mother!" "Let her speak." "Put her in the witness box and let her speak."

The usher was hustled back down the stairs by some women who had come out of their seats. Newspaper reporters were calling out that she must be given a hearing. She saw Jenny stand up with flapping arms.

Mr Hurst and Mr Trace were both urging her on but she was aware only of a ghastly vision of Francis suspended from a gallows. She pulled her skirt from Jack's grasp and fumbled her way down the stairs and found herself propelled by many hands to the witness box. She couldn't believe she was doing this but here she was.

The judge was giving orders to arrest people who left their seats but nothing was done. She found she was clasping the rail in front of her and calling out, "I know why it has come to this. Before God I can tell you the truth."

The clerk of the court was looking to the judge.

"There will be a riot, Your Honour, if she is not heard."

The judge gave a perfunctory nod, her name was demanded and she was sworn in. She found herself gazing across the court into Francis's eyes. They were anxious and perturbed but he was alive and he was going to stay alive.

Beyond him she saw the double row of jurymen, a blur of faces, but she felt their eagerness and excitement. It was they to whom she must speak, and please God, she would find the words.

"Gentlemen," she began, and her voice steadied as she spoke. She heard the breathless silence that had suddenly fallen. She drew strength from knowing that Francis's fate was now in her power. "Gentlemen, I ask you a question. Is it natural for a brother to take the word of a stranger against his brother? Especially in such a thing as an accusation of murder? Would you not have expected my son Billy to tell Harry Allthorp he was utterly mistaken? That Francis would never kill their uncle? Allthorp would have apologised and crept home and we would not be here wasting His Honour's time and yours. Did that not occur to you? Have any of you brothers? Do you love and believe in them as brothers should?"

The judge snapped, "We do not want a sermon. You said you were guilty and that is why you have permission to speak, irregular as it is."

"Oh, I *am* guilty. I am telling you what is *natural* behaviour. But there is nothing natural in the relationship of these two sons of mine. And it is *my* fault." She heard the squeak of a door and glanced in that direction.

The door to the witnesses' room was ajar and no one was stopping Billy, Sarah and Lily from standing there and listening. It was a shock to see them but Dee felt the stronger for their presence. She knew the relief when she had told Jack her secret sin. This would be so much greater. This would be freedom.

She turned back to the jury. "Gentlemen, I do not blame Billy that he has not been a brother to Francis. They are in fact *half*-brothers and do not know it." She didn't look at Francis. "But that is not all. Billy is the son of a man who deserted me, whom I hated and whom I saw in the eyes and colouring of Billy from the day he was born and still see from time to time." She would not look round but she could *feel* reaction coming from the group in the doorway. She pressed on.

"But *that* is not all. Billy was always on my conscience. I lived a lie. The world thought he was Jack's son because I married Jack to save my reputation. So from the first Billy was my sword in the flesh. I couldn't love him. I fed him and fought for his life when he fell ill but I never loved him. He quickly became a troublesome boy and I made that my excuse for not being *able* to love him. When Francis was born all my love went to him. But Billy was capable of good feelings. He had love for the people he believed to be his grandfather and grandmother and this uncle whom he tried hard to save. And Francis loved his uncle and tried to save him. What Billy lacked was *my* love which he saw given wholly to his brother. Now gentlemen, do you begin to see why Billy did not immediately defend his brother against a false accusation? He let this trial go forward to see what happened, maybe to see his petted brother squirm a little, but I do not believe for a moment he would have let him hang. You heard him say he never saw a push. That was the truth. There *was* no push. My brother-in-law had a seizure, fell and drowned. No one is guilty of his death but I am guilty that this trial ever took place and I am truly sorry."

Now she did glance round. She couldn't help it. Billy was leaning against the doorpost, his shoulders shaking, and Sarah and Lily, in an astonishing combination, were trying to comfort him. The crowd, aware of this, was starting to shuffle and murmur. Some were sobbing. Now she looked at Francis and saw he too had tears running down his cheeks. He held his arms towards her.

The judge said, "Have you anything more to say?" His tone was icy.

"Do I need to say more?" She looked at Harry Allthorp who had had to remain in the prosecutor's seat all this time and who now seemed more shrunken than ever. "I do not blame you for bringing this case, Mr Allthorp. You thought it was your duty. The man you had just been speaking to in a friendly way suddenly fell into the river. A young man you didn't know was close behind him. Your eyes read it as a push."

He sat up and pleaded to the jury, "I did see it as a push."

"Enough," said the judge. "Accused, have you anything to ask this witness?"

Francis shook his head and then blurted out, "I love her."

"Very well," the judge said and then, as if nothing unusual had happened, "Gentlemen of the jury, you may now consider your verdict."

Their faces turned to each other with smiles and nods and they shouted out with one voice, "Not guilty."

The crowd burst into cheers while the judge tried to make the jury follow the proper procedure of the foreman answering his question, "Have you reached a verdict?" He was drowned out.

He stood up in a fury to make his exit but just remembered to tell the gaoler, "The prisoner is released. He is free to go without a stain on his character."

There was prolonged clapping.

Chapter 32

Dee

Dee was surrounded by jabbering people. The reporter from the *Newcastle Courant* was waving his notebook to attract her attention.

"Mrs Heron, ma'am. I have you verbatim. Are you content with that?"

She could only nod. Jenny appeared at a distance and shouted, "Dee, why didn't you tell *me* your story?" Dee shook her head ruefully and Jenny was pushed towards the doors in the rush. Now Jack and Mr Hurst and Mr Trace were trying to reach her and she glimpsed Francis, his back slapped by a dozen hands and his face kissed by several ladies. She could not see into the witnesses' room and there was no sign of Billy or Sarah. Lily, small and slight, was squirming her way to Francis and as soon as they were in each other's arms the crowd gave a concerted, "Aah!"

Dee crushed down a small pang of jealousy with the thought Lily is his future, not me. But then they were forcing their way to her and Francis was embracing her and they were all in tears of thankfulness.

"Are you not ashamed of your mother?" she asked.

"Ashamed when you were so brave!" Francis cried. "Never! I was going to my death till you spoke. But where is Billy? I want to speak with him."

Voices were commanding, "Clear the courtroom. Another trial is to start. All those with no business in it depart forthwith."

Dee saw an usher look in the witnesses' room and call, "Outside if you please."

Sarah emerged, all in black with her face shaded by the large brim of her hat, and as the crowd thinned she came straight up to Dee, who had now been joined by Jack with Mr Trace and Mr Hurst congratulating her heartily.

Sarah eluded the embrace of sympathy which Dee thought to give her. "Well, Dee," she said, "I hope you'll not write any more Moral Tales after *that* revelation. Of course I had my suspicions when Billy was born so early but you brazened it out. I have a banker's draft to give you for your last stories and if you have any further dealings pray go direct to Mr Brandling." She pushed a paper at her and turned to go.

Dee stood still, shocked at her hostility. "Oh Sarah, are we not still sisters? I did wrong many years ago but now I grieve with you for Joe as Jack here mourns his brother."

Jack nodded vigorously.

"You and Joe have been so good to both my sons—" She broke off. "What has happened to Billy?"

"He'll not come out till they make him. He doesn't want to see any of you, only me. *I* can supply the mothering he lacked. And" – now she looked at Francis – "I will be following Joe's last wishes and will make Billy my heir."

"Oh Aunt, I never wanted your money."

"What, not to wed this girl?" She looked at Lily. "*You* will be paid off. I will give you a reference but I want you to collect your things today."

Dee wondered at this vindictiveness but her mind was now on Billy. She could not believe he wanted Sarah's mothering. But if he would not come to her she would go to him.

Ushers were hustling them all outside. She caught a glimpse of Billy trying to make for the doors without being noticed, but he was waylaid by reporters.

"Wait for me at the foot of the steps," she said to Jack. "Sarah, I will write to you. We cannot part like this." She glanced down then at the banker's draft which she had taken unawares. It was for one hundred pounds. "What! So much!"

"Yes, yes." Sarah was already walking away. She looked over her shoulder. "I've being doing the accounts the last few days. As your publisher I find I owe you that."

She hurried to the big doors and was briefly silhouetted against the sunlit square before she bobbed down the steps and Dee saw her wide black hat vanish round the corner beneath the soaring turrets of the castle. She would walk home alone to Heron Mansions. She would work hard and make a great deal of money but Dee pitied her with all her heart.

Billy had shrugged off the reporters and curious members of the public and she caught him trying to hide from her behind the first of the four great columns.

She grabbed at his sleeve and he was obliged to turn and face her.

"Billy, please, Francis wants to speak with you."

His face was pale and his eyes red. "I have nothing to say to him or to you."

She kept hold of him. "No word of forgiveness? You wept when I was speaking in the court."

He frowned. "That was not for you. It was for the childhood I missed."

The words stabbed like a knife. "Oh Billy, I know you are a man now but surely it is not too late? The lie is dead that lay between us. I want to love you if you will let me. Your *aunt* speaks of mothering you. That is fantasy, is it not?"

He shrugged. "If it pleases her. Should I choose to finish with mining I can go and live there, she says."

"But Billy, cannot we – Jack and I and you and Francis – can we not be a family now, whether or not you quit mining?"

"No." He pulled from her grasp. "I don't belong to you. Just tell me one thing. Who was my father?"

"Don't ask. He was a deceiver. He faked love thinking I was an heiress."

Billy gave a harsh laugh. "That will not be *my* mistake. If I ever again find one to love *I* will have the money."

"I pray to God you *will* find love." She was looking at him over her clasped hands. She dare not fling her arms round him; he was too aloof and cold.

"You haven't given me his name."

"I wish to forget him. He is dead. He was Ralph Barnet – Sir Ralph Barnet in fact."

"My God, a title! Am I heir to it, I wonder? Aunt will be delighted." He saw Jack and Francis hovering at the foot of the steps. "Your family is impatient. I may try to trace my father's kin and need your help. Otherwise I will not be in touch."

"But Billy, you will be next door."

"You won't stay in that hovel. Did Aunt not give you some money? She said she was going to."

"Yes, she did, enough to rent a much better place away from the coal mines."

"Then do."

"We will, if it will not upset your father to seek for new work."

"I am glad he is *not* my father. He has no backbone, no ambition. For those qualities and for your courage today I admire *you* but I can never *love* you."

He dodged round the pillar, walked obliquely down the wide steps to avoid Jack and Francis and disappeared into the crowds still hanging about.

Jack came rushing up to her as she stood, blind with tears, one hand on the stone pillar, unable to move. "My angel, your leg. I will carry you down."

The leg had not existed for her all this while but was now suddenly agony. She let Jack sweep her up in his arms and negotiate the stone steps. Amazingly Mr Hurst and Mr Trace were there on the cobbles with a hired cab.

"I have given the man directions to the schoolhouse," Mr Hurst said. "There you can refresh yourselves before the afternoon stage to Wylam. Mr Trace and I will walk but you and your husband and Francis must ride, away from prying eyes. The reporters are rushing to their offices with their accounts but they'll not beat the newssheets which will be on the streets before nightfall, and as for the gossip about town, heaven knows what tales will be told! But fear not, you will come out as a heroine."

In the cab Dee rested her leg on the opposite seat next to Francis while Jack took her hand and caressed it on his knee. She was utterly spent. The scene with Billy had drained away all her joy and relief, but now, alone with the two who loved her without reservation, she could feel a great wave of thankfulness. There was her boy alive, out of all danger, looking at her with such concern and tenderness. What had happened to his Lily? Where had she gone? She asked him.

"She met her mother and they'll go home when she's fetched her things from Aunt's. She'll find a new place and we'll be wed when I finish my apprenticeship."

It was said with such quiet certainty that she felt her throat contracting. His future was restored to him. He would work at his chosen profession. He would marry a sweet girl and they would have children whom, God willing, she would live to see.

She began to weep.

"Not more tears," cried Jack. "I thought all was well now."

"It is, it is. These are tears of gratitude to God for answering our prayers."

Jack broke into his most radiant smile. "You are right, my Dee." And he put his hands together, raising his eyes like a child to the roof of the cab. "Thank you God for making all come well again." Then a little puzzlement came into his eyes and he looked at Francis. "But it wasn't God. It was your mother, wasn't it?"

Dee laughed – when had she last laughed? – and shook her head. "Nay, *He* made me stand up. *He* gave me the courage and the words to use. He has freed me from the burden of my deception all these years – for which you, my son, have uttered no word of reproach."

Francis became very solemn. "Mother dearest, I suffered nothing from not knowing that story. That was why I wished so much to speak with Billy. I want to tell him I will be ten times more his brother after this. I am determined to make such an opportunity and, God help me, I will."

Dee realised the cab had stopped. The driver was opening the door and lowering the step. Jack looked anxious. "Have we any money to pay him?"

"That's all right, sir," the man said. "T'other gentleman paid."

As they descended to the pavement Dee saw they were at the gate of a pretty garden with a gravelled path leading to a green front door. It opened as she looked and a lady appeared, exclaiming, "Oh Francis, you are free!"

"Mrs Hurst," Francis muttered, unlatching the gate.

Jack was dumbstruck so Dee, gritting her teeth at the pain, stepped towards her, holding out her hand. "Dee Heron, ma'am, and my husband Jack. Our apologies for arriving like this but your kind husband sent us ahead in a cab to escape the attention of the crowds. There was a deal of confusion but a joyful outcome. He and Mr Trace will be here presently. We knew nothing of his plan till the cab was there."

Mrs Hurst, who seemed an easy, comfortable person, laughed. "That's his way, an impulsive man of action. Come in, come in. I am so happy for you, though I must say I never doubted the verdict." She waved them into a sunny sitting-room and disappeared 'to give a few orders in the kitchen'.

Dee sank into a chair. She wondered, Could Jack and I ever own a pretty house like this? Mr Hurst has done well with his school. There are enterprising men all over the north-east making money from coal mines, ironworks and shipping and they can pay well to have their boys educated in a modern way. My poor Jack! Will he ever earn more than he earns now? I must be the enterprising wife. Let but this sore leg heal and I will take our lives in hand.

It would take longer for her sore heart to heal. She relived the scene with Billy. What future joy could she ever feel if he parted from them like that?

Jack and Francis were sharing the sofa and talking in low voices, respecting her exhaustion. Then Mr Hurst and Mr Trace arrived and they were all invited into an adjoining dining-room where a feast of cold meats, a salad, a plate of buttered bread and bowls of fruit awaited them.

"The girl and I have just thrown something together," Mrs Hurst said. "All it lacks is a bottle of wine from the cellar, Edmund, to drink Francis's health. And you must tell me how it all came about over the meal."

All? Dee wondered. Of course her husband will tell her all privately. She will indeed read it in the newspapers. I never thought that I was laying myself bare before all the world. How many respectable people will react like Sarah? But it is not so much my fall into temptation that I am ashamed of. It is my cruelty to Billy that a warm-hearted woman like Mrs Hurst will find abhorrent. She struggled to eat.

They spared her during the meal. They talked of the judge's haste to be finished, his bias that had roused the crowd to frenzy and how nearly he might have drawn a guilty verdict from the jury if Dee had not bravely stood up and showed them the true way to interpret all the facts.

Mrs Hurst clapped her hands. "You should take up advocacy, my dear Mrs Heron. They tell me that in London courts lawyers do the pleading for their clients and charge high fees. Who knows? One day women may prove as good as men at such professions."

The men laughed and Dee had no need to say anything. All she now wished was to be at home and hear Billy next door and go in and not be rejected.

Chapter 33

Billy

Billy sat in Sarah's parlour drinking unpleasantly sweet chocolate. He planned to walk back to Wylam, not wait for the afternoon stage which he expected his family to take. He was hungry and he knew his aunt would be happy to feed him but as soon as he had appeared at her door he had felt her tentacles reaching out for him.

She sat opposite him now, perched on the edge of the best upholstered chair, leaning eagerly towards him.

"I have sent Gertie to the lawyer's office already and he will be with me tomorrow to make a new will. You will stay the night of course before you give notice at the mine and settle here permanently. I will let you have two rooms here in Number One on the first landing as soon as I can be rid of the tenant there." She gave him a smile which he found positively sinister. "And I will never charge you rent. Of course I will lose some income but it will be worth it to have my nephew at hand." She gave a little laugh. "I know you are not my nephew by blood but I still look upon you as such. You shall sit in my Joseph's place for meals, which will be very cosy."

She fastened her eyes on his, her head poked forward like a grinning vulture approaching its meal. He knew he was supposed to say something but what could he say? The prospect appalled him, but till she had made her will it might be wise to concur. She needed someone in her new loneliness and he ought to feel sorry for her.

As he had walked from the Moot Hall he had tried to crush emotion with the thought of freedom, freedom from all ties. He had looked down at the river and imagined enlisting in the navy and seeing the world. He had looked up at the sky and seen the blue of limitless space beyond the streamers of smoke from the chimney fires. Utter freedom was his, like that sharp east wind from the sea that could blow where it listed. And then he had felt hungry and the freedom had felt as hollow as his stomach.

He said, "You are very good, Aunt. I'll have to make my plans."

She nodded. "You do that. Let them know at the mine."

And then Gertie knocked and put her head round the door to say a luncheon was ready in the dining-room.

Had Lily already gone? he wondered. Lily had laid a hand on his arm when he had been overwhelmed with pity for the boy who had wanted to fight everyone and everything, especially laden corves and coal seams. He had brushed her hand off. She belonged to Francis and had already spoken of her dismay at not being called as a witness. "Ma'am," she had pleaded to Sarah. "Tell them we are here. I want to speak up for him."

Sarah had snapped, "They'll call us if they want us," and had seemed mightily relieved *not* to be called. "Your brother will want me to say Joe was ill," she had said to Billy, "but how do I know if he was ill that day? He was well enough when you and he set off together."

She too had patted his back when he wept but he had sensed embarrassment rather than compassion in the gesture. It shamed him now to think that he had given way like that. There was shame too that he had ever yearned for Lily. He had looked at her in the witnesses' room and contemplated her dispassionately. Her bonnet had been put on in haste; her shawl was awry. Her brows were set in an anxious frown and her mouth twitched. She couldn't sit on the benches by the wall but kept moving about. The stillness, symmetry and perfection he had first seen in her were nowhere at all and what use were they in judging character?

The image of his mother, standing up and shouting over the din, and then half-tumbling down the stairs in her haste, came before his eyes as he sat down in his uncle's place and looked across at his aunt. Her hands were pressed together and her eyes closed. Sanctimonious hypocrite, he thought. She is saying grace.

She opened her eyes. "When we are settled I will teach you the words your uncle used."

Billy ate because he was hungry but her presence was oppressive, stultifying. He couldn't believe he had hinted to his mother that he wouldn't mind his aunt mothering him. He had recently laughed to himself that he and Sarah were two villains who could happily mingle their lives in the service of money-making. But now he felt disgusted at the meanness of her evil-doing. She had shown no remorse when she told him, "I have something for your mother and then we can break away from her altogether and I don't want to hear that business mentioned ever again." She was cold and selfish.

Ma was passionately sorry for her ill-doing, confessing it to the world. He had told her he admired her for it and he was glad he had said that for she needed comforting. She must face the world now like a skinned rabbit.

He pushed away his empty plate and stood up.

"Thank you for that but I must report to the Viewer by the end of the shift."

"Dear me!" She pushed back her chair. "You could have coffee and sweetmeats and fruit."

He shook his head.

"Will you be giving in your notice at once then?"

"I must certainly make my plans."

She looked at the clock. "The stage doesn't go for another hour and a half."

"I am walking. I need the air and the exercise. Goodbye, Aunt."

She followed him to the door, protesting, but when it was obvious he was going, she grabbed his arm and hissed, "Just tell me, you did this because you wanted Lily. Would you have let Francis hang?"

He pulled away. "He wouldn't have. It was a feeble case. And I have no feelings for Lily at all."

He got himself out into the street, more determined than ever that he would not make that his home. She wanted not only his presence but his inner being and he would not let her have that. But she had no one else to put in her will and he was the only one who knew she had stolen from his mother for years. She had given her something back and Ma, with no knowledge of publishing, would trustingly accept it.

He still had power over Sarah Heron and she knew it.

He walked fast, covering the miles, trying to drive away her last query to which he couldn't give an honest answer. Ma had said in her speech to the jury that she was sure he would never have let Francis die. What right had she to be so sure? Down by the river it had come into his mind that he could contrive his brother's death without guilt to himself. In the court when asked if he saw a push the word 'yes' had stuck in his throat and come out as 'no'. Did that exonerate him from the name of murderer? He had an elusive memory of a verse in the Bible that having murder in one's heart was the same as committing it. How would he feel now, walking home, if he had left his brother in a condemned cell awaiting hanging?

His forehead broke into a sweat. He turned quickly to the roadside ditch and vomited into it. His legs were buckling under him and he had to grab a branch in the hedgerow to keep upright. He wiped his brow with the back of his hand and took several deep breaths.

Shocked at himself, he resumed walking and soon became aware of a rumbling sound behind him. He turned and saw the stage coach, a small box-shape with a blur of movement in front made by the four horses. Would the family be on it? There was a gate further on and he might dive into the field and dodge behind the hedgerow. The coach was coming at pace. There wasn't time and he would be seen running away. He would just keep walking steadily along the grass verge.

He couldn't help his head turning as it drew near. There was a shout. "Billy!"

Francis was one of the top passengers, waving and shouting to the driver, "Stop, coachman! It's my brother. We have a space on top. Oh, pray pick him up."

The coachman brandished his whip in a negative gesture and the whole contraption rattled by. Francis's head was turned and he went on waving.

Billy's hand seemed to be drawn upwards. He waved back.

Walking on, his steps were freer and stronger, his heart a little lighter.

Francis

Francis had chosen to ride on top though there was a seat inside. "I've had enough of confinement in small spaces," he said, and, cold as the east wind was on his back, he exulted in the fresh air and wide views. To be alive was everything.

Another passenger turned to him and said, "They are not allowed to stop, you know, only at coaching inns."

Frances nodded. It didn't matter. That wave of Billy's was surely a sign.

He thought, I can be magnanimous in forgiveness. Ma blames herself, but to me she is above criticism. If Da feels no resentment that she only recently revealed her secret to him, why should I? And as for love, in my lifetime I never saw much in Billy to love but I believe in the hurt his father caused her and if we could draw a transformed Billy back into the family, I can see no smudge on the clear horizon of my life.

At the Wylam coaching inn they soon drew a crowd avid for news. Relief that he had been freed was the prevailing view, though one wag yelled, "Well, well, Saint Francis has his halo back."

"Where's Billy then?" some asked. "Did Billy get you off?"

His mother called back, "Yes, Billy did it. He's on his way."

His father looked askance at her. "It was you, my angel, wasn't it?"

"Billy didn't back Harry Allthorp," she said.

His father nodded but with his habitual frown of puzzlement on his face.

A cart was offered so that his mother wouldn't have to walk the half mile home and he and his father pulled it, though his father took the main weight when he realised how sore he still was from his injuries. When Burn Cottage came into view Francis couldn't restrain his tears.

"I thought I'd never see it again," he said, as they lifted his mother down and she hobbled inside to sink into the rocking chair, where she too sobbed with relief.

They had a good fire going and the kettle singing when they heard Billy go in next door. Dee tried to rise but Francis held up his hand. "Sit still, Ma. I'll bring him. Da, will you brew the tea in the big brown pot? He will be parched."

Thinking of that wave, Francis walked into Billy's place without knocking and said, in the most natural way, "You're to come in and drink tea with us, our Billy."

The room felt very cold after theirs and Billy looked as if he had been about to fling himself on his bed. He straightened up and swung round, meeting Francis's ready smile with an astonished stare. Francis thought he had never seen Billy so taken aback in his whole life, but he mastered himself at once with a shake of his shoulders.

"Well, I *am* fair parched."

"Come on then."

Francis stepped outside again, took the two paces to their door and held it open for him. Billy seemed to be drawn forth on a string. He came, just pushing his own door too with an unconscious hand and walked in, his head turning from Mother in the rocking chair to Father carrying the teapot to the table. Both turned smiling faces to him and Francis saw how Mother's eyes were shining.

"Sit down, our Billy," Father said, and set four mugs on the table. Billy said not a word but sat down at the end of the table furthest from the fire.

"Will you not come this end," Mother said, "and get warm?"

He shook his head. Francis thought, We are being too quick for him. He has pride as big as an elephant to swallow. Swallowing tea, though, was not beyond him. He drank mug after mug as Da, chuckling, kept the kettle boiling on the hob and filled the teapot up several times. Frances understood that it was enough for his father that the four of them were together in their warm home and no one was quarrelling. He chatted to Billy, telling him they had been to Mr Hurst's house and Mr Trace had gone there too and had given Francis the rest of the week off.

Billy gave a small nod from time to time. When he could drink no more he stood up. "Got to report to Mr Burns," he managed to say and went out.

They looked at each other. "He's like my father," Da said. "Not much to say for himself. But he was mighty thirsty."

Chapter 34

Dee

Next morning Jack had gone at his usual early hour to the farm and Dee was sitting in the rocking chair with Francis, carefully unwinding the bandages from her leg, when there came a single tap at the door and Billy walked in, carrying a knapsack.

"Oh!" He shrank back when he saw her nightgown turned up to her knee.

"No, stay." The sight of him thrilled her. "I fell on the rail – on – on the day your uncle died and it's slow to heal." Francis removed the final dressing.

Billy dropped on his knee and looked at the wound and then up at her face with shock in his eyes. It was the most natural reaction that she had ever seen on his face since he became a man.

"But that's horrible, Ma. It must be agony." He stood up, still aghast. "And yesterday! That walking about! How—"

She smiled. "I never heeded it till afterwards. It's better than it was. The doctor lanced it."

He shuddered. "I've seen injuries not half so bad with lads moaning and groaning."

She said to Francis, "We'll leave it uncovered for a while. If you didn't mind facing the village folk again you could let Doctor Ransom know I am at home if he would like to come and see how it does."

"I'll go," Billy said.

"But hasn't your shift started?" Then she noticed he was not in his pit clothes.

He shook his head. "I only came in to tell you I'm finished with mining."

"Finished!"

"Tell Ma," Francis said, "while I run for the doctor." He took down his coat from the back of the door and was gone in a moment.

"You could brew some tea, Billy," she said. "I would love a drink and you could have one yourself. You may not have lit your own fire yet."

"I wasn't going to. Yesterday I told Mr Burns I'm leaving." He gave a short laugh. "He wasn't pleased."

As he spoke he was using the ladle to fill the kettle from the bucket. He set it over the fire. His movements were neat and controlled, so different from Jack's and more confident than Francis's. She looked at his well-brushed dark hair and the back of his neck and broad shoulders. She wanted him living with them, a new man, civil, competent, even cheerful, in a new spacious place of their own. Was he thinking of a clean, less dangerous job? Why had he brought in a knapsack, packed she supposed with his few possessions? He would have to give up his room of course if he was no longer employed at the pit. Was he hoping to live under this roof as he had as a boy?

"You are an Overman now," she said. "You would be better paid."

He spoke to the fire. "I need a new life away from here, that's all."

A sickening dread seized her. He was proposing to go just when she was learning to love his presence. "Oh Billy, don't go away. What will you do?"

He shrugged his shoulders. "Join the navy or the army. See the world."

"But they are not recruiting since the war with France ended. I saw a one-legged man begging in the streets of Newcastle. You have so many talents. Doesn't your aunt want you to help her with her houses?"

He sat back on his heels and looked at her. "I suppose I must keep in touch with her for the sake of her money. It should come to you."

"Me! She thinks me a wanton, a woman of ill-repute. She told me so as she handed me a hundred pounds. You must have some, Billy, to help you to new work."

He jumped up. "Not a penny. I have some more to give you." He felt in his pocket and counted out forty banknotes onto the table.

"Billy! If the mine have given you this for your services it is yours."

He laughed. "I get nothing since I have given no notice. It is from Sarah too. Ask no questions. It is rightly yours."

The kettle bubbled over with a hiss of steam and he made the tea.

Dee looked at the notes in some distress. "But Billy, you gave me ten pounds for the coach. I can pay you that back. I have never handled so much money since I was a young girl. How can this be mine?"

He poured her a mug of tea and placed it on a stool beside her.

"I want nothing from you," he said. "I must make my own way. You earned money from your writing."

She nodded slowly. "Sarah said something like that. She'd been doing the accounts since Joe—"

"Yes, yes. It's yours, Ma." He stood by the table, drinking his tea. Then he said, "I'll be away soon so tell me more about my father."

He *was* planning to leave them. Oh, she could understand it, but when? How soon? She heaved a sigh. If his time was so short she had no wish to speak of Ralph. She yearned to unloose his thoughts about Francis. This was a different Billy from the one who had brought a constable to arrest his brother for murder. But that other Billy lurked somewhere and might still emerge.

Briefly she sketched in the courtship of Sir Ralph Barnet, who had inherited a baronetcy, purchased in the days of James the First, but since wasted by profligate holders of the title. "If you tried to claim sonship," she warned him, "you might be liable for all the debts he left. My parents, then wealthy themselves, didn't care that he was in trouble. They fancied their daughter as Lady Barnet." She admitted she had given way to Ralph's passion, believing their marriage imminent, but his professed love had ended in a lawyer's letter when her father's bankruptcy had become public.

Billy was thoughtful for a whole minute. Then he said, "But you loved him at first?"

"I did. He was handsome and charming and professed to love me. How could I not? I never dreamt he could dissemble like that." The memory of how her love had transformed into bitter hatred could still hurt. She covered her face with her hand to hide her tears.

"I've upset you," he said. "I thought it was all dried up in the past."

She looked full at him, letting tears fall. "Billy, it is a terrible thing to hate so bitterly. I should have let it go when I had Jack's love. If only you,

Ralph's baby, hadn't reminded me of him! That was how the hatred didn't stay in the past."

"Have I inherited his character?"

She didn't hesitate. "No."

"What? Not my love of money? Not my telling lies? Not my cruel nature?"

"Billy, I don't believe all that is how you want to be. You lacked love. That was the root of all those things."

"Did you hate me?"

"Sometimes." She was sobbing now.

"I hated you – sometimes. It's so much easier to hate than to love."

"You loved Lily."

"No. She was an idea in my head. I *think* I could truly love someone one day."

"What would she be like?"

"Like you."

"Oh Billy, me! When I failed you so shamefully!"

She set down her mug on the stool and reached out her arms to him. He took a step towards her and she was sure he was about to kneel down and hug her but at that moment they heard quick footsteps on the gravel and Francis ran in, breathless.

"Oh Ma, Billy's men are coming in a body. They know he's quitting and they blame you. Oh, and Doctor Ransom will come later. He's with a dying patient."

Billy stiffened. "My men?"

"Your shift. Mr Burns has put someone else in charge of them and they've walked out. They're angry. They trust you and only you. I heard them when I came past the pit yard."

Billy's expression, Dee thought, was a mixture of pride in their devotion and regret that he must disappoint them. He was not going to change his mind. That was cruelly evident.

"Here they come," Francis said.

There were shouts of "Come on out, Dee Heron. We want words with you."

Dee pulled her nightdress over her legs and drew her bedgown round her. "I'll speak to them." She tried to stand but her sons said in unison, "No you don't, Ma!"

Billy stepped to the door and opened it. There was silence at the sight of him.

"What the hell is this?" he shouted. "My mother is in bed ill. Do you come in a mob to a defenceless woman? Are you men?"

Subdued murmurs came back: "Ain't she driving you away?" "She's got her pet baby there, hasn't she?" "You got him off but she only wants him."

"Who told you I got him off?"

"She did. She told my ma. We lent the cart to carry her back yesterday."

"The jury let him off. My brother was rightly found not guilty. None of it has anything to do with my leaving here. I'm done with mining, that's all."

"How's that, Billy Heron? Mr Burns made you Overman."

"He's mighty cross, we can tell you."

"You've let him down."

"You've let us all down."

Dee could hear that the voices were growing menacing.

One, in a pleading tone, said, "But mining's in your blood, Billy. I mind when you saw your Grandfather William get crushed wi' a fall of rock."

Billy's voice came through, thick with emotion. "When you've read all the papers you'll know he was *not* my grandfather. I am not a Heron. I am not accountable to anyone but I have been down the pit since I was a child and I intend to do something else with my life now, so clear off, the lot of you. Get back to work. And if I hear any one of you speak or act against my mother I'll beat you within an inch of your life."

There were mumbles of "All right, Billy," and some surprised murmurings of "He's not a Heron!"

Then one voice spoke up. "Ay, the night coachman said Dee confessed in court that her boys was half-brothers. It's all over the Newcastle papers. That's what it is. Billy didn't know it. It was a shock. Haway, lads, leave him be. Leave them all be. They're nowt to do wi' us."

Another voice said, "Here's Farmer Jack coming at a run." The tone was scornful.

Dee looked at Francis and mouthed, "They won't hurt *him*."

Billy was still standing in the doorway, a fierce presence, till they all dispersed. Then he came back in, making way for Jack, who was asking, "What did they want? I was worried when I saw them round our door and then I saw our Billy was dealing with them so I knew my angel was safe." He looked about with his radiant smile. "Eh, I'm minded it's like the old days with my father and mother and Joe and me. A family with two lads. But poor Joe's gone, hasn't he?"

Billy said, "And *I'm* going. Here's my knapsack packed."

"Where are you going, Billy?"

"Newcastle first. I'd better call on old Sarah and keep her sweet."

"I promised to write to her," Dee broke in. "When you go – if you must, Billy – you could take my letter."

He shook his head. "I can't wait. I'll tell her to expect it."

He's going *now*! Dee yearned to throw a chain about him and hold him fast.

"And where after Newcastle?" Francis asked. He is not so upset, she thought, at his brother's going.

Billy shrugged. "If I find a collier shorthanded I'll get to London and who knows then?"

Dee reached out a hand to him. "You'll write to us?"

"Is there any point? You'll go away from here. They know too much about you. You'll go where no one knows you."

"I don't want to go far. I don't want to *hide* from what happened. Indeed this is the biggest *moral tale* I have to tell the world."

"Put it in a book then." He threw that out casually and then looked at her intently. "But change the names."

A quiver of excitement ran through her. She could. She could write a novel. The characters would be different but the theme of a deception, a failure to love and disastrous consequences would be the same. She might write under a man's name. Women authors struggled for notice.

She saw Jack dithering in the doorway and knew the conversation had run away from him.

"I ought to go back to the farm," he said. "How is your leg, angel?"

"Francis went to ask the doctor to come and look at it. He will but he was with a dying patient. Go, and tonight we will speak of farm work for you in a better place than this, where we can sleep separately from our cooking space and I can have a little desk to write at and Francis and Billy can come and stay and each have a bed."

Jack stood, perplexed, biting his thumb. "You would like that?"

"I would love it."

He scratched his head. "I know not if I can provide all that."

"Ma will manage it," Billy said and held out his hand. "Goodbye, Jack."

"Oh!" The name shocked him but Dee could see his mind sorting it out and accepting it with slow nodding of the head. "Goodbye, our Billy." He turned at the door. "We'll see you again soon."

"It's a statement of his hope," Dee said as Jack walked back across the fields.

Billy said, "How do you endure him, Ma, clever as you are?"

She looked at him wistfully, aware of his own sharpness of brain and praying his new life would use that to the full. "I rest myself in his love."

His dark brows lifted and a smile played about his mouth. Envy or scepticism, she wondered, or a little of both?

He turned to Francis. "Can I take your waving from the coach to mean you are willing to shake hands with me after all that has passed? It will be the last time."

"But I *wanted* time," Francis said. "I wanted time for us to be brothers as we should have been." He grasped Billy's outstretched hand and made as if he would embrace him but Billy, with the slightest movement of his shoulders, prevented him.

"Don't pretend you can love me after all I have done to you. You can't begin to imagine the loathing I felt for you all our lives. It's gone now, thank God. I can see you as a decent lad but – there, that's enough." He released his hand and turned to his mother.

She knew he was desperate not to break down and he would prefer her too not to weep. He wanted to be gone as swiftly as possible and she must not even try to persuade him to stay. No word of forgiveness would be spoken on either side but it was there in the air around them.

She moved to stand up and he protested strongly. "Nay," she said, "now you can kiss me without crouching down." He did and she felt a tear drop on her cheek.

"Take care of that leg," he snapped.

"I'm walking to the door with you."

He hoisted the knapsack onto his shoulders.

At the door she gripped his arm.

"You *must* write. We will not go far from the Tyne. Jack will want the river and his waggonway, but you know Francis is apprenticed to Mr Trace the engineer in Heaton. And Mr Brandling – you know, the printer in Newcastle – even Aunt Sarah – I will try to befriend her – you will always be able to find us."

He nodded at each name and then pulled his arm from her grasp. "Goodbye, Ma."

She couldn't hold him. The moment had come and he had turned away before her choked out "Oh Billy!" had passed her lips.

He strode away eastward along the track into the morning sunlight, his eyes steadily forward.

"You will always be my son," she said aloud, her heart screaming for him to turn round and come back.

Francis came and put his arm round her waist and watched with her till Billy was out of sight.

He helped her limp back to the rocking chair and put a rug round her.

"Don't cry, Ma. It's for the best."

"What do you know?" She sat sniffling and shivering. "Make up the fire and add some hot water to the tea. *He* made it."

"And it was a good idea of his that you should write a novel." Francis briskly stirred the fire and put the kettle back on.

His words broke through her sobs. She sat up and held her hands out to the blaze. "It was. It was a good idea. *His* idea. Yes, yes, I see it. In my novel I shall have a happy ending. There will be an epilogue in which the suffering hero will appear in time for his brother's wedding, bringing with him a beautiful loving wife."

Francis poured her a fresh cup of tea.

"Thank you, pet."

She leant back in the chair and surprised him with a sudden, almost hysterical laugh. "Yes, my lambkin. All my Moral Tales have happy endings. My public expects it."

Francis grinned at her. "Good idea, Ma. A happy ending."

Lightning Source UK Ltd.
Milton Keynes UK
UKHW041430030122
396549UK00001B/54